FOOL'S MOON

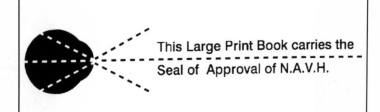

This Large Print Book carries the
Seal of Approval of N.A.V.H.

A TAROT CATS MYSTERY

FOOL'S MOON

DIANE A. S. STUCKART

WHEELER PUBLISHING
A part of Gale, a Cengage Company

GALE
A Cengage Company

Farmington Hills, Mich • San Francisco • New York • Waterville, Maine
Meriden, Conn • Mason, Ohio • Chicago

Copyright © 2018 by Diane A. S. Stuckart.
Wheeler Publishing, a part of Gale, a Cengage Company.

LIBRARY OF CONGRESS CIP DATA ON FILE.
CATALOGUING IN PUBLICATION FOR THIS BOOK
IS AVAILABLE FROM THE LIBRARY OF CONGRESS

ISBN-13: 978-1-4328-6259-6 (softcover)

Published in 2019 by arrangement with Midnight Inc, an imprint of Llewellyn Publication, Woodbury, MN 55125-2989

[handwritten signature]

Printed in Mexico
1 2 3 4 5 6 7 23 22 21 20 19

To all who are brave enough to set off
on their own Fool's journey.

ONE

"It's too hot! I can't breathe," Ophelia yowled. She lifted soft black paws to claw with desperation at the cardboard prison that trapped them. "We're good cats . . . the old woman always said that. So why did the man do this to us?"

"Because he's a bad human," her brother, Brandon, growled back. "Even the old woman didn't like him, and he was her son."

His words were muffled because his mouth was dry as the Palm Beach sand that stretched behind their old home and all the way to the ocean. But they were far from that safe sanctuary now. Instead, his keen feline nose and ears told him they had been dumped beside a road somewhere in a neighborhood redolent of bacon grease and burning coffee and canine poop. Why, he couldn't even smell a welcome bit of salt and stinky fish in the air any longer.

If only they had a bowl of water!

He paused to paw a bit of oily cardboard from between his teeth. It had been only a few minutes since their prison box had tumbled from the man's car and landed on the concrete with a bruising thud. Even then, Brandon had held out hope that the box would suddenly spring open, that the man would change his mind and gather them back into the vehicle that smelled of leather and fake pine trees, and take them back home again. Instead, he'd heard the man's car screech like a wounded chicken, followed by the sound of the man's car roaring off into the distance.

And so he'd spent the past minutes frantically gnawing at one of the long, narrow holes that allowed a bit of air into the box and hinted at a possible escape. As he chewed, he could taste the residue of the long yellow fruit — *banana,* the humans called it — that once had filled the container.

Bitter. No, sweet. No, both.

But that didn't matter. Good taste or bad, he had to keep on tearing at the box until he made a hole big enough for him and his sister to wriggle out of it.

He sank his teeth deeper into the cardboard and gave a mighty pull. A chunk of cardboard peeled off with a satisfying ripping sound.

"Look," he cried, spitting out bits of paper. "I made it through the first layer. It won't be much longer until we're free."

He shot an anxious glance over his furry shoulder at his littermate. Ophelia sagged against the other side of the box, her small paws still clawing at the cardboard, but to little effect. She was a slightly smaller mirror image of him — sleek black fur, bright green eyes, long legs and soft paws tipped with razor sharp claws. The one difference that humans noticed was their tails.

Hers was a silken black rope that swished and swirled and floated, depending on her mood — long enough so that when she sat upright, she could wrap it all the way around her front paws with tail to spare! His tail, however, better befitted a canine. It was perhaps a third the size of his sister's, not even long enough to touch the ground, and when he was angry it flared like the bottle brush that the old woman's housekeeper used sometimes with the dishes.

Squirrel, one of the smiling humans at the place of cages where he and Ophelia had lived as kittens had called him. Even at a few weeks old, he'd been insulted to be compared to a fuzzy gray rat-like creature. He had been pleased when the old woman who'd adopted them had dubbed him *Brandon Bobtail* — a far more dignified moniker.

But tail size was of no importance now. There was barely enough room in the box for two full-grown felines to sprawl comfortably, let alone both attack the same spot. Still, he knew better than to tell his sister to step aside, that he had this. She might be smaller and less muscular than he, but she had a spirit as big as a feline twice her size, he thought with pride.

He gave the oily cardboard another bite. If he kept track of time like humans did, he would guess it had been less than an hour since the man had lured them both into the box with a tin of sardines. While they nibbled at the stinky goodness — the old woman had never given them so tasty a treat! — the man had shoved another box over them like a cover. Then Brandon had heard a ripping sound going round and round the box. He'd recognized the noise as coming from a roll of the sticky stuff the humans called tape.

The man was sealing them inside the box so that they couldn't escape!

Brandon hissed as he recalled the man's treachery. He'd tried to reassure a yowling Ophelia that the man simply was taking them to the place of cold steel tables and sharp needles. Of course, he didn't really believe that. *She* always carried them there in a soft container with fluffy towels on the bottom and sides they could see out of. *She* would carefully strap them onto the back seat of her sleek yellow car that purred just like them, instead of shoving them into a hot, dark compartment that stank of oily smells and growled at them like an angry pit bull.

They'd fearfully crouched together in their suffocating prison until the car had skidded to an abrupt halt. A moment later, daylight and fresh air had flooded the compartment, leaking into their prison box. Where they were, he wasn't certain, but he could tell from the sounds and smells that it wasn't the veterinarian's office.

Maybe he changed his mind, Brandon had told his sister in relief as the man lifted the box out of the trunk. *Maybe he brought us back home again.*

But, of course, he hadn't.

Brandon had heard the man sneezing, like he always did when he was around them. *Allergic,* the son always reminded the old woman, voice filled with contempt. *You'd rather have those damned cats around than me.*

Then the box had dropped and landed

11

with a hard thud onto what felt like a sidewalk. While they untangled themselves from the unexpected impact, they'd heard the sound of the trunk slamming once more. Then the car sped off with a growl and a roar and a blast of smoke, leaving him and Ophelia behind.

Where are we? Ophelia had mewed in fear while Brandon pressed a green eye to one of the slits in the box in hopes of learning that answer.

All he could see was a bit of broken sidewalk and a battered garbage can that, even from a distance, smelled like rude dogs had peed all over it. Other smells drifted to him . . . burning coffee, rotting food, old shoes.

Not home, he'd told her. *Somewhere hot and stinky and ugly.*

Now Brandon paused again and pressed his eye against the small opening that finally was large enough for him to stick a forearm through. It was early in the morning, and the time of year that humans called spring, so the air outside the box wasn't yet unbearably hot. But he'd heard terrible stories when he was a kitten in the place of cages about animals — mostly canines — that got left in cars or trapped in sheds or boxes and cooked to death. Unless they could chew

12

out of the cardboard prison, that would happen to him and Ophelia.

They didn't have much time, he realized in a panic, and started gnawing even faster. He already was feeling as dizzy as if he'd chased a string in a circle too many times. Pretty soon, he'd be slumped on his side like his sister, panting as he tried to keep cool.

When it reached that point, they would simply have to lie there in their dark, broiling prison and hope to be found by a passing human . . . or wait to die.

"No!"

With an angry yowl, he gave a mighty rip of the cardboard with his teeth. And with that, a section of the inner box ripped free, allowing in a sudden little burst of cooler air. He gave another tug, and the outer box tore as well. Now he'd made a hole large enough to stick his head through — maybe even his whole body, if he shoved hard enough.

He paused a moment to gulp down nice cool breaths of air; then he turned to his sister. "We did it! Look, we can get out now."

Ophelia opened her green eyes just a crack.

"I knew you'd do it," she mewed. "Quick,

get out."

"You, first."

"No, you. Make sure the hole is big enough."

Brandon would have argued, but there wasn't time. Instead, he shoved his head through the hole; then, squeezing and twisting and gasping, he popped out of the box and tumbled onto the broken sidewalk.

Free!

Relief swirled about him just like the gaggle of tiny sparrows who lived in the green bushes at home taking flight at the merest fright. He squinted against the burst of morning sun. A second later, his eyes had adjusted to the glare, and he stared in wonder. Where were they?

This wasn't home, not by any means. Not with all these tiny buildings painted in strange colors, their cracked windows hung with ugly black bars and sagging like catnip mice missing most of their stuffing. Where he came from, the houses stretched wide and tall, in soft colors like sand and sky, with roofs made of rounded red tile that only sure-footed felines dared traverse. There, walls of thick green shrubs and tall palms and big thorny bushes with giant flowers that smelled like the old woman's perfume separated the houses from each other. But here, each squat building clung to a narrow strip of pebbles and brown grass so short that it couldn't even bar a rat from passing.

The only green he saw was a single stubby palm tree barely taller than he. Just as he had squeezed out of the prison box, the palm had somehow squeezed from a gap in the ground between the sidewalk and a metal building whose windows had been covered with big pieces of wood, like it was waiting for a hurricane to happen. If it ever grew big enough to be a real tree, instead of a few leaves, maybe it could protect the building when the winds next came.

"Brandon, where are you?"

Ophelia's soft wail drifted to him, the fearful tone snapping him from his momentary daydreams.

He shoved his furry face against the hole in the box. To his alarm, his sister was still lying where he'd left her.

"I'm right here," he meowed. "Come on, it's your turn. Climb out, and we'll find somewhere nice and cool to lounge until we figure out what to do next."

"I can't," she mumbled, eyes still closed. "I'm too tired."

"You have to! Hurry!"

She made no reply to that last, and Brandon felt his bobtail bristle in fear. Even if he could squeeze his way back into the prison box, the hole was far too small for him to be able to drag her back out with him again. And the minutes were flying by. He could try chewing a larger hole, one big enough for them both to fit through, but in the time that would take, it might be too late for her.

In a flash, he made a decision.

"Me-OOOOOOOOOOOOW!" he cried. "Ophelia, listen to me. I'm going to find a human to help you. I'll be right back. Will you be okay alone?"

He saw the faintest flick of her whiskers — *yes.*

"I'll be back soon. Don't give up."

With a flick of his fuzzy tail, he swung about and surveyed the street again. *No humans.* But he could see that at the far end of the next block, the barred front window of one squat yellow building buzzed with big flashing red letters.

PAWN.

What that human word meant, he had no clue. What he did know was that lights meant people, since with their inferior eyesight they needed that extra brightness even in the daytime. But they had hands instead of paws . . . hands that could tear away tape far faster than he could chew

16

cardboard. Maybe someone in that building was clever enough to follow him back to Ophelia and free her from the box.

With a quick look around for canines and cars — any feline knew enough to avoid both — he bounded down the sidewalk. Pausing a moment later at the crosswalk to crouch and look around again — both cars and canines were good at springing out from behind closed doors and around corners — he darted from one curb to the next. Then, with a final look back at the prison box that held his sister captive, he rushed on silent black paws in the direction of PAWN.

Brandon, where are you?

Ophelia opened her green eyes just a crack. Her head was buzzing, and her black fur felt hot as the oven where the old woman had always cooked her meals. Except now it felt like she was the one being cooked inside this terrible box that the man had made into a prison. And if she didn't get out soon . . . well, it would be what the humans called going to the bridge.

Of course, she knew that word actually meant *dead* — dead like a mouse caught in a trap, or a lizard in the mouth of a big black snake. Humans were the ones who used

17

words to make things all pretty. But going to a bridge might be nice. She could look down into the water and see fish splashing, which was always amusing. And maybe when she died, she would see the old woman again. She'd heard that humans and animals could meet up in whatever life came after this one. If that was true, the first thing she would do would be to jump into the old woman's lap and raise her chin for a soft scratching. And then, when the old woman laughed and obliged with a little scritch, Ophelia would lift a paw. Careful to keep her claws sheathed, she would give the old woman a gentle tap on one wrinkled cheek, which made her laugh again.

She missed that. She missed the old woman.

But the old woman wasn't the only one gone. Where was Brandon?

Ophelia tried to meow, but her tongue seemed stuck to the inside of her mouth. *Wait, he's looking for a human to help,* she remembered. And maybe he would bring a bowl of water when he came back. But what if he couldn't find her again? She needed to make sure he could see her.

Rallying a bit at that, she opened her eyes wider and rolled over, so that she was beside the hole that her brother had chewed. She couldn't drag herself out — she was far too tired to twist herself about like those wily rats that could fit into any space big as their nose — but she could shove her forearm through the gap and wave it about. And so, with a mighty effort, she slid a sleek black leg out of the hole.

Abruptly, something warm and wet brushed against her paw.

A tongue!

Squeaking in alarm, she yanked her forearm back into the box and gave it a sniff. Not Brandon. But she was so dizzy by now, that she was having a hard time figuring out what it was that had licked her. Outside the box, she could hear sounds now . . . sounds of a human talking. And then the box rolled about, and she heard the sharp ripping noise of tape being pulled off cardboard.

Brandon had done it! He'd found a human to help.

But her relief faded as she caught another sniff of her forearm. The slobber that dampened her fur smelled vaguely familiar . . . smelled suspiciously like . . .

Abruptly, the box lid was pulled off, and sunshine beat down on her. In the instant it took for her feline eyes to adjust to the change of light, she felt something hot and wet splatter onto her face. Then her vision

19

focused and she saw it — a broad white muzzle filled with sharp canine teeth looming over them. The jaws were open, and a long pink tongue lolled out.

"Pit bull!" she shrieked before everything went dark as a mouse hole.

Water. Cool and clear.

It wasn't real, Ophelia realized from some faraway place inside her head. She was in a dream, back again at the old house where she and Brandon had lived since they were kittens. And water . . . the water in her dream was everywhere.

Not the scary ocean that lived beyond the high stone wall and past the broad ribbon of hot sand. That water was a steely gray, and most mornings it roared and crashed on the rippled sand like an angry wolf in search of prey. That water frightened her, the way it tried to sweep away humans and birds and cats, alike. She didn't like *that* water.

No, the water she loved lived in the big rectangular pond safely inside the walled yard of their home. It was a nice, quiet water — still as a mouse, except at one end. There, a broad curtain of clear liquid spilled from a flat rock and joined the other water, splattering a little and sending out wet sparkles

20

that turned colors in the sun.

In her dream, she reached out a paw to tap its cool surface. It was a wonderful pond, indeed, with a broad ledge on all four sides so that she and Brandon could race around the water without getting wet. As long as one didn't actually jump in, the water was friendly and welcoming. The pond itself was pretty, too, with lots of small rocks arranged in funny patterns just above the water's surface.

The only thing bad about the pond was the giant fish with the long nose, like a pointed stick, that lurked at its bottom. The giant fish never moved, just waited down there for things to fall in.

And, lots of things fell.

When that happened, the water was still pretty, but wasn't quite so nice. In the year that Ophelia and her brother had lived with the old woman, they'd spied any number of mice and lizards — even one time, a long black snake! — floating in that large clear body of water. Sometimes, the creatures were still alive, paddling frantically to stay afloat and away from the scary fish at the bottom. That was the fun part, watching them splash about.

Ophelia mewed in amusement, remembering. Her brother, Brandon, would crouch on one side of the pool and she on the other. They would paw at the water, each trying to snare the swimming creature first, before Luciana the housekeeper appeared with her big net. If they could pull out the lizard or mouse, themselves, they'd have a fun toy to bat about for a time.

But, clever human that she was, Luciana usually won their game. Wide red lips tight as the long black braid that dangled enticingly over her thin shoulder, she would gingerly scoop out the mouse or lizard before the cats could retrieve it. Then, while they mewed in disappointment, she would unceremoniously dump the rescued creature into the tangle of vines and palm trees at the pool's far end. That way, it could dry off out of reach of feline paws and then run away.

But some floating creatures were not so lucky as to be snared by Luciana's big net in time. Instead, tiring of the struggle, they would take a final breath and slowly sink to the pool's bottom. When that happened, the two cats would wait at the pool's edge to see if the scary fish would swim over and eat the dead thing.

But the housekeeper was always faster than the scary fish, too. *Tsk'ing,* Luciana would scrape the big net along the pool's bottom, snatching up the corpse and dumping it into a plastic sack. That sack, in turn, she would hide in a giant plastic box near the place where the cars lived. And that would be that, until the next creature lost its battle with the water.

Usually, it was the mice that died, but once it was one of the big white birds with a long, curved beak.

An ibis, Luciana had called it. She sighed as she stood there with the cats watching the pretty winged creature on the bottom of the pond beneath the curtain of falling water. Birds were amusing only when they flapped and dashed about, and Ophelia had been sad to see it lying so close to the scary fish. Still, the water's motion made the bird's wings slowly drift up and down, so that Ophelia wasn't quite convinced it was dead, until Luciana scooped it out.

The old woman had looked much like that ibis on a morning not too long ago, when Ophelia and Brandon had found *her* lying at the bottom of the pond.

In her dreams, Ophelia once again saw that terrible sight. The old woman's sparse white fur, usually curled tight like a pug dog's tail, floated gently away from her head. The long white clothes that she wore — *a nightgown,* the old woman always called it — drifted about her, the fabric slowly flapping just like the dead ibis's wings. And Ophelia had known that something was very wrong.

Frantic, she and Brandon had pawed at the water, trying to make the old woman swim up to the top again. Ophelia knew the old woman could swim. She'd seen her glide across the water's surface many times, wrinkled white arms and legs moving but barely splashing at all. Indeed, Ophelia had always been impressed by this strange human talent.

So why was the old woman down there with the scary fish instead?

Luciana had heard their splashing and rushed to see what was the matter. When she saw the old woman, she screamed and screamed, scaring both cats off the ledge. They'd crouched in the nearby bushes, waiting to see what she would do with the old woman now.

But unlike with the mice and the lizard — and even with the ibis — the housekeeper didn't get the net. Instead, she rushed back into the house. Not very long after, other humans had arrived. They'd carried the old woman out of the water and laid her on the hard ground. One of the humans had breathed into the old woman's slack mouth, making her chest go up and down, like they were pretending that she was breathing. But by then, Ophelia could have told them that it was no use.

Like the ibis, the old woman was dead.

Two

"Ophelia, wake up! I heard the door open. Humans are coming."

The yowl came from the orange tabby in the cage beside her. Uncurling herself from the threadbare towel that served as her bed, Ophelia stretched one thin black forearm, then the other.

She was back in that place called the shelter — the same place where the old woman had found her and Brandon when they were just kittens and taken them home. Except Brandon wasn't with her this time. The human that had found her in the box had taken her away from the street before he could return. She was here, and he was still out there somewhere . . . alone.

She'd almost forgotten what it was like in the shelter. The cramped, cold metal box that held her; the harsh smell of something the humans called bleach; the terrified yowls of the other cats locked in their own metal boxes.

Wearing bright shirts covered with pictures of smiling dogs and cats, the humans tried their best to be nice to them. They gave frequent head-scratches with the litter box changes, and handed out the occasional little toys.

Only temporary, they would assure each new feline that arrived there. *You'll have a forever home soon.*

And, in the few days she'd been there, she'd seen excited humans come into the room and take away one of the felines — usually, a kitten, just like she and Brandon had once been — to live with them. All the remaining cats would cheer, for it meant there was a chance that a human might pick them, too.

But she'd also seen sick cats and injured cats taken away by one of the humans who worked there. They'd go to another room . . . the room the cats who'd been there awhile called the PTS room, though they didn't really know what that meant. The shelter worker would come back later, looking sad as she gave out more head-scratches than usual.

The cats, however, never came back.

"Quick," the tabby urged Ophelia, who had yet to uncurl her sleek black length. "If we want to get out of here, we have to make a human like us. They want cats who purr and bat their paws, not cats that lie about like dead mice."

"Oh, for kibbles' sake," Ophelia mewed back — this being the only epithet that her brother (being the elder by two minutes, and thus arbiter of such things) approved of her using. Still, she condescended to move to the front of the cage, though she complained, "What's the use? They want kittens, not full-grown felines. And no one wants black cats."

It was true. The humans who worked there talked about that all the time. And so they'd put pretty collars on the black felines, hoping to make them more appealing to finicky human eyes. That was why Ophelia was wearing a pink collar with a tiny pink bell. She hated the way the collar felt around her neck and the constant tinkling sound the bell made, but the humans put it back on her every time she pulled it off. So, for now, she deigned to wear it.

Now she could hear footsteps and the sound of human voices. It was a signal to the other caged felines — at least, the newer residents — to stick their paws through the bars and start meowing, *Me, Me, Me!*

Sometimes, the ploy worked. But most

times . . .

Ophelia sighed to herself. Black cats didn't have all the bad luck. The felines who'd been there longer knew the drill. They didn't bother with the pawing and meowing. Like her, they knew that humans looked for pretty cats first, ones whose pictures would look good on that thing they called the internet. And they liked cats who meowed just a little, but not too much.

The footsteps drew closer. This shelter human was Ophelia's favorite, the one named Shanice. She was tall and thin, with long hands made even longer by the bright blue claws that she sported. Best of all, she wore her long black fur in a mass of tiny braids that Ophelia couldn't resist batting at when Shanice bent to give her fresh food and water. Ophelia was careful never to use her claws, so that the human female always laughed and gave her an extra scratch.

Walking beside Shanice was another human female who was shorter and plumper than Shanice was. This one wore a short black dress that matched narrow black eye things — *spectacles,* the old woman always called them — that perched on her short nose. She looked young enough to be the old woman's granddaughter, if she'd had one. But while Shanice's smooth skin was almost as dark as Ophelia's fur, this new female was even paler than the old woman. More strangely, her light brown fur that barely reached her shoulders was streaked on one side with blue, almost like she'd rolled in berries.

But that didn't matter. When she spoke, Ophelia immediately recognized her voice. She was the human who had freed her from the terrible box!

"I had to know that she's okay," the female said, sounding apologetic. "Poor thing, she was so hot I thought she'd die of heat stroke before I got her here. I poured my bottle of water on her to cool her off, but she never moved once I put her in my car."

"You did just fine, Ruby," Shanice assured her. "If you hadn't of brought her here so fast, she might not of made it. But it's been almost a week now, and she don't seem to have any permanent issues. We've already got her up for adoption."

"So you didn't find her owner?"

"Actually, we did."

By now, the humans were standing in front of their cage. Ophelia flicked her ears in alarm. If the shelter found out about the old woman's son, they might send her back to him. And what he'd do to her this time, when the box trick hadn't worked, she didn't want to guess!

"We scanned her, and she had a chip," Shanice went on, her brow crinkling like a Shar-pei's. "Turns out this little girl originally came from our shelter as a kitten. I checked her records and she had a brother who looked just like her, except he had this funny little half tail. They were adopted out together about a year ago, to an elderly lady by the name of Hilda Givens out on Palm Beach. According to the paperwork, she named this little girl Ophelia and named her brother Brandon."

She paused and made a noise like she was eating some particularly tasting tuna. "Mm, mm, mm. Talk about rich. That Mrs. Givens, she was one of those Society ladies. You know, with her picture always in that weekly section of the *Palm Beach Herald* where they talk about coming out balls and fundraisers and such. Girl, I wish she could have adopted *me*!"

The two humans exchanged grins, though Ophelia wasn't sure what was so funny. She'd never heard of a full-grown human being given away to a different family, even though it happened with felines and canines all the time. Then Shanice's expression turned serious again.

"Anyhow, I called to let her know Ophelia had been found, and her son answered the phone. Turns out Mrs. Givens passed away a few weeks ago. Mr. Givens was under the impression that the housekeeper was still taking care of his mother's cats. He had no idea they'd gone missing until I told him we had Ophelia. And when I told him she'd been found in the box, well, he was pretty upset. He thought maybe someone in the lawn crew did it for a sick joke or something."

"*Wrong!*" Ophelia meowed in outrage, though she knew the humans couldn't understand her.

The ones who took care of the old woman's lawn were scary, with their loud cutting and blowing machines, but they weren't bad humans. When they stopped making all that noise and sat in the grass to eat their food when the sun was high, they would always toss a crust or two her and Brandon's way. No, the son had done this all on his own.

"Wait," the girl who Shanice had called Ruby interrupted, her bright red lips puckering like she'd taken a lick of lemon. "So the other cat — the one name Brandon — is missing, too? Do you think maybe he was in the box with his sister? It had a hole in it big enough for a cat to squeeze out, so maybe he escaped and he's still on the street somewhere."

"Maybe. All I know is that he hasn't shown up here yet. Which could be a good thing . . . or a bad one."

Ophelia felt a shiver run through her straight from nose to tail. She knew all about bad things that happened to felines. But just because Brandon hadn't come back before the Ruby human had taken her away didn't mean something had happened to him. And what must he be thinking, wondering what happened to *her*? He had to be frantic with worry. But how would they ever find each other again, with her caged up like this?

"So when is that Givens guy going to pick up this little girl and take her back home?" Ruby asked.

Shanice got the furrowed look again. "He said he travels a lot for business, plus he's allergic to cats. So he said it would be better if someone else adopted her. But he did promise to mail a big check in his mother's name to us."

"I guess that's decent enough of him," Ruby said as she leaned toward the cage and slid in blunt fingers as if to pet Ophelia. "Hi, pretty kitty. Remember me?"

"Decent?" Ophelia yowled, ignoring the

human female. "The son was the one who tried to murder us! Shanice, the son is the bad man. You should go after him!"

"Wow, she's talky," Ruby observed, her thin dark eyebrows raising at the sound of Ophelia's rant. "I wonder if she's part Siamese."

"Maybe. I've always heard that the most likely result when you breed one of them with a regular old domestic short-hair is a black cat."

"Part Siamese or not, she sure is pretty. And a black cat would be perfect for where I work. But if she's always going to be this noisy, I'm not so sure. I mean, with the customers and all, well, she can't be running around disturbing things."

"Quick," the orange cat hissed in Ophelia's direction. "This human is talking about adopting you, but she won't take you if you keep yowling. Shut up and do something to make her like you."

"But what if I don't want her to adopt me?" she meowed back, skittering to the rear of the cage and out of human fingers' reach. "I need to stay here, in case my brother shows up. I don't want to go off with this Ruby person."

The tabby gave a disgusted snort. "Don't be dumb as a mouse. If she adopts you, all you have to do is wait for her to hold a door open too long, and then you can run away and go looking for your brother. But if you stay here, there's no guarantee he'll show up. And even if he does, what if they already took you to the PTS room?"

Ophelia opened her green eyes wide. What the tabby said made sense. The only way to find Brandon was to break out of the shelter. And if it took pretending to be quiet and sweet so this human would take her away, then so be it.

With a nod of thanks for the other cat, she went to the front of her cage again, only to see that the two humans were headed back toward the door . . . away from her!

"I mean, I'd have liked to take her," Ruby was saying, "but I live in my sister's place. If — when — she ever comes back to town . . . well, she'd probably be okay with a quiet cat, but not one like that."

The shelter worker gave her a comforting pat on her arm. "I understand. And it would be worse if you took her now and then had to bring her back in a few months. I'm sure we can find another home for this little girl, and maybe another more docile cat for you, so don't you worry."

Ruby was leaving, Ophelia realized in shock. And taking with her Ophelia's best chance at escape!

"Wait!"

With that piercing yowl, she stuck a forearm through the bars of her cage. "Wait, human, come back! Take me with you!"

But by now, the other felines in the room had joined in the chorus, their combined meows loud enough to drown out hers. She shoved her other forearm through the bars and frantically shook both paws.

"Wait, human!" she yowled again. "Don't leave! Please come back for me."

"It's no good," the tabby said with a philosophical sigh and flopped down on his side. "They can't hear you over —"

"Well, I'll be."

The tabby halted in mid-protest as the human words drifted to them over the cacophony of cat cries. Shanice had turned and was staring back at them.

"Check that out, Ruby," she said, pointing her blue claw. "The little girl kitty is calling you."

Ruby turned, too, and then gave her head a vigorous shake. "Oh, no. Surely not."

"Uh-huh. Yes, she is."

With those no-nonsense words, Shanice caught the other woman by the arm and marched her back in their direction. Ophelia stared at them, wide-eyed. Had she been given another chance?

"Time to be quiet," the orange tabby hissed at her. "You've got to show her you would make a good house feline."

Nodding, Ophelia pulled her arms back into the cage and settled into a seated position, spine straight and tail wrapped neatly around her paws. Still as she was on the outside, however, she could feel herself quivering inside, as if she were poised to pounce upon a wayward mouse. The other cats in the room seemed to realize that something important was about to happen, for they subsided as well, save for an occasional random mew.

"Look," Shanice said. "Don't she look elegant? Like something straight out of an Egyptian tomb."

"She *is* really pretty," the other female agreed, gnawing on her bright red lips. "And so cute with that little pink collar. It looks like she can be very well behaved, if she wants. If she posed like that in the shop, the customers would be impressed. I mean, I'd like to . . . I really would, but . . ."

"Break out the big guns," the tabby instructed, his hiss just loud enough for Ophelia's fuzzy ears. "You know what to do. Humans love that."

On cue, Ophelia raised a soft paw and

gently slid it through the bars, holding it high, as if she were about to bat at something. It was a silly trick that canines did, shaking paws, and she felt foolish every time she did it. But the gesture always made humans *ooh* and *ahh,* like they did when they saw a human baby. She needed to make this Ruby human feel the same sort of protectiveness toward *her.*

Then, just as she was afraid the gesture hadn't worked, Ruby reached out her hand in response. Feline fur and human flesh brushed together, and Ophelia saw the young woman smile.

It worked! I did it!

And, something else.

Ophelia blinked. She'd always been able to tell from a single touch from a human if they were good or bad — or really bad, in the case of the old woman's son! The old woman had been very good. As for this Ruby person . . . strangely, her touch reminded Ophelia a bit of the old woman. Maybe it wouldn't be so terrible, staying with her for a few days. Just until she escaped to find Brandon.

Ruby, meanwhile, was saying, "You know, now that I think about it, it's like I was destined to find this kitty. That morning, something told me to park down the block and walk the rest of the way to the coffee shop. And if I hadn't been walking, I never would have noticed that banana box on the sidewalk."

"What about your sister?"

Ruby shrugged. "Well, Rosa always tells me that I shouldn't ignore signs from the universe. She's a Santera," she said by way of explanation, though Ophelia had no idea what *that* meant, "so she should know."

"Works for me," Shanice answered with a wide grin. "Now, speaking of signs, how about we sign some papers so you can take little Ophelia to her new home?"

THREE

"What's with all this career crap?"

The young Latina seated across from Ruby pointed a long bejeweled fingernail at the Tarot cards arranged between them on the threadbare yellow velvet tablecloth. Her scarlet lips curled in disgust, and for a moment Ruby feared she might start tossing cards, or kicking the table over or something. Fortunately, the young woman confined herself to giving an evil eye that was darned impressive, considering she was sitting on the client side of the wooden table in the tiny curtained alcove that served as the shop's reading room.

Technically, the only one supposed to be able to do that evil eye thing here in Botanica Santa Rosa was Ruby Sparks, *Tarot Card Reader Extraordinaire.* That was what the sign in the window called her. If she were honest, Ruby thought — and not for the first time — she would have modified it to read, *Tarot Card Reader Fairly Competent.*

Her client's name was Carmen. Her real name, Ruby had already decided. She'd already learned in her two short months running the store all by herself that some people were so embarrassed to consult a Tarot card reader that they would give an alias. Kind of like they were checking into one of those by-the-hour motels.

The alias thing always made her, Ruby, feel a bit embarrassed herself — like she was doing something pervy, reading the cards. When that happened, she reminded herself what her much older Cuban half sister, Rosa López Famosa, had told her. *We provide a great service,* Rosa had intoned in the dramatic, singsong voice she often affected. *We offer guidance and spiritual counseling to people who cannot afford a psychiatrist anytime they have a life issue.*

That had been Rosa's chief bit of advice before leaving Ruby in charge of her Botanica — the Cuban/Haitian version of a New Age shop — while she took a sabbatical in New York City. Her other advice, given in a decidedly non-singsongy voice, had been basically for Ruby to get over herself.

Ruby grimaced a bit at the memory. Normally, she would have been insulted at

41

that last. But the truth was, she'd been telling herself the exact same thing long before she'd been unexpectedly reunited with Rosa.

"Well?" Carmen snapped, bringing Ruby back to the present.

The other woman's dark eyes had been lined and shadowed into perfect cat eyes, just like in the YouTube tutorials that Ruby had tried but never could duplicate. Squinting for a closer look at the cards, so that she momentarily resembled a nearsighted Cuban Grizabella, Carmen went on. "I don't care about no new job on the horizon. I asked you about my man. I wanna know, is he doing the dirty with that *puta* at the *cafetería,* or not?"

Translation — *is he cheating on me with the ho down at the coffee shop?*

Ruby's skinny, black-framed eyeglasses had slid down her nose, and she gave them an exasperated poke back into place. The adage about the customer always being right did not apply to Tarot readings. Bottom line, the cards said what they said, no matter how much the client protested.

Still, there was always room for interpretation.

"Well?" the young woman persisted. "Tell me what you see. Jeez, what kind of a Tarot card reader are you, anyhow?"

"Let me take another look."

Ruby gave Carmen her best attempt at Rosa's trademark serene smile — the one she'd seen her half sister use to great effect on rattled clients. Rosa had full repertoire of expressions she could summon on cue, some benign and some borderline scary. Ruby hadn't mastered them all yet.

Heck, she didn't even have the outfit down pat. As a Santera — a female priest of the Santería religion — Rosa tended to dress all in white, especially when on the clock. Knowing that particular wardrobe was religious in nature and indicated someone who'd been through years of training, Ruby didn't dare emulate that look. Instead, she opted for variations on the stereotypical New Age reader regalia. Today's outfit was baggy red harem pants topped by a vintage white peasant blouse decorated with multi-colored dingle balls and sashed around the waist with a length of soft yellow leather.

While Carmen snapped her gum and ostentatiously checked her cellphone, Ruby again studied the spread — the stylized arrangement of cards — before her. As usual in a more detailed reading, she was using the traditional Celtic Cross. Six cards were laid in a cross shape representing the client's past, present, and near future, and another four cards were arranged in a column beside the cross to indicate the client's inner resources and potential. For this client, she was using the Morgan-Greer set of seventy-eight cards. It was one of her favorite decks to read with, borderless with a bright '70s vibe that tended to appeal to both former hippies and younger clients.

Unfortunately, a second look at the cards didn't change what she'd seen the first time. Fully half of the ten cards she'd drawn for the reading were pentacles, also known as coins — the Tarot suit associated with money, business, and generosity. A six of wands held the top spot on the column, indicating some sort of monetary reward to come. But not a single card hinted at a romantic relationship, let alone a stormy one.

So, what to do? Lie and tell Carmen what she obviously wanted to hear, that her man was two-timing her? Or, stick with the original reading that had nothing to do with her question?

"Oh, for kibble's sake! The answer is right in front of you!"

Ophelia shot an exasperated look at Ruby, who was busy gnawing the red coloring off her lips instead of talking to the other human. The cat was in her usual spot in the reading room, atop a short white column in the corner. Previously, the small pillar had held a statue of a dark-skinned female human wearing a crystal crown and dressed in blue and white, with a long necklace of tiny seashells draped over her shoulders.

Yemaya, she'd heard Ruby call the figure. But on her first day living in this strange new place, Ophelia had decided that the column was an ideal spot to laze about on. She had nudged the statue off onto the thick patterned rug below to make room for herself, earning a shriek and a *bad kitty!* from Ruby.

It took kicking the statue off the column twice more before Ruby had been properly trained. With an exasperated *fine, you win,* the human had retrieved the statue from the ground a final time and put it up on a high shelf, leaving the column permanently free for feline lounging.

Ophelia thought it an even trade for her condescending to continue wearing the silly pink collar that the shelter human, Shanice, had put on her.

Now Ophelia slid with smoke-like silence off the column and padded over to the table. Over the past two weeks that she'd been living there at the store, she'd watched as Ruby used the brightly colored pieces of cardboard to tell a story to whichever human was sitting with her. A couple of times, Ruby would leave the cards lying on the table while escorting the person she called *the client* back to the front of the shop. Ophelia took those opportunities to jump into Ruby's chair and peer more closely at the pictures, using a paw to spread them out on the table so she could see them all.

It didn't take long before she had memorized every image, along with the meanings that Ruby gave to them.

Pausing near Ruby's chair, she stealthily stretched along one table leg so that she could just see over the table's edge. She snaked a paw to where the remainder of the Tarot deck was neatly stacked at Ruby's elbow. Then she batted the deck, so that the top card flipped over and landed face up on the cloth beside the pentacle-heavy spread.

Three of Swords.

Satisfied that her work was done, at least for the moment, she slipped to the ground again and trotted back over to the column. By the time she had leaped up onto the column again and settled into a comfortable sprawl, emerald eyes squeezed tightly shut, Ruby was staring at her in amazement.

■ ■ ■ ■

Did that seriously just happen?

Ruby's gaze swept from the small black cat practically melting off the column in the corner and back to the Tarot card that said cat had just all but tossed into her lap. There had to have been a bug or something on the table, she told herself. No way had her new pet deliberately come over to flip a card to help her out.

Or had she?

Deciding to reserve judgment on that until later, Ruby turned her attention to the new card with its printed image of a plump red heart pressed against a blue sky.

The heart covered a blazing sun so that only a narrow ring of gold rays could be seen, while a threatening black storm cloud loomed above. But, most telling, three gold-hilted swords pierced the heart, one driving straight from the top, and the other two crisscrossed behind it. Not that the card was particularly gory, for only a moderate trickle of blood slid down the blade of the center sword. Still, the image got its point across.

Perfect!

She suppressed a relieved sigh. This card was her favorite of the minor arcana, that

47

portion of the Tarot card deck comparable to the ace through king cards in a regular poker deck. This card spoke of all manner of things — loss, broken relationships, sacrifice — as related to love gone bad. And it also served as the proverbial wake-up call when it came to romantic betrayal.

The *get over yourself* card, as Rosa likely would have put it.

Sending a little mental *thank you* to Ophelia, Ruby cleared her throat to get Carmen's attention back.

"As you can see, I've pulled a clarifying card," she said, holding up the Three of Swords so the young woman could take a closer look. Totally ignoring the spread of pentacles, she added, "I'm afraid your suspicions are correct — your boyfriend is cheating on you."

Cellphone forgotten, the young woman's kohled eyes widened in dismay as Ruby spent the next few minutes explaining the card's meaning, giving her the doleful message about the bad while elaborating on the encouraging aspects of meeting challenges and overcoming obstacles. When Ruby had finished, Carmen's eyes narrowed again.

"I knew it! Why, that son of a —"

She switched over to Spanish and sputtered on for several outraged moments. Like most non-Cubans in South Florida, Ruby's Spanish vocabulary was pretty well limited to curse words and menu items. Thus, while she had a fair idea of what Carmen was saying right now, she'd be pretty well out of the loop had the conversation been about anything other than boyfriends gone bad. It didn't help that Cuban Spanish differed slightly in some expressions and spellings from the Mexican/South American Spanish she'd taken for one semester in high school. The diminutive *chiquitico* with the "co" on the end instead of a "to" being an example.

As for the whole boyfriend thing, she didn't blame Carmen for the outburst. One reason she, Ruby, had ended up at the Botanica had to do with kicking a jerk of an ex-boyfriend to the curb. Though, to be literal about it, *she'd* been the one ending up on the street, since the lease to the condo had been in said jerk's name. And that was why, after a fortuitous reunion with her long-estranged half sister, she'd ended up moving in with Rosa a little more than a year earlier.

Carmen wound down finally and gave her a fierce, teary smile.

"Thanks. When I first sat down I thought you were, you know, kind of fake. Not like Rosa. But you did a good reading. I might

49

come back just for you."

Ruby managed a smile in return. Not exactly the review she'd want to see on Yelp, but she'd take it.

They both scooted back from the table, and Ruby pulled open the heavy black velvet curtain that separated the reading room from the main shop.

"Remember, stay strong when you confront him," she said, gesturing her client on out. "He's the bad guy, not you. Now, do you want any prayer cards or anything?"

Ophelia waited until she heard the curtain drop back into place; then she opened her eyes again and addressed the reading table.

"Don't you ever get tired of listening to these humans and their silly drama?"

The answer came in the form of a snort and snuffle, and then the yellow velvet tablecloth began to sway. A moment later, a compact white pit bull crawled her way out from under the piece of furniture. Getting to her paws, she stretched and yawned.

The pit's wide open jaws, complete with lolling pink tongue, would have looked fierce to anyone who didn't know her. But after her fright at first seeing the pit bull that memorable day of her rescue, Ophelia had discovered the truth. The canine was as sweet as her name, Azucar, which translated from the Spanish to "sugar."

Zuki, as she had told Ophelia most humans called her, finished her yawn and gave herself a shake that almost took out the table.

"I never listen, not even when it's Rosa doing the talking," the canine said in her usual soft voice. "I just go to sleep. It's nice and cozy under there."

"Well, I don't know how you can sleep with all that yowling going on," Ophelia complained, leaping from the column onto the table in a single graceful bound. "Humans! With all that whining and complaining they do, I don't understand how they seem to be in charge of the world. Felines — or even canines — would do a much better job of running things!"

"I heard somewhere it's because they have hands with thumbs, and we just have paws." Yawning again, Zuki changed the subject, adding, "My tummy is rumbling. I think we should go ask Ruby for a snack."

"Canines! You'll do anything for food."

Still, Ophelia leaped down from the table and padded after the pit bull. *She* wasn't going to beg for treats like a silly dog, but if Ruby offered . . .

By the time the pair left the reading room,

Ruby was finishing up at the cash register, while Carmen — small brown bag in hand — was headed for the front door. She opened it and then paused for a moment, calling back something to Ruby.

But Ophelia didn't hear what she said. Her bright green eyes widened, and she stared at the strip of outdoors that was visible beyond the woman. If she acted now, she could fly past the woman and out into the street, where she could start her search for her brother.

Zuki must have read her mind, however. The pit bull gave a sharp little bark that distracted Ophelia long enough for the woman to walk out. The door slammed shut behind her, the string of paw-sized brass bells that hung from the door's knob jangling like Ophelia's belled collar.

She glared at her canine friend. "Why did you do that? That was my chance to make a break for it."

"Hmmph! More like your chance to run out into the street and get squished by a car." Padding toward the counter, Zuki added over her shoulder, "You need to come up with a better plan than just sneaking out."

"What would you suggest?" Ophelia snarked back at her. "If I could dial Ruby's cell phone, I guess I could put an ad in the newspaper. Oh, wait, no one reads the paper anymore. I guess I could post on that Face-booker thing humans like. *Trying to find my brother. He looks like me except he's a boy. And his tail is shorter.*"

She didn't want to admit, however, that one part of her was secretly relieved the door had closed before she could slip out. It wasn't that she didn't want to find Brandon. She'd never been without her brother, and it was almost like she was missing a paw with him gone. Some days, she didn't want to get up from her naps, knowing he wasn't there to run and tumble with her. But *Outside* was scary, particularly since she had only a vague idea where she was compared to the location of their old home.

Ophelia sighed. Even though Zuki was a canine, maybe she was right. She needed a better plan.

Hearing her own tummy abruptly rumble, Ophelia trotted over to the register where the pit bull was already sitting, one paw raised. Ruby looked up from the piece of paper she was making marks on, glanced at the big round timepiece on the wall behind her, and then gave them both an indulgent smile.

"What, snack time already? Give me a

53

minute to clear the space, and then I'll see about your treats."

While they waited, Ruby reached beneath the counter and pulled out a tall, skinny plastic bottle with a fancy label on it. She pressed something on top of the bottle that made it spray a cloud of scent. As the fine mist drifted down to her, Ophelia sneezed.

What is that? she had demanded the first time Ruby had spritzed the strange-smelling stuff about. *It stinks worse than mice feet!*

Zuki had explained that it was an old fashioned human perfume called *Florida Water.* Or, more accurately, Flower Water — *agua de flores,* she'd called it, giving those words a perfect Spanish accent. (Ophelia had learned her first day there that Zuki understood Spanish as well as English.) Then, being a typical canine and proud of her olfactory skills, Zuki had started naming ingredients the stinky flower water contained.

Water, alcohol, lavender, lemon, cloves, cinnamon . . .

Ophelia didn't hear the whole recipe, for she'd padded off midway through the recitation. Later on, she'd heard Ruby say something about using the flower water for space clearing, though of course that made no sense to anyone but a human.

54

Now Ruby finished making the place smell like sour flowers and put the bottle back beneath the counter. Then she headed through a door behind the counter, returning with a pair of small-lidded crocks.

Knowing what was in the containers, Zuki gave a happy wriggle, her whip of a tail thumping against the tile floor.

"Who's a good girl? Who's a good girl?" Ruby demanded in the squeaky little voice humans normally reserved for their infant offspring.

Ophelia suppressed a snort. It was a silly question to ask, since all three of them knew that she meant Zuki. Just another pointless human ritual, like all the spritzing! Zuki didn't seem to care, however. She happily crunched the tiny bone-shaped biscuits Ruby tossed her. Then Ruby reached into the second, much smaller container that rattled when she shook it.

"How about you, Ophelia? Does the pwitty kitty want a treat, too?"

"Ugh, really?" she mewed in reply.

Still, her velvety black nose wriggled reflexively at the thought of the tiny fishy squares the jar held. When Ruby gave the container another shake, she decided she could suffer with the silly talk if it meant a tasty snack. And so she bounded onto the counter and gave a sharp *meow.*

Ruby laughed in response. "Actually, you deserve a handful," she exclaimed as she counted out the usual three little treats and then added a fourth. "You sure saved my butt on that reading, sticking your paw up there like that and knocking out the Three of Swords. I had no clue you knew how to read Tarot cards. I might have to hire you to help with the clients."

Ophelia's mouth was full as she crunched the treats, so her *like I don't have better things to do* came out muffled. Zuki heard her, however, and snickered.

"Maybe we should put your name on the sign in the window, too," the pit bull said as she snuffled up a few stray biscuit crumbs. "I bet humans would pay a lot of money to have a cat tell their fortune."

"I'm sure I could do much better than Ruby," was Ophelia's lofty reply. "But I don't want to. Besides, what would I do with money?"

"You could give it to Ruby. She's going to school to get smarter, and it costs lots of money. I've heard her say that before."

As if hearing what the pit bull had said, Ruby slid the treat containers aside and then pulled out a large book. She set it down with a thump beside the cash register.

Scooting onto the tall stool behind the counter, she sighed loudly and flipped open the text.

Curious, Ophelia leaned closer to take a look. It was boring as far as books went, since it appeared to be all little black marks that she knew stood for words, and had not a single picture of a feline that she could see. No wonder looking at it made Ruby sigh.

She flicked a whisker. Perhaps she should consider helping Ruby with the Tarot card readings after all. Anything to make a human smarter was a good cause. Perhaps she'd consider it! But first, she had to figure out how she was going to track down her brother.

Part of the problem was that the son had left them in a strange part of town, so that at first she'd had no idea of where she was in this human world. Zuki had helped her understand the situation one night by pulling down a book with a fancy picture of the area. A map, she'd called it, adding, *Humans need these pictures to find their way around, because they don't have a sense of direction built into them like a canine does.*

Although Ophelia had known about the ocean that lay beyond their old house, she'd thought it was everywhere. But the picture showed something quite different. *This is the Atlantic Ocean,* the pit bull had explained, pointing at a big empty section of blue to the far side of the page. Moving her paw to the left, she pointed at a long skinny pale shape, like a fat worm. *And this is Palm Beach, where the rich humans and their fancy canines — and felines — live. That's where your old house is. This here* — she pointed further left, at a big splotch that took up almost half of the page — *is the city of West Palm Beach. That's the not-so-fancy side where we live. And this* — she indicated a snaky section of blue between the big splotch and the skinny worm — *is the Intracoastal. It's like a big river that separates the fancy from the not-fancy. If you want to go back to your old house, you have to walk over long bridges to get there.*

The explanation had been enlightening . . . and more than a bit frightening. And realizing how big their world really was had been one reason she hadn't yet gone searching for Brandon.

Making sure now that Ruby was paying attention to her book and not them, Ophelia lightly jumped from the counter. Zuki had finished her biscuits and was now sprawled on the wooden floor. Ophelia gave a casual stretch and a deliberately unconcerned lick of one paw. Much as it went against everything she'd learned since kittenhood, she was going to ask a canine's help.

"Uh, Zuki," she ventured, "you said I needed a better plan. I'm sure I can think up something on my own, of course, but sometimes it's good to have another perspective. So, how do you think I should go about trying to find Brandon?"

Zuki gave a little snuffle as she considered the question. "Well, I do know a few canines around town. I can talk to them. They know things."

"Things? What sort of things?"

"Things like, what's going on in the streets . . . what dogs are new in town . . . and has anyone seen a short-tailed black cat roaming around? I could put out the word and see if anyone bites."

Then, when Ophelia reflexively bristled at that last word, she hastily added, "I don't mean literally. And I'll make sure they know that if anyone sees him, that he stays safe from any strays out there. And they should tell him where you are, so he can make his way here."

"That might help. But I should do something, myself. I *need* to do *something.*"

That last ended in a yowl. At the sound,

Ruby looked up from her book.

"Ophelia, are you all right?" she asked in concern, peering over her black-framed glasses. "Did Zuki accidentally step on you or something?"

When the pair blandly stared back at her, she shrugged and returned to her reading. Ophelia tried again.

"I appreciate your help, Zuki, but I need to do something myself to find Brandon. The problem is, I can't think of what to do besides sneak out and go looking for him."

"I do have another idea," the dog replied, getting to her paws and giving herself a shake. "Let's go to the courtyard and ask Philomena."

"Philo-who?"

"Never mind, you'll see. Come on."

Collar tags jingling, Zuki padded her way behind the counter to the open doorway beyond. With an exasperated hiss, Ophelia scampered after her.

Her first day in the Botanica, Ophelia had been both confused and a little under-whelmed by her new digs. She was used to the old woman's sprawling house that was filled with sofas and chairs and tables and beds, all of which made for excellent cat lounging. In contrast, Ruby's house was no larger than the small cottage behind the old woman's house where Luciana the house-keeper lived. It had taken Ophelia only a few minutes to slink through every room in the new place. She found it an odd amalgamation of spaces that, strangely, did not include a living room or a dining room.

Zuki had explained away some of the muddle.

The Botanica was actually what Zuki — who knew all sorts of interesting things — told her was called Mission Revival style. It had a yellow stucco exterior, arched windows, and terra-cotta tiles on the roof. The house dated from the 1920s . . . almost the beginning of time, Ophelia had thought in awe. A wall between what once had been the living room and small dining room had been taken down, and the space filled with shelves where the merchandise they sold was all arranged. This, and the small reading room which had once been a bedroom, made up Botanica Santa Rosa.

The remainder of the house — a kitchen and bathroom through a door beyond the shop area, and two bedrooms and a bathroom upstairs — was where Ruby actually lived. Not much room for running and exploring, particularly when Ruby did not allow her to play with the interesting books and statues and rocks that lined the store shelves and were good for a paw smack or two.

But the courtyard!

Ophelia purred now at the thought. It was almost as nice as the old woman's walled backyard with its giant rectangular pond and rows of swaying palm trees. Of course, Ruby's courtyard was much smaller; still, the paved square of ground did have a giant tree that she could climb, and a small pond where she could splash at the water. The pond was partway above the ground, its stone walls tall enough so that a human could sit comfortably on it like a bench . . . or a feline could lie in the broad shadow it threw. A few white water lilies floated on the pond's surface, putting out a faint scent that reminded Ophelia of the spray that Ruby spritzed about.

To be sure, the courtyard's stuccoed walls were rough and not good for scaling with cat paws, so she had yet to find an escape route from there. Still, the courtyard was an excellent place for one to lounge and watch lizards. There was even a concrete table and benches covered in bright multicolored tile in a starburst pattern that was cool for sleeping on.

But, best of all, in the far corner of the courtyard beneath a strangler fig tree was a stack of three wire cages, each one of which was home to a bright red rooster.

Of course, those chickens didn't live full-time in the cages. Every morning, Ruby would come out to the courtyard to open their doors and give the trio fresh food and water. The roosters spent the day crowing and pecking about the place, and eating the bugs that, by rights, should have been Ophelia's to play with. And at night, the human would herd them back into their cages to sleep. Boring, useless creatures! At least if she'd been allowed to chase them . . .

Ophelia sighed. The first time she'd seen them out in the courtyard, she had done what any respectable feline would do. She crouched low so that she was flat against the cool stone, wriggled her butt . . . and then pounced!

Unfortunately, Zuki had intercepted her leap, so that all she got was a single shiny black tail-feather as the roosters scattered in a flurry of squawking. Before she could prepare for another launch, the pit bull had warned her in stern tones that the roosters were Ruby's pets and thus off-limits for hunting. Ophelia had sulked a bit but agreed to follow the rules, though she kept the feather as a trophy to bat about when she got bored.

But despite the "no hunting" directive, the courtyard was a very fine place, indeed. Getting to it, however, was a feat for any cat.

Ophelia trotted down the short hall, past the black-and-white-tiled kitchen and the pink-and-black bathroom where her litter box was located. At the end of that corridor was the door leading outside. Ruby had installed in one of its panels a dog door that let Zuki — and now Ophelia — wander in and out during the day.

The compact canine had no fear when it came to barreling through the flapping plastic that covered the opening. For Ophelia, however, finding a way around the evil flapping thing was always a trial. If she tried to squeeze past, its rough edges always yanked a bit of fur. If she barreled through like Zuki, that flapping plastic curtain always slapped her rump before she could clear it. And then, when she was ready to come back inside again, she faced the same dilemma.

Being outside in the courtyard, however, was worth the suffering.

Even so, when she reached the door, she halted and waited until the flapping plastic rectangle settled back into place. *Pulled fur or a smack, which was worse?*

64

Then she heard the sound of gravel crunching in the outside parking area. That meant a customer was coming in, which meant Ruby would be busy for a while. And depending on how long it took to talk with this Philo-whatever (cat? canine? bird?), it was probably best that Ruby be otherwise occupied.

Steeling herself for the smack of the plastic, she bounded through the flap and out to the courtyard where Zuki awaited her.

FOUR

Ruby heard the sound of dog tags jingling and looked up from her text book. Zuki had padded behind the counter and was trotting out toward her doggie door and the courtyard beyond. Ophelia, black tail waving like a silky serpent, was following after.

Ruby smiled.

It was good to see the two of them getting along, rather than fighting like — well, cats and dogs. Not that she'd been worried about Zuki. Despite the fearsome reputation that clung to her breed, Zuki was one of the best-tempered dogs that Ruby had ever known. She never snapped or growled at any of the various furred and feathered creatures that had passed through the Botanica. Indeed, Zuki had been the one to find Ophelia trapped inside that box on the sidewalk. When the poor cat had collapsed from the heat, the pit bull had begun licking her motionless form, seemingly in an attempt to revive her.

And when Ruby had returned from the animal shelter and set down the pet carrier holding Ophelia, Zuki had pranced about in what Ruby could only describe as the canine version of the Happy Dance.

Of course, Ophelia had been harder to win over.

Ruby's smile became rueful. The first few days with a new kitty in the place had consisted primarily of hiding and hissing on said kitty's part, along with the occasional swat in Zuki's direction. But the pit bull had gamely hung in there, and after about a week, the pair suddenly had been as tight as if they'd been raised together.

Unfortunately, Ruby was still working on being BFFs with the cat. Despite what she'd been sure was a connection between them there in the shelter, she and Ophelia were still nothing more than acquaintances. Ophelia deigned to be petted at meal time, but as yet there was no lap sitting, and no warm snuggly kitty on the foot of her bed.

"I'll win you over yet, my pretty," Ruby intoned in her best Wicked Witch voice as she watched the cat vanish out the pet door.

Still smiling, she returned her attention to her book. She was sitting atop a wooden stool at the glass-fronted counter there at the back of the shop — her usual spot when not otherwise occupied with stocking or customers. The counter stretched almost the width of the room, cash register in the center and flanked by two small baskets of impulse buy items (this week, two soy mini candles for the price of one). The counter's shelves held rows of bright-colored prayer cards, as well as stones and crystals (natural and carved), along with a large variety of Tarot and oracle cards.

From her vantage point, she could look down every aisle and keep an eye on the front door as well. Even though her clientele supposedly were spiritually inclined, shoplifting was always a possibility. Though, surprisingly — or perhaps, not — she'd had little problem with theft in the store.

Ruby glanced at the wall behind her. Between two hand-lettered signs, one reading *No Checks Accepted* and the other *All Sales FINAL,* hung a life-sized oil portrait of Rosa. Seen from the waist up, she was dressed in her usual Santera white, her long black hair almost completely hidden beneath a white headwrap. Her strong, sharp features were set in an unflinching expression and always reminded Ruby of a Cuban Frida Kahlo. And even though she was a good two decades older than Ruby, no way did she appear anywhere near fifty years old.

Ruby shook her head. Despite the fact they shared the same mother, Ruby had yet to find any familial resemblance between her and her half sister, save for the same wide, full mouth. Definitely, the woman in the portrait projected a "don't jack with me" vibe that Ruby had yet to cultivate. If Rosa's reputation in the neighborhood wasn't sufficient to keep sticky fingers in pockets, the way her painted eyes seemed to follow people about the room likely did the job.

She was just settling into her biography of Mary Wollstonecraft again when the front door gave a warning jangle. *So much for studying before lunch.* But in the next moment, she saw it wasn't another customer after all.

"So, anyone up for food?"

The newcomer strode down the main aisle toward the rear counter where Ruby sat. The skirt of her brightly patterned Lilly Pulitzer halter sundress swung with every step. A bright yellow crossbody purse added to the outfit's tropical vibe and allowed her to carry a large white paper bag. She raised the sack so Ruby could see it was stamped with the name of the local Chinese food emporium.

Ruby shut her book, slid her glasses back up her nose, and grinned. "Do you really have to ask? I'm always up for food. Seriously, I've put on five pounds since I've been stuck here in this shop," she complained.

She slid off the stool and rushed around the counter to give her friend and former Florida Atlantic University roommate, Johanna "JoJo" Jones, a side-hug that barely missed the bag.

JoJo returned the hug and then stepped aside, shooting her a look of mock dismay. "You're so lucky, Rubes," she exclaimed, using her longtime nickname for Ruby. "You gain weight, and it goes to your butt or boobs. Me, I put on a pound, and it goes right to my belly."

Ruby rolled her eyes. They were the stereotypical opposites when it came to looks — JoJo being slim, blond, and leggy, and Ruby being sturdy, brunette, and not leggy. If there was an extra pound anywhere on her friend, Ruby darned sure couldn't see it. Aloud, however, she said, "I'm sure whatever you brought is low cal as well as being delish."

She paused for a look at the faux skull beside the register. The digital clock embedded in its forehead read 11:53 a.m.

"I can break for a couple of minutes. Let me lock up, and then we can sit in the kitchen."

Ruby went to the front door and flipped over the *Open* sign so it read *Will Return* before turning the lock. JoJo, meanwhile, was prowling along the main aisle poking at the merchandise.

The other rows held the more workaday merchandise: spell books and prayer pamphlets; baskets of ritual materials (shells, herbs, and the like); shelves of colorful candles guaranteed to bring luck in anything from love to the lottery. The shelves down the middle, however, were an orgy of statuary.

All denominations and sizes were represented, from tiny gold Buddhas wearing serene smiles to a life-sized rendering of a half-naked, crutch-wielding St. Lazarus and his dogs. Since the shop was technically a Botanica, the greatest portion of the statues represented the Santería pantheon, along with a variety of Roman Catholic saints. But Rosa was a shrewd businesswoman, and so in recent years she'd begun catering to New Age and Wiccan clients as well.

A good quarter of what the shop now offered included such popular items as essential oils and witchy T-shirts, as well as singing bowls and hanging chimes. Basically, a one-stop shop no matter one's esoteric preferences. Ruby had expanded the New Age offerings even further. Now everything from pastel-hued fairy figurines to gnomes to variations of the Three Wise Monkeys lurked among the various saintly representations on the statuary aisle. She'd also just stocked a series of modern witch statues, each figure wearing the stereotypical pointed black hat, but dressed in the outfit of her mundane job function.

JoJo picked up the blond witchy version of Lady Justice. The palm-sized statue was wearing a mini-skirted black suit that matched her hat and was holding the Scales of Justice in one hand, an upward-pointed sword in the other.

"Ha, all the little law clerks at the firm would probably say this is me," she said with a sour look as she raised the statue in a toasting gesture and then set it back on the shelf. "You can get me this for Christmas — assuming I don't say screw it and quit to stay home while Blake supports me in the style I'd like to become used to."

Blake being Dr. Blake Gormley, handsome young dermatologist to Palm Beach's richest, and JoJo's fiancé.

"You're not going to quit the law firm,"

Ruby assured her as she gestured her friend toward the kitchen. "The whole four years we were roomies at FAU, and the three years of law school after, all you could talk about was how you couldn't wait to be a criminal defense attorney. And how many other new lawyers did you beat out for this, and I quote, *super-duper plum position* that pays you more money than God?"

"Yeah, well, plans change. Besides, *you* were going to get your master's, and then your doctorate, and then teach wide-eyed college freshmen all about great eighteenth- and nineteenth-century women's literature. Instead, you moved out to California to try to be a screenplay writer for a couple of years. Now here you are back in Florida, pushing thirty and running your half sister's woo-woo shop."

"This isn't a woo-woo shop," Ruby countered, not for the first time. Reverting to her default statement of purpose that she'd crafted, she went on. "I'm running a retail establishment that specializes in traditional artifacts used primarily in Caribbean-based religious rites."

JoJo halted and swung about to face her. "Seriously, Rubes? You're selling naked people candles and live chickens. It's a woo-woo shop."

"They're roosters, and they're not for sale," Ruby shot back.

To be honest, however, the roosters *had* been on the block, until about five minutes after Rosa left town. Not willing to sell a hapless bird for ritual sacrifice, no matter if it was done humanely, Ruby had slapped a "quarantine" sign on their cages, telling anyone who inquired that the trio had been diagnosed with bird flu. She'd been trying ever since to find a poultry rescue to take them. In the meantime, their continued presence meant waking to a cacophony of crowing most mornings, but the loss of sleep was more than offset by a clear conscience.

And only some of the candles she sold were in the shape of naked humans!

This time, it was JoJo who rolled her eyes; still, her tone was apologetic as she replied, "Fine, I'm sorry. What you're doing makes sense. You get free rent and a salary, and you still have time to take a couple of classes and work on your master's thesis. I just worry about you being alone, with some of the people who stop in here."

"Ninety-nine percent of our customers are lovely, everyday people . . . and thanks to you, I've got Zuki for that last one percent who aren't."

A year earlier, JoJo had risked literal life and limb to steal Zuki, then a scrawny puppy, from the backyard of a lowlife who'd bought her to use as a bait dog in a dogfight ring. But since JoJo's condo association — just like the majority of HOAs in South Florida — didn't allow bully breeds, she couldn't keep the pup herself. Fortunately, Rosa had a soft spot for dogs, and so she'd not objected when Zuki had come to live with Ruby instead.

"So where are the fur babies?" she wanted to know as they settled at one end of the galley kitchen. "I can't believe they're not here trying to mooch our food. Is everyone getting along okay?"

"Ophelia and Zuki ran off to the courtyard before you came in," Ruby replied as JoJo unpacked the food — moo goo gai pan, along with an order of garlic shrimp, the requisite white rice, and a side of spring rolls. "And, yes, they're getting along fine."

She pulled a couple of vintage turquoise Fiestaware plates from the cabinet. She set the dishes on the red Formica and chrome dinette table that sat beneath the window. As always, she couldn't help but mentally contrast the narrow galley setup with those oversized farm kitchens in the home magazines with acres of cabinets and miles of counters and islands.

The first thing one saw as one walked through the kitchen door was a big painted hook, where Ruby hung Zuki's leash and a small tote that contained dog walking accessories: folding water dish, poop bags, and a half-bald tennis ball for chasing. On the opposite wall from the door and to the right of the dinette were glass-front white cabinets. These old-style fixtures hung over a couple of white-tiled countertops on either side of the white enamel sink (Rosa had yet to install an automatic dishwasher). To the right along the short wall was an old gas stove and an almost-as-ancient refrigerator. Together with the cabinets and stove, they formed a tidy, L-shaped cooking/prep area.

Set against the opposite short wall was a tall, pierced-door pie safe. The piece was original to the house, its chippy white paint a result of age rather than the work of a clever up-cycler. That cabinet held linens, pots and pans, and extra dishes. Beside it in the corner sat a large blue-glazed round planter on a wheeled base. The pot held a ponytail palm — a bulbous-trunked succulent with a swath of long narrow leaves sprouting from its top in a crazed fountain of green. The plant was Rosa's pride and joy, and so Ruby had been frantic the first time she'd seen Ophelia nibbling at one of the leaves. Luckily, a quick flick of water from the sink had scared her off, and so far there'd been no further signs of feline chomping.

All in all, it was a homey space. Even JoJo, who was proud owner of one of those miles-and-acres farm kitchens, often remarked how cheerful she found it.

Reaching into the aforementioned icebox, as Rosa called it the fridge, Ruby grabbed a couple of bottles of sparkling water. Then, slipping into one of the dinette's matching chrome and red upholstered chairs, she added, "Ophelia was a bit hissy the first couple of days, but that was to be expected. Now that she's had time to settle in, she and Zuki are best buds."

"What about you and her?" JoJo asked as she dumped half the moo goo gai pan onto her plate and then passed the cardboard container to Ruby. "Does she sit on your lap while you read Tarot cards?"

"Not exactly. She's still a bit standoffish with me, but she's getting better. But I do think she has a career ahead of her as a Tarot reader all by herself."

Ruby added a bit of garlic shrimp and part of the container of rice to her plate. Then, between bites, she told her friend about the earlier reading with Carmen, and how Ophelia had saved the day.

"It was pretty uncanny," she finished, waving her wooden chopsticks for emphasis. "I mean, what are the chances she could turn over the exact card that made sense?"

"Well, depending on whether or not you believe that sort of thing" — JoJo was, Ruby knew, quite the skeptic — "I'd say almost no chance. So your new kitty must really be a prodigy."

As they continued to eat, they moved on to other subjects — starting with the latest update on JoJo's attempts to secure the perfect wedding venue (two churches and a nature center had thus far been eliminated), and then on to Ruby's love life (or lack thereof).

"Speaking of which," Ruby said through a mouthful of garlic shrimp, "I need a pinkie swear or something that you won't try to set me up with another of Blake's friends ever again."

"What? I thought you and Bobby got on just fine."

"Oh, yeah . . . if by *fine* you mean that I should ignore what he told me about being nervous around girls who have unnatural hair color. And how the one little blue streak in my hair is the first step toward a full tattoo body suit and major facial piercings. Nope, no more of those clean-cut professional guys, thank you very much."

JoJo gave a martyred sigh. "Well, you didn't like the spin instructor from the gym either. Too peppy, I think you said? And you told me that the cute barista I found for you at CoffeeCoffee" — she named the nearby Starbucks knockoff — "was too needy. Seriously, I'm running out of single guys to dangle in front of you."

"And thank goodness for that," Ruby shot back, stabbing a hapless shrimp with her chopstick.

Then, tempering the words with a smile, she added, "Not that I don't appreciate your concern, but I'm calling a halt to dating for a while. Between the shop and studying, I barely have time for a casual dinner out once a week, let alone a steady guy."

"What, and you think I have time for a fiancé and a wedding on top of working sixty hours a week?" JoJo countered with a snort. "But I make time for him — for us — because it's important to me. And I want my best friend to find a great guy and be worn to a happy frazzle, just like me."

"Uh, thanks?" Ruby laughed. "Believe me, until further notice I'm perfectly happy to live vicariously through you and your fairytale relationship with Blake."

"Okay, if that's really what you want . . . but just as long as it stays vicarious. Oh, crud."

That last was directed not at Ruby for settling for a secondhand romance, but at Jo-Jo's cell phone, which had started binging. Wiping duck sauce off her fingers, the attorney swiped the screen and read the incoming text. Then she frowned.

"Work?" Ruby commiserated.

"Yep . . . so much for a leisurely lunch."

Sighing, JoJo snatched a final shrimp with her chopsticks and then reluctantly pushed back her chair. "Emergency meeting back at the office. All hands on deck and that kind of thing. I've got to get moving."

"You want me to pack up the rest of the food for you to take home to Blake?"

"No, you go ahead and save the leftovers for dinner tonight," her friend replied as she gathered her purse and looped it back over her shoulder. "Besides, one of those spring rolls is for Zuki. Give the fur babies a hug from me and tell them Auntie JoJo is sorry she didn't get to love on them today."

"Don't worry, I will."

Ruby walked her friend back to the front door, where they parted with mutual promises for lunch and shopping and happy hour

later in the week. Since no potential customers were lurking outside, Ruby relocked the
door after her and headed back to the
kitchen to finish the last couple of bites of
her lunch. Then, leftovers refrigerated and
dishes done, she picked up a spring roll and
a piece of shrimp — sauce carefully washed
off — and headed for the courtyard.

FIVE

"It's."

"The."

"Cat!"

"Be —"

"Ware."

"Brothers!"

The call came from the three courtyard roosters who had paused in mid-strut at Ophelia's approach. Usually, she ignored them lest the sight of their dancing tail-feathers be too tempting for even the strongest of felines to resist. They didn't have individual names, at least not that they shared with outsiders. Zuki called them Roosters One, Two, and Three, though Ophelia had no idea which one was which, since they looked identical.

Most times, the birds cackled and crowed among themselves out there in the courtyard. When they spoke to anyone else, it was as if there were three heads controlled by a single rooster brain. *More like bird brain,* she thought with a snort. Each bird clucked out one word, in turn, until as a group they had managed a full sentence. That made for boring conversation, in Ophelia's opinion, which was why she rarely engaged them.

But today, feeling particularly out of sorts with worry over Brandon, she slanted them an evil green look and let loose with a little *hisssssss.*

The three birds gave a collective *Squawk!* Then, wattles and combs wobbling, they flapped and fluttered their way to the safety of the side yard where Rosa grew her herbs.

Ophelia flopped onto the ground, laughing, her bad mood momentarily relieved.

"I should — do that — more often," she gasped out, waving sleek black paws in amusement. "It almost — makes up — for not being able to chase them!"

"That was mean," Zuki scolded, though Ophelia saw her cover a grin with one big paw. "You'd better be much nicer to Philomena."

Sobering, the cat got to her paws again. "All right, let's meet your friend and see if she can help me find Brandon. Though I'll probably do just as well looking at Ruby's Tarot cards."

"Forget Tarot cards. Philomena can tell

you anything just by looking at you. She's psychic."

Ophelia had lived in the Botanica long enough to know what *that* meant. She rolled her green eyes. "For kibble's sake, you've been hanging out with the human too long. You expect me to believe this Philomena can predict the future?"

"And the present, and the past!" Zuki exclaimed. "She's very, very smart. Do you know, she's at least fifty human years old."

"Really?" That impressed Ophelia more than anything else Zuki had said. She'd never met a furred or feathered creature anywhere near that old before. "Fine, I'll talk to her. Where is she hiding?"

"There." The pit bull waved a paw in the direction of the pond.

Ophelia frowned. She didn't see anyone. "Where?"

"There!" Zuki pointed a paw again. "In. The. Pond," she clarified, speaking slowly as if Ophelia were as dumb as a mouse.

Ophelia gave her a slanted look. If this was the canine's idea of a joke, well, Zuki was in for some payback. "The pond? What is she, a frog?"

"Jump up on the ledge and call her, and you'll see."

Muttering bad words about bossy canines,

Ophelia lightly leapt atop the rocky wall that surrounded the pond. Sitting straight up and wrapping her long black tail around her, she ventured, "Philomena? Philomena?"

A few seconds ticked by, and other than a lizard dropping from the tree to the table, no creature appeared. Leaning closer to the water, she repeated, "Philomena, where are you?"

Nothing. She shot a look back at Zuki, who gave her an encouraging nod. She took a deep breath and yowled, "PHILOMENA!"

Without warning, the pond rippled, and a large, shiny white head topped by a splotch of scarlet breached the surface, splashing water and halting a few inches from Ophelia's velvety black nose. Scaly lips made smacking sounds, and then a watery voice said, *"You need not to shout. I was coming out."*

"Me-YOW!"

Skittering away from the largest fish she had ever seen, Ophelia stubbed her rear paw on an uneven rock and went tumbling off the wall. She caught herself in mid-fall and twisted about, so that she landed on all four paws. But that didn't keep Roosters One through Three, who'd apparently been spying on her and witnessed her mishap, from clucking with hysterical laughter.

"*The.*"

"*Cat.*"

"*Fell.*"

"*Serves.*"

"*Her.*"

"*Right.*"

Ophelia hissed in their direction, which put an end to the laughter and promptly sent the chickens scuttling to the side yard again. She gave her front paw a quick, displacing lick and then shot a look at Zuki.

"Did you see that? That fish friend of yours is pretty mean. She — she knocked me over."

"Well, actually, I think you fell all by yourself," the pit bull replied, looking suspiciously like she was trying not to laugh, too. "But as long as you're all right, that's what matters. And so you know, Philomena is not just any fish — she's a koi who came all the way from Japan to live here. Now, go ask her about Brandon."

Huffing, Ophelia jumped back up onto the ledge.

The fish — or, rather, koi — named Philomena was still there, face barely out of the water and lips smacking so that she was surrounded by a halo of sparkly bubbles. The rest of her body seemed to be covered in

86

the same pearly white scales as her head, save for a few orangey-red patches that matched the splotch atop her head. And she was BIG . . . almost as long as a cat, and far thicker. Ophelia could well believe that she was as old as Zuki had said. Though why she'd never noticed the fish before, she couldn't guess. The pond was obviously far deeper than it looked.

Feeling slightly more respectful now, she flicked her whiskers and tried again.

"Uh, hello, uh, Philomena. I'm Ophelia the cat. I live here at the Botanica now with Zuki and the human, Ruby."

"It is a pleasure to meet you, young cat. If Ruby wants you being here, that's that."

Another rhyme? Ophelia paused and glanced back at Zuki. She asked in a stage whisper, "Does she always talk like that?"

"Yes. Now ask your question before she gets bored and leaves!"

"Fine." Turning back to the fish, who had moved her attention to the nearest water lily, she said, "Philomena, I need your help. My brother is missing, and I need to know how I can find him."

While the koi contemplatively nibbled on the water plant, Ophelia explained how she and Brandon had been dumped on the street. She told her how Brandon had gone for help while she waited behind, and how Zuki and Ruby had rescued her before her brother returned. And how, after she had spent a week at the animal shelter, Ruby brought her home to live at the Botanica.

"It's been almost a month now since Brandon disappeared," she finished, fighting to keep her voice from dropping to a sorry little yowl. "From what Zuki said, we were dumped ten or twelve blocks from the Botanica. So maybe Brandon isn't too far away. I know he'd never give up looking for me . . . that is, if something wasn't keeping him from it. Can you tell me where he is, so I can go looking for him, too?"

What she didn't ask . . . what she was afraid to ask . . . was *can you tell me if he's still alive?*

The koi gave a quick spin, sending ripples across the small pond. *"A sad story, little friend. Let me think how it will end."*

With those words, Philomena sank beneath the water's surface, so that only her red cap was visible.

"Don't worry," Zuki said when Ophelia began a nervous flick of her long black tail. "She'll be back."

Sure enough, half a minute later the koi breached the pond's smooth surface again. Her round black eyes seemed to take on a silvery cast as she stared somewhere far past Ophelia's furry shoulder. Then, her watery voice suddenly clear, she proclaimed, *"The three golden balls, he wanders those halls. Yes, the boy cat be all right. But finding him, 'twill be a fight."*

With those words, the koi smacked a few final bubbles and then sank beneath the surface again.

"What? Wait!"

Ophelia stared into the pond at the red splotch on Philomena's head that was all that was visible of her now. That splash of color got progressively smaller as the fish drifted still deeper into the pond's surprisingly profound depths. Ophelia began frantically pawing at the water.

"Philomena, come back! You must tell me what that means! Where is he? Where's Brandon?"

"Ophelia, stop," Zuki cried. "I forgot to tell you, you can only ask Philomena one question a day. She won't come back until tomorrow, no matter how long you call for her. But she told you what you need to know."

"No, she didn't!" With an anguished yowl, Ophelia swung about and leaped from the pond edge. "She talked about balls and halls and fighting, but that doesn't tell me where

Brandon is. I can't sit around doing nothing anymore. I'm going to go look for my brother, and you can't stop me!"

On that frantic final cry, she made a run for the courtyard wall and began scrabbling up its rough height.

"Ophelia, no!" Zuki bounded after her, but the cat proved just out of paw's reach. "Wait," the pit bull persisted. "If you go running off all crazy like the roosters, you're sure to get hit by a car before you can find him. There's a secret way out of the house that Ruby doesn't know about. Wait until tonight, and I'll help you sneak out to go look for him. I promise."

"You do?"

Ophelia glanced over her furry shoulder to see Zuki anxiously staring up at her, wide mouth open and panting in concern. Once, she would have been afraid of the dog with her broad jaws and shiny white fangs. But over the past two weeks, she'd learned to trust the canine. And, looking down at her, she could see that Zuki's dark brown eyes were filled with sincerity.

She moved a paw and gave a mew of pain. The pads on all four feet were already raw from the rough stucco that made scaling the wall difficult. By the time she reached the top, her paws might be too scraped and bloodied for her to travel far on the streets beyond. Maybe it made sense to try Zuki's plan instead.

"Okay. I'll wait for tonight."

She managed to turn and leap back down again. Paws stinging, she lay on the cool bricks and gave the sorest of her four feet a rough lick. "Ouch."

"Here, let me do that."

Zuki crouched beside her and ran a soft tongue over the raw pads. Since everyone knew that dogs could heal wounds that way, Ophelia lay still and let her lick away the blood. Cleaning her hurt paws was the sort of thing that Brandon would have done for her, if he'd been there.

Despite herself, she couldn't help a little sad cry. *Brandon! Where are you?*

"Oh no, poor kitty. What's wrong?"

The concerned question came from the human, Ruby, who had entered the courtyard unnoticed while Zuki was playing nurse. She tossed a tasty smelling roll of some strange food to the pit bull, who paused in her first aid duties long enough to swallow it in a single gulp. Ruby, meanwhile, gently shooed away the canine and sat beside Ophelia. She dangled a single large shrimp before her.

"Here you go, little girl. I saved this just

for you."

Ophelia's smooth black nose twitched. *I can be sad and full at the same time,* she decided.

While Ruby gently scratched her ears, she made quick work of the tasty crustacean. Once she'd finished, Ruby scooped her up so Ophelia was sitting in her lap.

"Now what happened? Let me see." The human shoved her black spectacles, which had slid down her nose, back into place. Then, gently, she lifted Ophelia's foreleg and examined it.

"Your poor paws, they're all scraped. Come on, let's go inside and I'll fix that."

Clutching Ophelia more securely, Ruby got to her feet and started toward the door. Ophelia considered struggling free, but then changed her mind. She might be leaving on her journey to find Brandon tonight, but no reason that she shouldn't take advantage of the human's help, in the meantime. And so instead she tucked her muzzle into the crook of Ruby's arm and let herself be carried back into the shop. Zuki, still licking her chops over the spring roll that she'd swallowed, followed after.

Ruby brought her all the way back into the main shop and carried her behind the counter, to where its far edge was butted up against the wall. There, a short, deep book-case almost the same height was set behind the counter at right angles to it. The lower shelves were filled with arcane reference books placed deliberately out of customer reach. From what Zuki had once explained, the lady in the big picture on the wall oc-casionally pulled out and ostentatiously read from one of them when the situation called for it. These volumes weren't for sale, and Zuki had laid down the law that, tempting as the old leather covers were, no chewing on said books was allowed!

The top shelf had once held an aquarium filled with tiny turtles. Zuki had told Ophelia that Ruby's second act after "quarantining" the roosters had been to donate the turtles to a local elementary school. Thus, she'd saved the little shelled reptiles from ritual beheading after being purchased by certain of the Botanica's customers. With the aquarium gone, there'd been enough room for one of those doughnut-style cat beds that Ruby had bought just for Ophelia.

Not wanting to hurt the human's feelings, she'd lain in the fuzzy pink bed a time or two, though she much preferred the snug and dark reading room and her perch atop the white stone column. But she didn't protest now as Ruby set her there and then reached for the strange green plant with thick spiky leaves that sat on the counter nearby.

"Let's put a bit of aloe vera on you," Ruby said and snapped off the tip of one leaf. "But don't lick it — you won't like the taste."

So saying, she squeezed the spike until a thick clear gel oozed out of the cut edge. Lifting Ophelia's paw, she smoothed the gel on her raw pads. It felt cool and stingy at the same time, but Ophelia resisted the temptation to shake it off her paw. If she was going to hunt for her brother tonight, she needed to be 100 percent.

Settling more securely into her bed, she dozed off to the soothing clear notes of a New Age flute playing as Ruby turned on the CD player near the register. Adding to the soundtrack was a breathy rumble as Zuki snored on the floor nearby. But just as she found herself in a dream where she and Brandon were taking turns riding atop Philomena in their old swimming pool, the bells on the shop's front door jangled.

Ophelia opened a single green eye, just in case. From her corner vantage point, all she could see through the gaps in the shelves was that this new customer was a short, slim female carrying a large canvas bag over her shoulder. As she drew closer, Ophelia could see that the human's long black fur had been braided into a single fancy tail down the back of her head. And, oddly, something about the way she carried herself seemed familiar. But it wasn't until the woman reached the counter that Ophelia opened both eyes wide.

Luciana?

"Zuki!" she cried, leaping up in her bed. "The human who just came in — I know her! She's the old woman's housekeeper!"

Zuki immediately snuffled awake. "Really? Maybe she found out you were living here and came to tell you where your brother is."

Could it be? Excitement tearing through her, Ophelia stood poised to leap onto the counter and rush to the woman when a terrible thought stopped her short.

"Or maybe the son decided he didn't want me to live with Ruby, and he sent her to find me and bring me back!"

Heart beating rapidly, but from fear now rather than excitement, Ophelia abruptly crouched low in the pink bed. Now only her ears and eyes were visible over the rolled edges. Better to wait and see what the woman told Ruby before she rushed over to greet her. And if Luciana tried to stuff her in that bag . . . well, much as she liked the human, she was going to get a taste of Ophelia's claws!

"Don't worry yet," the pit bull told her. "The humans at the shelter aren't supposed to tell the old owners where we end up living. Maybe she lives nearby and just wants to buy some candles or something."

"Maybe."

Ears flicked forward so that she could hear every word, Ophelia waited as Ruby looked up from her book and greeted her.

"Welcome to Botanica Santa Rosa. Was there something in particular you were looking for today?"

A missing black cat, Ophelia silently answered for her.

But to her relief, Luciana instead replied, "I — I was hoping for a reading?"

Six

Just as her half sister had taught her, Ruby swiftly took in the appearance of this new customer. The faintest hint of a Cuban accent had colored her words, which were more question than request. She was dressed simply, in dark blue jeans topped by a neat oxford-style cotton blouse that was pale yellow with black pinstripes. She looked to be close to Rosa's age and should have been quite pretty, with her chiseled cheekbones and large brown eyes. But the dark smudges beneath the latter and sharp lines around her pale mouth muted her attractiveness.

Obviously, something was on her mind. Ruby went through the mental checklist to try to narrow the options.

Not sleeping, so bad enough to keep her up at night.

No wedding or engagement ring, so likely not marital issues.

What appeared to be a uniform — health-care worker, maid? — tucked into her bag, so possibly job-related?

Though old enough that maybe a grown child was involved?

She gave the woman an encouraging nod.

"Yes, we do Tarot readings here. My name is Ruby, and I'd be happy to help you. Would you like the basic thirty-minute session, or do you need something more?"

She ran through the rates with her new client, who gave her name as Luciana. *Real name,* Ruby decided, mostly since she could see a bit of an embroidered *"L"* on the uniform peeking out of her tote bag. She noted, as well, that the woman wore a small gold crucifix on a chain around her neck. Not unusual, she'd learned. Many of her Cuban clients supplemented their Catholic faith with a bit of Santería.

Luciana went with the standard session, but as she pulled out a small green purse from the tote bag and went to pay — Rosa always said to get the money up front — the woman hesitated, wallet still in hand.

"I — I'm not sure. These past couple of weeks have been so confusing. I don't know if I want to know the truth."

"Trust me, it's better to know," Ruby told her, meaning it. "What was that old public service announcement campaign they used to have on television? *The more you know . . .*"

When Luciana gave her a questioning look — obviously, the woman hadn't spent much time watching the "peacock network" — Ruby clarified. "You need as much information as possible to make an informed decision about anything. And since I'm guessing you don't want to confide in a friend about this particular problem, the cards let you talk about it to an impartial party like me."

Her rationale seemed to resonate, for the woman nodded. "You're right, I need to talk to someone about this."

She reached into her wallet and paid in small bills, ones and fives. The reading was probably a hit on her budget, Ruby realized as she rang her up. She'd give her a few extra minutes for free, and Rosa didn't need to know about it. But even as she made the decision, she could almost feel her half sister's gaze drilling into her back from the oil painting behind her. Shooting the portrait a defiant look, she walked around the counter.

"Come on, let me put the *Closed* sign up, and then we'll go into the reading room and see what the cards say.

■ ■ ■ ■

"Quick," Ophelia told Zuki as Ruby and Luciana walked off. "Go to the reading room and hide under the table before they get there. I'll follow in a minute. We'd better hear what they talk about. It might be important."

"Right," Zuki barked and scrambled to her paws. "So did you decide yet if you are going to let this human know that you're here?"

Ophelia shook her fuzzy head. "Not yet. She was always good to us, but now the son is her boss. I have to make sure first that she's on our side."

"Well, don't take too long to decide. She's getting the short reading, so she won't be here long. And then it will be time for our afternoon snack."

A growl that came from Zuki's stomach, not her throat, punctuated that last observation. Slinking as best she could for a round, forty-five-pound pit bull, Zuki softly trotted from around the counter and down the back aisle in the direction of the reading room.

Ophelia, meanwhile, stayed crouched in her bed, remembering. Luciana had always been kind to the old woman and seemed to like her — which situation, Brandon had once told her, was not always the way it went with humans who were the boss and humans who were the workers.

And Ophelia had been inside Luciana's little house behind the main house many times before. It had a good feeling to it, almost like the old woman's bedroom. It was always neat and clean, with soft colors on the walls and on the furniture. And Luciana had pictures of calm and smiling humans in every room, with small candles beneath them that she would sometimes light. The scent would make Ophelia sneeze, but she liked to hear the soft words in Spanish that she didn't understand but that reminded her of raindrops falling from leaves.

Luciana was a good human, she was certain — but the son was not. And so she would wait for her and Ruby to enter the reading room before she slipped inside to listen. Once she heard what Luciana had to say, she'd make the decision whether or not to reveal herself to the human.

A few moments later, Ruby was gesturing Luciana into the client's seat in the reading room. Fortunately, the Botanica's ancient A/C system — read, individual window and wall-mounted units — was working. When the air-conditioning acted up, the comfort level in the reading room could drop like a block of ice, or climb to sauna-like heights.

"Go ahead, sit down," she said with a welcoming gesture and took the chair across from the woman.

Her foot promptly connected with something large and furry beneath the table. She stifled a smile as a warm wet tongue wiped across her ankle. She should have named the pit bull "Nosy," given Zuki's penchant for hanging out around the paying clients.

Aloud, she asked, "Would you like to choose which deck you want me to use?"

Not waiting for an answer, she pulled out a basket which held half a dozen different boxed Tarot sets. She lined them in a neat row on the reading cloth so Luciana could see their illustrations. Their themes varied — angels, fairies, even erotic — including Ruby's favorite Morgan-Greer. There were at least another dozen decks in a box on the shelf behind her, but she'd long since learned that too many choices made the client nervous.

Luciana glanced over the offerings. "It's okay, you choose."

Ruby considered a moment and then reached for the tried-and-true standby, the

Rider-Waite-Smith deck. She'd found it to be the most popular deck when it came to the non-Tarot-reading public, and with good reason. It had first been published at the turn of the twentieth century, and its iconic imagery had been used everywhere from magazine ads to movies ever since. From her demeanor, Luciana's problem was serious and called for a straightforward reading that this classic deck always gave.

Putting the other decks aside, Ruby pulled out the Rider cards from their box and started shuffling.

"Now, do you have a specific question you'd like to ask the cards, or do you want a general reading?"

"I — I have a specific question."

This time, her hesitation was more obvious, and she glanced over her shoulder at the pulled curtain, as if debating whether or not to make a run for it.

"You can ask me whatever you like," Ruby assured her. "And if we get started and you don't think it's the right question, you can change it. Okay?"

"I know the question. I — I just don't know if I can say it. If I am wrong, speaking it will be a terrible thing . . . but if I am right . . ."

Infidelity.

That was usually the question that was so personal. And Ruby could understand how she would worry about accusing her man — fiancé, boyfriend? — of such betrayal, only to learn she'd been wrong.

"Well, let me keep shuffling. And if you don't want to say it out loud, you can just think it, and we'll see how that goes."

And that was when Ruby heard a soft *meow* behind her. Before she could say anything, a sleek black feline landed with a soft thud in the middle of the reading table.

Luciana gave a surprised little cry, and then laughed. "*Un gato negro* — a black cat," she exclaimed as Ophelia sat and stared at her. "Does the kitty tell fortunes, too?"

"She likes to think she does. Bad girl," Ruby scolded, rising from her chair and preparing to scoot the cat onto the floor. Before she could do so, however, Luciana's look of surprised amusement became an expression of shock.

"*Dios mío,* could it be? Where did she come from? The gato, she looks just like . . . *Ofelia?*"

The woman gave the name the softer Spanish pronunciation as she stared from the cat to Ruby and back again. Ruby, meanwhile, tamped down a sudden feeling of alarm. Didn't all black cats pretty much look alike? Still, how many black female cats named Ophelia could there be?

On the other hand, unless someone at the animal shelter was talking out of turn, the previous owner would have no idea who adopted a particular cat. It had to be co-incidence that Luciana seemingly knew this kitty. *Right?*

But before Ruby could confirm or deny the woman's suspicions, the cat took the situation into her own paws. As Luciana leaned forward for a closer look, Ophelia raised her paw; then, claws sheathed, she gave the woman a couple of soft taps on her cheek.

Luciana's brown eyes grew wider still, and she reached a tentative hand toward the cat. Ophelia obliged by rubbing her head against the woman's palm.

"It *is* her," the woman said in amazement. "Ofelia, she always does this" — she tapped her own fingers against her cheek — "when she wants to be petted."

Leaning back in her chair, she continued stroking the cat with one nervous hand while the other was clasped over her heart. Then she glanced about her.

"*Estoy tan aliviado* — I am so relieved. He said they ran away, but I didn't believe him.

And you have found her. The boy kitty, Brandon — is he here, too?"

Ruby shook her head and gave a quick explanation as to how she'd stumbled across Ophelia and eventually came to adopt her. Then, lest the woman wonder, she was careful to add, "She had one of those microchips, so the animal shelter knew who owned her. They did contact Mrs. Givens's son, and since his mother had passed away, he relinquished ownership of the cats. So Ophelia is legitimately my cat now."

"Bien, bien."

Luciana's earlier hesitation was gone, and to Ruby's relief the woman seemed to take her side.

"That is good," the woman repeated. "Señora Givens, she loved her *pequeños* — her little ones. But as for her *hijo,* he is not a kind man. I think if I see Brandon again, I will catch him and give him to you."

"That would be wonderful," Ruby agreed, ignoring visions of her sister's likely reaction when she finally returned home to find not one but two black cats now living in the Botanica.

She plucked a card from the mermaid-shaped business card holder on the corner of the table and handed it to Luciana.

"Here's the store number. I've got it set

to ring to my cell phone. Call me if you find him, and I can bring a carrier to put him in to take him home."

Luciana pulled out her phone, which was wrapped in a bright pink rhinestoned case, and added Ruby's number to her contacts before tucking the card into her tote bag. Then she sobered. "I am ready. I think we should look at the cards now."

"Right."

Ruby began shuffling the deck again. Ophelia, apparently realizing her work was done for the moment, slipped off the table and returned to her usual spot upon the column. The cards well-mixed, Ruby squared the deck and set it on the table again.

"Go ahead and cut the deck into three piles, and then restack them in a different order."

Luciana nodded, but didn't move to cut the cards. Instead, she remained looking down at her clenched hands resting on the table. The lighting in the reading room was dimmer, less harsh than the fluorescents in the main shop. The rosier glow, however, didn't hide the stark lines in her face which abruptly deepened. She stared downward a moment longer, before raising her head and abruptly focusing her anxious gaze on Ruby.

No, it wasn't worry in her eyes, Ruby realized with a sudden sinking feeling in the pit of her stomach. It was fear.

In a swift move, the woman split up the deck and restacked it. That done, she raised her gaze to Ruby again, her brown eyes looking black now in the dim light.

"This is my question," Luciana choked out in a voice little more than a whisper. "I want to know if Señor Givens murdered his mother."

SEVEN

"Murdered?" Ruby stared at the woman in disbelief. "That's what you want to know, if someone murdered someone else?"

At Luciana's firm nod, she persisted. "If you witnessed a crime, you should be talking to the police about it, and not me."

"I already told them all I knew, which was nada . . . nothing. All I could say was that I found the poor lady drowned in her own swimming pool. And so the police, they decided it was an accident. But I have the suspicion here" — she tapped a close fist over her heart — "that *he* is responsible."

"He? You mean, her son. But why do you think that? I mean, besides a feeling?"

Luciana shrugged. "The old lady, she was a good swimmer. She would go into the water every morning before I bring her the *café con leche.* And the phone calls. The hijo, he is always on his phone, but he hurries and hangs up if he sees me. And he looks, how do you say, suspicious. Plus there was some other things . . . things with papers . . ."

Papers? Ruby wondered as the other woman trailed off. *A contract? Or maybe a will?*

But before she could question this, Luciana seemed to rally. "If the cards say he did it, then I will look for a way to prove it. Then I go back to the police again. That is why I ask for the reading, to make sure first."

"All right, let me think how best to do this."

Ruby took off her glasses and distractedly cleaned them on the loose hem of her blouse, needing something to do with her hands while she considered the situation. Rosa had never given her instructions on how to deal with someone who claimed to have knowledge of a felony. And in all the Tarot books she'd read, she had yet to come across a spread entitled *Did He or Didn't He Commit Murder?*

Not that Rosa would have hesitated to tackle a question like that. But she, Ruby, was not the confident intuitive that her half sister was. No way was she going to open that can of metaphysical worms, not as a junior — okay, very junior — Tarot reader.

Not when the subject was murder, or the possibility thereof!

She glanced back at Ophelia, who was perched on the column watching. *Any insights?* she silently asked the cat, not really expecting an answer. Ophelia blinked her green eyes but had no other feedback to offer.

So, what were her options, then?

Ruby frowned. Maybe she could excuse herself and call JoJo for a bit of legal advice. But JoJo was in an emergency meeting at work and likely wouldn't be taking calls. So that left her two choices — give Luciana her money back and send her on her way, or do what she could to help the woman gather her obviously confused thoughts.

"All right," she said with a sigh and put on her glasses again. "You've paid for a five-card spread, so let's start with that. But asking if Mr. Givens murdered his mother is tricky. I think the reading will go better if you ask for general guidance regarding the situation."

She feared for a moment that Luciana would protest, but to her relief the woman nodded. "I understand. Yes, that is what I want, guidance. Por favor, continue."

While Luciana watched, Ruby sifted through the deck looking for a particular card. Finding the card she sought, she turned it face up on the table, facing Luciana. Then she dealt out five more cards, arranging them face down in a row beneath the first. She'd decided upon a variation of the standard five-card spread that Rosa had taught her. This one would give insight into the overall situation — and might, in the process, give Luciana a direction to pursue.

"Let's start with the card at the top," she began, lightly tapping a blunt nail on the Queen of Pentacles card that lay face up. "This is what we call the Significator, the card that represents someone — in this case, Mrs. Givens. I need you to concentrate on her."

At Luciana's murmur of agreement, Ruby went on. "I chose this card to represent her because pentacles signify money, and she was a wealthy woman. Beyond that, the Queen of Pentacles traditionally means someone who is nurturing . . . a mother. But look at her sitting on her throne."

She paused and traced a finger along the illustration of the elaborate seat upon which the queen was perched.

"It's a beautiful chair with all those carvings, and she's there in a meadow filled with lovely plants and flowers," Ruby continued, explaining the card's attributes aloud. "But look at her expression. See how she's all alone staring down at a single gold pentacle in her lap. It's the sign of her money, but she's not smiling. She looks a little sad. Maybe she realizes it should have been a child — a son — in her lap instead."

"I agree." Luciana gave a vigorous nod. "She would tell me that they did not have, what do they call it, a good relationship, and her eyes would have the tears when she said it."

Ruby nodded. *Pretty typical situation in wealthy families — heck, in most families. Parents and grown children not getting along. That's why they say money can't buy happiness.*

Refocusing her attention on the layout before her, she went on. "All right, let's move on to the other cards. For the first one, it represents what is known about Mrs. Givens's death."

She flipped over that first card, and Luciana gasped.

"Dios mío."

Ruby managed to control her own reflexive intake of breath, since she hadn't been expecting a card quite so in-your-face as the Ten of Swords. One of the minor arcana, its imagery featured a prone man, the lower portion of his body covered in a bright

113

red cape. Ten straight swords were thrust into him along length of his back, while his face was turned away from the viewer, instead looking at a calm sea.

Talk about a literal depiction of being stabbed in the back! And, definitely a card that bespoke "the end," she knew. Yet despite the dramatic portrayal — the other term associated with those swords was "overkill" — the image was bloodless, almost sterile. An end to be sure . . . but not necessarily a murder.

She explained all this to Luciana; then, as another thought occurred to her, she added, "Let's look again at how he's lying there already dead, but facing the water. That could indicate that Mrs. Givens was already in distress before she fell into the pool. So the initial reading is that things are just what they seemed — that her death was an accident."

Luciana nodded, but Ruby could tell from the hard set of her mouth that the woman was still unconvinced.

She flipped over the second card and said, "Now, let's see with this next card what is hidden about her death."

Ruby blinked as she took in the image of the Lovers. One of the major arcana, it usually indicated positive energy with its depiction of a floating angel against a bright sun, and an innocently displayed naked man and woman standing below. Alongside the female was an apple tree complete with serpent, and beside the male a tree of life. All very Adam and Eve-y. Normally, it signaled romance, or married love, or good choices . . . the whole "you complete me" thing, with the completion anything from a perfect mate to a satisfying career.

But the card in the current spread was reversed — upside down — which in a Tarot reading meant that the card's meaning had been similarly turned topsy-turvy. Ruby frowned as the various negative meanings flashed through her mind.

Bad decisions, divorce, a family breaking up, people marrying for the wrong reasons.

Or, depending on the other cards in the spread, it could mean someone thinking, not with their head, but with what was below their belt. Not quite the card — or the meaning — she would have expected to see in that spot!

She gave Luciana an overview of the card in both its positions and then said, "Since the Lovers are reversed, that could indicate that Mrs. Givens and her son had a falling out shortly before her death. Maybe he made some lifestyle choices she didn't approve of, or a business decision she thought was wrong. Or maybe he was seeing the wrong woman. The stress and the upset of fighting could very well take a toll on someone her age."

Luciana appeared to be thinking hard as well. "I think you may be right for this. There is this señorita — this woman — who started coming around. She was young and pretty but — how do they say it? — hard, like stone." She leaned in closer and added in a softer voice, "The hijo, he did not see it . . . or maybe he did not care. But Señora Givens, she did not like her at all."

"Did she say anything to her son about her feelings?"

"Perhaps. It was a week, or maybe two before she died. I heard the señora yelling at the hijo, calling the woman very bad names. But just that one time. The woman came back more times, but the señora, she did not yell about it again. That's when the thing with the papers happened. I think maybe she was afraid."

Afraid of this unknown woman? Afraid to confront her son?

Frowning, Ruby went on. "Let's see how the other cards fall, and maybe this one will make more sense. The next card should tell us if there is a motive for anyone to want to see Mrs. Givens dead."

Holding her breath and mentally crossing her fingers — *let it be the Sun, or the Ten of Cups, something all fluffy bunny and happy* — Ruby flipped over the third card.

Five of Pentacles.

More pentacles. Meaning, more money issues.

Ruby kept her features carefully blank, but she was starting to have a bad feeling about Luciana's suspicions. She'd never cared much for this card, with its unpleasant image of yet another man and woman. No nudity here, however . . . but no angels either. This time, the pair was clothed, but in obviously threadbare outfits. The old woman in the lead — representing Mrs. Givens? — was shown walking barefoot in the snow clutching a tatty shawl about her. Behind her was a seemingly younger man on crutches doing his best to keep up with his wife, sister . . . *mother?*

A depiction of poverty. Literally . . . or of the spirit, perhaps.

And there was more to this seemingly simple imagery. Rather than trudging doggedly like the woman, whose gaze was fixed on the path before her, the man appeared to be staring up at the stained glass window of the church they were passing. The win-

dow's design was that of five golden pentacles, symbols of material wealth. Actual
wealth that he'd lost — or maybe something
that he'd wanted but could not have. Either
way, the pair in this card was in their sad
state most likely because of bad choices that
they'd made.

Of course, the card could also speak to
financial insecurity, or an uneasy relationship with money. Or being hobbled by
money . . . hence, the man's crutches. Or
even the fear of being alone.

Ruby gnawed her lower lip as she stared
at the image. If she were watching a murder
mystery movie on television, this would be
the point where she'd be yelling at the
screen, *Can't you see, the motive is money!
Look, the woman can't see what the man is
doing behind her back!* But since she was
trying to offer an anxious client real-life
advice, Ruby picked her actual words a bit
more carefully.

"It seems like maybe finances — or the
lack of them — might have something to do
with her death. I don't suppose you know
anything about Mrs. Givens's will, do you?"

"You mean, who gets her money?" Luciana opened her eyes wide; then she shook
her head. "I had to sign once. You know, to
be the witness for her papers. The hijo, he

already has his money from when the old man died many years ago. The señora told me that. And she said when she dies that all of her money, it will go to the poor."

So helping his mother to drown in the swimming wouldn't have gained the hijo, as Ruby also was beginning to call him, any monetary benefit.

Wondering whether to be disappointed or relieved that this crass motive could be discounted — *no, truly, she was relieved!* — Ruby said, "If he doesn't inherit anything, then maybe we're back to the stress and disappointment. Maybe it wasn't that mystery woman who came between him and his mother. Maybe she thought he was making bad investments, or getting involved in risky business schemes. And he didn't like being criticized — see in the card how the man is following after the woman, but at the same time not paying attention to her? All that caused them to quarrel."

"So maybe it's not so bad?" Luciana asked, a hopeful note in her voice now. "Maybe he didn't have anything to do with the señora dying?"

"Let's look at the next card. That one will tell us who has knowledge of the situation . . . who can shed light on the subject of Mrs. Givens's death," Ruby said and

119

turned the fourth card over.

This card was another of the minor arcana, this time featuring the image of a smirking man carrying an armful of swords. Dressed in bright tights and tunic and a jaunty red fez, he looked more civilian than soldier. He was glancing over his shoulder at an enemy encampment as he tiptoed away in an exaggerated fashion, hauling his ill-gotten weapons cache with him.

The Seven of Swords.

"Interesting," she murmured. "Check out this guy. He's pulled a fast one, stealing weapons from an enemy camp. And look at his smug expression —"

"Just like the hijo," Luciana broke in, *her* expression outraged.

Ruby nodded. "He's smart . . . but sometimes that's his undoing. Notice that he's only carrying five swords, though this card is the Seven of Swords. He's left two of the weapons stuck in the ground behind him. He thought he could get away with his theft, but he got overconfident and tried to pull off too big of a scheme. So in the end, he had to leave two of the swords behind. His eyes were bigger than his stomach. He bit off more than he could chew."

Luciana rolled her eyes. "*Si, si. Mi sobrino* — my nephew — calls it, don't write a

120

check with your mouth that your rear end, it cannot cash. That is the hijo, always."

"Exactly. So maybe he knows more about his mother's death than he's saying."

Ruby let that last statement hang between them. A person could know something, but not be technically guilty of anything. Crimes of omission, rather than commission. She didn't want to accuse anyone of anything, but Luciana already had suspicions about the man.

"Let's see the last card," she said after a moment. "It will tell us what the outcome will be."

She turned over the fifth card and allowed herself a small smile of satisfaction. The card was one of the major arcana . . . Justice. Unlike the cutely modern witchy statue that JoJo had earlier admired, the Lady Justice in the card wore long red robes topped by a green cape. Instead of a pointy black hat, the lady sported a heavy gold crown bespeaking both privilege and burden.

Uneasy lies the head that wears a crown, came the Shakespearean quote to mind, yet Lady Justice didn't appear to have any qualms. She squarely faced the viewer, seated upon a stone chair positioned between twin pillars and against a backdrop of lush purple cloth. The victorious upraised sword in one hand and the scales in the other signified fairness and truth.

"Justice," Ruby said aloud, winning a small smile from the woman seated across from her. She described the card's attributes for Luciana — balance, consequences, honesty, decision-making, litigation — and then finished, "The truth about Mrs. Givens's death will be known, and justice will be served. That's the ultimate outcome according to the cards."

Luciana's smile slipped a little. "That is good . . . but what does all this mean for me? We still do not know if the hijo, he is guilty. Should I spy on him and try to find evidence? You know, like they do in the *telenovelas.*"

Ruby considered that last for a moment. She had never seen any of the Spanish-language soap operas before, so she had no clue just what sort of detective work Luciana thought she might attempt. The one thing she did know was that she, Ruby, had to be very cautious as far as what she would say next. It was one thing to counsel a client regarding her love life or career goals. It was quite another to encourage a distraught woman to play the Cuban version of Miss Marple in a situation that was as grave as possible murder.

She thought back to the framed disclaimer hung on the wall outside the reading room door: *Tarot Card readings are for entertainment purposes only and are not guaranteed to be 100 percent accurate. No reading is intended to offer, or take the place of, medical, legal, or psychological advice.*

Weasel words, Rosa had loftily termed that notice. But necessary, she had also conceded. That was why it was posted where any person who set foot in the reading room had to walk past it. The same statement also appeared on the reverse of Ruby's business cards, and at the bottom of every receipt she handed out. And while that wording seemingly gave her plenty of wiggle room as far as liability, she wasn't anxious to test her culpability in a court of law should something go south.

Besides, the Tarot card reading had been less than clear about any actual crime having been committed.

"It's possible that Mr. Givens had a hand in his mother's death," she replied. "But it's equally possible that old age and stress caught up with her and her body just gave out. Since the cards indicated that justice will be served, perhaps it's best that you step back and let the future unfold as it's meant to . . . without interference."

A series of emotions flashed across Luciana's face, and for an uncomfortable moment Ruby feared the woman was going to rebel against her advice. But then, to her relief, Luciana nodded.

"I will step back . . . but I will watch, too."

She gathered her purse and tote bag, ready to leave, and then paused for a look in Ophelia's direction.

"Mi sobrino, my nephew, he lives just a few blocks from here, and I visit him sometimes. That is how I found you. Next time I see him, do you think I might stop by to say hello to the *gatico*?"

"To Ophelia? Of course," Ruby exclaimed with a smile, rising as well. She had almost forgotten the cat's presence, so still had she been during the reading. "And you don't have to wait to visit your nephew to come back. I'm sure Ophelia would be glad to see you anytime."

As if understanding those words, the cat leapt from her column perch and landed with light paws atop the reading table. Luciana chuckled and gave Ophelia another scratch under the chin.

"I will keep an eye out for *tu hermano,* your brother. Now, you be a good girl for Señorita Ruby, and I will come back and see you soon."

Ophelia watched as Luciana and Ruby made their way from the reading room; then she whipped back around and stared down at the Tarot cards the humans had left behind.

"What's wrong?" Zuki asked as she snuffled her way out from under the table. "Luciana seemed like a nice human. Why didn't you follow her to the door?"

"No time," Ophelia spat. "I need to look at the cards first."

"Why? Ruby already did that."

Ophelia shot her canine friend a sharp green look. "Ruby isn't as clever as she thinks she is. She forgot to ask the cards the most important question . . . what will happen to Luciana if she watches the son too much!"

With a soft growl, Ophelia reached out a paw and flipped over the next card on the stacked deck. *The Devil.*

"No! Bad!"

Hissing again, she pawed another card from the deck. *The Tower.* Even worse! If only Ruby had looked at these next cards, she could have warned the housekeeper that something wasn't right. But she hadn't, and now it was up to her, Ophelia, to sound the alarm.

"Wait, Luciana!" she yowled, leaping down to the floor. "You're in danger!"

Paws skittering against wood, she dashed past the velvety curtains of the reading room and out into the main shop. The small bells hanging from the front door were still softly jingling.

Too late! The housekeeper was already gone.

EIGHT

"Luciana!" Ophelia wailed, rushing to the door. Balancing on her rear paws and stretching to her full length, she wrapped her paws around the glass knob and tried to twist it. "Come back! I must warn you!"

"Poor kitty, what's wrong?"

Vaguely, she was aware of Ruby's concerned cry behind her. But her attention was fixed on the glass knob, which kept slipping from her paws no matter how hard she tried to hold onto it. And then, just when she finally managed a firm grasp, a pair of plump hands swept her up.

"Silly cat, you know you can't go out," Ruby gently scolded her, flipping her over and cradling her like a human baby. "I'm sure you miss your friend, but she'll be back to visit. Why don't I get you and Zuki a little snack, and —"

"No!"

With a yowl and a sharp twist, Ophelia

struggled her way out of the human's grasp. Landing on all fours, she ran for the door again for a last try at the knob. When that attempt failed, she spun about and flew like a mouse on fire through the store toward the back door. The plastic flap never touched her as she dived through the doggie door and out into the courtyard. There, she flung herself belly down onto the bricks, all four legs sprawled wide as she gave another yowl of frustration.

The plaintive sound was promptly echoed by crowing as Roosters One, Two, and Three trotted in from the side yard to stare. As usual, they each clipped out a word, in turn.

"Look."

"At."

"That."

"The."

"Cat's."

"Flat."

The last word was followed by a chorus of squawks that Ophelia knew was chicken laughter. But this time, she didn't even bother to hiss. Who cared what stupid roosters thought, when now she had to worry about Luciana as well as Brandon? Worse was the fact that even if she'd been able to catch the human, she wouldn't have been able to make her understand the danger.

By now, Zuki had bounded through the dog door as well and was giving her a concerned nudge with her broad muzzle. "What's wrong? Why are you so upset?"

"Didn't you see the cards?" Ophelia replied with a sigh, eyes closed and fuzzy chin resting on her paws. "They were bad. Something's going to happen to Luciana. She'll die just like the old woman did."

Zuki gave an inelegant snort. "That's silly. You know what Ruby says. The cards don't tell the future. They just talk about what you already know. I think you're all worried over nothing."

"You do?" Ophelia opened one eye and gave her a questioning look.

Zuki gave a firm woof in return. "I'm sure. And maybe after we find Brandon, we can go back to your old home so you can see Luciana is fine, too."

Ophelia opened the other eye. "Maybe you're right. It's just that I'm so worried about my brother."

Before Zuki could reply to that, they heard the back door open. Ruby walked out carrying a sealed jar that Ophelia knew contained fish pellets. But the human had also been known to toss a pellet or two their way. Certain she'd feel better if she had a little snack, Ophelia dragged herself into a sitting position and watched expectantly as Ruby approached.

"There you are, silly kitty. You had me worried, running off like a crazy cat. Why don't you sit by me over at the pond, and you can watch me feed Philly."

She didn't even have the lid off the jar before a red-capped head rose from the water, fishy lips making loud smacking sounds.

"I swear that koi is psychic," Ruby said with a laugh as she tossed a handful of pellets onto the water's surface. "How in the heck did she know I came out to feed her?"

A small feeding frenzy was ensuing as she asked the question, and within fifteen seconds every scrap was gone.

"Good Philly," Ruby said in approval. "You get the clean plate award."

Then, when Ophelia gave her a small meow by way of reminder, she added, "Sorry, didn't mean to leave you two girls out."

She tossed a couple of pellets each of their way. Zuki caught hers in midair and had them swallowed even before her broad jaws had clamped shut. Ophelia let hers bounce onto the brick before she leaned over and delicately nibbled at the tiny fishy morsels.

To her disappointment, she saw that Ruby was also sharing a few pellets with the roosters, who pounced upon them as if they'd not eaten for days.

Ophelia was just about to suggest that Ruby toss her a couple more pellets, too, when the pit bull broke in with an excited bark.

"Look," Zuki exclaimed, "I think Philomena is going to speak!"

Ophelia flicked a fuzzy black ear. "I thought you said she only answered one question a day."

"I know. But look . . ."

Sure enough, the koi was doing her spinning routine. As before, she halted and smacked a few bubbles before her black eyes once again took on a silvery sheen. In a burbling voice, she proclaimed, *"Another message for the cat. You must beware the human rat."*

"What?" Ophelia rushed over to the pool's edge. "What are you talking about? Rats aren't human . . . and humans aren't rats. What does that mean?"

But, of course, Philomena was already sinking back into the depths of her pool, meaning no explanation forthcoming.

"Oh, for kibble's sake," she muttered. What good was it having a psychic fish

131

around when nothing she said made sense? "Wow!"

This came from Zuki. The pit bull's tone held admiration as she went on. "That's the first time Philomena has ever talked twice in one day. She must really like you."

"I'm sure it's nothing," Ophelia countered, though she could feel her ear tips heating up in pleased embarrassment. While she'd never thought she would care one way or the other what a fish thought, it was obvious that Philomena was no ordinary koi. And it was nice to be in the official "Philomena likes me best" club . . . even if the fish in question spouted silly words.

While this exchange was going on, Ruby was busy screwing the lid back on the jar. With fond looks for her and Zuki, she said, "If everyone is back in a happy mood, I'm headed inside again. Don't forget, I'm leaving for class in a couple of hours."

She left them outside in the company of the roosters. Zuki promptly flopped in a sunny spot. "I'm taking a nap," she unnecessarily explained — mostly because she already napped numerous times a day, anyhow. "If we're going to spend the night looking for your brother, we should be all rested up."

Ophelia nodded her agreement. It would

be just a few more hours before darkness fell, plenty of time for a snooze. And so she curled up next to Zuki and rested her chin on the pit bull's outstretched paw. A minute later she was fast asleep and dreaming of Brandon chasing around the three golden balls that the koi had previously mentioned.

Ruby glanced back over her shoulder as she reached the door, smiling in approval at the sight of her pets snoozing. *Poor Ophelia.* Seeing someone from her past had to have been confusing for the little cat. With luck, by tomorrow she would have forgotten the encounter with the woman.

But she, Ruby, wouldn't forget so quickly.

Ruby made her way back to the reading room to straighten up the table that she'd left covered by the card spread. Had time permitted (*thirty minutes does not mean thirty-one minutes,* she could practically hear her half sister pontificating in her ear), she could have spoken even longer about the cards she had pulled for Luciana. Maybe she should take a picture of the spread with her phone and look at it again later, when her thoughts had settled. For although the cards had seemed straightforward enough individually, they'd been a bit vague overall. If she let the images steep awhile in her brain, she might find that —

She broke off in mid-thought as she took in the Tarot spread before her. Now, in addition to the original cards — the Significator and the five lined up beneath it — two more cards lay faceup to one side of that layout.

The Tower and the Devil . . . majors, and perhaps the most unsettling images of the entire deck. Those cards had not been there when she and Luciana had left the room. So where had they come from?

"Ophelia?"

The clever cat had seemingly helped her with a reading once before. Could she have unwittingly flipped over a couple of cards when she jumped off the table? But Rosa would say that there were no accidents.

She seated herself back at the table and took another look. The Devil card featured the titular dark angel . . . a Pan-like figure with a goat's legs and head, and bird-like talons for feet. He presided over the same nude man and woman as was found in the Lovers card she'd previously pulled for the spread. The difference here was that the naked couple now was chained by the neck to the rocklike throne the Devil perched upon. Though if one looked closely at the card, he might notice that those chains were loose enough that, had the pair truly wished it, they could pull the chain up over their heads and be free. A card speaking of temptations, lies, manipulation.

A card concerned with the baser things in life, rather than the spiritual.

As for the Tower . . .

Ruby soberly studied that image. That card carried with it perhaps the greatest warning of any of the major or minor arcana. It depicted a tall stone tower being blasted by a literal bolt from the blue. The lightning had split off the tower's crownlike dome and set the edifice on fire. At the same time, two frantic figures — perhaps the same now-clothed couple from the Devil card — were plunging headfirst from the blazing structure, headed for their likely deaths. It was a card of shock, destruction, and immediacy.

And had she seen those two cards while Luciana was still there, her advice to the woman would have been far different.

"You read the cards you draw," she reminded herself aloud. "No second guessing allowed."

The one saving grace was that tonight was a school night. For a couple of hours on this particular evening, she would be concentrating on a lecture comparing British female authors of the late nineteenth century to their American counterparts. A topic guaranteed to distract her from the disturbing imagery laid out before her.

But as she gathered the deck back together and tucked it back into its box, she knew she was fooling herself. Chances were that no matter how informative the lecture, she was going to spend the whole night second-guessing herself.

"Be good girls, and don't tear up anything in the shop. I'll be back from school in a few hours."

Ruby hoisted her backpack onto her shoulder, and Ophelia gave her a quick look. The human had changed from her usual flowy clothes and instead wore what she called jeans — faded blue pants that looked like an angry feline had shredded them at the knees. Ruby's shirt was strange, too . . . black with a big red mouth with its tongue hanging out, reminding her of Zuki, the more so because a sprinkling of the pit bull's white fur decorated it. She had never understood why humans had to look different every single day.

Ruby grabbed up her keys and turned out all the lights except for a lamp in the shape of a chicken sitting on a table in the front window. With a couple of air kisses, she slipped out the front door and closed it behind her. Ophelia waited until she heard the distinctive click as the human locked them in. Then she turned to Zuki.

"Okay, Ruby's gone. Now we can go find Brandon."

The pit bull didn't immediately respond, but instead trotted over to the front window and sat up so that her paws were resting on the sill. She cocked her blocky head and waited a moment, ears on alert. Then she nodded.

"Her car just turned the corner. *Now* she's gone."

"Good. Show me this secret way out so we can start looking for my brother."

"I will . . . but not until you promise."

"Promise what?"

Zuki padded back to where Ophelia sat and leaned in close to her. "You have to promise that you'll listen to me and do exactly what I tell you to do. I've been on the streets before, and I know what goes on out there. No hissing and puffing up, and no running off on your own. And don't even think of talking to a canine out there unless I tell you it's okay."

Ophelia gave a little hiss and puffed her tail just a little. "You're not the boss of me.

Don't worry, I can handle myself."

Zuki rolled her brown eyes. "You've never been out on the streets except for when we found you in that box. I know you're brave, but you have to be smart, too. And if you don't promise, I'm not going to show you the way out."

Ophelia hissed again, but then she nodded. "Fine, I promise. But just for tonight."

"Fine. Now, come on."

The pit bull led the way out to the courtyard. A few tiny solar lights put out a soft glow near the pond, turning the water's surface as silvery as Philomena's eyes when she spoke. Roosters One, Two, and Three were in their respective cages. They clucked and muttered a bit as Ophelia and Zuki padded past them, and then promptly fell asleep again.

"This way," the dog whispered, heading to the narrow side yard that was the roosters' daytime domain.

It also was where Rosa grew her herbs in big boxes above the ground. At the very front of that yard, a table made of metal and pine, with lots of shelves, was set up against the stucco wall. It blocked a wooden gate that now was permanently locked.

Ophelia eyed the table, frowning. She could easily leap atop it, and would be in jumping range of the gate's top edge. The only problem was that the wooden slats were cut so that they were all pointy on top like big knives. If she wasn't careful, she might get stuck on one of them. But Zuki . . .

She gave the dog a pitying look. The pit bull might be muscular, but the leap from ground to tabletop would be awkward. And no way could she jump over the gate. So how did Zuki expect them both to get out?

"Not up there," the pit bull said, seeing where her gaze was fixed. "There!"

Climbing beneath the potting table, she pawed at a section of gate behind the narrow wooden plank that connected the table's back legs and held them steady. To Ophelia's surprise, a rectangle of pickets moved outward, reminding her of the doggie door that led from the house to the courtyard.

All a canine — or feline! — would have to do was crawl beneath that long piece of wood and shove their way outside.

Zuki gave her a smug canine grin. "Ruby doesn't know about this. A long time ago, some human cut a dog-sized door in the gate. It used to swing both ways, but because the potting table is pushed up against the gate, the door can only swing out, not in.

139

And there's a bunch of vines growing on the other side, so humans never notice the door, and neither do the street canines."

But Ophelia had already seen a problem with Zuki's plan. "So you can get out . . . but how do you get back in again?"

"Whenever I sneak out, I roll that rock" — Zuki pointed a paw at a baseball-sized chunk of white coral rock near the table leg — "so that it keeps the door from closing all the way. That way I can stick a paw in to open it and squeeze back inside again."

Ophelia gave the dog an admiring look. Truly, she was almost as smart as a feline.

A few moments later, they were out on the darkened street. Despite her earlier brave words, Ophelia was glad that Zuki was with her. Not that the darkness bothered her — of course, she could see almost as well as she could during the day — but the sounds and smells were different, scarier. Even the houses and shops around them that looked cheerful in the daylight had put on sly shadow masks that made them seem somehow foreboding.

Zuki paused in the shadow of the Botanica and sniffed the air. "Felines the next block over," she declared. "Let's start with them and see if they know anything about Brandon."

Ophelia trotted alongside her as they rounded the block and, after carefully watching for cars to pass, crossed the street. She spied the cats before Zuki did . . . two gray tabby toms lazing atop the wooden bench where humans waited for the giant stinky car they called a bus. The toms spotted them, too, and they gave small yowls of warning as she and Zuki drew closer.

"No worries," the pit bull assured them, halting a respectful distance away. "We're looking for some canine or feline who might know my friend's brother. He's gone missing on the streets, and we're trying to find him."

"He got a name?" the bushier of the toms asked, ignoring Zuki and addressing Ophelia.

"It's Brandon. Brandon Bobtail. He's black like me, but a little bigger, and he only has half a tail."

The two gray tabbies exchanged glances.

"Maybe we've seen him . . . and maybe we haven't," the second feline with one ragged ear said. "If you can hook us up with some tuna, maybe our memories will improve."

Ophelia's long tail reflexively bristled in irritation. What, did they think she carried around cans of cat food with her whenever

141

she went walking? But before she could spit out an insult, Zuki broke in.

"If you have some information that leads us to him, I can get you a can. But I don't do payment in advance."

The first tom hissed. "Yeah, well, we don't give out information in advance. So I guess you're out of luck."

"Why, you —"

The rest of what Ophelia was going to say was muffled by Zuki's big paw abruptly covering her mouth.

"That's fine," the pit bull said. "We'll be in the neighborhood for a while. If you change your mind later and decide you know something, we can make a deal. C'mon, Ophelia, let's go."

The dog waited until they were out of earshot of the toms and then added, "I told you no hissing and bristling. You have to know how to talk to the street dogs and cats if you want to learn anything useful."

"They didn't know anything about my brother," Ophelia said with a sniff. "They just wanted free tuna."

"Probably. But you never know. Look, there's a beagle in that doorway. Let's see what he knows."

The half-blind beagle was no more help than the tabbies, and so they continued walking.

"You do know how to get home again," Ophelia nervously asked as they crossed yet another street, narrowly avoiding being hit by a skinny green motorcycle that whined like a giant mosquito as it flew past on a single wheel.

Zuki gave her a reassuring nod. "Of course. Did you ever hear of a canine who couldn't find her way home again?"

Since the pit bull was the first canine she'd really ever known, Ophelia couldn't answer that, but she was willing to trust her friend. Even so, she did her best to watch for landmarks as they moved about, in case they got separated.

She had just paused and crouched for a sniff at a section of sidewalk that smelled familiar — *was that the lingering scent of bananas? And a very particular kind of dog pee?* — when she heard it. Drifting to them from the next block over was a drawn-out, fur-ruffling caterwaul that pierced the night air.

Mee-yowwwwwwww! The screech was angry but also frightened, the patented cry of a feline ready to do battle.

And it was a voice that she recognized.

"Zuki!" she yowled. "That's my brother! That's Brandon . . . and he's in trouble!"

143

NINE

"MEEEE-YOOOOOW!"

Another frantic, angry feline screech ripped through the night. Ophelia, who'd been momentarily frozen by the first cry, leaped to her paws. "C'mon, Zuki! We have to save Brandon!"

"Hop up and grab my collar! It'll be faster!"

With a nod, Ophelia sprang onto the canine's back. She sunk her claws into the heavy mesh of Zuki's black collar, gripping the dog's muscular flanks with her rear paws as Zuki took off like a pit bullet in the direction of the cries. They rounded a corner, and the cries grew louder. Now Ophelia could hear yips and growls . . . dogs, goading and taunting the cat.

"That way!" she shrieked in Zuki's ear, pointing with one paw toward a dark, narrow opening between two boarded-up shops midway down the block.

The pit bull swung right and zipped into that gap, slowing her pace a little as she dodged discarded boxes and broken bottles. A few feet later they reached the buildings' rear corners. There, the gap opened up onto an alley that ran in either direction the length of the block.

Zuki halted so quickly that Ophelia had to sink her claws into the dog's flanks to keep from flying over her blocky head.

"Sorry," she said at Zuki's reflexive yelp. "Look, over there!"

The alley was dark except for the reflected light of a distant street lamp, but Ophelia didn't need the bright half-moon above to clearly see what lay to either side of them. To the right, the alley led to the side street where the streetlight stood. To the left, where it should have opened onto a second side street, it instead was blocked by a chain-link fence topped by curls of wire twined with pointy bits. Not a fence that a reasonable feline would attempt to scale . . . not unless she — or he — were desperate. Against that fence squatted a broad, rusty green trash container almost as high as a human's head and twice as wide, so that it nearly touched the stucco buildings on either side of it.

But that was not what held Ophelia's attention.

Three street dogs — a stocky boxer mix, a rangy German shepherd, and a tiny black-and-white terrier — were pacing at the dumpster's base, barking and snapping. She caught an occasional word . . . *territory* . . . *intruder* . . . *dead.* But what sent a chill through her was who stood atop the trash container. There, perched upon the dumpster's closed plastic lid, was her missing brother.

Brandon! Found!

Even though she'd recognized his voice, she had to blink several times to be sure the feline held at bay was really he. But her joy and relief were swiftly supplanted by fear as she assessed his danger.

Brandon was pacing like a cat on patrol, his bobtail bristling like a brush as he yelled back at the dogs. Where Brandon had taken refuge, he was safely out of biting range . . . at least, for the moment. But he wouldn't stay safe for long.

Though skinny, the shepherd had a look of wiry strength. While the dog appeared content now to merely taunt his prey, making little mock leaps that brought his black snout even with the dumpster's edge, Ophelia knew that wouldn't last. She had seen shepherds in action at the shelter. If this dog put an effort into it, he doubtless could make a leap high enough to scramble onto the dumpster's lid. With the other two mutts patrolling below, and the chain-link fence with its wire barbs behind him, Brandon would have nowhere to flee to.

The ending for her brave brother would be horrific.

Even as this frightening scenario whipped through her mind, she saw the flash of green eyes. Brandon had noticed her! His green eyes grew wider still and he halted his pacing. But rather than call to her, he commenced yowling again, so that the pack's barking grew more frenzied.

Holding the street dogs' attention. Smart.

By now, Zuki had also spied Brandon. With a whispered "Hop down and stay behind me" to Ophelia, the pit bull padded closer to the dumpster.

Brandon saw the canine then, and shot Ophelia a shocked look. Not only had he not expected to see her there in the alley, he obviously hadn't expected her to be with someone else . . . especially not a dog!

Ophelia gave him a reassuring blink in return.

This one is a friend.

Brandon must have understood, for he

blinked back. Then he began prancing about the dumpster lid, giving Zuki time to get into position while the dogs kept up their threatening act. Keeping low, Ophelia followed after her friend. She might not be able to tackle the boxer mix or the shepherd, but at least she could take on the yappy terrier, if it came to that!

Zuki moved in so that she was directly behind the three street dogs now, yet far enough back that they couldn't readily lunge at her or dash around her. Ophelia took up the spot behind her, deliberately puffing herself up so she looked double her size. She wasn't sure if Zuki could best three dogs at once, but she was certain the clever pit bull could outsmart them.

She braced herself, ready for action . . . and Zuki didn't disappoint. She let loose with the deep, long bark of a larger canine.

"Leave! Cat! Alone!"

The powerful barks made the three street dogs woof in surprise. Snapping their jaws shut, they swung about, eyes glowing in the moonlight as they took in this unexpected threat. Realizing it was but a single canine that confronted them, they exchanged glances. Then the boxer mix spoke up.

"Hey you, pit bull. You're sticking your snout in other canines' business. This is our turf. Turn around now, and we'll let you go peacefully."

"No, wait," the shepherd broke in before Zuki could speak. Jaws opening in a wide grin, he went on. "Look, she brought us another cat to play with. Isn't that nice? Bobo, go get it."

"No!" Zuki barked out, slamming a large paw on the ground for emphasis. "Both these felines are under my protection. No street dogs are going to hurt them. Let the black cat on the dumpster go, and there won't be any trouble."

"No trouble, eh?" came a higher-pitched bark. "I don't think you heard my friend, Sammy, there. This is *our* turf."

This from the terrier, who had scampered out in front of his two much larger friends. He sat, hind legs jauntily shifted to one side, and bared his crooked teeth in what Ophelia assumed was supposed to be a threatening expression. Instead, it made him look like a human child's goofy toy.

This is the leader of the pack?

Ophelia shot him a suspicious look. His wiry black-and-white fur was matted in spots, and he wore a frayed yellow collar that still had an old rabies tag dangling from it. Obviously, he'd been someone's pet once, though whether he'd been dumped on the street or simply had run away from his human, Ophelia couldn't guess. But any sympathy she'd normally have for him was lost in the fact that he was threatening her brother.

"Here's the deal, pit bull," the terrier went on. "You take your little kitty cat and go, and we'll pretend none of this ever happened. But if you're not out of here by the time I bark three, Bobo and Sammy will take care of you, and then we'll have some fun with this new cat before we chomp up the first one. Got it?"

"I don't think you want to do that," Zuki softly replied.

"Really?" The terrier got to his paws, while the other two canines silently closed in behind him. "I think I do. *Bark.*"

One.

Zuki gave an exaggerated snort. "Are you boys sure you want to mess with a canine that was made to join a dogfighting ring as a pup and lived to tell about it?"

"You're bluffing. *Bark.*"

Two.

"I wouldn't be so sure about that."

"Yeah, and I used to race at the Palm Beach Kennel Club," the terrier countered with a sneer, naming the spot where humans made greyhounds run the track. "Time's up. *Bar—*"

"Wait, Rally!" The German shepherd gave his terrier friend a nudge before he could finish the count. "She's a pit bull. It could be true. Ask to see her scars."

Rally replied with an irritated growl, "So what's the big deal if it's true? There's three of us, and only one of her."

"Wrong!" Ophelia yowled, stepping forward so that she stood right next to Zuki. Raising a paw with all claws extended, she said, "There's two against three."

"No!" came an echoing yowl from behind the three street dogs. Puffing himself out to twice his usual size, Brandon exclaimed from his perch on the dumpster, "It's three against three."

Zuki, meanwhile, had moved to one side, so that the moonlight reflected off her snowy white coat. Now Ophelia could better see what she'd noticed before but never had been rude enough to mention: a series of dark pink scars along one shoulder and flank. *Bite marks.* They shone like stripes of honor, testifying to the pit bull's fighting spirit, even as a pup.

The street dogs saw the scars, too, and Ophelia saw them exchange glances again. A good fighting dog could easily take on two canines at once and finish the battle victorious. And even if the fight ended in a draw, there would be bites and blood to spare . . . mostly on the street dogs' side.

After a few seconds of silence, Rally the terrier gave an exaggerated yawn.

"Whatev," he said in imitation of young humans Ophelia had heard, waving a skinny paw. "We've got better things to do than mess with felines all night long. You're starting to bore us, pit bull. Why don't you take your black cats and leave?"

"Thanks, I'll do that."

Keeping her gaze fixed firmly on the street dogs, Zuki added, "Hi, Brandon, I'm your sister's friend, Zuki. Why don't you hop on over here, and the three of us will get out of these fine canines' fur."

"Sounds good to me."

With that brash reply, Brandon backed up to the rear edge of the trash container, took a running start, and then sprang. As Ophelia watched in amazement, he sailed over the street dogs' head and lightly landed on the alley surface a few feet past them. Never breaking stride, he bounded over to Zuki's opposite side and said, "What are we waiting for?"

"Walk like normal," the pit bull instructed in a low voice meant only for his and Ophelia's ears. "If you run, they might change their minds and give chase."

Nodding their agreement, the two black cats swung about and began padding toward the gap in the buildings where Zuki and Ophelia had first entered. The pit bull brought up the rear, though she glanced back a time or two to make sure the street dogs weren't going to make a cowardly rear attack. Only when they rounded the building and were on the street again did Zuki quietly command, "Run!"

At that, the trio took off, flying down the sidewalk like cats and dog with tails afire. They didn't stop until they reached the wooden bench where Ophelia and Zuki had earlier spoken with the gray-striped toms.

"We should be all right now," Zuki panted out. "Brandon, are you okay? Those canines didn't hurt you, did they?"

"I'm fine . . . but they could have ripped my paws off and I wouldn't care. All that matters is that I'm back with my sister again!"

With a joyful meow, he jumped atop Ophelia and playfully knocked her over.

"I thought I'd never see you again," came his happy yowl as he gripped her with all four paws and rolled about the sidewalk with her in a mock fight. "I came back for you that day we were in the box, but you were gone. I went out looking for you every single night afterwards. When I couldn't find you, I was hoping a nice human took you home."

"A nice human did!"

Meowing in happiness, Ophelia broke free of the play fight so she could explain about Ruby and the Botanica.

She swiftly told him the basics . . . how Ruby and Zuki had found her, half dead, in the box and carried her to the shelters. She also told him how, when the shelter people called him, Mrs. Givens's son claimed he had no idea how his mother's two cats had vanished and wanted Ophelia put up for adoption.

"When no one brought you to the shelter, too, I knew my only chance to find you again was to let a human adopt me so I could run off and look for you. Tonight was the first time I found a way out onto the streets, thanks to Zuki. So where have you been all this time? Hiding from canines?"

"I was staying with a human, too," Brandon explained. "It's a strange place called PAWN. The human likes me because he thinks I keep the mice away, and he doesn't care if I go out at night. If we keep walking, we'll go right past it. Look, you can see the sign now."

He pointed a paw. A block away, Ophelia could see the glow of red light against window glass. If she remembered the landmarks she'd been watching, the place wasn't that far away from the Botanica. Brandon had been in yowling distance all this time, and she hadn't known it!

Brandon, meanwhile, had turned his attention to Zuki. "I guess I should thank you for saving me from those street dogs. Would you really have fought them?"

"If I had to do it to save you or Ophelia, yes," the pit bull said with a small shudder. "But other than that, I'll never fight another dog again."

"Zuki doesn't have to fight," Ophelia informed him, worried that her friend was remembering things even worse than a suffocating box in the street. Trying to cheer her up, Ophelia added, "She's the smartest canine I've ever seen, almost as smart as a feline."

To her relief, the pit bull snickered, obviously amused by the compliment. "That's pretty high praise, coming from a cat."

"Well, it's true." Ophelia gave her whiskers a quick preen. Then, changing the subject, she said, "So, do you think Ruby will let Brandon stay at the Botanica, too? Remember, Ruby told Luciana that she would take

155

him if Luciana found him."

"Luciana?" Brandon echoed, velvety black nose twitching in puzzlement. "You mean our Luciana who lived with us in the old house? You've seen her?"

Ophelia nodded. "She came to the Botanica — the place where I live now. It's a long story, and there's some bad stuff I have to tell you. I think she's in trouble. I know she needs help, so that's our next job, now that we've found you. But we should probably go home first. Ruby will be back from the school place soon, and we don't want her finding out that we sneaked out. Besides, the street dogs might get brave again and come looking for us."

With that, the three trotted down the sidewalk at a quick pace, ducking into a doorway or behind a trash can whenever a human drove or biked past. Every so often, a ragged-looking person would rise from the shadows like a street dog, giving Ophelia a start. Unlike the three canines they'd just encountered, however, those people cared nothing for two cats and a dog on the prowl.

She was limping a little now. Her paws made sore from climbing the stucco wall earlier in the day were now even more raw from their mad dash escaping the street dogs. But no way was she complaining!

156

Scraped paw pads were a small price to pay for having her brother back safe with her.

By now, the half-moon was higher in the sky, and by its light Ophelia saw in relief that Brandon appeared just the same as last time she saw him. Maybe a tail's worth thinner, but no scrapes or scars to show for his adventures on his own.

Still, Ophelia shot her brother a concerned look. She hadn't thought beyond finding him. But maybe he liked this PAWN place where he'd been living and wouldn't want to leave it. That would mean she would have to abandon Ruby and Zuki and the Botanica and go there. But then, what if the PAWN human didn't like *her*?

She gave a soft, uncertain mew. Of course, she could stay where she was, and Brandon could remain in his new home, and they could visit each other sometimes. But things would never be the same. It would almost be worse than if they'd never found each other again!

"Look," Brandon exclaimed before she could figure out this puzzle. They had drawn even with the building with the red light in the window, and he waved a dramatic paw. "We're here. This is PAWN."

Letting herself be distracted, Ophelia

stared up at the sign made of red light. What PAWN meant, she had no clue. But then she noticed something else about the window.

"Look, Zuki! It's the three golden balls that Philomena talked about! She really did know where Brandon was staying."

She pointed a paw. Beneath the bright red PAWN was a dark blue bar of light. Below that bar, like oranges hanging in a neat row, were three balls of yellow light.

"Remember what she said, Zuki?"

Not waiting for a reply, she squinted her eyes as she sought the exact words.

"The three golden balls, he wanders those halls. Yes, the boy cat be all right. But finding him, 'twill be a fight," she triumphantly recited. "The golden balls meant the place called PAWN, and we *did* have to fight to get Brandon back!"

Zuki shrugged. "I told you Philomena knows what she's talking about."

"Who's Philomena?" Brandon wanted to know.

Ophelia shrugged. "You'll meet her . . . that is, if you want to come home with me and Zuki."

Fearful of hearing his answer, however, she distracted herself by raising up and, front paws on the windowsill, peering inside the shop.

This was a strange place, indeed! While the Botanica had long since closed for the evening, this place was lit within and appeared to be, as Ruby would say, *doing business.* She could see two or three humans milling about, and another two leaning over a counter near the store's front. Like the Botanica, the shop had shelves filled with things, but the goods were nothing like what Ruby sold.

Tools and suitcases and musical instruments and even computers.

Brandon raised up and peered inside the window with her. As if reading her mind he said, "It's a strange place. People bring stuff in, and the human — his name is Luis — buys it from them. And then after a while he sells the same things to other people. But it's fun to wander through and see what's there. Though he has scary stuff, like animal heads that have been nailed to pieces of wood!"

Ophelia gave a little shudder. The son had a giant fish — rather like the fish at the bottom of the pool — mounted on a piece of wood that he hung on the wall of his room at the old house. Even though she liked eating fish, something about hanging the fish's body like a picture was frightening. She'd never want to live in a place like PAWN that had so many unnatural things.

Luckily, it seemed that Brandon felt the same way . . . or did he? But before she could ask him again if he would come live at the Botanica with her and Zuki, the pit bull barked, "The street dogs followed us! Quick, we need to run!"

TEN

Ophelia shot a frantic look over her furry shoulder. Two blocks behind them, but swiftly gaining ground, were the boxer mix and German shepherd, Bobo and Sammy. Rally the terrier trailed a distance behind, short legs churning as he did his best to catch up with his compatriots.

"Follow me," Zuki woofed. "I know a shortcut."

Once again, the threesome made a mad dash for safety, though this time the danger was far more immediate. Zuki's earlier bluff had worked, but only for as long as it had taken for the street dogs to decide they'd been played. Apparently they'd decided they weren't going to let this intrusion on their turf go unpunished.

"Quick, around this corner," the pit bull commanded, making a swift right. Brandon and Ophelia banked and turned, too, though the quick spin on battered paws made the latter mew in pain.

Almost home, she told herself, panting. *You can stand the pain a little long—*

Abruptly, her paw caught on a bit of broken sidewalk concrete, and she went tumbling toward the curb.

"Ophelia!" she heard her brother yowl.

Help! she tried to yowl back, but she couldn't catch her breath. But she knew she was rolling straight toward the busy street. She could hear the roar of automobiles rushing right to the spot where, at any moment, she would be sprawled. And then everything merged into a single earsplitting cacophony . . . *a blast from an auto horn . . . a squeal of brakes . . . Brandon yowling in fear.*

And then, as headlights pinned her in place and car tires spun relentlessly toward her, she was snagged by the nape of her neck and swung skyward.

In the next instant, Ophelia found herself lying in a small strip of weeds next to the curb as a small red car with one broken tail light roared past her. Zuki was standing over her, pink tongue lolling from her jaws as the pit bull stared down at her in concern. Just like that very first time Ophelia had seen her.

Brandon, meanwhile, had rushed to her

side. "Zuki saved you! That car would have run you over if she hadn't been so fast on her paws and dragged you back onto the sidewalk. Are you all right?"

"I — I'm fine," Ophelia insisted in a valiant tone, though she had a bump behind one ear, and two of her paws were now bleeding in earnest. Then, remembering why they'd been running in the first place, she choked out, "The street dogs! They'll catch us!"

"Not if we run faster!" Zuki shot back. "We're still a couple of blocks ahead of them. But I'd better carry you the rest of the way."

Before Ophelia could protest, the dog had caught her by the nape again and, with a quick move lightly tossed her over her shoulder and onto her back again.

"Hang onto my collar like last time!" she ordered as Ophelia regained her balance. To Brandon, she barked, "Stick by me! There's too much traffic now to try to dodge it. We have to wait for the right moment, even if we lose some of our lead."

Brandon nodded and crouched, ready to spring the instant the pit bull gave the word. Ophelia sank her claws into her friend's collar and stayed low so that she wouldn't throw the canine off balance. Behind them, she could hear the street dogs baying, and she dared to take a quick look back.

The boxer and shepherd were getting closer, long legs covering ground faster than the sturdy Zuki could move with her shorter limbs. Now she could see their tongues lolling and their eyes gleaming each time they dashed past a streetlamp.

Too close for comfort, the thought flashed through her mind.

Maybe too close to outrun!

But before she could warn Zuki, the pit bull gave a harsh bark. "Go!"

The canine sprang into the street, Ophelia clinging to the dog like a burr on a kitten and Brandon at her heels. The trio dashed across the first two lanes and halted on the concrete median to let a rusty blue truck and a smoke-spewing two-door car rumble past.

"Wait! Wait!" Zuki barked, while Ophelia glanced back again to see that the street dogs had almost reached their original crossing point. Then, as another gap in traffic appeared, the pit bull yelped "Go!" and took off.

"Go, go!"

Ophelia heard the high-pitched word echoing behind her as Rally the terrier urged on his faster friends. She squinted her green eyes shut. She didn't want to see the pair overtake them, didn't want to see her brother caught in their jaws, didn't want to see slashes of blood on Zuki's white fur. Before that happened, she vowed, she'd release her grip on the pit bull's collar and let the street dogs go after her, so that Brandon and Zuki could make their escape.

"YIIIIIPE!"

The high-pitched shriek of an injured canine pierced the air just as they reached the safety of the far corner. Zuki halted on the curb and swung about. "Look!"

To Ophelia's shock, the boxer mix who a moment early had been in full chase mode now lay in the street. Half a block down the road, a boxy black sedan slowed for an instant as a human stuck his head out the window. The head promptly vanished, followed by the squeal of tires as the sedan shot forward, leaving the injured dog behind in the gutter.

"He's hurt," Brandon meowed in concern. "Should we —"

"He's just clipped," Zuki cut him short. "His own fault for not watching for cars. Don't worry, his friends will take care of him. Come on!"

She swung about again and started running, Brandon at her side. Ophelia managed another look back. The boxer, Bobo, was slowly getting to his paws again while Sammy the shepherd stood guard, barking at approaching cars to warn them off. She gave a reflexive sigh of relief. While neither dog would have hesitated to sink fangs into her, she couldn't help but be glad the big mutt hadn't been killed.

Though he definitely deserved a bruised flank and a limp!

"You dummies!" she heard Rally yapping in the distance. "You let them get away-y-y-y-y!"

By the time Zuki rounded the corner to their block, the street dogs' barks had faded. A moment later, she dashed into the side yard of the darkened Botanica, headed for the fence.

"Hurry," she barked, halting to let Ophelia slide off her back again. "I can hear Ruby's car. We need to get inside the fence before she drives past and sees us."

The doorway in the fence was still propped slightly open courtesy of the rock, just as they'd left it. Zuki shoved a big paw behind one picket and lifted the wood so that Ophelia and Brandon could crawl past. The pit bull squeezed in after them, then knocked the rock aside so that the doorway could swing completely shut. It had just settled into place when headlights flashed across the fence, and they heard Ruby's bug car — Beetle, Ophelia heard it called — pulling into the driveway.

"Ruby's home," the pit bull said unnecessarily. "Quick, let's get inside before she unlocks the door."

A few moments later, they'd dashed from the courtyard through the dog door and were trotting down the short hall toward the main shop.

"Sightsee later," Zuki told Brandon as he gazed about the place, nose twitching and green eyes wide as he took in the aisles of herbs and crystals and statues. "Go hide behind the counter while we figure out how to introduce you. Ophelia, pretend you're napping or something."

She cut short her words at the sound of jangling keys at the door and flopped onto the tile floor, feigning sleep. Ophelia leaped onto the counter and curled into a tight ball, trying not to snicker as she heard Zuki pretend to snore. Brandon, meanwhile, had followed orders and was but a shadow against the back wall.

"I'm home," Ruby called as she pushed open the front door, letting in a swath of light from the street beyond. Swiftly relocking the door behind her — apparently the streets after dark weren't always safe for humans either — she set down her backpack on the counter.

Zuki gave a little woof, like she'd just awakened, and extended all four legs in a mock stretch. Ophelia contented herself with flexing a paw as the human gave her a quick head rub before bending to pat Zuki.

"Good girls. I knew I could trust you to behave. I don't know about you, but I'm starving. Why don't we go into the kitchen for a snack?"

Zuki, who never turned down food, gave a bark of approval and stood. With a happy meow — all this running about had made her hungry, too — Ophelia scrambled to her paws as well. Letting the pit bull take the lead, she waited until she and Ruby had gone into the hall before she peered over the opposite side of the counter.

"Follow us," she whispered to her brother. "Food makes everyone happy, even humans, so this will be the best time for you to meet her."

"Are you sure?" he whispered back. "I thought Zuki was going to tell me when."

"Zuki isn't the boss of us," Ophelia replied in a lofty tone. "Just because she's been here longer doesn't mean she knows everything."

"Right, but she saved both our tails tonight, didn't she?"

Since she couldn't contradict that fact, Ophelia merely shrugged and lightly leaped down again. Limping only slightly on her sore paws, she made her way to the black-and-white-tiled kitchen, Brandon quietly shadowing her.

After a couple of hours out on the darkened streets, the light streaming from the trio of red balls hanging from the kitchen ceiling made her blink. Ruby was already standing at the little red and silver table, Zuki crouched expectantly at her feet.

Ruby reached for one of two familiar jars sitting there and poured a few little fishy-smelling squares onto a tiny blue pottery plate she'd pulled from a cabinet, which she set on the floor. "Here you go, Ophelia."

Not waiting to be asked a second time, the cat made a dash for the saucer and began crunching treats. Ruby, meanwhile, pulled a couple of the usual bone-shaped snacks from the second jar and tossed them, one at a time, toward Zuki's open jaws.

"Good catch," she praised the canine as Zuki plopped to the floor and began her own crunching. "Now, let's see what's in the fridge for me."

Leaving the jars behind, Ruby went over to the big white cold box where she kept most of the human food. While her back was turned, Ophelia swallowed her last crumb and glanced back over her furry shoulder toward the doorway. She could just see Brandon's nose and his glowing eyes watching them from around the door jamb. Feeling a little guilty that she'd munched down all the snacks without offering to share, she gestured him into the room.

"Sit by the plate and pretend you're me," she hissed. "Maybe she'll pour out some more treats."

While Brandon took her spot, she slipped behind the large, squat urn in the corner of the kitchen next to a tall cabinet. That blue-glazed pot was home to an enticing plant with a fat belly half-buried in dirt and dozens of skinny long green leaves sprouting from its pointy top and dangling almost to the ground.

A ponytail palm, she'd heard Ruby call it. Only the fact that Ruby had rudely doused her with water the one time she'd sniffed at the plant kept her from taking a nibble each time she walked past it. As it was, she couldn't resist giving its leaves a quick bat before she crouched behind it to see how the human would react.

Zuki, meanwhile, had finished off her crunchy bones and noticed that the black

170

cat sitting near her was not the same feline that had been there a moment ago. Rolling her brown eyes, she muttered, "I know humans aren't very observant, but I think Ruby will figure out you're a different cat."

Brandon didn't have a chance to reply to that, however. Ruby turned from the refrigerator, a small yogurt container in one hand, and smiled as she caught sight of a black cat sitting beside the plate.

"Ophelia, you're such a little Greedy Gus. You just had your snack, and now you want more." Shaking her head, she set down the yogurt on the table and reached for the treat jar. "All right, just a couple more, but that's it. I don't want you getting fat."

Brandon got to his paws and, as she set out the promised two more, gave her denim-clad leg a quick rub by way of thanks. While he crunched away, she put aside the jar and gave him a pat in return, running her hand down his sleek back.

"Such a sweet girl," she observed in a fond voice, only to break off with a gasp. "Wh— What happened to your tail? Half of it is gone!"

Just as swiftly, the momentary panic that filled her voice was replaced by suspicion.

"Wait, your pink collar is missing, too. And if I didn't know better, I'd say you got a little bigger since I left earlier this evening. So what's going on here?"

Pushing her glasses firmly into place, Ruby rose and stared at the black cat at her feet. Right color, she told herself. But, unless she'd gone blind or crazy, definitely not the same feline she'd left behind.

Wondering if JoJo could have snuck in somehow to play a joke on her while she was gone at class, Ruby glanced from the strange cat to Zuki. The pit bull obviously knew something was amiss, for she wore the patented doggie look of guilt that Ruby knew translated to *Sorry, please don't be mad at me, Mom.* And then she heard a small mew that did not come from the cat before her.

Something black and furry was crouched beneath the cascade of narrow green leaves spilling from the ponytail palm in the kitchen's far corner.

"Ophelia?"

Then, when the fuzzy black form unfurled itself to reveal a familiar, small black cat with a pink collar and long black tail, Ruby dragged her gaze from her pet to the cat sitting at her feet. Definitely a second black cat . . . and this one larger and collar-free with a distinctive bobbed tail.

"Brandon? OMG! Ophelia, is this your

missing bother?"

She didn't expect a reply, of course, but Ophelia gave a loud, high-pitched *yow* that she had no choice but to take as a *yes*.

"I don't believe it," she exclaimed and bent to pick up the purring beast.

He was as soft as Ophelia, but beefier, and his purr was less the gentle buzz of his sister and more a throaty rumble. And unlike Ophelia, who could be reserved, this new boy had no problem snuggling into her arms as she pulled out a chair and sat at the dinette with him perched in her lap.

"Well, Zuki, you've got some 'splaining to do," she informed the pit bull in a playful tone, invoking the old '50s sitcom tagline. "Where in the world did this boy come from? Did he climb in over the wall or something?"

Zuki gave a few quick barks that might have been an explanation. Unfortunately, Ruby didn't speak dog, so the story behind Brandon's sudden appearance at the Botanica would likely always remain a mystery. Which left only the most important question . . . what to do with him?

"Rosa will kill me if she comes home and finds two cats here," she told Ophelia, who had run over to the table where she and Brandon sat.

Ophelia appeared unconcerned by this announcement. Brandon, meanwhile, squirmed out of her grasp, knocking her glasses slightly askew in the process before jumping from her lap to join his sister on the floor. Ophelia gave him a mock swat of one paw, and then the two tumbled together in playful battle, rolling and kicking their way across the black linoleum.

Ruby shoved her glasses back into place and groaned.

"Ugh, what am I going to do?" she asked Zuki, who was woofing along as color commentator to this round of big time cat wrestling. "I can't send the poor thing to the shelter, and I sure can't put him back out onto the streets. Though he does look in pretty good shape for a cat that's been on his own for a month. He must have been sweet-talking someone into feeding him all this time. Maybe he'll leave on his own?"

She said the last in a hopeful tone. Watching the two cats interact, however, she doubted that the boy kitty would leave of his own volition. It was obvious that he and Ophelia were BFFs. Mentally, she threw up her hands.

"What's the old saying, ask for forgiveness, not permission? Ophelia, show your brother where the food and water and kitty box all are, and we'll deal with Rosa when the time comes. I need to finish up some stuff online and then get to bed."

First finding a spoon to go with her yogurt, she made a quick detour into the shop to grab her backpack. She checked the front door a final time before closing the door between the Botanica and hallway. She usually let Zuki and Ophelia have the run of the place at night, relatively confident that they wouldn't damage anything in the shop. But with another cat added to the mix, she didn't want to risk the merchandise . . . at least, not the first night. A broken statue or gnawed candle would not help endear the kitties to Rosa.

A small crash in the kitchen, which was tumbling cats bumping into the pie safe, confirmed the wisdom of that decision.

"C'mon, Zuki," she called. "Beddy-bye."

With the pit bull at her heels, she headed up the narrow built-in staircase leading to the second floor where Rosa and she each had a bedroom. Rosa's, of course, was the larger of the two. Ruby had never actually been inside her half sister's bedroom before, though she'd caught a glimpse of it when she had first moved in a year ago.

From what little she'd seen, the design style could best be described as "minimalist on steroids" — empty white walls, bare wooden floor, a Mission-style single bed with white linens, and a matching chest of drawers, atop which sat a single large conch shell. She was pretty sure that Rosa had a personal altar set against the wall whose view was blocked by the door. But said door had been locked ever since her half sister's departure weeks earlier. Even if she'd been tempted to snoop, she couldn't.

Ruby's bedroom was across the narrow hall from her sister's and alongside the pink-and-aqua-tiled bathroom that, save for a slight difference in tile color, was a mirror image of the downstairs facility. She had the same set of furniture as Rosa, though the comforter on her bed was a swirly pattern of ocean blues. In keeping with the beachy theme, she'd added a sand-colored rag rug to the floor (since, pale as she was, she didn't spend a whole lot of time at the actual beach). The top of her dark-stained wood dresser was crowded with Florida-kitsch souvenirs she'd found in local thrift stores: old hotel postcards, flamingo figurines, alligator ashtrays, even a radio shaped like an oversized Florida orange.

Her favorite touch, however, was the framed prints — no way could she afford the original oils! — of Highwaymen art that hung on her pale yellow walls. She'd always loved the flamboyant colors of those mid-century Florida landscapes painted by self-taught African-American artists. Decades earlier, those men (and a couple of women) had hawked their canvases on Florida's tourist byways for a few dollars. Now, their work sold in the high thousands, some even for five figures.

Needless to say, there were no shrines to be found behind *her* door.

Once in her room, Ruby set the yogurt on her side table and pulled her laptop out of her backpack. Leaving Zuki curled up on the rug, she settled cross-legged atop her bed and fired up the computer.

Her usual routine after class was to pull up that evening's lecture notes she'd taken and flesh them out while the material was still fresh in her mind. But tonight, *A Comparison of the Secondary Characters in the Works of Dickens and Doyle* was pretty far down the list of important things. Instead, she opened a web browser and typed three words:

Hilda Givens Obituary.

ELEVEN

Elderly Palm Beach Socialite Drowns in Pool.

Ruby winced. Even knowing what had happened, it was still a shock to see that blunt headline pop up as the first result in her web search. She clicked the link and was taken to a *Palm Beach Herald* news article dated a few weeks earlier, along with an accompanying photo of Mrs. Givens.

Following the trend of using vintage photos of the elderly deceased, the black-and-white headshot was of a handsome woman in her early fifties with 1980s-era sky-high permed blond hair and deep dimples. The photo obviously had been taken at a social event, for her jewelry — dangly earrings and a choker necklace — appeared to be diamonds, and what was visible of her gown had lots of lace and tulle. Somehow, seeing the dead woman in her prime made the situation more tragic, though Ruby couldn't explain why.

Straightening her glasses, she took a deep breath and started reading.

Police are investigating the apparent accidental drowning of a long-time Palm Beach resident Friday morning. Eighty-two-year-old Hilda Givens, wife of the late real estate developer Walter W. Givens, was found unresponsive in the pool of her Poinciana Lane home. According to police, Mrs. Givens's housekeeper, Luciana Torres, discovered the woman around 6:45 that morning and immediately called 911.

Attempts to resuscitate Mrs. Givens were unsuccessful. She was rushed to St. Elizabeth's Medical Center, where she was pronounced dead a short time later. Her only son, Terrence W. Givens, who lives in the same residence, was not at home at the time of the incident.

So far, the account jibed with what Luciana had told her. Ruby read on.

Mrs. Givens had been a fixture in Palm Beach society ever since her marriage to Walter Givens in 1960. The two were known for both their dazzling parties and their philanthropic endeavors, including a major donation in 1989 to the Care for

Kids Foundation that allowed the building of one of the first children's hospice homes in the Palm Beach area.

Ruby skimmed the rest of the story, which mentioned the death of the old woman's husband a dozen years earlier and detailed Mrs. Givens's social life and charitable endeavors before and after. She paused, however, at the news account's final paragraphs.

The daughter of Sioux City, Iowa, banker Ralph Franklin and wife Rose, Mrs. Givens first met her future husband in Melbourne, Australia, during the 1956 Summer Olympic games. Mrs. Givens, who had attended Mt. Holyoke College, was a member of the 1956 US Women's swim team. Her specialties were the 100 meter backstroke and the 400 meter freestyle. Mr. Givens was attending the Games as a spectator.

According to her son, Mrs. Givens was eliminated early in both her events at the 1956 Games. Additionally, she gave up a spot at the 1960 Games in Rome in order to marry; still, she considered her short tenure as a US Olympian as one of her proudest moments.

"Hey, Zuki, what do you think of this?"

she asked aloud. "Mrs. Givens was once a world-class swimmer. Pretty ironic that she died by drowning."

The pit bull made a little mumbly sound in return and then snuffled back to sleep again.

Ruby frowned. Of course, good swimmers drowned all the time. And, at eighty-two, the woman obviously was no longer an athlete of Olympic caliber. But still . . .

She scrolled down the article a bit more and found a couple of related links. She clicked on the one that said *Givens Drowning Ruled Accidental* and began reading aloud.

" 'Palm Beach police said Tuesday that last week's death of prominent Palm Beach Resident Hilda Givens has been ruled an accidental drowning. Results from the coroner's autopsy listed a head injury consistent with a fall. Although there were no witnesses, a police investigation concluded that Mrs. Givens, eighty-two, slipped on the pool deck and hit her head before falling into the pool sometime between midnight and 6:45 a.m. when her housekeeper discovered her body. According to the first responders, the victim was wearing a nightgown at the time of her death. A statement made by her son indicates that

Mrs. Givens had been prone to sleepwalking in the past, which might explain her presence outside the house at that hour.' "

Sleepwalking. Slipped on the pool deck and hit her head, Ruby silently repeated.

It sounded logical. Old people — heck, young people! — fell all the time. And a wet pool deck was all kinds of hazardous. Neither of the stories mentioned a bathing suit lying about, so it seemed the old woman hadn't been planning to take a midnight dip. Though, to be fair, she had friends who swam naked in the privacy of their own pools, mostly so they weren't constantly having to rinse chlorine out of an expensive swimsuit. But Luciana had said that the old woman swam daily, and surely she would have included the whole "sans bathing suit" thing had that been Mrs. Givens's habit. And she hadn't mentioned sleepwalking either.

Or maybe the old woman simply had insomnia and liked to enjoy her courtyard at night. Nothing wrong with that. And, apparently, the cops hadn't found anything suspicious about it.

She skimmed through the rest of the article, which basically was a rehash of the previous one. Halfway through, however, it included quotes from both Luciana and

Mrs. Givens's son.

"We're all devastated by her loss, of course," her son, fifty-three-year-old Terrence Givens, told the Palm Beach Herald reporter. "She lived a remarkable life and did much on behalf of numerous local charities. I warned her many times not to swim by herself, but Hilda did things on her own terms."

The quote from Luciana, however, was far blunter.

"Señora Givens, she had a very strict routine," stated Luciana Torres, the Givens' live-in housekeeper who discovered her employer's body. "She took her swim the same time every morning. I told the police I cannot think why she would be out in the night."

It seemed that Luciana had her suspicions from the start, Ruby told herself. Still, there was nothing in either account that made the old woman's death sound anything other than accidental. The housekeeper's reaction, however, was understandable, for it was obvious she considered Mrs. Givens more than just a boss.

Ruby sighed. She'd lost a college friend in

183

an automobile accident a few years back. Within hours of hearing the news, a group of the dead girl's mutual friends — including Ruby — had formed a spontaneous grief support group. They'd spent the days before the funeral creating scenarios to explain their friend's tragic passing as more than a random event.

Maybe some creep was chasing her, and she'd crashed trying to escape.

Maybe someone had walked out onto the road in front of her, and she'd deliberately wrecked rather than run him down.

Maybe she'd witnessed a crime, and the Mob/Government/MS-13 had silenced her.

In the end, however, she and her friends had had to accept the truth — that Madison drank too much that night and climbed into her car before someone could take away her keys, and subsequently plowed into a concrete barrier on the Interstate.

Recalling those raw emotions and outright denial, she definitely got where Luciana was coming from.

Returning her attention to the current situation, Ruby backtracked to her original search results. More out of curiosity than from any true feeling that she'd stumble over something to contradict the official findings, she reentered the query as *Hilda*

Givens Palm Beach.

This time, the hits mostly were to links from the *Palm Beach Herald*'s society pages.

She spent the next half hour reading through the articles and looking at pictures of Hilda that spanned a period from her college years until just a couple of weeks before her death. She particularly enjoyed the swim team pictures of Hilda and her teammates dressed in old-fashioned one-piece bathing suits, their hair covered by rubber swim caps. A few photos were of the Givens estate, both now and in the past, and Ruby was impressed despite herself.

"Check this out, Zuki," she said aloud as she took in the gracious mid-century architecture and glimpses of highly manicured grounds. "Poor Brandon and Ophelia. Coming to live here sure was a step down for them. Actually, about ten or twelve steps!"

She kept clicking, finally pausing at a series of photos from a soiree that had occurred a couple of weeks before the old woman's death. *An Evening in Black and Blanc,* the main headline read — black and white apparently being the event's theme.

As befitted that motif, the pictures she found of Hilda were of the old woman dressed in a long-sleeved V-neck ball gown in white and black taffeta. Instead of diamonds, she wore multiple strands of pearls around her throat, while a cluster of pearls the size of Ophelia's paw dangled from each ear. The hair was white now, and gently waved about her face, the dimples almost hidden among the wrinkles. Even so, her features remained as handsome as in her youth . . . most likely because her smile exuded warmth that came through even in a newspaper photo.

The first photo showed Hilda elegantly posed alone beside a staircase. The next were group shots. According to the accompanying captions, one was of Hilda with a prominent local surgeon, the surgeon's husband, and a grizzled man who'd apparently been a popular singer in the late '70s. All were wearing the requisite black and white. Another photo had Hilda posed between two much younger men, both in sleek black tuxes and with poufy white hair, their smiles wide. Hilda's name was listed along with theirs: *Mr. James Hudson and Mr. Bart Jennings-Hudson.* Married couple, Ruby surmised, though she couldn't decide if the hair thing was their usual style, or if they'd bleached their matching pompadours just for the event.

The last photo, however, was the one that

held Ruby's attention. Three people were in this shot as well. First was Hilda, standing to one side and looking surprisingly grim. Beside her was a smiling man in a black tux who, according to the picture's caption, was her son, Terrence.

This was the first photo she'd seen of him, and Ruby squinted a little through her glasses, looking for the familial likeness. She could detect a bit of similarity in the strong, square features, but chances were the man more closely resembled his late father. He was handsome enough for his age, despite the thinning blond hair, though in Ruby's opinion he would have been far better looking had his smile held half the warmth of his mother's.

A third person stood to Terrence's right, a woman probably twenty years his junior and wearing a sleeveless black gown split almost thigh-high. Terrence's arm was draped awkwardly around her waist, and it was hard to tell from her closed-lipped smile if she appreciated this attention or not.

Joan Ratzen, according to the caption. She was pretty, Ruby conceded, if not particularly striking, with long dark hair that had been twisted into a deliberately messy updo. A size 2 or smaller, but with boobs that probably were not original equipment, given their size and gravity-defying properties. Was this maybe the woman Terrence had brought home, and who Luciana claimed Hilda had not approved of?

Succumbing to plain nosiness now, Ruby skimmed back through some of the older event photos where Hilda had been a guest. Sure enough, Joan showed up a few more times . . . once at a benefit for hurricane victims, and again at a children's cancer fundraiser. At the latter, she was photographed between Terrence and another man about the latter's same age. The second man look thrilled to be in the photo, likely because Joan was wearing yet another gown slit down to there and up to here.

Feeling nosier still, Ruby did one more web search, punching in Joan's name. As with Hilda, numerous hits came up, but of a different sort. She saw in surprise that the woman worked for a prominent West Palm Beach investment firm. Her LinkedIn profile presented a far more staid photo than her social ones: business suit, glasses, and hair straightened into smooth submission. Her background was impressive, too: MBA, Ivy League school, and membership in several prestigious professional organizations.

"Wow," she muttered, feeling more than a bit outclassed. Why Hilda would have objected to this version of Joan dating her son, she couldn't guess.

So much for that, she decided, stifling a yawn.

She closed down the browser, but not before bookmarking the search . . . just in case. That accomplished, she carried the laptop over to her small desk beneath the window where she usually did her class-work. Her view was of the not-so-scenic street, Rosa having the room with a window overlooking the picturesque courtyard. Still, when the room was dark, she rather enjoyed peering out past the curtains at the activity below. In this part of town, things never entirely shut down for the night.

She plugged in the laptop so it would recharge, wishing she could as easily revive her positive outlook. But now that she'd done her internet sleuthing, she had to admit that she did feel a little better about Luciana's situation. Best as she could tell, the housekeeper's concerns were based more on passion than on any sort of evidence. Perhaps after a couple more weeks, when her emotions about her employer's passing were less raw, the woman would come back in for another reading that would give her some relief.

And even better, she could tell Luciana

that the missing Brandon had been found and had been reunited with his sister.

As if hearing that last, a small questioning mew came from the vicinity of the bedroom door. She glanced in that direction to see a small fuzzy black head push past the door jamb.

"Ophelia?" she asked with a smile. "Do you want to come in?"

The cat gave a little yowl of agreement and padded through the doorway, followed by her brother. Zuki opened one eye and gave the pair a welcoming woof before settling back down again.

"Make yourself at home," Ruby told the pair as she rose and started for the bathroom. "I'm going to get ready for bed.

When she returned a few minutes later with teeth brushed and wearing a long black nightshirt emblazoned with an image of The Fool, both cats were curled in tight balls at the foot of her bed. Obviously, the "make yourself at home" invitation had been taken literally.

Grinning, she plucked off her glasses and set them on her bedside table. Then, flipping off her lamp that was in the shape of a pineapple, she slid beneath the covers, taking care not to disturb the snoozing felines. Tomorrow, she'd contact Shanice over at the animal shelter to let her know that Brandon had somehow managed to find his sister, and that he now had a new home at the Botanica, too.

Ophelia waited until the soft sound of Ruby's even breathing indicated that the human was sleeping. Then she gave her brother a nudge.

"Ruby left her laptop on. You heard what she was telling Zuki while we were listening outside the door. She was looking up things about the old woman and Luciana. Remember, I told you she needed help. We should go see what Ruby found out."

Brandon opened one green eye. "I don't know how to do a computer," he protested. "Besides, I'm sleepy after all that running tonight. Maybe tomorrow you can explain everything."

He clamped both eyes firmly shut again and started snoring, just like Ruby.

"Fine," Ophelia muttered.

Slipping shadow-like off the bed, she made her way to the desk where the computer sat. Just like Ruby, it was asleep . . . but when she gave it a little nudge with one paw, it woke up and began a soft hum. A close-up picture of Zuki, long pink tongue lolling, abruptly popped up, making her jump back a little.

Dumb canine.

She gave her paw a lick, pretending that she'd not been at all startled. She glanced over her furry shoulder to make sure that the sudden light from the screen hadn't disturbed the snoring human; then she settled in front of the keyboard. Imitating what she'd seen Ruby do, she poked a paw at one of the little black squares with squiggly white lines on them.

The screen promptly changed, filled now with words and a few small pictures. Ophelia squinted, nose almost touching the screen. What any of this meant, she wasn't certain. Hesitantly, she touched a paw to one of the lines of words, and new things appeared. This time there were more pictures, including one of the old woman!

Mom!

She blinked back a bit of moisture in her green eyes. Even though Ruby was very kind, she still missed the old woman who had raised her and Brandon from kittens. If only Luciana had found her in the pool sooner, maybe they would all still be together.

Ophelia gave the picture a fond pat with her paw, and the screen changed again. This time, there were several big pictures of the old woman, some of them by herself and some with other humans. She gave a reflexive hiss at one picture which had the son standing next to her.

Bad human! Someone should put you *in a box*!

And there was something funny about that picture, she decided. In all the other pictures, the old woman was smiling . . . but in this one, her mouth looked all flat, like she had bitten into a dried mouse. It had to be because the son was standing next to her and she knew what a bad man he was! Even the other human female in the picture did not look happy standing next to him.

Ophelia squinted at that third person. She wasn't sure she'd ever seen this person before. This human female looked about the same age as Ruby and also had dark fur, though hers was longer and didn't have that strange blue streak in it. She looked nice — but with humans, you couldn't always tell.

She poked a few more keys, but she found no pictures of Luciana anywhere. And no pictures of the old woman floating at the bottom of the pool, so that she could study it and figure out if Luciana was right.

With a little hiss of frustration, she stared at the screen awhile longer until it went black again. Then she jumped off the desk and climbed back onto the bed.

Feeling the covers shift, Brandon slitted open a green eye and whispered, "What did you find out?"

"Nothing much."

"Were there pictures of Luciana?"

Ophelia sniffed. *Now* he was interested in what she had to tell him. She shook her head. "No. But I don't think Ruby looked very hard. There weren't pictures of anything important. Computers obviously aren't much good."

With that lofty declaration, Ophelia plopped down beside him, her chin propped on his shoulder. She couldn't sleep, however. Every time she started to doze off, she would see the street dogs pinning Brandon atop a dumpster, or chasing the three of them down the street. And then there was the matter of Luciana.

Ophelia sighed. Even though Ruby and the computer turned out to be an empty mouse hole, she wasn't going to give up. The cards she'd pulled for Luciana were bad, and it was up to her and Brandon and Zuki to watch out for the housekeeper. That's what the old woman would have done.

Another message for the cat. You must beware the human rat.

Abruptly, Philomena's words from earlier that day popped back into her mind. The fish had been right about finding Brandon at the three golden balls, which was the place called PAWN. And she'd been right about the fight, too. So she must be right about this human rat . . . whatever . . . whoever that was!

Ophelia frowned. She knew only one human who acted like a rat, and that was the son. She tried picturing him with a pointy nose and round ears and a long scaly tail, and she had to shove a paw over her mouth to keep from laughing out loud. But in real life, he wasn't funny. He was cruel to felines and had yelled at the old woman. And Luciana was afraid of him, even though she was mad at him, too.

But if a human couldn't deal with him, how would a cat put him in his place?

But it wouldn't be just one cat, she reminded herself as she finally drifted off to sleep. There would be two cats and a canine . . . and surely together they could outwit one measly human.

TWELVE

"Your coworker needs a Tarot card reader for a bridal shower she's throwing? Where, how long, and when?" Ruby asked next morning as she and JoJo sat outside in the courtyard at the concrete table.

At the center of the table's red, blue, and yellow tiled starburst pattern sat a pasteboard box containing a baker's dozen of doughnut varieties. Ruby's "outside" Tarot deck — a cheap Rider-Waite that she played with in the courtyard, not caring if it got dirty — lay stacked at her elbow. The chipped gray onyx box that she kept it stored in sat next to her phone, which was protected by a bright yellow faux leather case.

It was just after 7:30 a.m. Since the Botanica didn't open until ten, Ruby had been indulging in her usual morning routine. First came taking Zuki for a quick walk down the block. Food was next — previously for a single dog, but now for two cats as well, with a yogurt for herself. The remainder of the routine consisted of sitting outside with her smartphone or laptop reading the headlines on her newsfeed, or finishing up a bit of homework. That, or she did practice spreads with her Tarot cards while drinking coffee — not that she needed the caffeine wake-up with three roosters on the premises.

JoJo, who knew her schedule, had called a few minutes ago on her way to work to say she was stopping by. She'd arrived at the Botanica's front door dressed for her job at the law firm in a coral-hued version of a skirted power suit. In one hand, she'd held a box from which wafted the irresistible smell of sugary fried delights.

Now, JoJo swiped a few cruller crumbs from her chin and broke off a bit of her pastry for Zuki. The pup was sitting patiently among the three gently clucking roosters hanging out beneath the table and awaiting their respective shares of human food. Zuki caught the tossed piece with a snap of her broad jaws, while the roosters scrambled for the stray crumbs that went flying.

"The *where* is Palm Beach," JoJo replied. "Lucky you, you get to hang out with the rich folks. The *how long* is two to three hours, but you get all the snacks and wine you want while you're working. As for the *when* . . ."

She paused for another bite of cruller, then continued. "Courtney already had a Tarot card reader booked, but Madam Babushka apparently had a family emergency and had to cancel. And it seems the bride really, really, *really* wants a Tarot card reader at her bridal shower. So Courtney needs to find a substitute pronto *becausetheparty'stonight,*" she finished in a rush.

Ruby lowered the baseball-glove-sized apple fritter she'd been nibbling on — hey, the yogurt cancelled it out! — and stared at her friend. "Tonight? As in, *tonight* tonight? Jeez, now I know why you brought doughnuts. This is a bribe, right?"

"Kind of," JoJo admitted as she popped the final bit of cruller into her mouth and folded her hands together in a praying gesture. "Please, please, *please*!" she went on, putting a little whine in her tone for good measure. "Courtney's helped me out bigtime twice this month, so I'd really like to return the favor. Besides, remember that this is Palm Beach. She and the rest of the bridesmaids pooled their resources, and they have a pretty hefty entertainment budget. I think you'll like the pay."

The figure JoJo named made Ruby gasp.

"Seriously? For two or three hours? Heck, I'd stay all night for that," she exclaimed with a grin. "Tell Courtney I'll be there. Just let me know the time and address."

"I'll confirm it now. What do you need from her as far as a setup?"

There was a quick discussion of the particulars — hostess to supply a table, two chairs, and a quiet spot to put them; Ruby to bring the fancy tablecloth, some crystals and incense, and the cards. Then Ruby settled back to enjoy the final five minutes of cool weather before the day's temperature hit the usual mid-80s typical of a West Palm Beach spring day. JoJo, meanwhile, pulled out her phone and called her friend.

"Hey, girl, I got you your substitute Tarot card reader," she said without preamble. "Let me tell you what she needs, and then give me the party details."

While Ruby made quick work of her fritter, JoJo scribbled a few notes on a pad she'd pulled from her cavernous designer bag.

"Uh-huh . . . uh-huh," she agreed, still scribbling. "Okay, I think I've got everything. Don't worry, Ruby will be there on

199

time, and she assured me she'd dress the part. Yes, I promise, you'll love her. Okay, buh-bye."

She pressed the end button on the cell and ripped the top sheet of paper from the pad, sliding it across the table to Ruby.

"There you go . . . time, names, address. It's a gated street, so you'll need to stop at the guard house and give the guy your driver's license. Don't worry, the guard'll have your name on file. And then, when you get to the house, punch that four-digit number right there" — she pointed to a code written at the bottom of the page — "into the box at the gate, and it will open automatically. She said you can park with the rest of the cars and come in the front door."

"You mean I don't need to walk around to the back door like the rest of the hired help?" Ruby asked with a grin.

JoJo grinned back. "Heck, no. Madam Ruby, Reader Extraordinaire, only uses the front door. And make sure you dress all exotic. No FAU Owl T-shirts," she said with a pointed gesture at the college jersey Ruby wore over a pair of jeans. "Lots of sparkly stuff and plenty of eye makeup. These girls are used to no-holds-barred kind of events, so don't be afraid of going over the top with how you look. But try not to take the mood down with a bunch of dire predictions."

"The cards reveal what the cards reveal," Ruby intoned in her best imitation of Rosa. Then, when JoJo rolled her eyes, she added, "Don't worry, I'll bring all my cute girl-power and fluffy bunny kinds of decks. I'll make sure the bride and all the bridesmaids have fun."

"Great! I wish I could be there to see you in action, but unfortunately I'm not on the invite list. I'm just the facilitator." JoJo gave Zuki a pat and then looked around. "So where's little Ophelia this morning . . . sleeping in?"

"Probably. And you are not going to believe what happened last night."

While JoJo started on her second dough-nut, Ruby told her how she'd come home from class only to find that the cat population at the Botanica had doubled while she was gone. And, even more amazing was the fact that the new cat in residence was none other than Ophelia's missing brother.

"Rosa is going to kill me, of course," she finished, "but I've already decided that if she complains, I'll pull a 'her' on her and talk about Fate and Karma until she agrees both cats were meant to be here."

"Your half sister's created a monster, and

she doesn't even know it," JoJo replied with a grin. "Seriously, you get more woo-woo every day."

Glancing at her phone, she added, "I can't wait to meet Kitty Number Two, but I've got to get to work. Shoot me a text tomorrow and let me know how it went with Courtney's girls."

"I will. Here, I'll walk you out." Ruby grabbed the cardboard box with its remaining doughnuts — you never left any food sitting outside unprotected in Florida unless you wanted to attract fire ants or lizards or other creepy crawlies! — and then headed with JoJo back inside.

Ophelia waited until the door closed after the two humans; then she crawled out from behind the tangled-root base of the strangler fig tree and gestured Brandon to follow. At the sight of the cats, the roosters startled and then scattered in a flurry of flapping wings to the side yard.

"We should have come out earlier and said hi to Ruby's friend," Brandon complained, watching the retreating chickens with interest. Ophelia had already warned him that the birds were off-limits; still, a feline could look!

"If you didn't make us hide," he went on, "maybe we would have gotten a bite of doughnut like Zuki did."

Ophelia made a little grumbly sound deep in her throat. "We weren't hiding, we were collecting information on the down-low," she told him, proud that she'd been able to use that strange human expression in front of her brother.

She lightly leapt onto the tile-topped concrete table that Ruby and JoJo had just vacated. "We don't have time for yakking with humans," she went on. "I told you yesterday that Luciana was in trouble. We need to start working on a plan to help her."

Brandon jumped on the table to join her, flopping atop the tile surface so that his stub of a tail hung off the table's edge. "But I thought Ruby said last night that everything was all right."

"Hmmph. Who are you going to believe, her or the Tarot cards?"

She didn't wait for Brandon to ask who *Tarot Cards* was. Instead, she pawed at the deck that Ruby had left behind, flipping over a few of the thin pieces of cardboard as she began explaining to Brandon what Tarot did.

Humans need them to help figure out things, since they can't see or hear what we felines can! They look at the pictures on these cards and tell stories about them. See, look. These

203

are the bad cards that mean something awful will happen.

She sifted through and found the same cards from yesterday, the Tower and the Devil. Those, she pushed to the edge of the table, near where her brother was sitting. With them as illustration, Ophelia told Brandon how people came all the time to the Botanica, sometimes to buy statues and books and pieces of plants with funny smells. But sometimes they came to have Ruby tell them stories about the cards.

She didn't dare mention — at least, not yet — that she, Ophelia, seemingly had her own knack for interpreting these strange human symbols.

"That's what Luciana came for," she explained. "You remember the night we rescued you from the street dogs, how I told you that Luciana had come to the Botanica. She wanted Ruby to look at the pictures and say what they meant. She was happy to see me, of course. She said I should stay here, and that she'd keep looking for you. She acted brave about that, but she was scared as a mouse when she talked about the son. She thinks he killed the old woman, our human mom. That's what she came to ask Ruby about."

Brandon had been only half listening to

her explanation about this thing called Tarot. He was more interested in watching a pale brown gecko change color as it walked across the yellow case of Ruby's phone, which she'd left behind on the table, and then onto the gray stone box. But at the mention of Luciana's name and talk of their first human mom, he forgot the lizard and sat up.

"What?" he exclaimed, tail bristling. "That can't be right. I thought the old woman fell into the pool, just like the birds and the snakes and the mice did. If he pushed her on purpose, not just for a game, we have to tell Ruby so she can tell other humans!"

"But Ruby doesn't think he did it," Ophelia hissed back. "And Luciana didn't see him do it. But she knows he's bad, and she's looking for something she called *proof.* I think she even figured out he was the one who put us in that box!"

"Then he might try to put Luciana in a box, too! And maybe no one will find her. You're right, we have to help her."

Brandon bristled his fur, ready for action. Ophelia, meanwhile, leaned to look under the table at Zuki.

"Brandon and I need to sneak out again tonight while Ruby is gone. Do you want to come with us, back to our old house?"

The pit bull had been sitting at her spot beneath the table staring at the back door Ruby and JoJo had gone through with the pastry box. Reconciled to the fact that the doughnuts weren't going to return anytime soon, she crawled out and put her front paws on one of the benches, so she was nose-to-nose with the cat.

"Go with you? No way. Even if you knew how to get to your old house, it would take you all night to walk there, and then you'd have to walk back again."

"So what? If we get tired, we can take a nap."

Zuki snorted. "You won't get much sleep. There'll be lots more street dogs like the ones from last night, plus big roads with lots of cars. All you'll be doing is running and hiding."

Ophelia snorted back. "Me and Brandon, we're not mice. We're not scared of dogs and cars."

"Well what about mean humans with their shooting things?" Zuki countered. "You might never make it back here."

Ophelia squinted her green eyes. What the pit bull was saying was true. It would be a dangerous trip . . . and in the end, they might not be able to do anything to help Luciana. But they had to try!

And then Brandon poked his fuzzy face over the edge of the table, too. "It wouldn't be too far to go if we drive a car."

Zuki gave a howl of laughter and tumbled off the bench. "Drive . . . a car," she choked out, raising both paws like she was holding an invisible steering wheel. Giving said invisible wheel a few twists, she added, "But you . . . don't have . . . a driving license."

"Hey, this is serious business! Quit laughing at my brother!" Ophelia gave her friend a stern frown, even as she shot Brandon a look that said, *Are you for real?*

Brandon, meanwhile, gave his short tail an imperious flick. "I didn't say *we* would drive. The PAWN human, Luis, has a picking up truck. And he goes to our old neighborhood at night all the time."

"He does?"

Zuki quit laughing and stared at the cat. "How do you know?"

"Because I went with him one time." Brandon gave his paw a quick lick, like he was embarrassed. "I didn't mean to. You see, he's got one of those hard tent things on top of it —"

"A camper top," the dog helpfully supplied.

"— and since that makes it nice and shady, one day I thought the truck would be a good place to take a nap. I guess I was real tired because when I woke up, it was dark out and he was driving! We went all the way to Palm Beach, and we even drove past our old house. I've never gone so fast before. Ophelia and I could sneak into the truck and let him drive us over."

"Brandon, you're brilliant!" Ophelia cried, doing a quick figure eight around him.

Zuki, meanwhile, sat pondering. "But how do you know he's going to go there again? What if he drives the truck somewhere else, like to the ocean?"

"He'll go there," Brandon insisted. "I heard him tell this other human in the store — a fat man with pictures drawn all over his arms — that he had a sweet deal on the island and was making lots of money. And that he could go there every night if he wanted to. If it's sweet, maybe he's selling doughnuts."

"Or tuna," Ophelia suggested, since that obviously made more sense.

Zuki snorted. "I bet he's not selling doughnuts . . . or even tuna. I've heard humans talk like that, and it usually means they're selling drugs."

Then, when Ophelia and Brandon gave her twin puzzled looks, she clarified. "You know, the bad medicine that makes humans happy and sick all at the same time. And then the police come and put the humans that sell it in cages so they can't do it anymore."

Brandon's whiskers drooped a little. "But Luis seems like a nice human. He gives me food and water, and he lets me stay behind PAWN. He even gave me a new name, Gato."

"That just means 'cat' in Spanish," Zuki told him, the explanation making Brandon's whiskers droop even more.

Ophelia shot the pit bull another annoyed look. To her brother, she said, "Don't listen to her. Zuki doesn't know everything. If the human fed you, he can't be all bad. And we don't need Zuki. We can do this plan all on our own. We'll sneak out after Ruby leaves, and we'll be back before she knows we're gone."

Zuki cleared her throat. "What about the street dogs? If you two go alone, they're bound to spot you."

"So we'll run fast. They won't catch us."

"But they caught Brandon, remember?"

The two cats exchanged glances. Then Ophelia said, "Well, maybe we could use a guard dog to walk to PAWN with us. You could wait there until we come back from checking on Luciana if you don't want to ride with us, and then we'll walk back here together."

"I'll think about it. Right now, I'm going back inside to see if Ruby will give me another piece of doughnut."

So saying, the pit bull slunk off, whiplike tail hanging low.

"I think you hurt her feelings," Brandon observed. "She looked sad when you said we didn't need her."

"Oh, for kibble's sake. She'll get over it, just like any other dog. Besides, she was making you feel bad, first."

Still, Ophelia couldn't help feel a tiny bit guilty. Zuki was a good friend, for a canine. And she was right that the street dogs might be a danger, particularly since they probably blamed her and Brandon for the boxer mix getting hurt.

"I'll talk to her," she decided. "But first, I'd better straighten up these cards before Ruby comes back outside again."

Swiping at them with her front paws like she was scratching litter, Ophelia swiftly pulled the scattered cards into a semblance of a pile. All except the Tower and Devil cards, which still lay at the table's edge. Before she could scrape them into the pile, she heard the back door of the Botanica squeal open.

"Quick, it's Ruby," she hissed to her brother. "Hop down and get under the table, and pretend you're sleeping."

In a flash, she and Brandon hit the literal bricks. In the process of jumping, however, Ophelia accidentally kicked the two orphaned cards, sending them fluttering to the ground.

Ruby will notice them. But no time now to worry about that!

Instead, she and her brother curled up side by side on the bricks beneath the concrete table, feigning sleep. After a few seconds, Ophelia slitted open one green eye and watched as a pair of short, denim-clad legs advanced on them. And then came Ruby's voice saying, "Aha! There you are."

For a moment, she thought the comment was directed at her and Brandon. Then she realized that Ruby was talking to her phone — something that humans did quite often, she'd noticed, even when there wasn't another human talking back to them. She saw Ruby's hand as she tucked the phone into her jeans pocket. But instead of turning and heading back inside, Ruby stood there a moment.

"What the heck?" Ophelia heard her mutter.

Act innocent, she told herself, and blinked

that same message to Brandon.

Ruby stared at the Tarot deck sitting on the tiled tabletop. "What the heck?" she repeated. Her glasses had slid down her nose again, and she gave them an impatient poke back into place. But that adjustment didn't change what she was seeing.

When she'd left the courtyard a few minutes earlier, the cards had been neatly stacked alongside her cell phone. Now they lay in an untidy heap, as if someone had taken a large hand and smeared the cards into disarray, then gathered them back into some semblance of a stack again.

Except for the Tower and the Devil — the same two cards that she'd found turned up beside the Celtic Cross after her reading with Luciana the other day. They lay faceup on the brick beside the table, as if they'd been tossed, or dropped. *But how . . . who? . . .*

She glanced around; then, gripped by sudden suspicion, she peered beneath the concrete table.

Where Zuki and the roosters had earlier been, two black cats now snoozed. The little girl, Ophelia, opened her green eyes and yawned, revealing a neat, pink mouth and plenty of tiny, sharp white teeth. Her brother opened his eyes as well and gave front and back legs a long stretch. Both felines looked sleepy and innocent.

Too innocent.

Despite herself, she smiled.

"All right, my little Tarot cats," she said as she retrieved the two errant cards. "I know you've been playing with my deck. That's fine, but try not to lose any, okay? A deck's not much good if some of the cards go missing."

To her surprise, the cats each gave her a small mew before settling back down to sleep again. Had they truly understood her, or were they simply responding to her voice? Even though she knew she was being fanciful, she couldn't help but think it was the former.

Leaving the cats to their naps, she squared up the cards and stowed them back into their onyx box. She tossed a few pellets of fish food into the pond, earning a round of bubble-smacking from Philomena. The roosters heard the shaking of the fish food container and came running for their share.

By the time the finned and feathered portion of the menagerie had all had their snacks, it was well after 8:00 a.m. Time to do a bit of reshelving and general checking of inventory in the shop before she opened up. She wouldn't have time for shop duties after closing, she reminded herself, not if she wanted to get costumed and out the door to the party on time.

But even with a surprisingly busy day of sales and readings at the store, Ruby couldn't stay focused on business. Instead, her thoughts kept drifting back to the two recurring cards, the Tower and the Devil, that she'd first seen turned up next to the reading she'd done for Luciana. What were the chances that the cats had knocked those same exact cards out of a second deck that morning?

It had to be a coincidence, she was still insisting to herself as 5:00 p.m. came and she was locking up the Botanica for the night. Of course, Rosa would have taken such a happenstance in stride. She could almost hear her half sister intoning one of her favorite catch phrases: *Coincidence is the Universe making a point, so you'd best listen.*

Ruby snorted. She liked the late, great Yogi Berra's quote better: *That's too coincidental to be a coincidence.*

But when she was back upstairs in the shared bathroom applying hair glitter to her blue streak, she found herself again worrying over Luciana and those two cards.

"Stop that," she said aloud to her reflection, giving her head a shake so that the glittery blue lock caught the light. "You did your part with the reading. Everything else is up to her now. Besides, she knows how to find you if she wants you to take another look at the cards."

An hour later, Ruby was properly bangled and veiled and carrying a velvet bag that held a couple of bridal-shower-appropriate Tarot decks. She called a quick goodbye to Zuki and the cats, frowning when they didn't trot out for their usual round of petting before she left for the night. No doubt they were in the courtyard digesting their supper which, because she felt guilty for leaving them alone for two nights running, was heartier than usual.

That, or she was getting the silent treatment for same.

"I'll make it up to you," she called to them, adding a couple of air kisses for good measure. "I promise, I'll be a stay-at-home-pet-mom tomorrow night."

A few minutes later, she was in her powder blue Volkswagen Beetle heading down the darkened side streets. Her plan according to her GPS was to hit the main drag — in her case, Dixie Highway — and head to the nearest bridge over the Intracoastal waterway and into Palm Beach. Her immediate destination, however, was the chain drug-store for a refill of breath mints, an item Rosa had told her to always keep on hand for an event like tonight.

Your client won't be paying attention to what you're telling her about her love life if you're breathing a Cubano all over her.

She had, of course, been referring to a sandwich — one of the go-to lunch menu items made by the Cuban locals. Similar to a grilled ham and cheese sandwich, it stepped up the game with sliced pork, pickles, and mustard atop Cuban bread and was squashed, panini-style. Ruby indulged in one at least once a week. Picturing the tasty sandwich now made her stomach rumble, since she'd foregone supper based on JoJo's promise of appetizers at the party.

Caught up as she momentarily was in thoughts of food, she almost missed the glimpse of white canine rump trotting down the sidewalk and vanishing around the next corner. A rump that looked oddly familiar.

Ruby hit the brakes. If she didn't know better, she would have said the dog butt in question belonged to Zuki.

Impossible.

When she'd left the house, the pit bull was either inside or else out in the enclosed courtyard, which had no accessible gateway in or out. It had to be another white pittie she'd spied. And, unfortunately, it wasn't uncommon to see abandoned dogs — or dogs belonging to irresponsible owners — wandering her neighborhood.

Sending out good thoughts that the pup in question stayed safe from speeding cars, Ruby accelerated in the direction of the big neon *Rx* sign the next block down.

Thirteen

"I don't think I like this plan. Too much can go wrong."

The doleful sentiment came from Zuki, who was crouched beneath an oily drop cloth in the bed of the battered black picking up truck belonging to the PAWN human, Luis. Brandon and Ophelia had been beneath the drop cloth with the pit bull, but now that the truck was moving, they'd crawled out from under it and were peering over the closed tailgate at the passing traffic.

"The plan has gone fine so far," Ophelia pointed out as she glanced back over her furry shoulder at the canine. "We made it to PAWN without seeing any street dogs, and we got into the truck without the human seeing us."

With that last, it had helped that the camper top was missing its rear window, so that the truck bed was open even if covered.

Ophelia and Brandon had each bounded inside with a single leap. Getting Zuki into it, however, had taken a bit more effort.

After a bit more conversation on the way to PAWN, the canine had decreed that no way was she letting Ophelia and Brandon make the dangerous journey alone. Fortunately, the overhang where the truck had been parked also sheltered a few metal boxes and wooden crates. The pit bull had used them as stairsteps, gripping the top edge of the tailgate with her strong paws to pull herself in. But there was no guarantee that wherever they stopped would have the same convenient setup; hence, that portion of their plan that left Zuki waiting in the truck.

"Let's make sure we all understand," Ophelia went on. "When the human stops at the house to do his deal — we'll be like Army felines and call it the drop-off spot — Brandon and I will jump out. We'll run to our old house to check on Luciana and make sure the son hasn't stuck her in a box. Zuki will wait here in the picking up truck until we get back. She'll also see if she can figure out what the human Luis is doing. Then we'll all ride back to PAWN together and run home before Ruby gets there."

She gave her tail a quick flip, like a snapping whip, for emphasis. "Easy as a mouse eating cheese."

"But I should go to the house with you, in case there's trouble," Zuki protested.

Brandon shook his fuzzy head. "Once you climb out, there's no guarantee you can get back into the picking up truck again . . . at least, not without someone seeing you," he pointed out. "Besides, you can't go walking around the streets of Palm Beach with us. We can fade into the shadows, but you'll stick out like a sore paw with that white fur. Dogs don't run loose there, not ever. Particularly not . . . well, dogs like you."

"You mean, pit bulls?" Zuki asked in a small voice, ears drooping.

Brandon nodded, looking a little embarrassed. "No offense. But you know how humans like to judge canines. If someone sees you, they'll call the animal shelter people, and a truck will come after you. And if they catch you, they might not call Ruby to come get you. And then . . ."

He trailed off, but they all three knew what he meant. The life expectancy of a pit bull at the animal shelter wasn't long.

Ophelia rushed over and gave her canine friend a quick head rub. "Don't worry, nothing's going to happen to you if you hide in the truck and wait. The plan's a good one. And you have a job, too, keeping an eye on Luis."

"But what if you and Brandon don't make it back to the truck before the human leaves again? It's not safe for you to try to walk home again all that way. What if you fall off the bridge and drown in the Intracoastal?"

Ophelia rolled her green eyes. Seriously, didn't Zuki know that cats never fell into anything? Besides which, like all other domesticated animals, she and Brandon both had a built-in sense of time as accurate as any human clock.

Aloud, she said, "That's easy. If you and the picking up truck are already gone before we get back to the drop-off spot, we'll run back to the old house and stay with Luciana. She'll hide us and keep us safe from the son. She'll probably even drive us back home to Ruby."

She realized as she said it that she was thinking of the Botanica as home now, rather than the old house. The notion made her whiskers twitch just a little. She'd never forget her first mom, the old woman, but now that several weeks had passed since her death, her image was slowly fading in Ophelia's mind. But her soft scent — a combination of lilacs and talc — and her gentle touch were still strong in her memory.

The truck gave a sudden lurch, and Ophelia quickly returned her thoughts to the matter at hand.

"Look, we're going fast now," she cried, running back toward the tailgate. Clinging tightly with her front paws and peeking over its edge, she added, "And I can see the water. Wheeee!"

"Shhhh!" Brandon warned. "Luis might hear you."

"Wheee," she repeated in a whisper, obediently lowering her voice as she stuck her velvety nose to the wind.

Now she understood why humans liked to drive around in these big metal cans instead of running about on their own two paws. It was exciting, feeling the air ruffling her fur and watching the scenery rush past. It didn't even matter that they were looking backward, so that objects seemed to be rushing away from them.

And the sprawl of city lights was something she'd never seen before. She blinked in amazement at the way the countless small bright lights looked like a careless heavenly canine had dumped all the stars from the sky onto the ground. It was almost as beautiful as watching the morning sun dance on the blue ocean.

With such fantastic things to be seen,

maybe they should go driving around in the picking up truck every night!

Zuki joined them at the tailgate now, pink tongue flapping in the breeze as her jaws lolled open in a big canine grin. Ophelia gave a quick purr of contentment, glad that her friend had accepted her apology after their spat earlier that day. Even though the pit bull would have to stay behind in the picking up truck, Ophelia couldn't help but feel safer knowing that she'd be nearby. And if something bad *did* happen, she had no doubt that Zuki would find a way to come to their rescue.

A few minutes later they were over the bridge and onto the island. Even while she enjoyed the sights, she was careful to keep watch on where they were. Like a canine, a feline had an excellent sense of direction and could find his or her way back from any place. But, just in case, she wanted to make very sure she knew where they were.

Now Ophelia could smell familiar scents in the air — fish, salt, night-blooming flowers. Beside her, Zuki was eagerly sniffing, too, her black nose quivering. Doubtless, the canine was sorting through all the smells with the same speed and efficiency as Ruby's laptop sorted data. All Ophelia knew was that the air was different here from that of the streets near the Botanica.

They were getting close to their old home!

The truck slowed, and then abruptly stopped. Brandon rushed to the front of the camper top and peered through its window, which allowed him to see through the truck's rear windshield to what was happening beyond.

"What's going on?" Ophelia softly asked, padding over to join him. "Are we already there? I didn't see our old house go by yet."

"We're at a gate. I remember it from last time," Brandon whispered back. "Luis had to talk to the human in the little house next to the street. They were laughing about something for a while, and then the human opened up the gate so we could drive in. He did the same thing when we left."

Before he could explain more about the gate, headlights abruptly flashed behind them, momentarily silhouetting them both against the topper's window.

Ophelia gave her brother a quick nudge. "Get down," she hissed. "We'd better make sure that no one sees —"

"Duck!" Zuki yelped from her spot at the tailgate as she followed her own command and swiftly flattened herself against the picking up truck bed. "That car behind us . . .

it's Ruby's bug car! And I think she saw me."

"Are you sure it's her?" Ophelia hissed as she crawled on her belly toward the tailgate. "Maybe someone else has a bug car like that."

Zuki shot her an exasperated look. "I'm sure. I can tell her car sound from everyone else's. Besides, she has the top down, and I can smell that froofy perfume water she likes to spray."

"What's she doing?" Brandon wanted to know as he, too, scrambled toward the back of the truck. "Is she following us?"

His question was directed at Ophelia.

"I don't think so. But I'll take a look." She eased herself up so that only her eyes and flattened ears rose over the tailgate's edge. Enough light came from the gate guard's small house that, to her feline eyes, it was almost bright as day where they sat parked. Luckily, the car had pulled up close enough now to them so that she could see past the twin beams shooting from the big round lights that gave the car its bug-eyed look.

For her own part, Ophelia squinted so that her eyes wouldn't give out a telltale glow and draw the human's attention. From her vantage point, she could clearly see Ruby, who was wearing a strange red cloth wrapped around her head. She appeared to be ignoring the picking up truck and was instead searching through a big black bag on the seat beside her.

"She's not looking at us at all," Ophelia reported in a whisper as she ducked back down again. "Remember, she's supposed to be at that party that JoJo told her about — the one for a bunch of human females. She must have driven the car somewhere else, first, and then she drove here. That's why she's behind us."

"I hope you're right," Zuki said in a doleful tone, squeezing her eyes shut and covering them with her paws for good measure.

Ophelia rolled her own green eyes. Zuki reminded her of a statue of three monkeys that Ruby had for sale in the Botanica. She didn't know why a monkey would put its paws over its eyes, but with Zuki it seemed she hoped doing that would make her invisible to any human.

Before Ophelia could helpfully point out the futility of that, the truck abruptly moved forward again. She popped her head up again. "I'll keep looking to see if she follows us, just in case."

She watched as the gate swung shut behind the truck, trapping the round-eyed bug car behind it. She kept on watching while the truck moved steadily forward and the round lights got smaller and smaller. If the bug car ever made it past the gate, she told herself, Ruby would have to drive very fast to catch them!

The truck slowed as they reached a corner where a thorny white-flowered bougainvillea hung over the top of a tall gray stucco wall. Red lights on the back of the truck flared and then flashed. Ophelia had figured out during the drive that this signaled to other humans that they were stopping and turning. Not a smart trick if you were trying to hide from someone! Though, of course, the PAWN human could not know about Ruby.

Still watching what was happening behind the truck, Ophelia saw the gate — which was now far behind them — open long enough to let Ruby's car through. The bug's round lights, which had shrunk almost to pinpricks, began to grow larger again as the small vehicle headed toward them.

Brandon also had stuck his head up past the tailgate to keep watch. Now, as the truck swung around the corner, he observed, "She's driving too fast. Do you think she's lost us?"

"She never found us in the first place," Ophelia pointed out, "so it would be hard for her to lose us. But let's see if she takes the same turn."

They watched the intersection, waiting for the headlights to appear. A few moments later, the bougainvillea lit up from the beams shooting from the bug car's eyes, but to their relief Ruby's car kept on driving past.

"She didn't turn," Ophelia triumphantly told Zuki, who was still doing the "see no evil" routine with paws over eyes. "See, she's going to the party, just like she told us. C'mon, you can get up now."

The pit bull obediently dragged herself to a seated position again, though she kept her ears low as she kept a wary look out the back. "Are we there yet?"

"Almost," Brandon replied, sticking his nose over the tailgate again. "Our old house is . . . there!"

He waved an excited paw in the direction of a tall, sand-colored wall spilling over with green palm leaves.

Ophelia leaped up so that her front paws were on the tailgate's edge. "Home!" she yowled. "I almost forgot what it looked like."

She stared wide-eyed as the truck drove along the high wall — so tall that a human couldn't look over it — that separated the grounds from the street. Though, of course, she could barely see the wall, since it was hidden behind a long green stretch of hedges that was almost as tall as it. Near where the wall started was an opening where a wide trail of smooth rocks led from the street all the way to the small houses where the cars lived. But, as always, that trail was blocked by a heavy black iron gate that kept everyone out who didn't belong.

As they drove past the gate, she glimpsed the son's long black car, the one that growled and roared depending on how fast it was going. Parked, it was silent, but that didn't mean she trusted it. As for the old woman's yellow car, she didn't see it, though maybe it was in its small house where she used to keep it.

Too swiftly, the truck drove on, passing a smaller gate that looked like the first but was only big enough for a human to walk through. As they left the house behind, it was all she could do not to leap out into the street and run back to the gate. A glance at her brother told her he was thinking the same thing, though he shook his fuzzy head at her. They had to wait until they reached the place where the human was going first; then they would come back.

Fortunately, the truck slowed again a couple of blocks later, rear lights flaring red as it turned into a short driveway. As with the old house, the driveway here was blocked by a black gate made of metal sticks with points on their tops.

"This must be it," Brandon whispered, peering through the camper top window and the rear windshield to see what was happening beyond. "He's entering the code to get inside."

Ophelia hurried to join her brother at the window and watch. Besides the back of his head, this was the most she'd seen so far of the human, Luis — a bare, muscled arm with a light covering of black fur. He was reaching out the truck window toward a big stucco column where a small silver box covered with numbered squares was mounted. He started pressing the squares, and she watched with interest as light glinted off the big silver ring that he wore on one finger. Next came the faint sound of grinding metal, and the big iron gate began a slow slide to one side.

Zuki tilted her blocky head. "If you're going to go, you'd better jump out now before the truck starts moving again."

"Right." Brandon nodded and then turned to Ophelia. "It's not too far to the house. I can go by myself, if you want to stay in the truck."

"No way." Ophelia gave a little hiss and trotted back to the tailgate, calling over her shoulder, "I'm sticking to you like a mouse stuck in a trap. Now hurry up."

"Remember the plan," Zuki urged, worry tinging her words. "Run to your old house and check to make sure that Luciana is all right. Then come back here and wait at the gate until you see the truck. You can jump inside again while the gate is opening. Brandon told me that the human doesn't stay too long when he does his deals, so don't get sidetracked chasing lizards."

"For kibble's sake, we're not kittens. You're worse than Ruby with all your worrying," Ophelia yowled.

Then, seeing Zuki's ears droop, she gave her friend a quick purr and added, "Don't worry, we'll be fine. You're the one who's taking a risk, hiding inside the truck. Be sure you stay out of sight."

Brandon, meanwhile, had his head out the back of the camper top doing a quick reconnoiter of the street. "It's clear. Ready, go!"

With a synchronized leap, the pair bounded out of the truck and lightly landed on the concrete drive. Their black fur momentarily glowed red as they were illuminated by the truck's brake lights. So they wouldn't be spied, they ran off to the other side of the truck, concealing themselves in the shadows spilling from the second stucco column.

By now, the gate had opened wide enough so that the vehicle began moving forward. Zuki raised up in the truck bed, sticking her white muzzle over the tailgate's edge.

"Be careful," she softly called as the gate began closing again.

Ophelia and Brandon waited a few moments until Zuki and the truck vanished down the drive; then, wordlessly, they bounded down the strip of grass along the roadside headed back in the direction of their old house.

A few minutes later, they reached their destination. As before, the human-sized gate was closed, but it was no barrier to a sleek feline intent on entry! Besides which, it was away from the lights at the big gate that made the slick stone path almost glow in the night, making it a safer spot to begin their mission.

Brandon squeezed between the upright bars, while Ophelia flattened herself and slid on her belly through the gap between gate and ground. And just like that, they were back at their old home again.

Except that it wasn't home . . . not really.

"It — It feels funny," Ophelia mewed in

surprise as she glanced around the expanse of lawn bisected by a Y-shaped concrete drive. "I — I don't like it here anymore."

"I know what you mean," Brandon whispered back as he also looked about. "It's like all the good things went away, and rats and mice filled the spaces."

Though, of course, Ophelia knew he meant that statement symbolically, as Ruby would have said — rather like a picture on a Tarot card. There weren't any mice or rats around. The son never would have allowed it.

She and Brandon crouched in the shadow of the gate and surveyed the familiar grounds. Tall palm trees — some that had coconuts in them, others with fluffy fronds that looked like fox tails — were planted in circles of red wood chips in various spots in the grass. At the foot of each tree were rings of yellow and red and green bushes just tall enough for a feline to easily hide in them. Lights hid in them, too, shining upward at the tree tops at night. When they were on, they were so bright that a keen-eyed feline could see every sleeping frog or lizard on every frond all the way to the sky.

A faint breeze began to blow, and the palm trees rustled, like they were trying to speak. Ophelia's ears went straight up.

Once, she had found that sound comforting. Now, however, she realized she was afraid of the voices talking through the leaves.

At least the house didn't talk. It was the same sand-colored stucco she remembered, with red half-circle tiles on the rooftop. The same red tile in the shape of a little roof hung over some of the windows, most of which were tall and rounded on the top, like mouseholes that had been stretched up high. She'd almost forgotten how the giant wooden front door to the house was the same pinkish color as the salmon the old woman sometimes would give them.

Thinking of the fish made her stomach growl.

No time to worry about food. With that firm reminder to herself, she continued surveying. Except for the usual tree frogs and fat toads, no creature was moving about the grounds. In front of that door was a big covered space, like a room with no walls, where the cars stayed when they weren't in their little houses in back.

And here, Ophelia spied something different.

In addition to the son's car, she could now see a second vehicle parked there. This car was smaller and crouched low to the ground like a lizard, though it was red and not green. It didn't have a top, just like Ruby's blue bug car sometimes didn't. She knew it didn't belong to Luciana, for the housekeeper's car was like a small gray box, with dents on one side. Maybe it belonged to the other female human . . . the one that Luciana had told Ruby about.

She whispered as much to Brandon, who nodded.

"That's good. That means he'll be busy playing with his friend while we go looking for Luciana. Come on, let's find her."

They slipped through the shadows and made their way through the front yard. They kept low, remembering how giant bright lights from the house sometimes lit up the darkness if a cat walked in the wrong spot. And when the lights came on, the son would always stick his head out the door to look.

Ophelia had almost forgotten how the dark green grass there felt: cool and soft and even, almost like a living rug. If they weren't on a mission, she would have stopped and rolled about, enjoying the short-cropped blades lightly scratching against her fur. Except that the grass was wet, she realized in dismay. The raining machine that came on at night must have turned on before they got there.

Giving her fuzzy legs a reflexive shake, she followed in Brandon's paw-steps. They both were careful to avoid the spots that turned on the lights, safely making their way to the driveway. From there, they started toward the building where the cars lived. Luciana's small house — the cottage, the old woman had called it — was right behind it.

But as they approached the housekeeper's quarters, Ophelia halted. A short stucco wall separated the driveway and car houses from the place where the pool was. She peered through the gate of iron sticks, half expecting to see the old woman.

She wasn't there, of course.

Ophelia frowned. She knew that dead was dead. But she thought she could smell the old woman's perfume. And the pool looked strange, too. As usual, it was lit from below the water's surface, so that it glowed in the darkness, the water shimmering as the waterfall splashed about. But the glow looked different this night, almost like the pearls that the old woman used to wear when she would go out to a fancy party.

You're imagining things.

Still, she couldn't help but move a few steps closer to the gate — close enough now that, if she wanted to, she could stick her head between two of the metal sticks, even squeeze all the way in. Maybe she should forget about Luciana and Ruby and Brandon, and just stay here. The son wouldn't have to know. She could hide during the day, and at night come out and dance around the edge of the pool, dipping her paw into the pearly water. If she did, maybe the old woman would come back. If she did, maybe —

No!

Shaking her head so hard that her ears flapped, she scampered away from the gate. Brandon was already at the little house where Luciana lived. He was standing on hind paws, his front paws balancing on the stucco sill as he peered in the long narrow window to the side of Luciana's door. Deliberately shoving aside thoughts of the pool, she stood and peered inside the window, too.

"It's dark in there," Ophelia observed in a whisper. She meant, of course, dark for a human. "Have you seen Luciana?"

"No, but I thought I heard someone moving around. Wait. Hide!"

That last came as the door knob jiggled and turned. The pair turned and scuttled beneath one of the short, broad cat palms that ran along the stucco wall. They'd barely concealed themselves in the fronds when the door opened and Luciana stepped out.

FOURTEEN

Ophelia stared at Luciana in amazement. She was used to seeing the housekeeper in her uniform pants and matching long top; that, or else slacks and a blouse, or else a dress on Sundays. But tonight, Luciana was dressed like she was going on a mission, just like her and Brandon. She wore long black pants and a long-sleeved black shirt, and her hair was braided tight against her head.

"She's all in black, just like us," Brandon softly hissed, noticing the same thing about her appearance. "Do you think she's going to spy on the son and his female?"

"Maybe. Let's follow her and see."

They waited until Luciana walked past. At first, Ophelia thought she was going to the door by the pool, but then the woman walked past the gate and continued up the driveway in the same way that Ophelia and Brandon had come. The pair exchanged puzzled glances; then, keeping deep into the shadows, they softly padded after the woman.

Luciana moved almost as quietly as a feline, slipping around to the front of the house and staying close to it as she, too, tried to avoid making the bright lights shine. Since a tall wall surrounded the property, the old woman had rarely closed the curtains at night. The curtains were open now, and Ophelia guessed that the son had kept up his mother's habit.

By now, Luciana moved past the cars to the far window, the cats at a safe distance behind her. The window looked into what the old woman had called the parlor, though Ophelia remembered that the son had always sneered at her for that.

The nineteenth century is calling, Ma. They want their jargon back.

It was a clean and cozy room with pictures of monkeys and palm trees and pineapples, with everything in it the colors of sand and sky and water. This was where the old woman brought her guests. Felines were not allowed, the woman had kindly but firmly told her and Brandon. And, most time, they obeyed that request.

As they watched now, Luciana sidled up to that window and, nose barely past the window frame, peered inside the house. The room must have been empty, for she immediately moved to the next set of windows. Brandon and Ophelia quietly padded after her.

This time, Luciana was looking inside the movie room — the place with lots of reclining seats made of soft black cow skin and a giant glass rectangle hanging on the wall that played all sorts of interesting pictures. Anytime the pictures lit up the screen, the curtains would be drawn. But they were open now, which meant no pictures were playing. So why was she looking?

Ophelia puzzled over that even as she snuck a bit closer, trying to peek in herself. That room once had been one of her and Brandon's favorite places to nap, for the chairs stayed cool even if it was hot outside. And because the pictures played there, the room had been made into what the son called "soundproof," which meant it was very quiet. Of course, the son did not allow them inside that room either, but they had discovered they were almost invisible curled up in those chairs, black fur blending into black leather. And so they'd lounged there with impunity, until one time —

Ophelia softly hissed at the memory. They always had tried to follow the old woman's rules and only scratch at the special fuzzy posts she'd given them. Brandon, however, sometimes gave into temptation and sunk a claw into something he shouldn't. Unfortunately, the time he'd decided to try his claws on the leather seat backs, the son had chosen that moment to stop in the room to do what he called "checking the scores." Catching Brandon in the act, he'd yelled and flung a hard-soled shoe that missed Brandon by a whisker. Though they'd managed to escape the room before the son could throw anything else, the fright had been enough that they'd never dared enter that room again.

"What's going on?" her brother whispered now, craning his neck from his hiding spot behind a clump of fuzzy long-leafed plant that she knew was called fountain grass. "Is she watching a movie?"

"No," Ophelia hissed back, moving a shadow closer for a better view. "The room looks empty. No, wait! I see him. I see the son . . . and the female human is with him!"

She padded closer still through the damp grass, knowing that Luciana was far too intent on the action within the house to notice a sleek black shadow almost at her feet. In fact, the way the housekeeper peered into the movie room looked like how Brandon had peered into *her* window.

At the thought, Ophelia smothered a snicker with one paw. Then she reared up on her hind legs for a better look inside the window at the female that the old woman hadn't liked.

I won't like her either, Ophelia had already loyally decided.

To her surprise, this was the same woman she'd seen in the picture on Ruby's computer — the human she'd thought had looked nice. But she suspected the old woman had been right in her judgment. The female didn't look friendly now, not with the way her thin mouth twisted as she seemed to be yelling at the son. She was tall and skinny, like she didn't eat enough kibble, with dark hair almost as long as Luciana's. Her nose was long, too, and pointed like a collie's. She looked like she might have been Ruby's age, but Ruby was far nicer.

She flicked her ears forward, trying to eavesdrop through the glass, but to no avail. The only sound she heard was the faint rustling in the fountain grass behind her as Brandon moved about for a better view. She shot him a warning look — *you're too loud, Luciana will hear!* — and then turned back to the window.

Now the son looked like he was yelling back at the female, and they both were waving their arms about like branches in the wind. Ophelia was glad not to be part of it. Yowling humans made her nervous, as a feline never knew what they might do. Besides, Luciana looked worried as she stood there watching. She knew that the other humans were talking about something bad . . . perhaps something really bad, like what happened to the old woman in the pool.

A shudder ran down Ophelia's fur, making her tail bristle. What had Philomena said? *Beware the human rat.* Maybe the female didn't look like a collie after all. With her pointed nose, maybe she looked like a rat . . . which meant that if the koi fish was right, this human was bad, just like the son!

"Brandon?"

Startled, Ophelia hastily dropped back down to all four paws. The whispered word hadn't come from her, but from Luciana. Her brother had been spotted!

Momentarily forgetting rats, Ophelia sunk into the shadows to see what would happen next. Luciana was staring over her shoulder at the clump of fountain grass, which was still rustling. And with her feline keen vision, Ophelia immediately saw the problem.

Although his head and body were carefully concealed within that foliage, Brandon's distinctive bobbed tail stuck out to one side of the bush.

Luciana had noticed the tail, too.

"Brandon," the housekeeper whispered again, though of course she couldn't be heard inside. "*Ven aqui,* gatico. Come here, little cat. I take care of you."

Brandon popped his head up out of the fountain grass while the housekeeper began slowly moving toward him, now softly clapping her hands to summon him to her.

"What should I do?" he yowled in Ophelia's direction. "If I let her catch me, she'll carry me inside, and you'll have to go back to the truck alone."

"Oh, for kibble's sake. Run and hide somewhere else," Ophelia yowled back, hoping that the housekeeper thought her cries came from Brandon. "Maybe if she doesn't get a good look at you, she'll think you're a different cat. Once she gets tired of searching and goes back to looking in windows, we'll decide what to do next."

"Me-OW!"

With that shout of agreement, he bolted from the bushy grass and back toward the driveway.

But the housekeeper, it seemed, wasn't

going to give up so easily. "Dios mío," Luciana muttered in a voice loud enough for Ophelia to hear. "Come back, chiquitico. Good boy."

Then, with a quick look back at the window, she took off in the same direction he'd gone. She'd gone only a few hurried steps in that direction, however, when two things happened simultaneously.

Luciana slipped in the wet grass and went sprawling . . . and blinding white light abruptly flooded the grounds around them.

"She fell into the bad spot and made the light shine!" Ophelia yowled to Brandon as she squinted her eyes against the glare. Then, as her vision swiftly adjusted, she added, "Quick, hide before the son comes out to see what's wrong."

Not waiting for her brother's response, Ophelia all but flew to the same clump of fountain grass where Brandon had been hiding moments earlier. She waited for the housekeeper to do the same. But as soon as Luciana scrambled to her feet, she dropped to the grass again with a sharp cry of pain and clutched at her ankle.

"The human is hurt," Ophelia cried, hoping Brandon was close enough to hear. She stuck her head out of the grass for a better look at the woman. Despite the danger, she hadn't moved.

Not good. A similarly injured feline could have simply bounded away on three good paws. But with one foot injured, the housekeeper was as helpless as a sparrow with a broken wing.

"Brandon," she called again. "We'd better help her."

"Too late," her brother yowled from his spot near where the cars lived. "The son is coming outside! We'd better stay hidden until we know what's going to happen. We can't help Luciana if he catches us, too."

Which made sense, Ophelia realized as she heard shouting from the direction of the front door. Peering out through the grass again, she could see that the son and his female were headed in the housekeeper's direction now, while Luciana tried and failed again to rise.

The son did not look pleased.

"Who's there?" he bellowed. Waving his cell phone in a threatening manner, he added, "I'm calling the police right now, so don't try anything. Wait . . . who is . . . Luciana?"

"*Si,* Señor Givens," the housekeeper gasped out. "It is me."

"And what are you doing, skulking about?"

247

His bluster became confusion for a moment as he shot an unreadable look at the female beside him. Then he advanced on the housekeeper, his manner threatening. "I think she was spying on us. I won't tolerate this! I won't —"

"No, no, Señor Givens." Luciana cringed back into the grass, expression suddenly fearful. "I wasn't spying. I thought I heard the gato — the cat of the señora. You know, Brandon, the boy cat who is missing. I came out to find him, and I — I slipped in the grass."

"I don't hear any cats," the son shot back. "Now tell me the truth. What were you really doing out here?"

But as Ophelia tensed, ready to spring to Luciana's defense with tooth and claw, the pointy-nosed woman rushed forward and put a restraining hand on the son's arm.

"Really, Terry, you're frightening the poor woman. And look, she's injured. Why don't you help her inside, and we'll discuss this like civilized people?"

Ophelia flattened her ears as she listened to this exchange. Though she wasn't prepared to trust the female, she appeared to be a more reasonable human than the son was.

While the son grudgingly helped Luciana

to her feet, the other woman stuck out a bony hand to assist and said, "We haven't formally met yet. I'm Joan, Terry's . . . friend."

"Yes, thank you, Señorita Joan," Luciana managed, taking the woman's hand and then quickly letting it drop. Then, expression still fearful, she glanced over at the son, who had released her to stand on her own.

Though standing wasn't quite the word, since she gingerly held one leg bent, toe pointed into the grass. She reminded Ophelia of one of those strange tall gray birds with long necks and pointed beaks that had sometimes landed in the yard.

Blue herons, the old woman had called them, forbidding her and Brandon to chase them. And so any time one landed, they'd had to content themselves with watching the bird balance on one long skinny leg with the other tucked high to its chest until it took flight again.

But, unlike a heron, the housekeeper didn't have big wings that would let her fly away fast!

"I — I am sorry I disturbed you," she went on. "Por favor, I go back to my rooms now."

"Nonsense." This from the Joan female, who gave the son a stern look. "Terry, don't just stand there. Help Luciana inside so we can see how badly she is hurt."

"Fine."

With that grudging word, he stuck his phone in his pocket and shoved a shoulder beneath the housekeeper's arm. Despite her soft protests, he half walked, half carried her to the front door and inside the house. Joan, with a final look around the yard, followed them inside.

Ophelia waited until the blazing lights that flooded the grass had dimmed again. Then, keeping low, she rushed from her hiding spot in the fountain grass toward where her brother was crouched near the garage.

Brandon met her halfway at the big open room. "The son took her," he meowed in concern, pacing in a circle with tail bristling. "We have to get her out of there, before the son puts her in a box."

"Not yet. Let's look inside first. The human Joan seems like she might be nice after all. She made the son help Luciana."

Brandon growled. "It's my fault she got hurt. We need to make sure she's safe."

Still, he followed her at a swift trot back to the windows. This time, the humans had moved to the parlor. Ophelia pressed her soft black nose to the glass in time to see the son lowering Luciana into a chair and then raising her injured leg up on a matching footstool.

Then they talked . . . or, at least, the Joan woman talked. The son stood there looking angry. As for Luciana, her chair was turned away from the window, so that all Ophelia could see of her was her arm and her leg.

"Can you hear what they're saying?" she whispered to her brother.

Brandon flicked his ears back and forth, then shook his fuzzy head. "I hear them, but I can't make out the words. Even though this isn't the soundproof room, the glass is still too —"

"Wait," Ophelia cut him short with a soft hiss. "Look, the son and Joan are leaving."

While they watched, the female smiled and nodded; then, putting her hand on the son's arm, she made him walk with her. She paused at the door, however, and turned. Giving the housekeeper a smile, she spoke while raising her finger in the air . . . a gesture Ophelia had learned that for humans meant *just a minute.*

But it seemed that the housekeeper wasn't willing to wait. As soon as the door closed behind them, Luciana tried again to stand. Ophelia could see her pushing up with her hand pressed down against the arm rest, her bad foot touching the ground.

"She's really hurt," Ophelia whispered.

"Look, she had to sit back down again."

Which was perhaps just as well, for the door opened again. The son came back in along with Joan, who was carrying a small clear glass half filled with brown liquid. Ophelia squinted for a better look, deciding it must be the same drink that the old woman used to make for herself.

Brandy.

As she and Brandon watched, Joan handed Luciana the glass and made gestures encouraging her to drink. A moment later, she gave a satisfied nod and took back the glass, which was empty now. Then she bent for another look at the housekeeper's ankle.

"Maybe the brandy will fix her," Brandon softly suggested as he peered through the window glass. "It always made the old woman feel better."

"I hope so," Ophelia agreed with a glance up at the stars to check the time. "Because we have to leave soon if we want to meet Zuki back at the truck."

But while they were whispering, the Joan female gestured the son toward the door again. They stood there for a few moments, heads close as they talked, and kept looking back at Luciana.

Planning something, Ophelia thought, green eyes narrowing. And then, the two

252

walked back over to the housekeeper again. A moment later, they had lifted her from the chair and were walking, one on either side of her, out of the parlor.

"Maybe they'll take her back to the cottage now," Brandon softly mewed. "Quick, back into the fountain grass."

Not waiting for Ophelia's reply, he dashed back to the grassy clump. She followed after him, slipping under soft green plumes just as the lights flared on again, illuminating the yard. The front door opened and the three humans came out. But instead of heading for the cottage, they paused alongside the red car with no top.

"Here, let's get her in," the Joan woman told the son, leaving him to support Luciana while she opened up the passenger side door. To the housekeeper, she said, "Don't worry, I'm going to take you to the emergency clinic. They'll fix your ankle."

Between them, they settled Luciana on the seat and closed the door again. The housekeeper made no protest to any of this, her head lolling back against the headrest.

"The brandy must have worked. She looks like she's sleeping," Ophelia hissed.

Brandon nodded. "I think they're taking her to the veterinarian."

"You mean to the doctor," Ophelia replied

with a snort. "That's where they take humans, silly."

Joan, meanwhile, was talking to the son. "Go to the cottage and get her purse. I'll stay here with her."

The son muttered something that Ophelia couldn't hear. As he walked off toward Luciana's quarters, the Joan female got into the driver's side of the red car. By the time the son had returned with a small green purse that Ophelia recognized from that day at the Botanica, Joan had made the car's black top rise up to cover her and Luciana.

"Here," the son said in a curt tone and dropped the purse through the window into Luciana's lap.

He walked around to the driver's side and leaned into the window. What he said to Joan, Ophelia couldn't hear. A moment later, he straightened and stepped back from the vehicle, then started for the house again.

"I promise you, it's the right thing to do," Joan called after him.

The words were loud enough for Ophelia and Brandon to overhear, but the son didn't turn around. *Pretending to ignore her?*

By way of response, the car emitted a loud metallic crunch that made the son scrunch his shoulders in apparent pain. Ophelia winced, too. Once, she'd heard the son yell at a deliveryman who made that same sound with his truck. *Grinding the gears,* he'd called it. But apparently he didn't care that the Joan female couldn't drive any better than the deliveryman. Instead, he made his way to the front door and went inside without looking back.

The car crunched again and then lurched forward.

"They're leaving," Brandon whispered unnecessarily as the vehicle with the two females rolled down the driveway. It paused at the front entry while the iron-barred gate slowly opened.

Ophelia gave her brother a nudge. "Quick, before the gate closes."

Together, they raced down the darkened driveway to the entrance. By the time they got there, Joan's red car already had squealed out onto the street, while the gate had started to close once again. They reached the entry with seconds to spare, bounding out onto the grassy strip alongside the road just as the bars all clanged shut.

"There they go," Ophelia said.

She waved a paw. It was the same direction they'd be going, too, once they made it back to Luis's truck. The red lights on the back of Joan's car glowed in the dark, looking like rodent eyes. But at least Luciana was safe from the son now, and going someplace where the human doctor would fix her hurt leg.

"We'd better hurry," Brandon replied. "We need to get back to the other house where we left Zuki before Luis leaves, too."

But it was too late for that. They'd barely made it a block when Ophelia spied the black PAWN truck coming down the road, headed in their direction.

FIFTEEN

"What do we do?" Ophelia mewed in concern as the truck drew closer. The human hadn't stayed long at the other house at all, she thought with a worried look at the stars.

Brandon's whiskers drooped as he swiftly considered the problem.

"I don't know," he meowed back. "The truck is going too fast for us to jump inside when it passes by. But with Luciana gone, I don't think we should stay here alone with the son."

Then he bristled his tail in excitement as another idea occurred to him.

"Wait, maybe there's still a chance. See that big bump in the road? Luis will have to drive over it. Maybe when he does, he'll slow down enough that we'll have time to jump inside the truck bed."

Sure enough, just a few feet away Ophelia saw what looked like a big flat concrete log lying in the street. *The bump.* But she wasn't sure about the slowing down part. All the way here, the truck had seemed to go as fast as a bird flying. She didn't remember Luis slowing down for anything.

Trying to keep the doubt out of her voice, she agreed. "All right, let's do it."

They kept to the shadows as the truck approached, though Brandon gave a warning yowl to Zuki, riding in the truck bed.

We're here! We're going to jump into the truck at the big bump!

While the human wouldn't have heard the cry, Ophelia knew that the canine's sensitive ears would surely pick up on Brandon's caterwaul and would be watching for them. Sure enough, a faint whine drifted to them on the night air.

Be careful!

Brandon snapped his fangs. "Get ready. As soon as the truck reaches the bump, we'll run out behind it, and when it slows down, we'll jump in together."

But the truck wasn't slowing. In fact, it was moving faster now, its crooked headlights, like a cross-eyed Siamese, bouncing in the darkness. Ophelia could see Zuki's white muzzle peering around the camper top's edge.

"Watch ou-u-u-ut!" the canine howled as the truck never paused but took the bump at full speed, all but tumbling Zuki out the back.

Ophelia and Brandon stared after the truck as it sped on down the road, tail lights flaring and splashing Zuki's blocky white head with a red glare.

"He didn't stop!" Ophelia yowled. "What do we do??"

A high-pitched canine howl, something that human ears couldn't hear, drifted back to them. "Wa-a-a-a-it for Ru-u-u-u-by at the ga-a-a-a-ate."

The two cats exchanged glances; then, like they were being chased again by the street dogs, they bolted down the road in the same direction.

"Zuki's right," Brandon gasped out as they ran. "It will be a while before Ruby's finished at the party. We can wait at the little house with the wooden arm and jump into the back of her bug car while she's waiting for it to open."

"But what if she put up the top? How will we get in?"

"We'll jump on the back and sink our claws into the cloth roof. We'll hang on just like the surfer humans. It'll be fun."

Ophelia gave a yowl of agreement but saved her breath for the remainder of their run. The truck lights had already rounded the turn, leaving them in the dark — which was only half-light to felines. Both were out of breath by the time they reached the guard house some time later. They found a palm tree surrounded by a ring of yellow and green shrubs right behind the shack and collapsed there beneath the concealing leaves.

Once she'd caught her breath again, Ophelia rolled on her back and waved her paws in the air.

"Wake me up when Ruby gets here. I'm going to take a nap," she said and shut her eyes.

What seemed just a minute later, but according to the stars was a human hour, Brandon was poking her in the side.

"Come on, get ready. I hear Ruby's bug car coming."

A cool breeze tugged at Ruby's fringed red headscarf . . . one disadvantage of driving with the convertible top down. She brushed the annoying threads away from her eyes and stifled a yawn as her car approached the guardhouse on the way out of the neighborhood.

The evening had been, in her humble estimation, a rousing success. Though she'd been a bit nervous about hobbing with the nobs, the bridal party had proved surprisingly warm and welcoming. Both the hostess — JoJo's friend, Courtney — and the bride had exclaimed over her vintage sequined ten-yard skirt and coin-trimmed hip scarf she worn in her Tarot reader guise. And rather than simply pointing her to a table and chairs, they'd actually brought in a tiny fortune teller's tent that looked like something Jeannie the Genie from the old television show would feel at home in.

The guests had seemed equally impressed. From the flower girl (a shy, cornrowed preteen) to the grandmother of the bride (a potty-mouthed octogenarian with spiked silver hair), all the major wedding players had been excited to receive readings regarding their love life. In between imbibing copious amounts of high-dollar champagne (except for the flower girl!), opening risqué gifts, and creating toilet paper bridal gowns, they'd eagerly filed one at a time to her tent.

To Ruby's relief, no errant messages about cheating or divorce had popped up in anyone's reading, most particularly the bride-to-be's. Even better, Courtney had been so pleased with the guests' enthusiasm that she'd vowed Ruby would be her first choice for entertainment at any future girls' night out parties.

Clutching the fat envelope filled with cash that Courtney had handed her at the conclusion of her session, Ruby had agreed that she'd be pleased to make an appearance at any of the woman's upcoming events.

She stopped the Beetle near the gate, next in line behind a dark green Jaguar — the most budget-friendly car she'd seen on the island besides her own VW. Well, except for the battered black pickup that had been in line in front of her when she'd first come through the gate, she reminded herself with a snort. She'd almost expected the guard to turn the driver away as an undesirable. Instead, he'd seemed to be chatting in a familiar manner with the guy, as if he were a frequent visitor. Maybe someone's hired help, or maybe just an eccentric rich guy who liked to slum when it came to his ride.

Though probably not the latter, she decided now with a grin. She'd been startled while waiting behind the truck to glimpse a white pit bull that looked surprisingly like Zuki peeking from its bed.

Not the sort of dog one found on Palm Beach.

She rather suspected that the rich folks on the island who wanted guard dogs went for Rottweilers or Dobermans. Pitties would probably be too "thug" for them. But when the pickup entered without issue, she'd been relieved. That meant her vintage but spotless Volkswagen convertible would pass muster, too. And so it had.

While she waited for the Jag to move on, she reached for her phone. She'd turned the ringer off during the party, and she'd received a couple of texts during that time. One was from JoJo — a big smile emoji and a thumbs up. The other was an automated reminder from her cell service provider that payment was due in ten days. She also had a call from a number she didn't recognize, along with a voicemail. Curious, she played the message.

"Ruby . . . I need . . ." the message droned, and then abruptly cut off.

Frowning, she listened to it again. It was a female voice, but not one that she recognized. The call had come about thirty minutes earlier, while she was winding up the readings and settling up with Courtney.

Maybe one of the women from the bridal shower had wanted to schedule another reading and had been too impatient to call the next day? She'd handed out her card to everyone there. Besides, the voice in the recording sounded distinctly out of it, like the person had had a few too many glasses of bubbly.

Funny, but also kind of creepy.

Shaking her head, Ruby set the phone down again. "Call me back when you're sober, girlfriend."

The Jag moved ahead as the gate arm opened, and Ruby eased her car even with the guardhouse doorway. She glanced over at its lighted interior and gave an inner grimace. The uniformed guy manning it was the same potbellied, middle-aged comedy school reject who'd taken her information when she'd arrived.

"Hey, it's the gypsy queen again," the guard proclaimed with a toothy grin as he checked her off on his clipboard list. "So how did the 'entertainment' " — he waggled his sandy eyebrows at that last word — "go tonight?"

"It went just fine. And you can see from the lack of frosting on me that I really didn't jump out of a cake," she replied, trying not to roll her eyes.

A typo on his list had shown her as entertainment for a bachelor party, and he'd pretended not to believe her explanations to the contrary. It had made for a few annoying moments, but she'd let it slide . . . mostly because he was the guy with the clipboard. Plus she had a bit of sympathy for him, stuck as he was in that guardhouse.

No doubt he had to be deferential when it came to dealing with actual residents, so the poor guy was probably looking for a bit of levity in his work. And since his comments had been more corny than outright sexist, she gave him a pass.

Still grinning, he nodded and hit the button to activate the barrier arm. "Glad it went good for you. You have a good night, now."

"You too, and . . . *oh!*"

"Something wrong, ma'am?"

Ruby glanced behind her, squinting into the darkness and seeing nothing back there but the empty street. She'd felt an almost imperceptible bump, as if someone had nudged the back of her vehicle. But unless the Invisible Man was behind the car kicking tires, she had to have imagined it. That, or her foot had slipped a fraction off the clutch and caused the bug to give a tiny lurch.

"Everything's good," she assured the guard, giving him a smile for emphasis. "Have a quiet evening."

She drove past the upraised barrier arm, taking care to keep to the posted speed limit, since Palm Beach was known for having zero tolerance for speeders. A minute or so later, she had reached the bridge that spanned the Intracoastal, heading back west.

"Whew," she muttered aloud once she was traveling on the main road again. "I was getting lightheaded breathing all that rarified rich people air. It's good to be back in the bad part of town."

As if in answer, an emergency siren abruptly sounded behind her. She pulled to the shoulder and waited as a West Palm Beach police car went flying past, followed by one of the county's truck-like Fire Rescue ambulances, and then one of the department's smaller fire trucks. Being a Friday night and the start of the weekend, between car wrecks and the obligatory gang shootings that ritual would probably be repeated a few more times before Monday morning.

She checked to make sure that no other emergency vehicles were behind those, then pulled back onto the road again. All she wanted to do now was get home and swap the gypsy fortune-teller duds for leggings and a big T-shirt. Then she'd pour a glass of white wine and scarf down the baggie of appetizers that Courtney had given her.

Though, of course, she'd share a couple of bites with Zuki and the black cats.

A few minutes later, she had turned the VW onto her narrow driveway and eased it into the tiny garage. She could hear Zuki's excited bark from the courtyard, and she smiled. With the pit bull on the job — and Rosa's reputation as a Santera well-known by a certain element — no way were any lowlifes going to mess with her or the Botanica.

But as the overhead door was closing behind the bug, and she was walking out the garage's side door into the courtyard, she heard a thump and a rustle that made her whip around.

Had someone come into the garage from the street?

Just as quickly, though, she gave a relieved sigh as she felt soft fur wrapping itself around her ankles.

"It's you two," she said with a smile as Brandon and Ophelia ran figure eights between her feet. "Have you been waiting for me here by the door all night?"

Then, as she hefted her tote higher onto her shoulder, her smile widened into a grin.

"Or maybe it's not me you're happy to see. I bet all you want is that bag of tasty *hors d'oeuvres* you can smell. Don't worry, you'll get your share. You too, Zuki," she added as the pit bull came bounding up through the shadows from the side yard. "C'mon, let's go inside and snack."

"You made it!" Zuki softly woofed as she followed Brandon and Ophelia back inside the house. Ruby had already rushed upstairs to change, so the kitchen was temporarily human-free. "I wasn't sure you heard me tell you to ride with Ruby."

"It was a great plan," Brandon conceded, trotting closer to give the pit bull a quick lick of approval on her jaw. "We got to the main gate in plenty of time, and luckily she had the roof down on the bug car. We jumped right in."

"Yeah," Ophelia agreed. "Brandon said that if the roof was up, we would pretend to be surfers and hang onto the back of it by our claws."

Zuki snickered at that, while the cat hopped onto the red kitchen table and balanced on her hind legs, front legs flapping as she pretended to "hang ten." The playing came to a quick halt, however, when Ruby came downstairs again.

Ophelia leaped off the table and padded over to the pit bull. In a soft voice, she said, "We'll tell you everything that happened as soon as Ruby goes back to her room."

But the human didn't look in any hurry to leave. She'd traded her fancy skirt with all the jingly things hanging off it for skinny pants and a big red T-shirt with a picture of a crown and white words on it. Ophelia silently sounded out the latter.

Kee-Pee Call-M and Boo-Gee On.

The phrase made no sense to her, but was probably something significant in human-speak. More important for now, however, was the clear plastic sack that Ruby pulled from her tote bag that she'd left on the kitchen counter. The mingled aromas of pork and fish came spilling out as she opened it up. Ophelia and Brandon gave appreciative sniffs, while Zuki's big pink tongue lolled.

"Check this out," Ruby exclaimed.

Grabbing a big yellow plate from one of the short closets hanging off the wall, she carried sack and plate over to the table. There, she dumped the contents of the former onto the latter.

"Talk about a haul! Prosciutto-wrapped scallops, bacon-wrapped dates, mini crab cakes, red peppers stuffed with goat cheese, some kind of flat bread thingies. Oh, and look, Courtney even wrapped up a couple of cheesecake bites, which are for me. But don't worry, I'll share the rest."

So saying, she pulled out four small blue plates from the same closet and a fork from the drawer. While the cats and dog watched with interest, she slid a couple of scallops onto each plate. Then she used the fork to split one crab cake between two of the plates and put two of the cakes onto the third.

"Bon appétit," she said and set the plates down in front of each of them, in turn.

Zuki polished off her share in two bites — being polite, as normally she could have cleaned her plate with a single swipe of her pink tongue. Ophelia and Brandon ate more slowly, gnawing quietly on each piece.

Well, except for Brandon. Ophelia rolled her eyes as she heard him making *nom-nom* noises while he chewed his portion.

Ruby, meanwhile, had poured a small glass of white wine from a box she had in the refrigerator. She returned to the table with her glass and put a sampling of all the snacks onto her own plate. To Ophelia's amusement, she rushed through them with the same speed and sound effects as Zuki and Brandon had, then pushed her chair back from the table.

"I could eat like a rich person every day. And there's even enough left for breakfast tomorrow."

They all sat in companionable silence for a few minutes more while Ruby finished off her wine. Then, while Ophelia, Brandon, and Zuki lounged underfoot, Ruby made quick work of storing the leftovers and taking care of the dishes. That done, she reached for her tote bag and flipped off all the kitchen lights, save for the tiny lamp in the shape of a seashell sitting on the counter.

"All right, my furry ones, I'm headed upstairs for a little studying before bed time. Come up when you're ready."

Zuki gave a whine of agreement and wagged her whip-like tail. But all three remained sprawled beneath the table until the sound of Ruby's footsteps on the stairs faded, and they could hear her shuffling around in the bedroom above them. At that, they rose and padded silently out the pet door into the courtyard, where they settled near the concrete table.

"So what happened?" Zuki asked with an eager pant. "Did you find Luciana?"

Brandon and Ophelia took turns explaining how they'd followed the housekeeper, only to see her get injured and the son discover her. And then there had been the introduction of the human female, Joan.

"But everything is all right," Ophelia finished the story. "Even though the son was yelling, the Joan female took Luciana away from him and drove her to get her paw fixed. So maybe we don't have to worry about Luciana anymore. Now tell us what happened to you . . . why was that PAWN human driving his truck too fast for us to jump in?"

Zuki shook her head. "I don't know. When we parked inside the gate and he got out, he was whistling like he was happy. He went inside and was gone awhile. Then he came out, and his phone rang. I could hear him saying bad human words, like he was mad."

"Aaand?" Ophelia urged, waving a paw in a *hurry up* gesture.

Zuki furrowed her brow, obviously trying to recall. "And then he drove off."

"That's it?" Ophelia asked. "He just drove back to PAWN, and then you walked home again?"

"Not exactly. He drove fast, and I could barely hang on. It was scary." The pit bull's ears drooped as she added, "I had to run all the way home because he was gone so long. I barely got here before you did."

Brandon gave the canine a reassuring purr. "You did just fine, and all the plans worked out. Even Ruby is happy. We'll miss Luciana, but I don't think we need to check up on her anymore."

"Whew," Ophelia said, flopping onto her side on the cool bricks. "I agree, it's time for the humans to take care of themselves. But Luciana said she'd come back here to visit, so maybe we'll see her again."

"I hope so. I liked her," the pit bull declared. Getting to her paws, she added, "I'm going upstairs to sit on the bed with Ruby. Anyone else?"

"Me too," Brandon agreed. "Ophelia, are you coming?"

"In a minute."

As soon as Zuki and her brother had pushed through the pet door, leaving her alone in the courtyard, she padded over to the koi pond. A quarter moon glowed through the branches hanging over it, so that the pool's surface reflected back at her, black and shiny. Paws on the stone edging, Ophelia leaned in for a look.

"Philomena," she whispered, "it's me, Ophelia. I wanted to tell you that you were wrong. The human rat turned out to be nice after all."

She waited a few moments to see if the fish would surface for a rebuttal or maybe a new prediction. All she saw, however, was a thin, silvery stream of bubbles rising from somewhere very deep in the pond.

Ophelia snorted.

Last time I listen to you, silly fish, she thought, wondering if the koi could hear what she was saying inside her head. Which, if she was psychic like Zuki had said she was, the fish should have been able to do.

But since she didn't pop out of the water to make one of her rhymes, that had to mean she wasn't that clever. Ophelia snorted again. Even Ruby was better at predicting the future than Philomena was, no matter that she was the oldest fish Ophelia had ever heard of . . . and even though the koi supposedly liked her best.

But, next morning, Ophelia couldn't help but feel a bit guilty about having made fun of the fish. After all, Philomena had been right about Brandon. And everyone — even a koi — was allowed to make a mistake once in a while. Maybe she should apologize.

Though, of course, that would have to wait until she was alone with Philomena. Ruby and Zuki had long since taken their walk while Ophelia and Brandon got in a few extra ZZZZs. Now all of them were sitting near the concrete table while Ruby ate her breakfast (the furry members of the family and the roosters already having had their food). As promised, they'd had some of last night's snacks again as a treat.

Along with her appetizers, Ruby had her computer with her — so she could do what she called "homework" before she opened the store. But right now, she was doing what she called "surfing" — looking at pictures, mostly of canines and felines doing silly things — and so all three furs had decided to indulge in an early morning nap.

Ophelia had just drifted off to dreams of boundless crunchy shrimp tails when she heard a sudden gasp from Ruby. Her green eyes flew open to see the human staring at her computer, her mouth round as the koi's was when she blew bubbles. Ruby's eyes behind her black glasses were round, too. She whispered "oh no" and kept staring.

Maybe she'd seen a bad picture, Ophelia thought. Sometimes the computer had pictures of hurt humans and hurt animals that made Ruby sad when she saw them.

She was trying to decide if it was worth jumping up for a look — sometimes those pictures made her sad, too — when Ruby's phone began playing a song sung by a scratchy-voiced human male talking about having friends. Ophelia had heard that song enough times to know that it meant Ruby's friend, JoJo, was calling.

Ruby answered the call, though she was still staring at the computer.

"Hi, JoJo . . . yeah, it went great. Thanks for setting it up. No, it really did go good. It's just that I . . . I just now had some bad news."

She paused, and Ophelia flicked her ears. Something was obviously going on with the

275

human, and she intended to know what that was.

"No, the family's fine," Ruby went on. "It has to do with one of my new Tarot clients, Luciana Torres. I was reading the local headlines on my homepage on my laptop when I saw a story . . ."

She trailed off for a moment, and then said in a rush, "The woman, Luciana . . . she — she was killed last night."

Sixteen

"I still can't believe it. I mean, I was just talking to Luciana two days ago, and now she's dead."

Ruby stabbed her straw at the icy remains of her sweet tea that she'd been nursing since noon. It was almost 12:30 now at the New Yawk Deli, a trendy little hole-in-the-wall restaurant not far from JoJo's downtown condo building. She and JoJo were finishing their lunches.

Or, rather, JoJo was. The blonde had already downed one of the deli's signature sky-high Reuben sandwiches and had turned her attention to the dill pickle spears and potato chips that accompanied it. Ruby's turkey version of the same menu item still lay on her plate, with only a single bite missing. She'd not really been all that keen on doing lunch, but her friend had insisted. *Look, Rubes, I'm sure the cats and Zuki are good listeners and all, but with something like this you really need to talk it out with a human. And, yes, even though I'm an attorney, I do qualify.*

That last had been designed to make Ruby laugh, and so she'd obliged with a half hearted chuckle and agreed to meet JoJo at the deli later. In the interim, she'd split her time between customers and refreshing the news websites trying to learn more about Luciana's death.

Frustratingly, the details had been sparse.

A hit-and-run, the police were calling it — car versus pedestrian, to be more precise. According to initial reports, Luciana had been on foot near downtown West Palm Beach and apparently tried to cross one of the busier streets against the light. Unfortunately, she'd stepped into the path of a speeding vehicle — a small, dark pickup, according to one eyewitness — whose driver had fled without stopping.

Based on the timeline given in the police report, the accident had happened not long before she, Ruby, had been driving back from her party. Reading that, Ruby had shuddered a little as she recalled the emergency vehicles that had gone flying past her. Given the hour and the proximity, those likely had been the first responders to Luciana's accident. Had she followed them, she might have ended up at the scene of the woman's death.

"Listen, Ruby," JoJo said now as she finished off her chips. "What happened to Luciana was awful, but you can't take it to heart. All you did was read the Tarot cards for her, and that had nothing to do with how she died."

"I'm not so sure. The cards that Ophe— I mean, that I drew as clarifiers to the original reading indicated something bad was coming her way. I should have tried harder to warn her."

She hesitated, recalling in particular the image of the Tower card with its lightning bolt — the literal bolt from the blue — blasting apart the tower and sending the people inside it flying. The hit-and-run accident, with the death vehicle barreling down the road as randomly as any lightning bolt, was an unsettling parallel to that violent scenario.

JoJo, meanwhile, was raising her empty tea glass in the bus boy's direction to indicate her need for a refill. That done, she returned her attention to Ruby.

"I know you're really into this whole Tarot thing, but you've told me a hundred times it isn't fortune-telling. And even if she thought it was, you don't have any legal

279

obligation to warn her about bad luck and juju and all that. In fact, you know the laws about fraud and so-called psychic services. The only way you'd be in trouble is if you were telling her bad stuff was going to happen and accepting money for getting rid of her bad luck."

Before Ruby could reply, she went on. "And it might seem callous, but Luciana holds some responsibility for what happened to her. Technically, she was jaywalking, crossing against traffic in the middle of the street when she got hit."

"That's what doesn't make sense. She has a car, so why was she on foot after dark? And why was she walking around there, of all places?"

"There's all kinds of things to be had in that part of West Palm," her friend pointed out. "Drugs, booze, guns, and all that. It's one-stop shopping out there."

"I can't believe Luciana would be into any of that. She's not that type of person."

"Are you sure?" JoJo took a swallow from her refilled tea and persisted. "I understand that you care, Ruby, I really do. And that's what I love about you. But remember that you talked to this woman for, what, an hour total? Bottom line is that you really don't know anything about her."

The words hung between them for a few moments as JoJo grabbed the last pickle . . . which deli staple, Ruby absently noted, perfectly matched the color of other woman's military-style blouse and matching green capris. By contrast, Ruby was wearing one of her official Tarot outfits, a white silk blouse topped by a long paisley vest in jewel tones (vintage, of course) and worn over a yellow broomstick skirt.

But fashion wasn't on her mind right now. Instead, she pressed her lips tight in a stubborn line. What her friend said made absolute sense, but she couldn't agree. Along with her growing skills with the Tarot cards, she'd developed a knack for analyzing people. And her instincts told her that Luciana wouldn't wander that part of town alone and on foot . . . at least, not voluntarily.

But while her death was a crime, it obviously had nothing to do with those suspicions about Mrs. Givens's death that she'd come to Ruby about.

"I suppose I have to let it go," she finally replied, which was as far as she would concede the issue. Glancing at her phone, she added, "I'd better get back to the shop. Saturdays are busy, and I've been gone almost an hour."

"Well, at least get a to-go box for that sandwich. I'm sure Zuki will eat it even if you won't."

They settled up their mutual bills; then, bidding goodbye to her friend (JoJo's next stop was a cake-tasting with Blake), Ruby walked the half block to where her VW was parked. But rather than head straight back to the Botanica, as she had planned, she found herself making a small detour and instead driving to the scene of Luciana Torres's death.

Once she reached the cross streets that the news stories had specified, Ruby pulled off onto the shoulder and opened her window to peer out. What she expected to see on the road before her, she wasn't quite certain. *Skid marks? Chalk outlines? Crime scene tape?*

In reality, had she not known that an accident happened at that spot, she likely would have driven past without a second thought. For all that remained on the asphalt to indicate anything untoward had happened were the remnants of several road flares. That, and numerous small splotches of yellow paint, the latter no doubt having been used to mark the evidence.

To mark where her body had landed, came the unwilling thought.

She shuddered. She could only hope that Luciana had never seen the vehicle that had hit her, that she hadn't known a final few seconds of terror.

A few feet ahead of where she was parked, Ruby spied something else. A bouquet of red roses lying on the grass between curb and sidewalk. It was a typical South Florida display of respect for those killed on the road, marking the spot with floral tributes. Later, no doubt, there would be more flowers . . . maybe candles and a stuffed animal or two.

"Something I can help you with, ma'am?"

The voice came from outside her open window . . . stern, female. Startled, she looked over to see a uniformed police officer — *T. Washington,* per her name badge — standing at a slight angle behind her. She clutched a small notebook but her gaze was fixed on Ruby, her dark features unreadable.

Double-checking the accident scene for more evidence, Ruby guessed. That, or waiting to see if the hit-and-run driver had returned to the scene of his — or her — crime.

"Sorry," she replied. "Luciana — the woman who was killed here — was a friend of mine. I — I just needed to see where it happened."

The cop's stern expression relaxed a bit as she tucked the notebook into her belt. Still, she was all business as she replied, "I understand. You don't mind if I take a walk around your vehicle, do you?"

"Not at all."

She waited while Officer Washington, hand on pistol, made a slow circle around the Beetle. She was looking, Ruby guessed, for recent damage to it . . . this despite the fact the witness statement indicated it had been a dark-colored truck that fled the scene. But then she'd watched enough crime shows on TV to know that witnesses statements weren't always correct.

The cop completed her inspection and, apparently satisfied, returned to the driver's side window. She gave Ruby a nod.

"Sorry about your friend, ma'am. Now, I do need you to move along. We don't want another accident here."

Ruby obliged. She'd keep an eye on the obituaries to see if a wake was planned, so that she could go and pay her respects. That, and maybe add one of the prayer candles Rosa stocked in the store to the makeshift memorial. Since the next day was Sunday, the Botanica was closed, so she'd have time to make the trip back again . . . hopefully not under the watchful eye of Officer Washington. The gesture wouldn't bring the woman back, but making the effort might give her, Ruby, a bit of closure.

But what about Luciana's suspicions regarding her employer's "accident"?

Ruby considered the question as she made the drive back to the Botanica. Had the housekeeper met her end in the same swimming pool as Mrs. Givens, she'd have been on the phone to the police in a flash. But Luciana's death, while suspiciously timed, was surely nothing other than a tragic coincidence. It seemed like at least once a week that she saw news of a similar death while scanning the Palm Beach Herald headlines online.

"Face it," she muttered, "you take your life in your hands any time you walk — heck, or even drive — in this town."

And while Luciana's death wouldn't make the headlines beyond a day or two, Mrs. Givens's death had received plenty of scrutiny . . . fair or not, simply because of her social status. Had there truly been anything nefarious about her drowning, surely the police would have found the evidence. It was probably best that she let both women rest in peace.

"Let it go," she softly sang, channeling

her inner Elsa from the movie *Frozen.* Time to accept the fact that advice wasn't always taken, that warnings weren't always heeded. In her role as Ruby Sparks, Tarot Card Reader Fairly Competent, she had met her responsibilities to the housekeeper.

But as she pulled the VW into the driveway, she couldn't help but add, "I promise you, Luciana, that next time I'll try to do better."

"We never should have let her leave with the Joan human," Ophelia mewed from where she lay beneath the concrete table in the courtyard. "Luciana is dead now, and it's all our fault."

"We should have gone with her," Brandon yowled in agreement from where he lay sprawled on the koi pond's ledge. "We could have jumped in the car and stayed with her. We could have told her not to walk into the street."

"But why did she run away from the place that was fixing her leg?" Zuki wanted to know from her spot lying next to the strangler fig. "Didn't the Joan human wait for her?"

Ophelia gave her tail an angry flick. "I don't know. I went up to Ruby's bedroom and looked at her computer, but I didn't see any pictures of the Joan female. So she must have left Luciana at the fixing place and gone home again."

Then, shooting a glare in the direction of the koi pond, she growled, "This is all Philomena's fault. If she's so smart, she could have warned us about Luciana instead of making silly rhymes."

She got to her paws and stomped over to the pond. Ignoring her brother, she leaped up onto the ledge and peered into the water.

"Philomena!" she yowled. "You're a fake. You don't know anything, at all! And I don't care if you used to like me best! I don't like you now."

Brandon sat up as well, staring from her to the pond's surface in interest. "I never did meet the koi. Maybe you can introduce me."

"Forget that! Who wants to meet a stupid fish, anyhow?" she spat in the direction of the water. "All she's good for is eating!"

With that last insult, Ophelia stalked back over to the table and lightly jumped up, making a deliberate turn of her back on the pond as she sat.

Zuki got up and padded over to the pond. "Philomena," she called, "don't be mad. Ophelia didn't mean it. Did you?" she added with a look over her shoulder at the cat.

Ophelia hissed. "I did so mean it. What's the good of knowing important things if you don't share them? We're the ones who should be mad, not her."

"But I told you before, that's how she is. Koi fish have a certain way of speaking, and we can't make them change. Just like you can't make a mouse not want cheese." Turning her attention to the pond again, the pit bull added, "Philomena, please, come talk to us."

Curious despite herself, Ophelia glanced behind her to see if there was any sign of the fish. Not surprisingly, the pond surface remained undisturbed.

Stupid koi was deaf, too.

And then Brandon gave a mew. "Look, I see something!"

Sure enough, the pond's surface shimmered, ripples making the water lilies dance. A moment later, a large, red-capped white head slowly rose above the water to the accompanying sound of smacking bubbles.

Brandon's round green eyes grew wider. "Is — Is that Philomena?"

"Yes, it is I. I cannot lie," the koi burbled.

Ophelia snorted. "Well, maybe you can't

lie, Philly, but you sure can't tell us anything we don't already know."

"Ophelia!" the pit bull snapped. "Be polite."

To the koi, she said in a reverential tone, "Please forgive the rude feline. And now, this new cat is Ophelia's brother, Brandon. He's been eager to make your acquaintance."

Brandon nodded. "Nice to meet you, Miss Philomena. I heard you were very old and very smart. Ophelia told me you knew without being told where I was living before I came here."

"That is quite true. I knew all about you."

"Well, then maybe you know about our human friend, Luciana," Ophelia shot back. "I heard Ruby talking on the phone. She said Luciana got run over by a picking up truck last night. She's dead."

"That is so sad to hear. It was my own worst fear."

Ophelia leaped off the table and rushed to the pond. "What do you mean, your own worst fear? You knew this was going to happen? Why didn't you say anything?"

The koi gave a little bob — her version of a shrug, since she lacked shoulders. *"You must ask the right question. That is just a suggestion."*

"Yoooowl!" Ophelia smacked the water with an angry paw. "Fine. All right, you dumb fish. Here is a question. Was Luciana's death an accident or something else?"

As in the past, Philomena began a slow spin while her eyes took on a silvery glow. She gave a final rotation and then halted. In a burbling voice, she intoned, *"The accident, it was intended. And the bad things, they have not ended."*

Ophelia exchanged shocked glances with Brandon and Zuki. Not only had the koi confirmed their suspicions, but she claimed that more bad things were to come. As that realization sunk in, they began mewing and barking all at once.

"We have to warn Ruby!"

"We should go back to the old house and get the son!"

"We have to tell the humans with badges and guns about Luciana!"

The roosters, hearing the commotion, came running from the side yard, adding their clucks and crows to the cacophony.

"What."

"Is."

"Wrong?"

"Can."

"We."

"Help?"

The only silent one was Philomena. She floated at the pond surface for a few moments longer before she began to sink back into its depths again.

"Stop!" Ophelia cried as she noticed the fish's retreat. "You have to tell us more. Who is behind all of this?"

"Just one question per day," the koi burbled. *"It is always that way."*

"One question? That's not fair! This is important. You must —"

"Wait," Brandon cried, cutting his sister short. "Is that one question a day, period, or one question a day per feline? Because I have a question for Philomena."

Philomena halted her downward progression. Resurfacing, she smacked a few bubbles and then gurgled, *"This time, I will allow it. But only if you meow it."*

"Meow it?" Ophelia sputtered. Normally, when more than one species was present, everyone spoke the same universal multi-species tongue rather than their own languages. "Do you even understand feline?"

Zuki nodded her blocky head. "Of course she does. Philomena understands every language . . . bird, mammal, fish, or reptile. She even knows insect talk."

"Fine. Brandon, go ahead and ask her a question in feline. But it's only one question, so make it a good one."

Her brother was silent a moment, considering. Then he nodded. "Okay, here it goes. *Meow, mew-mew. Meow-ow-ow. Mew. Me-OOW!*"

Which Ophelia translated for Zuki's benefit: *Where do we find the human who is responsible for hurting Luciana?*

The koi started to spin again, while the trio watched. Finally, to the accompaniment of the roosters' clucking, Philomena snapped a few bubbles and proclaimed, *"It takes a pill to fix what's ill. The rat may be bold, but the trail is not yet cold."*

Ophelia snorted. "That's it? You're talking about the 'rat' again?"

"Maybe there's another rat we don't know about?" Zuki suggested, earning another snort from her friend.

Brandon's whiskers drooped as the koi sunk from sight, leaving behind the usual trail of silvery bubbles. "I thought I asked a good question. Philomena likes to talk in puzzles, doesn't she?"

Zuki trotted over to the pond and raised a paw to give the feline a comforting pat. "That's just how koi are. Don't worry, Brandon, it was a good question. And we'll ask another one tomorrow. In the meantime, all of us — even the roosters — should keep our eyes and ears open to see if we can find this rat before it finds us."

Seventeen

Early Monday morning, Ruby had just unlocked the cash register when her cell phone tucked beneath the counter began to ring.

The sound made her jump. Other than a trip to Luciana's makeshift roadside memorial to leave a candle, she'd spent a quiet Sunday working on her thesis without a single phone call to break the silence. The cats had seemed unusually subdued, too, almost as if they'd understood her when she'd told them that something bad had happened to their human friend.

She'd noticed later that they and Zuki were spending a lot of time in the courtyard near the koi pond. What that meant, she had no clue, but as long as everyone stayed dry, she was fine with their curiosity. For herself, she'd needed the mental break that came with a phone-free day.

Now Ruby glanced at her cell's display

and realized the number belonged to the same unknown caller from the night of the party . . . the one who had left the drunken message. Maybe the woman had sobered up enough to make an actual appointment. Curious, she answered with her usual spiel.

"Thank you for calling Botanica Santa Rosa, this is Ruby, how can I help you on your spiritual journey?"

The caller was silent for a moment; then, as she was about to hang up, a man's voice asked, "What's your address?"

A man?

Several possibilities flashed through her mind. Maybe the female caller had been using this guy's phone instead of her own, and he was trying to figure out who she'd called. Or, more unsettling, maybe this was a jealous spouse or boyfriend trying to track down unknown contacts in his sig other's call history.

Or maybe the guy had simply been embarrassed the first time around to call for himself, and so had put a female friend up to it.

Since the unknown man's voice didn't sound particularly threatening, she gave him the address along with the major cross streets to look for. She had started on the parking explanation — they were fortunate to have three actual spots for the shop, but beyond that, it was street parking only — when he hung up on her in mid-sentence.

Maybe not threatening, but definitely rude.

"Have a good day, yourself," she muttered into the silent phone.

He might not even show up, she told herself. But, just in case, she tucked her phone into the pocket of her blue-and-black-striped harem pants where she could get to it quickly. She also made sure that a spray bottle of Florida Water — which substance, she knew from personal unfortunate experience, stung like heck when it got in one's eyes — was close at hand. And, of course, Zuki was behind the counter and could be in chomping range in seconds should things go terribly wrong.

But an hour later, she'd almost forgotten the call. It had been a busy start to a Monday. She'd made several small sales already — male and female candles to a young Haitian woman; a vial of "Come to Me" oil to Lana, the middle-aged trans woman who ran the antique shop the next block over; and a St. Mark prayer card and silver medal to an elderly Hispanic gentleman — as well as scheduled two readings for later that day. She'd just returned to her spot behind the counter, after doing a bit of stocking, when the bells on the front door jangled and a man in his mid-thirties strode in.

Her first impression was that he reminded her of a Cuban Tony Stark . . . the Robert Downey, Jr. character from the *Iron Man* movies. That was, if Tony Stark wore khaki cargo shorts and a black pullover with his name and company embroidered on it.

This guy had the same dark hair and eyes, similar chiseled features and lean build. He also affected the same razor-precise facial hair as the comic character . . . sharply cut goatee and thin, Fu Manchu-style mustache. But the scowl on his face better befitted another comic book character: The Incredible Hulk.

He stomped his way over to the counter and tossed down a business card. "This you?" he asked without preamble.

She didn't need to pick it up to recognize the card as one of hers. And though he'd spoken only two words, she didn't need to hear more to know that he was the same man who had called earlier. And it was obvious that he was not a happy camper.

"I'm Ruby," she confirmed. "Can I help you with something?"

She casually shoved her glasses into place while at the same time giving the snoozing

Zuki a nudge with one foot. The pit bull silently rose, positioning herself alongside Ruby. Unless the man leaned all the way over the counter, he'd never see the dog. That was, not unless he did something requiring an introduction to Zuki's not-so-sweet side.

The man's scowl, meanwhile, had deepened. Picking up the card again, he flapped it in Ruby's direction.

Now she noticed that he had a brightly colored tattoo on his right biceps, though she couldn't quite make it out, partially covered as it was by his shirt sleeve. Still flapping, he demanded, "I want to know why my aunt had this in her purse."

Ruby bristled, feeling rather like Brandon when his stubby tail went all bushy. She'd encountered a few people of this type before. Obviously a skeptic, which in itself didn't bother her. But she couldn't stomach the self-righteous types who not only proclaimed that the Botanica and everything associated with it was bunk, but also felt compelled to rail against anyone who believed.

Keeping her tone polite yet curt, she replied, "Where or when she got my card is your aunt's business. If you have any concerns, maybe you should ask her directly."

"Yeah. Well, I can't exactly do that."

He dropped the business card again and reached into one of the pockets of his cargo shorts, pulling out a phone. She doubted it belonged to him, given its bright pink case covered in rhinestones. And in the next instant, she realized with a gasp that she'd seen that very same phone case just a few days before.

"Her name was Luciana Torres. And the reason I can't ask her about you is that she's dead."

He slapped the phone down on the counter beside the business card.

"So now that we've settled that, I want to know why you were the last person she called right before some lowlife ran her down and left her to die on the street."

Ruby opened her eyes wide, as shocked as if he'd smacked her with the phone. *Luciana Torres was his aunt?* And then another realization struck her.

"Are — Are you saying Luciana was the one who left me a voicemail the other night?"

She stared from him to the pink cell phone as the pieces began falling into place. She recalled the garbled phone message she'd listened to as she left Palm Beach, remembered how she'd dismissed it as being from an intoxicated bridal shower guest. But, instead, the caller had been Luciana. And now the question was, why had she called . . . and, perhaps as importantly, why had she seemed so out of it?

As for the Tony Stark wannabe, he had to be the same nephew that the housekeeper had mentioned lived in the area. Ruby glanced at the embroidery on his shirt. *Gold Crown Pawn,* it read, with a cute logo of a crown atop three golden balls. Beneath it was the name *Luis.* Luciana hadn't mentioned that her nephew worked at a pawn shop, not that it had any bearing on the situation.

No doubt the police had turned over to him all the belongings of hers they'd recovered at the accident site . . . phone included. Obviously, the phone's "recents" list was how he'd connected Luciana to the Botanica. And while his attitude could use some adjustment, she could understand his need to track his relative's last moves.

"Look, Luis," she began, giving the name her best Spanish accent and emphasizing its second syllable. "I'm terribly sorry about your aunt. I only met her once, but I really liked her. As for why she called me —"

"It's *LEW-is,*" he broke in, giving the name the typical American pronunciation, accent on the first syllable. "And I'm not here for condolences. I want to know what sort of scam you were running on her."

"Scam? What in the heck are you talking about?" Conciliatory feelings vanishing, Ruby met his mistrustful scowl with a glare of her own. "Your aunt came in of her own free will and paid for a Tarot card reading. I gave her the reading, she thanked me, and then she left. The end."

"So why did she call you right before she was killed?"

"I — I don't know." Ruby hesitated. Should she mention the real reason Luciana had come to the Botanica for a reading? But already she could hear Rosa's voice in her mind emphasizing a major rule of reading Tarot cards . . . that what was said between reader and client was sacrosanct.

Just like a priest or a counselor, she would intone. *You cannot breach that confidence.*

Rosa hadn't indicated if that vow of silence extended beyond the grave. But for now, she'd make that assumption. Besides, the hit-and-run was a random accident and certainly had no connection to the Givens family.

"Look, *Lew-is,*" she repeated, "when Luciana called that night, I was in the middle of doing readings at a bridal shower on Palm Beach, so she went to voicemail. When I played the message on the way home, I figured the voice had to be one of the women from the party. I honestly didn't know your aunt was the one who called me until you said so."

"Yeah, so what was the message?"

"I haven't deleted it yet. I can play it for you, if you want."

Though would he want to hear it? The brief message was undeniably unsettling, the more so because it held what might have been Luciana's final words. Not something to spring on someone who was unprepared.

But, obviously, he was steeled for it. At his sharp nod, she pulled the phone from her pocket and pulled up her voicemail history. Putting the phone on speaker, she pressed the "play" arrow.

"Ruby . . . I need . . ."

The message cut off, and Ruby suppressed a shudder. Knowing now who it was, she could recognize the woman's soft, accent-tinged voice, distorted as it sounded. She'd assumed before that the signal had simply dropped, ending the call. But hearing it again, it occurred to her that maybe Luciana had been distracted making the call . . . and maybe that had been the moment she'd stepped into the truck's path.

She glanced up at Luis. The scowl was gone, replaced by a shuttered expression that told her he was thinking the same thing . . . and that he didn't want to be thinking it.

A wave of compassion washed over her, and she blinked back sympathetic tears. Whatever opinion he might have about Tarot and the Botanica, it appeared that his love for his aunt was genuine. Why else was he trying to retrace her final movements?

"Do you want to hear the recording again?" she asked.

He shook his head, frowning. "No. But do me a favor. Don't delete it yet, okay?"

She hesitated once more. The idea of having someone's last words permanently recorded on her cell phone voicemail was disturbing at best. But she'd oblige and keep the message for a while.

At her nod, he went on. "Is it just me, or did Aunt Lu sound drunk or something?"

"Definitely something. Do you have any idea what she was doing out on the street on foot?"

"That's the problem. She should have been at school — she was taking night classes — but I talked to her instructor. He said she skipped class that night." His frown deepened. "Either way, she shouldn't even have been walking at all. According to the cops, they interviewed her boss — whats-hisname, that Givens guy — and he said she'd sprained her ankle pretty bad earlier that night. Supposedly, Jo— er, Givens's girlfriend drove her to one of those doc-in-the-box places to get it looked at."

"You mean she took Luciana to an emergency clinic?" Ruby clarified.

Luis nodded. "Yeah, whatever. The girlfriend claimed that my aunt didn't want anyone to wait with her, so the girlfriend just dropped her off and then left. Problem is, the clinic doesn't have any record of Aunt Lu checking in."

Now it was Ruby's turn to frown. None of this had been in the online accounts of the incident.

"This clinic," she asked, "do you have any idea how far is it from where your aunt . . . from where the accident happened?"

"It's six, maybe seven blocks away. A pretty good haul for someone with a busted-up ankle to walk."

"That could explain why she sounded like she did. If she was in that much pain, it was probably hard for her to think straight, let alone talk. Maybe she was calling me for a ride or something? Though it would make more sense if she called you."

"Yeah, well, there's more. A witness said they saw someone matching her description near the accident site about fifteen minutes earlier. They said she was staggering around, like she was drunk. My aunt maybe took a glass of wine on a holiday, but as far as I know she never got plastered a day in her life."

Which was maybe why she was embarrassed to call her nephew? "Look, I really *am* sorry about Luciana. But I'm not sure there's anything more I can do. And I really need to get back to work . . ."

"Yeah, me too."

He retrieved the phone and business card, allowing himself the faintest of smiles. The movie star resemblance was even more apparent now, Ruby thought, pretending the sudden rush of heat that swept her was the A/C acting up again. Too bad the guy had attitude issues, because he was, to put it bluntly, a hunk.

As if reading her mind on the attitude part, he added, "Look, I appreciate your help, and I'm sorry if I came on like a jerk at first. I believe you that you weren't scamming her. It's just that this whole thing has been a pretty big shock, and — what the hell? You — You stole my cat!"

"I what?"

She turned in the direction he was pointing. At some point while she and Luis had been talking, Brandon and Ophelia had wandered into the shop. Without Ruby noticing, the pair had jumped onto the end of the counter nearest the hallway door where they now lounged, Brandon's stubby tail dangling off the edge. At the sound of the man's voice, the cat's ears flicked.

"That's him, with half a tail. He went missing a few days ago," Luis exclaimed. To the cat, he added, "C'mon, I'm taking you back where you belong."

He'd started toward where the cats sprawled when a soft but business-like growl stopped him short. Ruby looked over the counter to see that Zuki had made her quiet way around and now stood between the man and the cats.

Luis glanced from the pit bull to Ruby. "Seriously, you're going to sic your dog on me?"

"I'm not siccing her on anyone," Ruby mildly replied. "She did that on her own. She must think you're a threat, and that's why she's trying to keep you away from the cats."

"I don't know about the other one, but the cat with the short tail is mine. He's been living with me for a month. I rescued him off the streets, and I want him back."

Ruby suppressed a snort. "If he's your cat, what's his name?"

"His name?" The innocuous question seemingly took him aback. "Uh, Blackie. Yeah, it's Blackie."

"Right." Not bothering this time to hide her skepticism, she said, "Why don't you call 'Blackie' and see if he'll come to you? Maybe then I'll believe he's your cat."

"Fine. Come here, Blackie. Good boy. Blackie?"

Ruby folded her arms and waited. The cat gave Luis a quizzical look but remained where he sat. Obviously, Brandon wasn't buying the man's story either.

Smirking a little, she said, "It might help if you call him by his real name . . . which I happen to know, because he's the brother of my cat, Ophelia. If you'd had his chip scanned, you would have known it, too. Blackie? Please."

"Hey, don't make fun of my cat's name. And if he's really your cat, why don't you try calling him and see if he'll come to you?"

"Fine, let's give it a try. Brandon, come here. Come on!"

For an unsettling moment, she was afraid the cat was going to ignore her, too. And then, to her relief, Brandon rose from where he lay on the counter and quickly slinked over to her.

Told ya, was Ruby's reflexive thought as she stroked the cat's sleek fur. Aloud, she merely said, "I guess that settles that."

"Not so fast. Look, I have pictures."

He whipped out his own cell phone this time — which did not have a pink rhinestoned case — and began swiping through photos. "Here he is eating. And here he is, sleeping on the hood of my truck. And here's one in the shop where he's riding on one of those robot vacuums someone pawned."

One at a time, he showed the pictures to Ruby, who felt her triumph slowly slipping away. No mistaking the cat in the photo for any feline but Brandon. In addition to his trademark bobbed tail, he had the same couple of white whiskers mixed in with the black, just as Brandon did. The fact that Luis was a relative of Luciana's might have had some bearing as to why the cat had gravitated to him while on the run.

"Believe me now?" Luis demanded, stowing away his phone again.

Ruby slowly nodded. "I — I don't have a choice. But, look, while Brandon — okay, Blackie — has apparently been staying at your place, he ran away and ended up here with his sister. It's like he knew to come here. According to the animal shelter, these two have been together since birth, except for when they got separated when someone took them from their old home and dumped them on the street. How can you break them up again?"

"Easy. Come here, gato."

To Ruby's shock, Brandon wriggled out from under her hands as she was petting him and butted his furry head against Luis's arm.

Ophelia stared in shock from her spot safely out of anyone's reach. "Brandon, what are you doing?" she yowled. "Why did you go to the PAWN human?"

"He called me," her brother replied. "I told you, Gato is his name for me."

"And I told you that name means 'cat' in Spanish," Zuki reminded him from her position on the floor, where she was still keeping an eye on Luis.

Brandon flicked his whiskers. "But that's what he calls me. And it would have been rude to ignore him."

"Who cares about rude?" Ophelia yowled. "Did you hear? He wants to take you away from us."

Brandon shot her a steady look. "I don't want to leave. But didn't *you* hear what he said? He's related to Luciana. And I think he might know something about what happened to her. I'm going to go with him and play detective, just like in those shows on that screen on the wall that the old woman used to watch. I'm going to look for clues."

Before Ophelia could reply — things had not gone well when they tried that detective cat thing with Luciana! — Luis abruptly scooped Brandon up in his arms.

"Thanks for looking after Blackie for me," he told Ruby, "but I'd better take him home now." Glancing down at Zuki, he added, "Can you call your dog off?"

"Fine," Ruby muttered, nervously adjusting her glasses. "Zuki, back off. Let the man pass."

"Don't do it, Zuki!" Ophelia meowed.

The pit bull took a step back, glancing from Ruby to Brandon and back to Ruby again. To Ophelia, she said, "I — I have to listen to my human. She said to let Luis go, so I have to do it."

"It's okay, Zuki. I'll be fine. Do what Ruby tells you," Brandon meowed back.

To Ophelia, he said, "Don't worry, I have a plan."

"A plan?" She gave her tail an angry snap while Zuki backed out of the aisle. "For kibble's sake, what are you talking about?"

310

"Trust me. Give me two days, so Luis doesn't get suspicious. You and Zuki can come back for me the day after tomorrow, at midnight. Meet me outside of PAWN and I'll come back with you. And maybe I'll even have evidences for Ruby to give to the police."

"Are you sure?"

"I am. And there's something I didn't tell you," he called over Luis's shoulder as he and the human headed toward the front door. "Remember what Philomena said? Look at the picture painted on his arm."

While Ophelia leaped off the counter and hurried after them, Brandon rubbed his head against the human's shirtsleeve, as if simply snuggling up to him. But she saw that the gesture actually pushed up the shirt's fabric, which had been partially hiding what the humans called a tattoo.

At first glance, Ophelia couldn't quite tell what the picture on his arm was, since Brandon's ears were partially in the way. Then he moved his head to one side, and she saw it . . . a brightly inked picture of a sharp-toothed, grinning rat.

EIGHTEEN

"Where is he? Where's Brandon?" Ophelia hissed. "It's midnight, and we're here, just like he said."

She and Zuki were crouched in the shadows behind PAWN, in the open room where the Luis human parked his picking up truck. The truck was there, but the front of it was warm — warm enough for a feline to sleep on — and it was making little tinking noises. Which meant, she knew, that even though the truck was parked, it had been driving not that long ago.

Had Brandon gone driving in it, and been lost somewhere?

The bright red letters in the front window were still lit, along with the three golden balls, but there was a smaller sign with blue letters that read CLOSED. Ophelia knew that word meant all the humans were supposed to be gone. Unless Luis lived over the shop, just like Ruby lived over the Botanica.

She shuddered a little as she thought of Luis . . . the human with the rat painted on his arm. He had been loud and angry when he first came into the Botanica, but she didn't think he was a bad human. Not like the son.

That was, not until she'd seen the picture on his arm.

It had been a frightening moment, indeed. Here, Philomena the koi had warned them about a human rat, and yet Brandon had volunteered to go off with him! She'd been so stunned at his decision that, before she could demand more answers, he and Luis had been out the Botanica door.

And it had been all Zuki could do to make her wait like Brandon had wanted, instead of rushing around like one of the roosters and going after him. Ruby had been distraught, too, muttering to her and Zuki about making a mistake and even calling her friend JoJo to ask what she thought.

But the two days that Brandon demanded for his plan had finally passed. Once Ruby had gone to sleep, Ophelia and Zuki had sneaked out of the courtyard like last time. With no interference from any street dogs, they'd come to PAWN on schedule, only to find no sign of her brother.

Now the pit bull raised her blocky head and began sniffing, then flicked her ears about.

"The Luis human was here a little while ago," she confirmed. "Brandon was, too, but it's been a while. Maybe a few hours? But I hear something in the building moving around that sounds more feline than human.

Sure enough, a moment later, Ophelia heard the faintest whisper of paws on concrete coming from the other side of the truck. Almost immediately, she glimpsed green eyes glowing in the shadows right before a sleek black feline with a stubby tail popped out of the darkness.

"Brandon!" she softly yowled as she rushed over to her brother. Making figure eights around him and butting her head against his, she asked, "Are you all right? Did the rat human do anything to you?"

"I'm fine," Brandon purred. "Luis didn't do anything bad to me. But I did lots of investigating, just like on television. Come on, I'll tell you about it."

The trio settled in a spot near the open room's main entrance, but far back enough so they couldn't be seen. After making sure that no humans were lurking about, Brandon told them about his adventures.

"I found a clever way to listen to what Luis says to his friends," Brandon began. "He thinks its funny when I sit on that flat round thing that drives around the floor sucking up dirt —"

"A robot vacuum," Zuki helpfully supplied. "I saw that on television."

"— so I would ride around on it and pretend to be driving, but I'd actually be listening to them. And that's how I finally found out what PAWN is."

He explained the strange human custom of bringing something special — like a watch, or a big saw — to the shop. Luis would give the other human money in return, and then put the thing in the back of his store. If the human brought back the money, Luis would give them back their thing. If the human never came back, Luis would put the thing in the front of his store for other humans to look at, and would give it to whoever gave him money.

Zuki and Ophelia nodded. Living in the Botanica, they knew all about the paper and metal pieces that humans gave out in exchange for food and other things. This PAWN, apparently, was just another way to trade.

"But that's not all that Luis does. You see,

there are some humans that have lots of things, like the old woman did, but they don't have any money. So they have to trade for it . . . but they don't want to come to PAWN in case someone sees them. Luis said they'd be embarrassed. You know, like if you try to jump onto a table or a sofa, but slip and land back on the ground."

Ophelia and Zuki nodded again. They'd both experienced that sort of cringeworthy indignity before.

Brandon continued. "Since they can't come to PAWN, Luis goes to where the embarrassed humans live. He gives them money and takes their things. That's what he was doing the night we snuck into the back of the truck and went looking for Luciana."

"So he's not selling doughnuts or tuna or the bad medicine? How can you be certain?" Ophelia asked, green eyes narrowed in suspicion.

Brandon gave her a lofty look. "Because I went with him and saw all the things he brought out of the houses."

While Ophelia and Zuki listened in amazement, he explained about the trip from the Botanica to PAWN riding in the front seat of Luis's picking up truck. The human had laughed when he'd balanced his forepaws on the dashboard and stared intently out the windshield, watching the streets slide past. And that had given Brandon an idea.

That night, when Luis had closed the store and gone out to the picking up truck with his bag of money, Brandon had boldly followed after and leaped into the passenger seat. And rather than shooing him out, the human had patted his head and said something about shotguns.

"But don't worry, he didn't shoot anything. We drove around to big houses near where we used to live. And he showed me all the things the other humans gave him."

Check this out, gato, Luis had said after their first stop. *A diamond tennis bracelet, a Rolex, and a pair of emerald earrings.*

The next stop had yielded similar items. *Diamond necklace, diamond and ruby ring . . . stones are kinda small, though. And look, gato, here's a tiara.*

To Brandon's amusement, the human had put a circle of sparkly spikes on top of his head . . . looking, Brandon thought, like a picture he had once seen of the old woman wearing her fanciest clothes.

But with the last stop, Luis hadn't been laughing. He'd stayed there longer than at the other places. When he came back out, the only thing he brought with him was a big gold circle that fit on a human's finger. It was flat on the top with a picture of some winged human carved on it.

A signet ring, Luis had called it. And his expression was as flat as that ring.

Here's a lesson for you, gato. Don't get old. El viejo, the old guy who pawned this ring, you'd think he has lots of money living here. But his hija — his daughter — and her husband, they control everything. And he's in a wheelchair, so he can't just leave. He has to wait until they go out of town so he can call me and sell some of his things, so he has money for emergencies.

He'd stuck the ring on his own finger. *His papa gave him the ring back when he was in prep school, sixty years ago. It's worth a fortune to him, but best I could give him was full melt price. But don't worry, gato, I'll hold onto it and get it back to him someday.*

"And that's where we went," Brandon finished, as Ophelia and Zuki nodded soberly at that last story. "We didn't go out tonight, so I mostly rode around on the robot. But I did find something that looked like a clue on the floor under Luis's desk. Wait here."

He disappeared into the shadows again, returning a few moments later with a crumpled ball of newspaper in his mouth. He walked over to a spot where the moon was shining onto the concrete and, with a proud purr, dropped the bundle.

Forgetting the story of the old human, Ophelia walked over and nudged the paper with a careless paw. "A piece of newspaper? What kind of clue is that?"

"It's a good clue. Look."

Snagging the paper back from her, Brandon poked at it until he'd managed to smooth it almost flat.

"See its edges," he explained. "They're not ripped, like someone accidentally tore it off a bigger paper. They're straight, like a human cut it out with those scissor things."

Ophelia flicked her whiskers. "So the human cut up a piece of paper and crumpled it up. Maybe he was making a toy to bat around. Ruby does that for us sometimes."

Brandon gave an exasperated growl. "You're not looking hard enough. It's a picture out of the newspaper. And see the human in it?"

Ophelia leaned closer so that her nose was almost touching the page. Then, with a squeak of surprise, she jumped back. "It's him! It's a picture of the son!"

Then, squinting, she took another look at the paper. Tone suspicious now, she stalked a few feet away as she added, "What are all those little holes all over the picture? It looks like something with fangs was biting it."

Though she'd never seen a fang pattern quite like that, with single punctures randomly scattered about. Not that she blamed the unknown biter, she thought, momentarily baring her own glossy white teeth. If she ever saw the son again, she was going to bite him herself . . . for real!

"It smells like Luis," the pit bull observed as she walked over and gave the paper a sniff. "So why do you think he cut out a picture of the son? The way it's all wrinkled up, it looks like he tried to throw it away."

"There's writing at the bottom," Brandon pointed out. "Maybe you can read it."

Zuki furrowed her brow, brown eyes narrowed in concentration as she slowly sounded it out. "*Mr. Terrence W. Givens . . . and . . . Ms. Joan . . . Ratzen Attend . . . the Spring Opening of . . . the Gardens.* What does that mean?"

"Nothing important," Ophelia replied as she slid between the pit bull's front legs for another look. "But, see, the Joan female was in the picture, too. That's her shoulder and hair on the edge. Luis cut her out and only left the son. I wonder why."

"Maybe he didn't like her," Zuki suggested. She stepped around the cat and flopped onto the concrete. Then, brown eyes widening, she added, "Or maybe he liked her and didn't want to bite her picture."

"How would he even know who she was?" Ophelia countered. "I never even saw him come visit Luciana the whole time we lived there. But I bet she told him about the son, and Luis knew he was a bad man."

To her brother, she said in approval, "That was a very clever find, even though we don't know what it means. Did you discover any other clues?"

"Only one." Brandon's whiskers drooped. "I noticed it yesterday, after I jumped out of the truck. Come here and look."

Bobtail drooping, too, he led them to the front of the picking up truck and pointed with one paw. On the passenger side, the headlight was broken, and part of the front end crumpled.

The three exchanged silent glances while the truck gave a final *tink-tink* before going silent, too.

"No!" Brandon yowled. "I know it has to be what humans call a coincidence. She was his mother's sister. He wouldn't hurt her, not even on accident."

"What about the son?" Ophelia pointed out in a subdued voice. "He was mean to the old woman, and she was his mother."

"Luis isn't like that. I'm sure . . ."

But he *wasn't* sure, Ophelia knew from the uncertain tone of her brother's voice. Beside, Philomena had warned them about a rat, and the human had a big picture of one painted on his arm.

"Maybe he hit her with the picking up truck because he thought the old woman left Luciana lots of money. Maybe a hundred dollars," she suggested, naming the largest sum she had ever heard of. "And since the police people gave him her phone, maybe he thought he would get her money, too."

Brandon gave a softer yowl. "But he was nice to me . . . and he felt sorry for the old man in the wheeling chair."

"That doesn't matter," Zuki said with a shake of her blocky white head. "I've see humans do bad things, like make canines fight, but then they give some of the moneys they win to the good place they call church."

They lapsed into silence for another moment; then Brandon asked in a small voice, "Can we go home now? I — I don't think I want to be a cat detective anymore."

Nor do I, Ophelia decided. At least, not when it came to humans' problems. They were far too complicated and made too much of a mess of things . . . unlike felines,

322

who were always straightforward in their dealings. Even canines didn't cause this much trouble!

Leaving the picture of the son behind, they slipped out of the open room and onto the street. Keeping to the shadows, they padded quietly in the direction of the Botanica. Ophelia kept close to her brother, giving him a concerned look every few steps, but leaving him to his own thoughts. They'd barely gone two blocks, however, when a familiar growl sounded behind them.

"Hey, you. Cats, pit bull. You're on my turf again."

The trio halted and swung about to see the terrier, Rally, trotting on stubby legs down the sidewalk after them. He stopped as well, and bristled his wiry black-and-white fur in an obvious attempt to look larger.

"I told you to stay away, but you came back," he snarled, crooked teeth bared. "Now I — we — are going to have to teach you a lesson."

"We?" Zuki echoed, looking about. She gave a quick sniff and added, "I don't smell your friends anywhere around."

"Bobo and Sammy? Eh, they couldn't hack life on the streets. They let some rescue

323

group pick them up." Rally bristled even more. "But I don't need them. I've got other canines to help me."

Ophelia rolled her green eyes. "Are you sure? I don't see any canines besides you. Do you see any, Brandon?"

Her brother shook his furry head. "Nope."

Rally glared at them another moment, black eyes gleaming. Then his fur settled back into place and he plopped down on the sidewalk in a seated position, hind legs shifted to one side.

"Fine, you got me. Now have your laugh, and then go on back to your nice house and your nice humans."

"Oh-kay," Zuki replied, nodding for Brandon and Ophelia to come along. But instead of following, the two cats exchanged looks; then Brandon grimaced.

"We can't just leave him there," he hissed to the departing pit bull. "He thinks he's tough, but being on the streets alone is even tougher. I — I know about that."

Zuki halted. She stood there a moment before cocking her blocky head and turning with a sigh. "Go ahead, ask. But there's no guarantee Ruby will say yes even if he does."

Still, Brandon's whiskers flicked hopefully as he padded back toward the terrier.

"Uh, Rally," he began, "it wasn't too long

ago that I was on the streets alone, myself. Our owner died, and her son didn't want us. He stuck me and Ophelia in a box and dumped us out here. If I hadn't chewed my way out and found a place to stay, and if a different human hadn't found my sister before she had heat stroke . . . well, we would be dead now."

Rally bared his crooked teeth again. "And that's interesting to me because . . . ?"

Brandon hesitated, so Ophelia jumped in.

"Our human, Ruby, is really nice," she explained. "And we live in a nice place, too. We have our own courtyard, and we get extra snacks. So maybe, if you're tired of living on the streets, you might want to come home with us."

"Come home . . . with you?"

The terrier stared at them in amazement; then he threw back his wiry head and gave a howl of laughter.

"That's a good one, cat. What makes you think I'd want to do that?"

"Maybe because you're lonely without your friends," Brandon replied for her. "Or maybe you're hungry. Or maybe you're scared —"

"Oh, for kibble's sake," Ophelia spat, cutting him short. "He obviously isn't interested in our offer. This was a bad idea.

Leave the stupid canine where he is, and let's go home."

Not waiting for either one's reply, she stomped over to where Zuki waited. She glanced over her shoulder in time to see Brandon shake his head and come trotting up to join her and the pit bull.

"You tried," she told him in a softer tone. "That's all you can do."

But as they continued down the sidewalk and onto the next block, she thought she could hear the *snick, snick, snick* of nails on concrete behind them. She gave Brandon a nudge and whispered, "We're being followed."

He nodded. As if on cue, all three of them halted.

So did the *snick, snick* sound.

Smothering a smile behind her paw, she started walking again, flanked by Brandon and Zuki. The pattern continued for the rest of their journey home, the sound of pawsteps stopping and starting whenever the three of them stopped and started. By the time they reached the Botanica, however, Rally had dropped all pretense of subtlety. They stopped in front of the house and turned to see him strolling up to join them.

"I didn't say I wasn't interested," the terrier said, resuming the conversation as if it hadn't been cut short. He glanced about and nodded. "Kinda small, but I've seen worse. Maybe I'll stick around out here tonight and think about it. You know, just in case I get bored with that whole street warrior thing."

"Sure," Zuki said. "I can bring a little midnight snack for you, if you like."

The trio slipped back through the door in the wooden gate, leaving it propped open long enough for Zuki to sneak into the kitchen and carry out a couple of bone-shaped biscuits she'd been saving for later.

Setting the treats beside Rally, who gave an audible gulp but pretended not to notice them, she said, "See you in the morning."

"Maybe," the terrier replied, giving a little growl.

Probably so that they didn't think he was *too* grateful, Ophelia told herself.

And, apparently, he wasn't impressed enough with the place to stick around after all. The next morning, following her walk with Ruby, Zuki reported back to Brandon and Ophelia that there was no sign of the terrier.

"Though he did eat the dog biscuits," she added. "I guess if he changes his mind again, he knows where to find us."

"He's a grown-up canine," Ophelia said

with a shrug. "He knows how to take care of himself."

Though she was a bit disappointed not to see Rally waiting there. His visit would be a distraction from worry over what they'd learned the previous night. And even though, like her brother, she'd decided to give up detecting, she couldn't help but worry over Luis and what bad things he might have done. Brandon didn't say anything, but she could tell from his expression and the way he'd ignored the roosters that he was feeling much the same as she.

Still, the morning passed uneventfully. Ruby had been surprised and happy to see Brandon again, showering him with kisses and praising him for his cleverness.

"So I guess you decided you liked us best," she'd told him with a big smile. Even better, she seemed not to care when he enthusiastically rubbed his head against her cheek and knocked her glasses askew.

"I don't blame you," she went on, brushing black fur off her pink T-shirt with its picture of a lady with a crown holding a big stick in one hand and a flower in the other.

Queen of Wands Tarot card, Ophelia knew. Even better, in that picture she had a black feline seated nearby her.

"I mean, the guy couldn't even think of a

more original name for you than Blackie," Ruby went on. "But we'll keep your return on the down-low, okay? Last thing we need is word to get back to Mr. Pawn Shop that you're here."

And all went per Ruby's plan . . . that was, until it was almost time for their noon snack. Ophelia and Brandon had moved back inside the Botanica again to escape the noise of the roosters' fighting over a fresh crop of bugs they'd found in one of the planter boxes. The two felines were lounging on the register counter near Ruby, who was writing up what she called "inventory." Zuki was lying next to the pair of plaster dogs that were part of the life-sized statue of St. Lazarus, looking rather saintly herself.

Then the bells on the front door gave a violent jangle, disrupting the Southwestern flute music Ruby had playing for background ambiance. Zuki scrambled to her paws and gave a warning woof. Her warning didn't come soon enough, however.

The PAWN human, Luis, was striding into the store. He spied them at the register and pointed at Ruby, light glinting off the big signet ring he wore on that finger. In an outraged voice, he said, "I knew it! Someone kidnapped my cat last night, and that person is you."

NINETEEN

Ruby's first instinct at hearing Luis's accusation was to grab Brandon and clutch him to her, which she did. He gave a little squeak of surprise but fortunately didn't try to wriggle away.

"I didn't kidnap him," she protested in an offended tone. "When I got up this morning to feed the other animals, Brandon was with them. Apparently, he decided he *still* didn't like living with you. The fact that he keeps running away from you is hardly my fault."

"That's your story," Luis countered, expression still outraged. "I bet if I check my security cameras, I'll see you lurking around outside my shop with a can of tuna trying to lure him into your car."

"Seriously? That's insane. Now, I'm going to have to ask you to leave my shop."

"I'll be glad to . . . once you give me back my cat."

Time to break out the big guns.

Still holding Brandon tight, Ruby gestured at the stern portrait of Rosa behind her. "Dude, you live in this area. You *do* know who my sister, Rosa López Famosa, is, don't you?"

The question had worked before when she'd felt uneasy with someone off the street . . . mostly the substance-impaired, or those obviously scoping out shoplifting opportunities. Of course, she'd already surmised that Luis was a skeptic when it came to anything smacking of the spiritual. Still, there was the old expression about there being no atheists in a foxhole that kind of applied. She'd found that even those who professed not to believe in curses usually figured there was no point in taking any chances on being on the receiving end of same.

Luis's reaction to the Rosa revelation, however, wasn't quite what she expected. He took one look at the oil painting and chuckled in genuine amusement.

"*That's* your sister? No offense, but I'm not seeing much family resemblance. She's got that warrior queen look going, and you . . . well, don't."

Was that supposed to be an insult?

"Same mom, two different dads," she loftily replied, "not that it's any of your business. And she's a fully initiated Santera, as you can see by how she's dressed. I wouldn't laugh about that."

"I'm not laughing," he countered with a grin that said they both knew he was lying. With a glance down at Zuki, who was quiet but standing at full attention, he went on. "So the other day, you tried to sic your dog on me. Now you're threatening to have your sister put a curse on me. Who're you going to send after me next?"

"Hell-oooo . . ."

The familiar greeting accompanied by the jangling bells of the shop's front door made Ruby sigh in relief. Setting Brandon back down on the counter, she called, "Hi, JoJo. We're here at the register."

JoJo came briskly down the aisle, designer high heels clicking against the tile floor. Since it was a workday, she was dressed in her usual Florida version of a power suit: short skirt and fitted jacket, this time in a lime sherbet shade, beneath which she wore a paisley silk tank top. In one hand, she held a takeout bag; under the other arm, she had half a dozen thick, glossy-paged magazines.

JoJo stopped short when she noticed Luis standing there. She gave him a quick once-over, then turned her attention to Ruby.

"Sorry, Rubes, I didn't realize you had any customers right now. I didn't see any cars in the front spots. How about I go out to the courtyard and wait until you're finished?"

"That's okay, Luis was just leaving," Ruby replied with a pointed look at the man. "Oh, but before he takes off, I should introduce you two. Luis, this is my friend, Johanna Jones. *Attorney* Johanna Jones, to be precise. JoJo, this is Luis. He works at the pawn shop a few blocks from here."

"Nice to meet you," JoJo said, setting the magazines down on the counter and sticking out her hand. As they briefly shook, she asked, "So, did you get one of Ruby's fab Tarot card readings today?"

"No, actually, we were exchanging tips on cat care." He gave Ruby his own pointed look and added, "I have a cat, but he keeps running off."

JoJo frowned as she set the takeout bag down next to the magazines on the counter. "That's too bad. Seriously, you really should keep your cat indoors at all times. There's too many things that can happen to them if they're out on the street."

"JoJo's really big on animal rights," Ruby interjected. With a deliberately sweet smile, she added, "She even does pro bono work for some of the local animal rescues when they need legal help to remove an abused animal from a bad situation."

"Somehow, I'm not surprised to hear that," was Luis's dry reply.

JoJo gave an "aw shucks" smile and shrug and then pointed to the takeout bag. "I brought plenty. Do you want to join us?"

"He can't," Ruby broke in before Luis could reply. "He's got lots of work to do at the pawn shop. Besides" — she reached for JoJo's magazines and held up one so he could see the cover — "I'm going to be helping my bestie here with wedding dress suggestions. He'd probably be bored listening to that."

As she'd hoped, the sight of the bridal magazine worked on the man like a crucifix on a vampire. Luis took a step back, hands raised and palms out in a deflecting gesture.

"Score one for the psychic," he said, tone wry. "Thanks, Ms. Jones, but I'll pass."

Then, when Ruby thought he was going to leave without further incident, he glanced back at her.

"So, *Rubes,*" he continued, deliberately using JoJo's nickname for her, "how about I come back later this afternoon so we can finish our conversation?"

"Sorry, I've got readings scheduled all

afternoon. Besides, won't your boss be wondering about you?"

"Well, it just so happens I *am* the boss."

He paused and pulled a business card out of his shorts pocket, setting it down on the counter. Ruby pushed her glasses back into place and took a quick look at the slightly creased bit of gold cardboard. Sure enough, along with the logo and address, the card had his name — *Luis Ortiz* — and beneath that the word *owner.*

"So maybe I'll stop by later, anyhow, just in case you have a cancellation."

With that, he reached over to give Brandon a scritch under his chin, and then he strolled out.

"Wowza!" JoJo exclaimed as the bells jangled and the door closed after him. "I wonder if anyone's ever told him that he looks like Robert Downey, Jr.?"

At Ruby's snort, she grinned and shook her hand like she'd burned it. "Seriously, I can't believe you haven't told me about this guy before. If I didn't already have a hot fiancé of my own, I'd be down at that pawnshop every day trying to redeem my ticket . . . if you know what I mean."

"Not so fast," Ruby countered with a roll of her eyes.

She hurried around the counter and

locked the front door, then returned to the counter and picked up the takeout bag. "Grab the magazines and come into the kitchen, and I'll tell you all about him."

Ophelia waited until Ruby and JoJo were settled in the kitchen; then she whispered to the others, "Quick, outside to the courtyard."

A few moments later, they were gathered in their usual spot near the koi pond. Ophelia jumped onto the ledge for a quick look in the water. *No Philomena . . .* at least, not that she could see.

"What am I going to do?" Brandon asked in alarm, ears flat. "Luis knows I'm here now. What if he tries to make Ruby send me back?"

"He won't," Ophelia said with more assurance than she felt. "You heard how Ruby talked about JoJo. Now Luis knows she's a law person. If he tries to take you away, Ruby and JoJo will send him to court!"

Not that she was exactly sure what that meant, or how "court" actually worked. But the words seemed to make Brandon feel better, for his ears popped back up to normal again.

Zuki, too, appeared relieved.

"I was worried I was going to have to bite

him," she confessed, "and then they would have taken me away, too. But we'd better listen carefully when he comes back again, in case he tries to trick Ruby while JoJo's not around. He's pretty smart."

"We should take turns being lookout," Ophelia suggested. "And when we see him coming back, we all need to find hiding places where we can watch but he can't see us. Especially Brandon."

"I know a good place," he agreed. "And as soon as Ruby and JoJo are finished with lunch, I'll be the first lookout."

"You ask me, that's pretty messed up," JoJo declared. Poking a critical finger at the bridal magazine page she was scanning, the blonde went on. "Ruffles, on top of lace, on top of beading, on top of more ruffles. Seriously, it looks like a drunken fairy godmother barfed up a dress."

"Definitely goes in the *no freaking way* pile," Ruby agreed with a grin. Then, sobering, she added, "But that's not what I was asking about, and you know it. Now that you've heard the whole story, what's your take on this situation with our not-so-friendly neighborhood pawnshop owner?"

Telling the story had taken some time. They'd first split the veggie calzone with plenty of marinara that JoJo had brought. Then, while her friend leafed through the bridal magazines, Ruby had relayed the details about her initial meeting with Luis.

JoJo had been as shocked as she to learn that Luciana was his aunt, and dutifully outraged when Ruby explained how he'd accused her of scamming the dead woman. Ruby went on to admit that, after the initial bad blood, they'd seemed to come to an understanding — *heck, he even apologized for being a jerk.* That was, until he saw Brandon lounging on a shelf. At which point, Luis had claimed she'd stolen the feline from him and then essentially cat-napped Brandon back.

Though the last laugh had been on the pawnshop owner, Ruby pointed out, since Brandon had decided he preferred living with Ruby and found his way back to the Botanica again.

"Well, that's all pretty messed up, too," JoJo now conceded. "But I think as far as Brandon, you're okay. When you adopted Ophelia, you asked the shelter to notify you if her brother showed up. Since Mr. Givens already relinquished ownership, you were at the top of the list for adoption if Brandon was found. If Luis gives you any more flack about it, I'll have one of my rescue friends pay him a visit and explain the county laws about animal adoption."

Ruby sighed. "I'd appreciate that. But in the meantime, what if he shows up again this afternoon, like he said?"

"I doubt he'll try anything. Besides, doesn't Rosa have cameras in the shop?"

"Yeah, but they're the fake kind — you know, just to make people think they're being recorded."

JoJo rolled her eyes and muttered a few things to herself about *cheap* and *being sorry.*

To Ruby, she said, "Well, it wouldn't hurt to make a comment about the cameras being there. He won't know they're bogus. But the main thing is, he'll be guessing that you've already dished all the dirt about him to me . . . which you have. He'll know that if you go missing, his name is the one I'll give to the cops."

"Hey! That's not exactly the reassurance I was looking for."

JoJo grinned and shrugged. "Sorry, Rubes, I was only kidding. If he does come back, you've got Zuki as a first line of defense. And if that's not enough, if you feel too uncomfortable, just whip out that cell phone and call 911."

"Actually," Ruby replied with a cool smile,

"I have a better idea. Let me grab a deck. I'm going to pull a few cards and see what Madame Tarot has to say about Mr. Luis Ortiz."

Brandon's shift at the front window had ended, and Ophelia had just taken over when she saw a familiar black truck pulling into one of the front parking spaces.

"It's him . . . the PAWN human," she softly yowled. "Zuki, warn Ruby. Brandon, time to hide!"

The pit bull gave a few swift barks, startling the two Haitian women who were busy filling little bags with dried bits of plants that smelled good — *herbs,* Ophelia knew that Ruby called them. She saw in relief that Ruby was smart enough to know what the canine was saying, for she replied "Good girl" to the canine.

To the humans, Ruby explained, "No worries, ladies. I think it's just an ex-boyfriend stopping by. My dog doesn't approve."

The pair smiled and made comments about how animals always *knew;* still, they hurriedly finished their selections and came to the counter to pay. Ophelia, meanwhile, found Brandon snoozing on a shelf beside the boxes of seashells.

"Get up," she hissed and gave him a poke.

"Luis is back."

He immediately rose and padded toward the double-sided shelf nearest the register. The back half of it was filled with bagged shirts and dresses and other human apparel. The front half facing Ruby's counter was filled with reference books of various sizes and shapes. Brandon didn't hesitate but jumped up onto the piles of clothes — a strict *no-no* at any other time — and climbed over them and into the gap between bags and books.

"Clever," Ophelia purred in approval as she hurriedly followed her brother, leaving Zuki to take up position in front of the register.

The shelf with the books was far wider than most of the volumes were deep. That meant there was plenty of room for two cats to crouch behind them if they squeezed themselves into tight balls. And the books made a fine wall, with the short ones leaving holes like little windows that they could peer through, giving them a good view of the action without being seen.

By the time they had settled into place, the bells on the front door were jangling and Ruby was finishing ringing up her customers. The quiet drum and chant music that Ruby was playing in the background kept Ophelia from hearing any footsteps. Even so, she knew Luis was headed toward them from the way all three women looked in that direction, moving their heads as they followed his progress through the aisles.

The older of the two female customers leaned closer to the counter. She had long black fur worn in tiny braids, just like Shanice at the shelter did, though hers had little colored balls tangled in with the fur. Ophelia immediately approved of her.

"Baby, you want we should stick around for a minute?" the woman asked in a voice loud enough for everyone — including the PAWN human — to hear.

Ophelia saw Ruby smile.

"Thanks, but no need. This is a very secure shop. We've got cameras and every-thing," she replied, nodding toward one of the black plastic things with a big glass eye mounted high in the corner behind her. "Plus I've got my dog, Zuki."

"That sweet little thing?" the woman asked, earning a happy wriggle of her butt from the canine. Then, realizing what she'd said, the woman corrected herself. "I mean, she do look like a fierce dog. I bet she bites and everything."

"Only when someone deserves it." She put the women's herbs and one of her business cards into a bigger bag and handed it to the female with braids. "Thanks, ladies. Please come back soon."

The two women started for the door, though each one gave the PAWN human a good looking at as they went by him, like he was a particularly unappealing mouse. Or, rather, *rat!* He didn't say anything to Ruby, however, until they had gone out the door. Then he gave her a rat-like smile and said, "Cameras?"

She nodded. "Of course. We like to keep track of who comes and goes here."

He shrugged and made a rude snorting sound. "Not disagreeing . . . but, seriously, those have to be the worst fakes I've ever seen."

Then, as Ruby got the bristly look, like Brandon's tail, the man added, "Look, I've got a couple of sets of security cameras for sale at the shop that are brand new in the box. You want 'em, price is half off retail. I'll even help you set them up."

Ophelia and Brandon exchanged glances. "He's being nice," she hissed. "I wonder why?"

Ruby had to be thinking the same thing, Ophelia realized, for her expression was one of confusion. "Uh, sure. Maybe. I'll have to check in with my sister next time she calls.

But why — ?"

"Why am I being nice?" He shrugged. "I thought about it, and if the gato, er, Brandon, would rather stay here with his sister, who am I to break up a family? Besides, your lawyer friend is right. It's too dangerous for him running around the streets. He might get hit or something."

"Thanks," Ruby replied. "That's very . . . understanding of you."

"Sure, whatever. But that's not the whole reason. The other part is, I need a favor from you."

A favor? Ophelia and Brandon exchanged looks again.

"He's trying to trick her," Brandon whispered, getting the faintest woof of agreement from Zuki.

Ophelia nodded. "Probably," she whispered back. "Do you think Ruby knows that?"

But even as she asked the question, the expression on Ruby's face told her that she did. In fact, it was obvious that she trusted Luis about as much as they did . . . which was as far as you could toss a mouse. Which is why Ophelia was shocked when she heard Ruby say, "Sure, what's the favor?"

With those words, Ruby crossed her arms

and tilted her head in an exaggerated listening pose, waiting for his reply. How she'd manage not to gasp or faint or something, she didn't know. But better that she keep him off balance, at least until she had some idea of where this conversation was leading.

She was gratified, however, to see that the guy looked a little surprised himself. Obviously, he hadn't expected it to be that easy. She smiled inwardly as he cleared his throat and shuffled his feet a moment.

Ball's in your court, LEW-is.

Then he said, "Look, I've been trying to get hold of Terrence Givens since my aunt died. I want to clear out her things and send them to my mother up in Cleveland. He finally called me back and agreed I could come by tonight. Thing is, I still don't trust his story about what happened to Aunt Lu. I want to do a little poking around while I'm there, but I need someone to distract him."

"Meaning, someone like me?"

"Well, I could bring along Tomas, or Big Mike, or DeWayne, but that probably would make Givens nervous. You, on the other hand, would not."

He paused again and looked her up and down. "Well, except you've got that blue streak in your hair. Maybe you could put on

345

a ballcap or something? And try not to dress so hippy-dippy?"

Hippy-dippy? True, she was wearing a Tarot-themed T-shirt over batik print jeans, but that was hardly the most extreme outfit she wore on the job.

She gave him a look, but otherwise let his words dangle there a moment. Finally, she replied, "Let me see if I understand you. You'll let me keep my cat, Brandon, if I'll work as your decoy while you poke around on a Palm Beach estate. Does that about cover it?"

"Hey, I said I'd give you a deal on the security cameras, too. So how about it?"

"I don't know. I already had plans to meet friends tonight for dinner at the brew pub. It would be pretty rude to cancel on them last minute."

Not that he needed to know that the meeting was actually her regular weekly study night with some of her classmates . . . something she could beg off, if she needed to do so. And she was uncomfortable enough over the circumstances of Luciana's death that she wouldn't mind poking around a bit herself. Not that she had any clue as to what they might find.

But if her particular task was to be distraction, she *did* have an idea of how to go about that.

"So I'll throw in dinner too," he countered. "We have a deal?"

She glanced over the counter at Zuki, who was still patiently on alert. "I'll do it but only if we add one more condition. My dog comes along with us."

He shook his head in disbelief but said, "Fine . . . except she rides in the bed, not in the cab. I don't want her getting nervous halfway there and taking a bite out of me, and I sure don't want her leaving white hair all over my black upholstery."

Then, when Ruby would have protested, he added, "Don't worry, the bed has a camper top, so she'll be safe back there. So if that works for you, I'll pick you up at seven."

He didn't wait for her okay but headed toward the door again. But before he walked out, he called over his shoulder, "Don't forget the ballcap, okay?"

TWENTY

"How are you going to get into the truck?" Zuki wanted to know. "You'll have to run out where they might see you jump in. And you know if Ruby spots you, she won't let you come along."

"We'll figure out something," Ophelia assured her, while Brandon nodded his own agreement. "Because no way are we letting Ruby drive off with the PAWN human without all of us coming along to guard her."

For, even though Luis had claimed that he was going to let Brandon remain at the Botanica, no way did she believe him . . . not with that picture of a rat painted on his arm! Dumb fish or not, Philomena had been proven correct enough times that Ophelia wasn't going to doubt her again. And she wouldn't put it past Luis to somehow be making secret plans with the son to do more bad things.

And to cover up bad things, she thought

with a shiver, remembering the broken light on the front of the picking up truck.

"All right," Zuki agreed with a sigh. "It's almost time for him to be here. I'll go fix the gate so you can get in and out."

While the pit bull went to handle that part of the night's plan, Ophelia and Brandon trotted upstairs to check on Ruby. They found her already changed into new clothing: plain jeans and a black T-shirt and a gray version of what the humans called a "hoodie."

Spying the pair, Ruby grinned and said, "Hey, kitties, your buddy Luis thinks I need to wear a ballcap. You think he'll be okay with this?"

She reached behind the bedroom door, where many of her toys were hanging on hooks. She grabbed a pink hat that stuck out in front like a duck's bill and plopped it on her head, then turned so the felines could better see it. Sparkly little rocks on the top part made a word picture that Ophelia tried to spell out.

B-i-t . . .

She frowned in confusion as she finished reading, then exchanged confused looks with Brandon. Why would Ruby wear a hat that called her a canine?

Ruby must have come to the same conclusion, for she pulled it off and tossed it onto her bed.

"You're right, kitties. Wrong place, wrong people for that one. We'll stick with something nondescript."

Another hat in that same style was hanging on the back of the door. This one was blue and looked like it was made from the same cloth as her jeans. Instead of sparkly letters, it had the face of a mean-looking owl on it. Ophelia knew from another shirt and a coffee cup of Ruby's that the owl had to do with her school place.

Ruby twisted her hair up and stuck the hat on top of her head, then looked at herself in the mirror.

"Perfect," she declared. "No blue streak showing, just a little FAU school spirit. Nothing to offend . . . unless you hate the Owls."

To the cats, she said, "All right, you two. Zuki is coming with me tonight, so that means you two are in charge of things. You've already had your dinner, so I expect you to play nicely while we're gone."

She picked up a small version of her usual backpack, and the three of them headed downstairs again. Zuki was waiting at the door leading from the hallway to the shop. The pit bull gave the two cats a faint woof to indicate *mission accomplished.*

"You about ready, girl?" Ruby asked the dog, reaching around the kitchen doorway for Zuki's leash and tote bag. "Let's lock up now and wait for him out front."

Ophelia and Brandon waited until the two were outside and they heard the key in the front door click to lock it; then the two felines rushed down the hall and out the pet door into the courtyard.

The three roosters were already in their cages for the night. In sleepy voices, they asked,

"Where."

"Are."

"You."

"Two."

"Going."

"Now?"

"We're helping Ruby with something important," Ophelia whispered as they rushed past. "You're in charge while we're gone."

"We."

"Are."

"Boss?"

They answered their own question with a soft chorus of triumphant crowing that promptly cut off when Brandon and Ophelia both hissed the command *Quiet!* Leaving the roosters to their grumbling, the pair trotted down the side yard and crawled beneath the potting table. The pet door was propped open with a rock, courtesy of Zuki. Peeking out first to make sure the coast was clear, they slipped out and took up position at the corner of the house.

Since it was already mostly dark out — at least, to human eyes — the streetlight near the Botanica was lit, throwing a yellow glow on Ruby and Zuki. The latter cocked her blocky white head, obviously hearing the two felines. The three parking slots in front of the Botanica were empty right now, but Ophelia could see down the next block a single crooked headlight driving in their direction.

"That must be Luis's truck," Brandon whispered. "Get ready."

"For what?" a voice growled from the shadows beside them.

Ophelia and Brandon both jumped. The pair swung about with claws and teeth bared, only to see a familiar small fuzzy figure sitting on the nearby sidewalk, hind legs jauntily shifted to one side.

"Rally!" Ophelia yowled. "What are you doing here? We thought you'd gone away."

The terrier got to his paws and shrugged. "Eh, I decided to come back tonight in case

Zuki had some extra dog biscuits to share," he said, trotting over to them. "So, what are you waiting for?"

"The human in that picking up truck coming toward us . . . he's going to take Ruby and Zuki to our old house. We're going to sneak into the truck and go along with them."

"Hmmm . . . I have to say that biscuits sound better."

By now, the picking up truck was pulling in — not into a single slot, Ophelia saw, but parking across all three spaces. That meant the front of the truck was facing them, which also meant they'd have to run all the way past the passenger side without being spotted.

Ophelia gave Brandon a swift nudge. He glanced from her to Rally, and nodded.

"How about if we give you those biscuits when we get back?" Brandon hurriedly suggested. "But in return, we need a little help."

He whispered in the terrier's ear. Rally listened, and shrugged again. "I guess . . . whatev."

"All right, get ready," Brandon replied.

They watched as Luis stopped the truck, leaving it still running as he got out. He was dressed much like Ruby, the rat picture on his arm covered now with his shirt sleeve.

"Ready to go?" he asked her without preamble.

Ruby nodded. She had Zuki on the leash and was walking her around to the back of the truck while Luis lowered the tailgate. The pit bull gave an anxious look in their direction, and Ophelia popped out of the shadows long enough to give her canine friend an encouraging nod.

Don't worry. We've got this.

Zuki nodded back and bounded into the truck bed. At that, Brandon turned to Rally. "You're on. Make it good."

"Watch and learn, feline," the terrier growled back, and then gave a sharp, high-pitched whine of a bark.

Ruby had been concentrating on loading Zuki, but now her head shot up. Staring toward the front of the truck, she asked Luis, "Did you hear that?"

"Yeah. It sounded like a dog. There it is again."

For Rally had let loose another cry, this one even more high-pitched. As Luis shut the tailgate, Rally went into action. Rear paw held high, as if it had been injured, he hobbled on three legs into the headlight beam, giving a little shriek with each step.

"Look in front of the truck," Ruby exclaimed. "Poor little thing . . . it's hurt. Luis, we have to catch it."

"And do what with it?"

"I don't know — take it to the emergency vet? C'mon!"

Giving Zuki a quick pat, Ruby hurried toward where the terrier stood. Luis followed more slowly, shaking his head. Rally, meanwhile, was letting loose with pitiful little yips, backing away as Ruby moved closer.

Brandon gave a quick purr of appreciation. "He's pretty clever for a canine. Now, get ready. As soon as he lures them a bit farther away, we'll make a run for it."

"I've almost got him," Ruby called back to Luis as Rally halted to let her get within a few feet of him.

Luis had moved in front of the truck, too, though he was obviously letting Ruby do the hard work. "You better watch out," he warned. "You try to pick up a hurt dog, he might bite you."

"I'll get him by the collar, first, and then I'll see if he'll let me pick him up." To the dog, she said, "C'mon, little guy. Let me and Luis help you. Let me get just one more step closer, and — son of a gun!"

As Ruby bent toward him, Rally gave a sudden, loud bark and skittered backward. Then, all four legs suddenly functional and churning, he spun and went running down the street away from the humans.

"Now!" Brandon softly yowled.

With Ruby and Luis's attention fixed on the terrier, he and Ophelia took off like shadowy rockets. They raced past the truck and around to the back of it, bounding through the open camper top and into the bed, where Zuki waited.

"Good plan," the pit bull softly exclaimed, tongue lolling as she gave a wide canine grin. "I was watching through the back windshield. Rally should be a stunt dog in the movies!"

"Well, we did have to bribe him with more of your biscuits," Ophelia confessed. "He'll be waiting for them when we get back."

Then, hurrying to look through the back windshield and out the front, she added, "I think the humans have given up on chasing him. Look, they're coming back. We'd better stay low until we're driving."

Taking time to give each other a soft, congratulatory bump of their heads, she and Brandon crouched beneath the drop cloth which was still there from the previous time. Paws crossed for luck, they waited for Luis to drive off.

"Poor little dog," Ruby said as Luis held

the truck door open while she climbed inside. "I haven't seen him around before. Someone must have just dumped him."

"Don't worry, I doubt he went far," Luis replied as he closed the door after her. Talking through the open window, he added, "If you're lucky, he'll be waiting here when we get back."

That last was said with an obvious bit of sarcasm, but Ruby refused to bite. If the injured pup was still there later that night, she'd try again to catch him. Though the way he'd taken off when she'd attempted to grab him, he couldn't have been hurt *that* badly, she thought with a wry smile. Maybe she could contain him in the courtyard until morning when she could contact one of Jo-Jo's rescue friends to pick him up.

"Yeah, well, if nothing else, I'll see if I can help the poor fellow find a new home."

"Good luck with that. I like dogs and all, but that mutt is butt-ugly."

"Aw, I thought he was cute with that underbite."

Luis rolled his eyes but made no comment as he started around to his side of the truck. After a glance back in the bed to make sure Zuki was okay, she gave the interior a quick once-over.

It was in pretty decent shape for what apparently was a working truck, with bucket seats that were clean and rip-free. Unlike the vehicles of numerous single males she'd ridden with in the past, its passenger floorboard didn't serve as a trash can, though the interior *did* have a strong fast-food odor about it. An older model, it lacked the fancy built-in media center satellite radio and directional display. Instead, one of those portable GPS units was suction-cupped to the windshield.

In the time it took for her to make these observations, Luis had reached the driver's side and climbed inside. Putting the truck into gear, he pulled onto the street again. A block down, they hit a red light, and he took that opportunity to reach behind his seat.

Ruby froze.

Despite the lack of junk or bondage equipment or running chain saws inside the truck, once she'd climbed inside, she'd not been able to shake a feeling that something was slightly off. She couldn't put her finger on it. Maybe the truck rode funny, or the seat belt buckle was a little too hard to unfasten. But now, mental alarm bells were going off.

What was he reaching for? Guns? Knives? Rope?

She slid her hand into her mini backpack

and gripped her cell phone, ready to hit redial and send a panicked call to JoJo if things went sideways.

And then Luis dragged out a large paper sack stamped with a familiar fast food logo on it.

"Here," he said and handed the bag to her as the light turned green again.

The smell of fresh French fries and burgers abruptly assaulted her; hence, the fast food smell she'd noticed. Heaving a sigh of relief, she asked, "What's this?"

"I promised you dinner," he said with a shrug. "We're kind of on a tight schedule, so I got it to go. You've got your choice of a burger with the works, or else a chicken sandwich, plus fries. Oh, and there are large diet colas in the console between us."

"Uh, thanks?"

Feeling like an idiot now, she opted for the chicken. He ate his burger with one hand while steering with the other. He'd finished it off by the time they reached the next red light, where he took the bag back from her. He dumped both large containers of fries into it and stuck the cardboard containers behind the seat again. That accomplished, he set the bag on the armrest between them and reached into the bag for a handful.

"Easier this way."

"Yeah, easier," she mumbled through a mouthful of grilled chicken and bun. She took a token fry from the bag and left the rest for him. The smell of fresh-cooked fries was hard to resist, but the whole sharing-from-a-bag routine seemed a bit too intimate, given their decided lack of a relationship. And, her recent fear of kidnapping/murder.

As the light changed again, he glanced over at her.

"You look good. Uh, I mean, appropriate. You know, for what we're doing tonight."

Sounding a bit uncomfortable, he jumped to a change of subject. Indicating her ballcap, he said, "So you're an Owl? Me too. When did you graduate from FAU?"

"I got my BA four years ago, but I'm back now working on my master's in English Lit. I'm kind of taking the slow track."

He appeared a little surprised as he smiled. "Yeah, I know what you mean. It took me almost three years to get my MBA since I was taking all night classes."

"Well, uh, if you were working full-time, that's not surprising," she replied, trying not to sound as shocked as she felt.

MBA? Though, of course, any number of small business owners in this day and age had an advanced degree. Just because his business happened to be a pawnshop, she shouldn't have made the assumption he wasn't as educated as she.

Feeling a bit chastened by that — though, to be fair, he'd seemed equally surprised by her revelation — she took another fry as a symbolic peace offering.

For his part, he grabbed a handful from the bag and asked, "So, what's with all the luggage?"

"This?" She held up the tote bag. "This is Zuki's traveling kit . . . you know, poop bags and toys and stuff. The other one is just my purse."

She set down the tote again and picked up her mini backpack. "I brought something along that might help us tonight," she went on, reaching inside it and pulling out her Rider-Waite deck.

He glanced at the box of cards and frowned before refocusing on the road. "What are you going to do, chuck it at Givens if he gives us any flack?"

"Actually, since you said I was the distraction member of our little team, I figured I'd give him a Tarot reading. That'll keep him occupied for a bit."

Then, in a confidential tone, she confessed, "And I kind of stacked the deck. I put all the scary-ass cards on top so I can do a little sleight-of-hand with the shuffle. I'll give him a reading guaranteed to leave him with guilty nightmares."

"Yeah, well, assuming he can even feel guilt. But good thinking." He gave an approving nod, then glanced her way again. "Actually, I'm surprised you haven't tried to do one of those Tarot readings for me."

"Oh. Well, I kind of thought you were a skeptic. You know, the type who thinks Tarot is a scam?"

"I told you I was sorry about that. And, I don't know, maybe it would be interesting to see what you come up with."

"Uh, sure, I could do that sometime."

What she wasn't going to say was that she already *had* done a Tarot reading about him. She hadn't lied when she'd told him that afternoon that she had readings scheduled the rest of the day. In fact, she'd been so busy with those clients that she didn't have time to do a full reading for herself. But with her favorite Morgan-Greer deck, she'd managed between appointments to do a little five-card spread of her own creation that she called *What Kind of Guy/Gal is He/ She Really?*

It was a basic spread, with the cards fittingly arranged in an arrowhead shape.

Starting from the left with the first card, the second card stair-stepped higher, as did the third — the literal "point" that the cards were making. The fourth and fifth cards stair-stepped back down again. Each asked its own question, which could then be interpreted as a whole.

How does the querent see himself? How do others see him? What's his true nature? What's his worst flaw? What's his greatest virtue?

To Ruby's mind, the results had been surprising, if fitting. The card answering the first question — *how does he see himself?* — had been the Nine of Wands. The image was that of a dark-haired, bearded man who was a regular foot soldier, not a nobleman. He was in profile and carrying a weapon, which he let balance back against his shoulder. Though less traditionally lethal than a sword, his wand — or in his case, more correctly a cudgel — could still get the job of fighting done. He was striding past a row of another eight wands planted in the ground like a forest, and seemingly was ignoring their presence.

Ruby had always read the Nine of Wands as the card of "keep on trying." It reflected someone always striving, and always beset by other challenges, but with the fortitude

to face them and persevere. Though, sometimes, it also meant someone needing to
leave the past behind and move on to new
things. From the little she knew of the man,
it again seemed an accurate portrayal,
though Luis himself would have to speak to
that interpretation. That was, if she ever
dared share it with him.

The second card, *how do others view him,*
had been equally appropriate: the Six of
Pentacles, or coins. This image featured
another man, though blond now and clean-
shaven, facing the viewer. In one hand, he
held a set of scales (for weighing gold,
perhaps?) while with the other he smilingly
doled out coins to disembodied grasping
hands. An accurate depiction of Luis's
job . . . and perhaps showing that people
accepted the face he presented to them?

The third card, dealing with his true
nature, had been a bit more unsettling: the
Knight of Swords. Here was another dark-
haired, mustachioed warrior in profile view.
His pose was similar to the more humble
man in the Nine of Wands, but this knight
balanced a sword rather than a stick against
his shoulder. In the background was the
blazing edifice that was the frightening
Tower card.

Disconcertingly, the knight's sword was

tinged red — maybe a reflection of the burning building being left behind, or maybe lingering traces of a vanquished enemy's blood? Either way, it was a card of action, signifying a man willing to rush into danger, not caring what obstacles lay in his path. Though, taken too far, it could also indicate someone ruthless, confrontational . . . someone rash, controlling.

Yeah, that's not Luis — not at all, she'd thought with a snort.

The fourth card had been the spread's only major arcana — the Chariot, but its position was upside-down, or reversed. The charioteer, with his six-pack abs of a chest protector, was driving alone, though he wore a crown reminiscent of a king. His expression was confident as he guided the two horses — one black, one white — that were hitched abreast to his chariot. But a closer look at the steeds showed they each were pulling away in opposite directions, rather than running straight and true. And the fact that the card was reversed seemed to underscore the likely trouble that this loss of discipline foretold.

This, then, reflected Luis's major flaw — someone wanting to be always in control, and uncomfortable when not. A man needing to be in the driver's seat at all times, and not happy when plans are changed on him. That, Ruby could easily see.

As for his greatest virtue, that card had interested Ruby the most. She'd smiled when she'd turned over the Ace of Pentacles. Somewhere, she'd once read that as a sign of occupations, this card was associated with — surprise — pawn shops! But there was more to it than that.

The card featured a disembodied hand reaching out of a fluffy white cloud and holding a single gold pentacle coin. Perhaps he was accepting it . . . or maybe he was giving the coin away. The card was ambiguous on that point. But, traditionally, the card reflected wealth and new beginnings. The latter was symbolized by a path beneath the clouds that led to an arch, which, in turn, led to a mountain and then to the ocean beyond. Definitely a card symbolic of an optimist.

She'd felt a little better once she'd interpreted that spread . . . but she'd been surprised to realize that her positive feelings had dissipated once she'd got into his truck. Why that was, she'd been wondering for the past several minutes. But now, as a car with a burned-out headlight came speeding from the opposite direction toward them, she abruptly realized why she'd been feeling uneasy.

While she'd tried to catch the stray dog that had shown up in front of the store, she'd also gotten a look at the front of Luis's truck. What she'd seen in the process hadn't sunk in, distracted as she'd been. But she wasn't distracted anymore.

No way, she sternly told herself. But she had to put the question out there. Because it was possible that she might have interpreted the cards incorrectly. After all, she was merely *Ruby Sparks, Tarot Card Reader Fairly Competent.*

And so she gathered all the food wrappers and containers and put them into the now-empty French fries bag. Then, praying she wasn't about to open a really horrible can of worms, she said, "So, Luis, I noticed your broken headlight. It looks like you had a little fender bender recently. What happened?"

Twenty-One

"The broken headlight?" Luis echoed, and muttered a few uncomplimentary things about an unknown person's lineage. "The hell if I know. When I came back from a run the night that my . . . the other night, the truck was fine. But sometime overnight, some idiot vandalized it, just for the hell of it, I guess. Busted out the light and scratched up the quarter panel, too."

Then he shot her a suspicious look. "Wait. You didn't think . . . you weren't wondering if . . ."

"No, no, not at all," Ruby hurried to reply.

But hadn't the news accounts said a witness saw a black pickup truck fleeing the scene of Luciana's death? Not that she truly believed Luis would have deliberately killed his own aunt. But it seemed oddly coincidental that his truck had ended up damaged in the same way as the hit-and-run driver's vehicle likely was . . . and apparently that very same night.

They had just driven over the bridge to Palm Beach and were approaching the familiar guard house. Luis slowed the pickup, pulling in behind a small silver BMW already in the guest queue, while a black Ferrari slid past the automatic gate in the resident lane. He threw the truck into park and turned to her.

"Look, we'd better both get on the same page before we reach the Givens estate," he clipped out, shooting her an irritated look. "Here's a few things you should know. First, Aunt Lu was as much a mother to me as my own mom was. And, second, if you checked out today's news report, you'd see the cops figured out from the broken headlight pieces that the hit-and-run vehicle was a Chevy pickup."

He paused and pointed to the logo on the truck's horn. "This is a Ford."

"Oh. That's good. Really good."

Ruby sighed, feeling equal parts foolish and relieved. Not that she really had thought Louis might have been responsible for Luciana's death, but this was South Florida. The newspapers were filled with accounts of family members killing family members over burnt steaks, a lost remote control, a borrowed twenty dollars not repaid. This not to mention the surprising number of husbands and wives hiring hit men to kill their respective spouses.

"All right, so that's settled," he replied. "Anything else on your mind?"

Ruby took a deep breath and pushed her glasses back into place. She still hadn't told him why Luciana had come to the Botanica for a Tarot reading in the first place. It was probably time to break the Tarot reader-client privilege and let him know about his aunt's suspicions.

"There's something you should know before we get there," she began. "Luciana had a specific reason she wanted me to read the cards for her. She suspected that old Mrs. Givens didn't accidentally fall into the swimming pool and drown, like the ME ruled. She was afraid that Mr. Givens killed his mother and made it look like an accident . . . and she wanted the cards to tell her if that was the case."

"She what?" Luis gave Ruby an incredulous look. "Let me get this straight. Aunt Lu thought Givens offed his own mother, and instead of going to the cops with what she knew, she went to a Tarot card reader?"

"That was the problem," Ruby explained. "She didn't have any sort of evidence she could bring to the police, just a gut feeling.

She was hoping to learn something from the cards."

"Uh-huh. And did *the cards*" — he gave those last two words air quotes — "shed any light on all this?"

"Nothing about *murder,*" she replied, giving him air quotes back. "But the reading did point to conflict between the mother and son, and the fact he was a sneaky little so-and-so. Oh, and there were some sort of money issues going on. Maybe he was spending like crazy and she was trying to rein him in."

Luis's expression turned a bit thoughtful at that. "You might have a point. If Givens was hurting for cash, helping his rich, elderly mother have a fatal accident could fatten up his wallet in a hurry."

"Actually, that couldn't have been a motive. From what Luciana said, he already had his own money from his late father. Everything else belonged to Mrs. Givens, and she changed her will so everything of hers was going to charity upon her death. Luciana was one of the witnesses to the document."

"So it wouldn't have done Givens any good to kill her, since he wasn't going to inherit anything," Luis finished for her.

Ruby nodded. "Exactly . . . and Luciana

understood that. But she knew that the mother and son didn't get along, and she just had a bad feeling about the whole situation. Apparently Mrs. Givens had been an Olympic swimmer back in her youth, so your aunt thought it didn't make sense the old woman would die by drowning."

"Right, but the police said Mrs. Givens fell and hit her head first, before she ended up in the pool." Luis sighed. "I always told Aunt Lu she watched too many telenovelas. I think she was drumming up a bunch of drama here."

He looked like he would say more, but the guard arm blocking the BMW had opened and the car began pulling away. Putting the truck into gear again, Luis eased the vehicle up to the spot opposite the guard house door. A uniformed man with a clipboard peered out.

Ugh. It had to be Mr. Unknown Comic, Ruby thought with a grimace, recognizing him as the same pot-bellied guard who'd been on duty the night of the bridal shower.

"Hey, Luis," the man exclaimed. "I heard you lost your aunt in a traffic accident the other night. I'm real sorry about that."

"Thanks, George. I have to say, it was a pretty big shock. They still haven't found the hit-and-run driver."

George shook his head. "Tough break. I sure hope it works out and they catch the SOB." Then, condolences out of the way, he bent and squinted toward the passenger seat where Ruby was sitting. "And who's the lady?"

"Hi," she said, taking off the ballcap and letting her blue-streaked hair tumble down. "It's me, the gypsy queen from the other night. Remember?"

"Heck, yeah, Ms. Ruby." He grinned and then winked at Luis. "I didn't know you two were an item. I guess that explains why she drove in after you the other night."

"Wait, what?" Ruby demanded.

She whipped about to stare through the rear window at Zuki, who grinned back at her, pink tongue lolling. She'd forgotten about the black pickup in front of her at the gatehouse that night . . . a pickup which, now that she thought of it, looked identical to Luis's. Except for that truck having a white pit bull who looked suspiciously like Zuki riding in its bed, and Luis didn't own a dog.

So either Zuki was out joyriding on her own at night, or Ruby had simply imagined seeing a dog that looked just like her in Luis's truck.

Luis, meanwhile, was shaking his head.

"No jumping to conclusions, boss. Ruby's just a friend helping me out. We're picking up my aunt's things from the Givens estate."

"Right, right. Mr. Givens called and put you on the list." He raised his clipboard and scanned the names, and then frowned. "But I don't see Ms. Ruby's name on here."

"She's kind of a last minute addition. It was going to take me too long to try to load everything by myself, so I asked Mr. Givens if I could bring help. He said it was okay, but I guess he forgot to tell you. You can call the guy and confirm it, if you want."

"Nah, no point in bothering the man. Besides, I've got her info on file already. Oh, and you might want to get that broken headlight fixed so you don't get a ticket."

With that last bit of advice, along with a jaunty wave, George hit the button to activate the gate arm. Luis rolled on through.

The gate arm dropped again behind them, and Ruby snorted as she twisted her hair back up and put on the ballcap again.

"I guess your friend George didn't notice Zuki in the back of the truck. I have a feeling she wasn't on the approved list. And I'm guessing you didn't clear me with Mr. Givens either."

"Yeah, I kind of forgot to do that. As far

as he's concerned, you work for me."

"You got it, boss."

They made the remaining short trip to the Givens house in silence. Luis pulled the truck into the drive, halting before an imposing wrought iron gate that reminded Ruby of Courtney's main entry. He leaned out the window to punch in a code on the gate access control box. It slid open, and they drove on in.

The grounds were subtly lit, as was the main house. *A definite old Florida feel,* she thought, taking in the vintage mission-style that conveyed both grandeur and understated good taste. It wasn't as imposing as Courtney's more recently built mansion that had been all glass and sleek marble columns, but Ruby preferred it to that more modern look. The only jarring touch was the ostentatious black sports sedan parked in front beneath the portico.

Luis slowly negotiated the cobbled driveway, the glare from the truck's single headlight wobbling through the tasteful tropical plantings that lined it. No doubt it was tough on him, making this one last visit, Ruby told herself.

"Her place is there at the back, near the garage," Luis said, tone subdued. "I imagine they've locked up her rooms. Givens will probably meet us there with a key."

On cue, the darkened servants' quarters abruptly blazed with light. Luis parked at the far side of the garage pad, which was as close as he could get to the tiny house's front door. A short cobbled path led the rest of the way.

"What about your dog?" he asked as they climbed from the truck. "Will she stay in the bed, do I need to lock her in the cab?"

"And risk getting white hair on your upholstery? Kidding," she clarified as he quirked a brow at her. "If I tell her to stay, she will."

Leaving her purse and bags in the cab but taking her phone, Ruby went around to the back. Zuki stuck her blocky head out from the camper top.

Ruby gave her a quick pat. "Good girl. Now, you stay while I go inside with Luis. Sit and stay."

The dog obediently sat. Giving her a final scratch behind the ears, Ruby turned and followed Luis to the guest house.

"Are they gone yet?" Ophelia whispered, sticking her head out beneath the drop cloth and looking about.

Zuki turned from where she was gazing out from the camper top and nodded.

"They just went inside. The coast is clear."

"Come on, then," Brandon said, crawling out to join Ophelia. Front paws planted on the tailgate's upper edge, he added, "We need to keep an eye on Ruby in case the son — or Luis — tries something."

"Uh, I can't go," the pit bull said, ears drooping. "Ruby told me to stay here."

"So?" Ophelia retorted with a flick of her long tail. "Just because a human says something doesn't mean it's a law."

"Maybe not for felines, but for canines . . . well, it's our job."

Zuki heaved a big sigh, and Ophelia rolled her green eyes. She knew the rules were different for dogs, but this was an emergency!

"This is an emergency," she told the pit bull in a stern tone. "If something goes wrong for Ruby, we'll need you there to be the muscle . . . and the teeth!"

"But if nothing goes wrong, and Ruby finds out I left the truck, she'll be mad . . . or sad. Besides, Luis said they're packing things. That means they'll be going back and forth bringing out boxes. They'll notice I'm gone right away!"

Brandon nodded. "She's got a point. And we'll need a look out for us, while we're looking out for Ruby. You know, just in case the son sneaks back outside again and tries to catch us. Besides, it's not like Zuki would be far away. One yowl from us and she'll come running to help. Right, Zuki?"

"Right. If there's trouble, all the rules go out the window," the pit bull declared, puffing her wide chest so she looked most formidable.

Ophelia gave her a playful head-butt. "Okay, we get it. Scary pit bull. But that's a good plan, too. We keep an eye on Ruby, and you keep an eye on everyone. Besides, like I always tell you, with that white fur you stick out in the dark like a sore paw."

Leaving Zuki on guard, the two cats lightly leapt from the truck and trotted down the familiar cobbled path toward Luciana's little house. The breeze from the nearby ocean was cool this night, and smelled like Ophelia remembered . . . like salt and fish and perfumy flowers. *Too bad Ruby couldn't live here instead of the son,* she longingly thought. Then everything would be almost like it used to be.

Almost.

The light from the windows was bright, and she had to squint as she waited the couple of seconds for her feline eyes to adjust to the abundance of artificial light. She and Brandon crept through the edging of short, yellow and green bushes to reach the front window. They peered inside and were rewarded by the sight of Ruby and Luis . . . and, the son.

Ophelia gave a reflexive hiss. She'd like to see Zuki bite the son. Maybe twice!

Brandon nudged her. "Quiet," he murmured, straining his fuzzy black ears toward the window glass. "Can you hear what they're saying?"

She flicked her ears back and forth a couple of times. "Some of it. Boring stuff — *sorry for your loss, valued employee, blah, blah* — but nothing bad. But look at the son. He looks funny, doesn't he?"

For, though he was looking serious and nodding, she could see him making little quick moves with his hands. Almost like a mouse with a piece of cheese worried that another mouse was going to steal it.

Her brother nodded. "I know what you mean. He wants them to leave, but he can't say that to them." He snickered a little and added, "If he had a tail, it would be flipping about worse than yours."

Ophelia narrowed her green eyes and gave him a not-so-sisterly cuff that made him snicker even more. Her tail might be flipping just a little, but that was only because she was keeping the tree frogs in the bushes at bay. *She* wasn't nervous.

The son, meanwhile, was pointing at a stack of empty cardboard boxes in the middle of the room. Next to them were a couple of larger boxes that Ophelia could see were filled with the housekeeper's clothes. And Luciana's pictures of people in long robes were off the walls and propped like they were real live humans sitting on the couch and chair.

"Do you think that the son is going to help put things in those boxes?" Ophelia whispered.

Brandon snorted. "I doubt it. That would mean he had to work, and he doesn't like to do that. He likes to order around other humans, remember?"

As he said that, Ruby picked up a box and headed toward the small kitchen. The PAWN human took a box, too, and followed her. Not surprisingly, the only thing the son picked up was a bottle of water as he stared after them, like the three roosters did when waiting to spy a tasty bug to eat.

Brandon rested his chin on the window sill. "Maybe Ruby didn't need us after all. None of the boxes are big enough for a human, and no one is doing anything interesting."

"They just started," Ophelia countered. "Something is bound to happen soon."

As she said it, they both heard what sounded like music playing. The son reached into his pants pocket and pulled out a phone. He turned his back and whispered into it.

"I can't hear what he's saying," Brandon murmured, stretching out his ears. "Can you?"

Ophelia flicked her ears again. "No. He's too far away, and he's whispering like a mouse. Wait, look!"

As they watched, he put away the phone and went over to where Ruby and Luis were packing. They exchanged a few words, some of which Ophelia heard — *appointment, unavoidable, back soon* — and then the son walked toward the door.

"Quick, hide," Ophelia hissed.

The pair crouched in the bushes and watched him exit the little house. But rather than going to the big house, like they expected, the man instead walked over to the long black car parked beneath the open room. He climbed inside it and started it up.

Brandon and Ophelia exchanged confused glances as the car rushed down the driveway toward the gate, which was already opening. A moment later, the car was gone and the gate already closing, leaving them and the two humans — and Zuki, of course — alone at the house.

Ophelia blinked. "Are you thinking what I'm thinking?"

"As long as Zuki keeps watch."

"I will," came the pit bull's soft howl.

"Pa-a-a-arty!" Ophelia yowled as they rushed toward the gate leading to the pool.

"Did you hear a cat?" Ruby asked, straightening from the slow cooker she was wrapping and looking toward the door.

Luis shook his head. "Probably a night bird of some sort. There aren't many cats roaming around the neighborhood in this part of town."

"Maybe I should check on Zuki, just to be sure. Last thing we need is for her to be chasing after a stray."

Leaving Luis to keep packing up Luciana's dishes, Ruby set her box of pots and pans aside and hurried out to the truck. She found the pit bull sitting obediently in the truck bed, her broad muzzle resting on the tailgate's upper edge. From the dog's relaxed manner, it was pretty obvious there were no cats on the prowl.

"Good girl," Ruby told her. "For being such an excellent watch pup, you deserve a treat."

She grinned as Zuki's ears perked up at the magic word, *treat.* Going to the cab, she pulled out the dog supplies and poured part of a bottled water into the folding nylon water bowl. Carrying that and a couple of pieces of chicken jerky (the good stuff, made in the USA), she returned to the truck bed.

While Zuki snacked and drank, Ruby took a moment to gather her thoughts. Meeting Terrence Givens had been an uncomfortable experience, knowing as she did what Luciana thought of him. In person, however, he'd seemed a bit less, well, evil than she'd prepared herself for him to be.

His greeting to her had been polite if not solicitous, but he'd seemed genuine in his acceptance of her condolences regarding his mother. Fortunately, he'd not objected to her presence — at least, not aloud — though she could sense that he seemed on edge about something.

It had been immediately obvious, however, that he wasn't the type to be enticed by a Tarot card reading. She'd been a bit disappointed not to be able to use her pre-arranged deck to shake him up a little. On the other hand, she was glad she wasn't going to have to clobber him with the deck either, as Luis had facetiously suggested.

Luciana's quarters turned out to be what looked like an old guest house. While nowhere near the level of vintage luxury that the main house boasted, it had similar touches with its arched windows and Mexican tile accents. And the comfortable apartment was larger than it looked: a combination living room/dining room, a kitchenette, and a separate bedroom and bathroom.

She wondered how often Luis had been there before. Had he been a regular visitor, at some point he likely would have encountered the black cats, and vice versa. But man and felines had all seemed to be strangers to each other. So chances were that Luciana had done most of the visiting.

She'd been a bit surprised to see that some of Luciana's things had already been packed. Maybe the day staff had gotten started on it, she surmised. She was pretty sure good old Terrence hadn't been the one boxing his housekeeper's clothes and makeup.

She and Luis had barely gotten started with the rest of the packing when Givens took a cell call and then proceeded to leave. His excuse was that he needed to consult with a client who was having an emergency. Since she wasn't sure exactly what sort of work he did, or what sort of clients he had, she couldn't judge if his explanation was real or manufactured. What she did know was that it meant she could take off her ball cap . . . and she and Luis could sort through Luciana's small world without the man's cool blue eyes keeping watch.

Though Ruby had been amazed that Givens would leave her and Luis alone on his multi-million-dollar estate while he went gallivanting about elsewhere.

Not as big a deal as you might think, Luis assured her when she said as much. *Let's just say that I'm known on Palm Beach.*

Pawnbroker to the rich and famous? she had asked, earning a shrug from him and an echoing *Let's just say that I know where a few of the financial bodies are buried.*

Which statement had left her even more curious. But for the moment, what mattered was going through Luciana's things to see if perhaps the housekeeper had left any clue as to why she'd suspected Givens of wrongdoing. Because if it turned out that the man did have a hand in his mother's death, bringing him to justice could be one last favor she and Luis could do for both women.

TWENTY-TWO

Satisfied that Zuki was doing fine, Ruby walked back into the guest house to find that Luis had filled another box in her absence. Now he was starting on the upper kitchen cabinets.

"No cats to be seen, and Zuki is just chillin'," she reported. "You holding up okay?"

"Another couple of boxes and I should be finished in here," he replied, not quite answering her question.

She decided not to press it. After all, she barely knew the man, and it wasn't her place to help him through the grieving process. Instead, changing the subject, she said, "I guess Luciana liked to cook. She sure had a bit of everything as far as pots and pans and gadgets."

"Well, it's not surprising. In Cuba, you can't just run off to your local Williams Sonoma and pick yourself up a spiralizer when you want one. I think she decided to

386

indulge her inner chef once she arrived here."

Ruby looked at him, surprised. Somehow, she'd figured Luciana had been in South Florida most of her life. The way he'd put it, it sounded like she was a recent immigrant. "So how long was your aunt living here in the states?"

"Only a few years. I can give you the Cliffs-Notes version of the old family history, if you want to hear it?"

When Ruby nodded her interest, he said, "It started with my grandfather. He and my father escaped Cuba on a raft with eight other people back in the early 1970s. My father was five at the time, but they figured he was old enough to pull his own weight, so they took him along. Aunt Luciana, she was only two, maybe three years old, so she and my grandmother stayed behind on the island. And, miraculously, all ten of those refugees made it to US territorial waters and were rescued by the Coast Guard. They all applied for citizenship and were accepted."

Ruby nodded. "That's kind of how it was for my half sister. Her father came over on a raft, too."

But even before she'd connected with Rosa, life in Florida had by default given

Ruby some familiarity with the thorny laws regarding Cuban immigrants. She knew that, in the sixties, crossing the strait and reaching US waters had been enough. But in the nineties, things had gotten more complicated. The US government had compromised with the Castro regime to make immigration into the US harder, the result of which was the wet foot-dry foot law.

Despite its fanciful name, the policy was a dead serious reinterpretation that required Cuban immigrants to reach dry land before they'd be allowed to remain and apply for citizenship. Intercepted at sea — even in the shallows — and they'd be returned to Cuba. Unlike horseshoes and hand grenades, almost touching shore didn't count. But that stricter policy was recently rescinded by the previous president right before he left office.

Normalizing relations with Cuba, they had termed it. What it actually meant was that Cuban refugees trying to slip into the country without going through proper channels were now to be treated like any other illegal immigrants . . . meaning they were returned to their homeland if they were discovered.

Luis, meanwhile, had pulled down a mixing bowl and was wrapping it in brown paper. Adding it to the box, he resumed the story.

"My grandfather always thought he'd somehow get my grandmother and aunt out of Cuba and bring them here, but it didn't work out that way. But then, some years ago, Aunt Lu managed to find a spot on a boat with some friends of the family who had decided to escape. That group wasn't quite as lucky. They'd drifted north and were maybe twenty yards off Jupiter Island" — a township further up the coast from Palm Beach, Ruby knew — "and were racing the Coast Guard to shore when their boat overturned."

"Oh no," Ruby gasped. "Did everyone make it?"

"It was pretty much fifty-fifty. One guy drowned, and a couple more were pulled from the water by the Coast Guard and sent back to Havana. But Luciana and two others made it to shore, meaning they were home free. She met up with my parents in Cleveland, applied for citizenship, and then decided after her first winter there that she hated the cold. So, she came back down here to live and eventually found the job as housekeeper to Mrs. Givens."

Ruby nodded, not quite trusting herself to

speak over the lump that had suddenly formed in her throat. Talk about a cruel irony. Luciana had fled a Communist regime and survived a treacherous water crossing, making it to freedom, only to die in a tragic accident in her adopted country.

Clearing her throat, she managed, "Why don't I start on the bedroom while you finish here."

Mood thoughtful, she grabbed three more empty boxes and a stack of the wrapping paper and went into the tiny bedroom. Though most of Luciana's clothes were already packed, her personal items — statues, books, a rosary hanging on the wall — still remained to be boxed.

Ruby started with the books. A handful had already been pulled from the small bookshelf and dumped on the bed. Accounting textbooks, along with a CPA test prep workbook. *Interesting.* It appeared that Luciana had been studying for a career beyond her role as housekeeper. Maybe this was what Luis had referred to the other day when he'd mentioned that his aunt was supposed to have been at class the night she died.

She picked up the books one at a time and carefully shook each volume before boxing them. The antiques shop owner, Lana, had once told her that she'd always find at least one interesting item left between the pages in any box of books she bought. Sometimes, the original owners did it deliberately and for safekeeping, as with money. Other times, they simply used something as a makeshift bookmark — photos, news clippings, or even the electric bill. Either way, the items were forgotten and ended up the spoils of whomever got the books next.

The remainder of Luciana's library filled two boxes and were an eclectic mix of Spanish-language novels and biographies, English-language self-help and business books, and a couple of Spanish-English dictionaries. The most exciting thing she found hidden in any of them, however, was a coupon for a free chicken sandwich like the one she'd eaten on the way over.

Ruby put that freebie aside for Luis and set the third box on the bed, ready to start filling it. And then she heard Luis's voice from the kitchen.

"Ruby, come take a look at this."

Something in his tone made her drop the collection of throw pillows she was holding and rush into the other room. Luis was standing beside the kitchen countertop where, alongside a collection of canned and boxed foods, a fat stack of cash now lay.

Ruby's eyes widened and she leaned closer. "Wow! How much do you think is there?"

"It's two thousand, seven hundred and forty-two dollars, mostly in hundreds. I found it stashed inside one of those big stainless steel coffee tumblers sitting behind a bunch of mugs."

"Wow," Ruby repeated. Lowering her voice, she went on. "Do you think the money . . . I mean, did she get it . . . you know, is it . . . ?"

Luis gave her a pitying look. "We're talking less than three grand here. It's not bribe money, and it's darned sure not drug money. It's emergency cash . . . like for when your paycheck's late, or there's a hurricane and all the ATMs are down. I do the exact same thing. Besides, that's not what I wanted you to see."

Among the packaged pasta and rice and other staples was a tall box of generic sugar frosted cereal. Reaching into the box, Luis pulled out a gallon-sized, zip-style plastic bag. Except the bag wasn't filled with cereal.

As Ruby watched in surprise, he extracted a thick sheaf of letter-size paper that had been tightly stuffed into it.

"Now you can get all suspicious," he told her as he shuffled through the pages and then handed them to her. "I can't say for sure, but it looks to me like Aunt Lu had been doing a little auditing of Mrs. Givens's accounts."

Ruby took the papers which, at first glance, appeared to be photocopies of bank documents. "Auditing? Luciana?" she echoed. "How would she — ?"

And then she recalled the textbooks she'd just packed. She knew a few immigrants who'd been degreed professionals back in their home countries. But because of language barriers or lack of U.S. accreditation, these former white collar workers had been forced to take blue collar jobs to pay the bills.

And, too many times, people made assumptions about their educational level because of that.

"Wait," she persisted, giving him a wary look. "Any chance your aunt used to be an accountant back in Cuba?"

"Got it in one," he said with a nod. "She did my books on the side for a while, just to keep her hand in. But before she could go for her CPA here, she needed to take some post grad hours and work on getting more fluent in English."

"I bet it was pretty tough, trying to do that on top of being a housekeeper on an estate like this. She probably had to keep it secret so she wouldn't be fired."

"Actually, Aunt Lu told me that Mrs. Givens found out about her classes a couple of years ago. Instead of being mad, the old lady actually did a private scholarship thing for her, paying for her tuition and books."

A little *noblesse oblige* on Mrs. Givens's part, Ruby thought in approval as she took a closer look at the paperwork.

In addition to the copies of bank statements, she saw sections from ledgers, along with a couple of letters from what appeared to be charities. Accounting was definitely not her personal forte, so the columns of numbers were pretty well indecipherable to her. But someone — likely Luciana — had circled a number of large figures in red. And, interestingly, all those figures reflected negative sums.

"So do you think Mrs. Givens asked her to do the auditing? Do you think she was worried that someone was stealing from her accounts?" Ruby ventured.

But even as she asked it, the question sparked a memory of her conversation with the housekeeper. A couple of times during the Tarot reading, Luciana had mentioned something about "papers." Maybe she had been referring to bank statements. But if the old woman had requested the audit, why would Luciana have to hide her work?

Unless there was someone else on the estate who knew about possible irregularities because they were responsible for them.

Maybe someone like Mrs. Givens's son, Terrence?

Before Ruby could offer that theory, Zuki let loose with a series of warning barks from her vantage point in the pickup. A moment later, they heard an automobile transmission grinding as headlights momentarily flared in the guest house's front window.

"That doesn't sound like Givens's car," Luis said, tone suspicious even as he winced at the painful sound. "I wonder who else has an access code?"

"Maybe it's one of the day staff coming back to help with the packing?"

"If it is, you'd think Givens would have mentioned it. Quick, give me those papers."

But squaring them up and getting them all back into the narrow bag took a little more doing. Luis had barely dropped the bag back in the cereal box and tucked the flaps back in when the guest house door burst open. A young woman dressed in a sleeveless pink sheath dress and with dark hair pinned in a messy up-do came flying in.

"Oh, Luis, my poor darling!"

Ignoring Ruby, she rushed to the man and flung thin white arms around his neck. "It was terrible, just terrible," she cried. "I told Luciana I would stay with her at the clinic, but she insisted I leave her there alone. You know how proud she was. I think she was embarrassed for anyone to see her in pain like that. I never should have let her send me away. If I'd stayed, maybe . . ."

She paused and buried her head in his chest. Then she took a sobbing breath and finished. "I — I only hope you can forgive me."

Looking pained himself, Luis took her by both arms and gently but deliberately moved the woman away from him. "No one's blaming you, Joan."

Joan?

Ruby had been staring at the newcomer, watching her display of remorse in slightly horrified fascination, while at the same time certain that she somehow knew this person. Hearing her name, Ruby abruptly realized how. It was the same woman that she'd seen in those society photos standing with Terrence Givens. And, the girlfriend of Givens who'd taken Luciana on that ill-fated drive to the clinic.

In person, she looked even thinner, and

not quite so pretty. Maybe it was because without the benefit of a little digital retouching, her features appeared harder, almost unhealthy. But what struck Ruby most was the way she had clung to Luis.

Where she came from, Ruby thought with an inner snort, that kind of hugging was *way* too familiar for someone supposedly dating another man.

More interesting was the question, how was it that Luis and Joan apparently knew each other so . . . intimately? Chances were that Luis didn't attend many Palm Beach soirees, and she doubted Joan had ever set foot in a pawn shop. To be sure, it made sense that they might have a nodding acquaintance because his aunt had worked for the mother of the man Joan supposedly was dating. But it was obvious the pair had some sort of history beyond that. She'd have to question Luis about that later.

Luis, meanwhile, was saying, "I know you feel bad about this, but it's not your fault. You had no way of knowing what was going to happen when you dropped off Aunt Lu. As long as you told the cops everything you remember about that night, you've done all you can do."

"But I still feel so guilty, darling," she exclaimed and marched past him to the kitchen sink.

Tearing off a paper towel, she dampened the sheet under the faucet and patted her face with it before reaching into the gold purse she wore cross-body style. She pulled out a compact and did a bit of quick repair work; then, turning back around, she seemed to notice Ruby for the first time.

"Oh, hello," she said in a composed voice.

Tossing the used paper towel onto the countertop, she walked out of the small kitchen, pale hand extended toward Ruby. "I'm Joan Ratzen. Friend of the family . . . both families, actually. And you are . . . ?"

"Ruby Sparks," she replied, momentarily taking the woman's hand. *Bony, cold.* "I knew Luciana, so I'm helping Luis with packing her things."

"Well, isn't that kind of you." Joan tilted her head to one side, surveying her with the faintest of smiles. "That little streak of blue in your hair is simply adorable. I never could get away with something so bohemian."

Then, sliding her hand free, Joan gestured toward the boxes of clothes. "I suppose you noticed some of Luciana's possessions were already packed. That was me. I told Terry I'd get things started, just so poor Luis didn't have to sort through his auntie's things alone. And when Terry said that Luis was going to be here tonight, I hurried on back to finish helping. I didn't realize he'd be bringing someone with him."

"Well, I did," Luis broke in. "Look, Joan, Ruby and I have things under control, so why don't you go back to the house and wait for Givens to get back."

"No, really, I insist." She grabbed an empty box from the dwindling stack of packing supplies and marched over to the kitchen counter. Eying the cash, she picked up the stack with her free hand and, setting down the box, gave the bills a quick riffle.

"Auntie had a tidy little stash," she commented before returning the money to its spot and reaching for a bag of pasta.

Ruby frowned a little at the dismissive tone. Joan's too-familiar way of calling Luciana "auntie" somehow rang false, though she wasn't sure if it was a deliberate diss of the dead woman or simply meant to tweak Luis. Whatever history there was between the pair, she was pretty sure now that it wasn't romantic.

"I'm sure you don't need this food, darling," Joan went on, tossing the noodles into her box and reaching for the next container. "I'll take it all up to the main house and give the box to one of the maids tomorrow.

One less thing for you to worry about doing, and a nice charitable gesture."

"Well, actually, I kind of . . ."

Luis trailed off and exchanged an uneasy glance with Ruby as Joan reached for the cereal box with its secret cache of papers and added it to the rest. Ruby winced. The box was almost full now, and any attempt to rescue a particular item from it would likely draw suspicion. Then Luis gave her a fleeting nod, and she knew he was going to make the effort, anyhow.

"Seriously, Joan, I planned on taking some of it home with me. I could use the cereal, and maybe the rice, too."

"Nonsense." Seemingly oblivious to any dismay she was causing, the woman added, "If you're that hungry, darling, use your auntie's cash to buy what you need. You know Terry pays awful wages. I'm sure one of the girls will be grateful for a little something extra to put in her pantry. Your aunt would approve, too, I'm sure."

She hefted the box with surprising ease, given her slight build. With another cool smile — this one for Luis — she turned to Ruby and said, "Be a dear, will you, and get the door for me?"

Not waiting for a response, she marched on past Ruby, who shot Luis a panicked look. *What do I do?* He spread his hands in a *beats me,* gesture. And so, with no other option, Ruby was a dear and got it.

Once the door had closed behind the woman, however, Ruby swung about again. "Now what? She's walking off with any proof Luciana had against Terrence Givens."

"She's only taking the box as far as the main house. The day staff won't be back until around seven tomorrow morning, so she'll probably stick it somewhere in the kitchen for safekeeping. Give it a minute, and we'll find an excuse to go up there and see if we can't steal those papers back." Luis grabbed another box and filled it with the rest of the nonperishable food. "Here we go. Another contribution to the maids' fund."

For good measure, he picked up the cash and counted out two thousand dollars of it, which he stuck in the box, and then folded the remainder and put into his pocket. "A grand each for the maids," he explained. "I think Aunt Lu would want them to have a little something, too. C'mon, let's go get that cereal box back."

TWENTY-THREE

"Car coming," Zuki barked, raising the alarm from her spot in Luis's picking up truck. "Car, car, car!"

Ophelia and Brandon stopped in mid-chase around the swimming pool and scampered over to the tall iron gate where they'd squeezed in earlier. Through the heavy twisted bars, they could see beyond the driveway to the street. There, they spied headlights shining through the main wide gate at the driveway's end — the gate that barred entry from the street. A faint squeal sounded as it began to open.

Ophelia frowned. Surely this wasn't the son, back again already!

They'd seen him drive off a few minutes earlier, leaving Ruby and Luis alone in Luciana's little house. The human obviously had been in a hurry, since he hadn't even bothered to close the two big glass doors — the ones that led from the main house to the paved courtyard where the pool was.

Before Ophelia could say anything aloud, however, they heard an awful crunch of metal that made her ears flicker in sympathetic reaction.

"It's the Joan car," she exclaimed.

Sure enough, a squat red car came rushing up the drive and parked close to Luciana's place, just pawsteps from where she and Brandon were watching.

"Why do you think she's back, without the son being here?" Brandon wanted to know. Pressing his nose as far as he could through the bars, he added, "Maybe she came to help pack."

Ophelia would have agreed . . . except that the Joan human didn't go immediately to the door. Instead, once she'd turned off the car's headlights and climbed out, she sneaked quiet as a mouse to Luciana's window and peered inside.

Peering like a rat, Ophelia thought in sudden suspicion.

"Quick," she whispered to her brother. "Let's see what she's looking at."

They slipped out of the gate again and silently padded their way into the bushes outside Luciana's window. The Joan woman had managed despite her lack of feline dexterity to climb through the foliage. Now she was crouched to one side of the glass, her thin nose all but pressed to it. Careful not to rustle any leaves, the two cats climbed as high as they could in the branches to see just what it was she was watching.

Boring stuff, Ophelia promptly decided.

A glance at her yawning brother confirmed her conclusion. On the other side of the glass, Ruby was looking anxiously over her shoulder toward the door. Luis, meanwhile, was hurriedly stuffing a stack of pages into a bag. Then, even stranger, he stuck the now-full bag inside a box that should have held human breakfast food . . . this, according to the colorful picture of a bowl and spoon drawn on it.

Apparently, the Joan woman found the sight equally boring, for she abruptly straightened. While Brandon and Ophelia froze in place, pretending to be part of the leaves, she scrambled out from behind the bushes. Going right past the two cats without noticing them — of course, her human eyes weren't equipped to distinguish much in the dark — she walked to Luciana's door and let herself in.

They watched through the windows awhile longer. After a dramatic demonstration of overwrought human emotion on the Joan woman's part — for too many moments, she was hanging onto Luis like a puppy tugging a rope — they saw nothing other than Joan packing a box while everyone talked. The conversation was quiet enough that neither cat could make out much in the way of words, though it appeared that Ruby didn't care much for the Joan human.

And then, for some reason, Joan picked up the box and marched over to the door . . . which Ruby, with a funny look on her face, opened for her.

"What's going on?" Brandon whispered as the woman walked back to the main house with the box firmly gripped to her chest.

Ophelia shook her head. "I don't know — but Ruby doesn't look happy. I think we should sneak inside and spy on the Joan. Remember, the glass doors are still open."

"What about Zuki? Should we tell her what we're doing?"

"She'll figure it out," Ophelia replied, earning a soft distant bark of agreement from the pit bull . . . who, of course, had heard the felines' conversation. "Quick, before Joan remembers and closes the pool doors."

Running for the courtyard yet again, they squeezed back through the gate and swiftly bounded through the opened glass doors. The entry led directly into the main living area where once the two felines had slept and played. But it wasn't the same room that it used to be.

I don't like it here now, Ophelia told herself, looking about to see what had changed since they'd last been there.

It was colder and quieter than it had been when the old woman was alive. True, the two matching black leather sofas with their bright fabric pillows — just the right roughness for sharpening one's claws when no human was watching — were still there. But someone had taken away the fluffy white rugs that used to blanket much of the shiny gray tile on the floor.

Marble, the old woman had called it as she complained about it hurting her feet. But the fluffy rugs made her feel better. Sometimes, she'd take off her shoes and walk on them, barefooted like a cat, when the son wasn't looking. She'd laugh and wiggle her toes, telling Brandon and Ophelia that it felt like walking on a fuzzy cloud. The son had argued about the rugs, saying they looked ridiculous, but the old woman had been stubborn about it.

But now that she was gone, there was no need to worry about the marble hurting her feet anymore.

Ophelia suppressed a hiss. Even the old

woman's pictures that had always hung on the wall — the ones with bright colored houses and sunny beaches and prancing animals — were gone now. They'd been replaced by big white squares covered with ugly slashes of black and blue that didn't look like anything at all! It was as if the son was trying to pretend that the old woman had never even lived there.

They didn't have time for further exploration, however. She and Brandon barely had time to crouch behind a big silver pot with an even bigger green palm tree growing out of it when Joan made her way through the front door.

She was juggling the box with Luciana's food and muttering bad human words. For a moment, she stood there in the long open hallway just inside the doorway that the old woman had called the foyer. It wasn't its own room, but was separated from the living area by a series of tall white columns that once had been fun to chase around.

Ophelia doubted that Joan or the son ever ran circles around them like she and Brandon had. But now that she had a box of things, maybe . . .

Maybe she'll set it down and play with it right there, Ophelia hopefully thought, wondering if there was anything inside the container for a feline to snack on. But instead — high-heeled shoes clicking against the cold marble — Joan turned and carried the box through the open foyer toward the kitchen.

They remained in their hiding place and watched her go, both knowing there was no point in following her. While the kitchen was a fine place for leftovers from the humans' meals, it was all granite and mirror-like metal and open shelves with fancy dishes on them. There was no place in that broad expanse of stone and steel for a feline to conceal herself.

"We'll wait and see what she does next," Ophelia murmured, earning a nod of agreement from her brother.

A moment later, Joan returned, minus the box but carrying the same clear bag filled with papers that Luis had earlier stuck inside the cereal container. She was smiling now, like a mouse with cheese. She took off the gold flat box — *a purse* — that she'd been wearing over her chest and put it on the sleek black leather sofa. Then she sat down beside the small gold box and opened up Luis's bag that she'd carried in.

"What's so important about the papers?" Ophelia whispered as Joan spread the papers on the glass table before her. "Should we try to get closer and look?"

"Yes," Brandon whispered back. "If Ruby let Luis hide them, they mean something. We'd better find out what."

Ophelia gave an uncertain nod.

Unfortunately, unlike at the Botanica, there were no convenient shelves to duck behind while trying to go from point A to point B. Which meant there was no way to get from their current hiding place to the sofa without Joan readily spying them. They'd have to wait her out . . . which also meant risking Luis and Ruby leaving without them should Zuki not sound a warning bark soon enough.

That, or worse . . . the son might return and shut the doors, accidentally locking them in. But their problem was solved a moment later when a familiar chiming sounded.

"The doorbell," Brandon explained unnecessarily, adding, "It must be Luis or Ruby. The son wouldn't ring to walk inside, and no one else can come in without a code to the front gate."

Surely Joan must have realized the same thing, yet she looked upset, Ophelia saw. Maybe because she didn't get a chance to finish looking at her papers?

And, indeed, Joan scrambled to her feet. But rather than immediately heading for the door, she took care first to grab up all the papers she'd spread about and stuff them back in the bag. Then, as the doorbell sounded again, she hid the bag behind one of the sofa pillows.

Why doesn't she want anyone to know that she has the papers, Ophelia fleetingly wondered.

But the *why* didn't really matter. What did was the fact that Joan had seen Luis and Ruby with the papers and known they were important, and that she'd managed to deliberately take them away.

Now, patting the pillow back into place and smoothing the wrinkles from her pink dress, Joan gave a satisfied smile and went to answer the door.

"This is our chance," Ophelia whispered. "Ready? Now!"

Like twin shadows, the pair scuttled across the marble tile and leaped onto the sofa. In a swift move, Ophelia batted aside the pillow so that Brandon could grab the plastic bag in his teeth. Grip secure, he dragged the packet off the sofa and across the marble tile again. Ophelia propped the pillow back into place again so that Joan wouldn't notice, and then she bounded after him.

"No, not there," she hissed when he would

have returned to their spot behind the palm. "There, under the armchair."

Nodding, Brandon wheeled about and made a beeline to what had once been a favorite hiding spot of theirs.

It was the seat that the old woman had preferred to the sofas . . . a sturdy, high-backed chair covered in pale yellow cloth that was stamped with little gray pictures of cows and humans and trees. A ruffle of fabric in the same pattern wrapped around the chair's curved wooden legs like a tent, turning it into a cozy refuge for felines as well. At least once a day, she and Brandon would lounge beneath the chair while the old woman sat above, reading a book or listening to her music.

The son had hated this chair almost as much as he'd hated the rugs, Ophelia recalled. He'd called it old-fashioned and claimed it spoiled the look of the room. And yet, though he'd replaced the old woman's pictures and taken away her fuzzy carpets, for some reason he'd left the chair untouched in its original spot.

Maybe it was because a hint of her perfume still clung to it, Ophelia thought with a reflexive little mew. For a few moments, at least, she could pretend that the old woman was still alive and sitting on the chair while she and Brandon played beneath it. Maybe the son did that sometimes, too.

She didn't have time to puzzle over the son's vagaries, however. They'd barely squeezed beneath the chair, and the flap of fabric had just fallen back into place, when they heard Ruby and Luis talking to the Joan woman.

"What's taking her so long to answer?" Ruby asked in a low voice as they waited before the salmon-colored double front doors at the main house. Not caring if she was noticed, she tried peering through the narrow sidelight windows at either side of the entry for signs of movement. Unfortunately, white plantation shutters effectively blocked any view of the inside.

Luis juggled the box he was holding, indicating his own impatience.

"Who knows with her. Without Givens around, she's probably playing lady of the manor and letting us peasants cool our heels until she's ready to open the door."

"It doesn't matter, I guess, as long as we get that box with Luciana's papers back from her. Any ideas how to do that without raising suspicions?"

"A couple," Luis replied and rang the bell again. "Just follow my lead."

A few moments later, one side of the double front doors opened and Joan peered out, expression quizzical. "Oh, hello again. Have you finished packing your auntie's things already?"

"Not quite, but it's turning out to be more than I thought there would be," Luis explained. Indicating the filled box he held, he said, "And I decided you were right. At a time like this, it doesn't hurt to be charitable. The maids might as well take all the food with them."

"That's very kind of you," the woman replied with a cool smile, reaching out to take the box from him.

Ignoring the hint, Luis pushed past her, Ruby on his heels. "You put that other box in the kitchen already, right? Don't worry, it's been a couple of years since I've been here at the house, but I remember how to get there. Why don't I carry this one on back, too?"

Not waiting for a response, he turned and started down the open foyer. Joan quickly closed the door after them and then hurried after Luis, heels clicking against the marble.

"Really, darling, I can carry the box, myself. This isn't necessary."

"Of course, it is. Besides, Aunt Lu would slap me upside the head if she knew I let a lady carry something heavy like this."

Trailing the pair, Ruby tried not to roll her eyes. While she was sure Luis was putting it on for effect, she knew enough Cuban men to have witnessed firsthand the old chivalry routine that was second nature to most of them. And while she had nothing against common courtesy, sometimes the older men, in particular, carried good manners to extremes.

But she promptly forgot about manners as they walked into the kitchen. Almost as large as Luciana's whole quarters, it was an interesting combination of vintage and new, the high end stainless steel appliance and gleaming granite countertops set against glass-fronted wooden cabinets painted a cheery turquoise. The look shouldn't have worked, but it did . . . perhaps because there was not a stray crumb or a gadget out of place save for the box of food that Joan had left on the long expanse of kitchen island.

"I'll put this one right here next to the other box," Luis said, setting his box down.

Ruby shot a covert glance at the original packing container and inwardly gave a sigh of relief. The cereal box was still there. All they needed was a way to spirit it out of the mansion without Joan noticing.

Luis, meanwhile, reached into his box and

pulled out the cash. "Here's another little bonus for the ladies," he said, counting out the bills into two equal stacks and tucking one into each box. "I want to give each of the maids a grand from Aunt Lu. I'm sure they'll put it to good use."

Ruby glanced over at Joan. An expression flashed across her pale features that looked oddly like avarice, but the emotion vanished far too quickly for her to be sure. All she said, however, was, "Why, how thoughtful of you. I'll be sure the ladies get it."

"Thanks." Then, nodding in Ruby's direction, he went on. "Ruby told me not to ask you, but I knew you wouldn't mind. She's never been in a house like this before. Is it all right if she takes a quick look at some of the main rooms? That is, if you've got the authority when Givens isn't around."

The question hung there a moment, and Ruby obediently assumed an eager look. Luis was playing to Joan's pride, she knew. While she suspected from her expression that Joan was more than eager to be rid of the peasantry, no way would the woman want to admit that she didn't have the authority to treat the Givens estate like her own. And with Joan elsewhere in the house playing duchess-slash-tour guide, Luis would have ample time to pull the bag out of the cereal box, stick it under his shirt, and then meet up with them again at the door.

As Luis had no doubt expected, pride won out. With a gracious bow of her head, she said, "Certainly. Come along, Ruby."

Then, when Luis casually remained where he was, leaning up against the kitchen counter, she added with just a bit of regal steel, "You too, darling. You'll want see the changes Terry made since . . . well, since he became sole owner. Really, I insist — you must come along."

He could hardly refuse without arousing suspicion or looking ungracious. With a shrug, he straightened and followed after them.

The woman took them on a brief but — Ruby had to admit — impressive tour of the first floor. Her favorite room was actually the sunken bathroom. With its geometric yellow-and-black-tiled floor, yellow stucco walls, and freestanding tub, sink, and toilet, it reminded her of the bathroom in the old Hemingway House down in Key West.

The tour ended back in the main living area . . . a rather sterile room, in Ruby's opinion, save for a definitely shabby chic wingback chair in yellow and gray toile that

416

had an undeniable charm to it. Joan, however, seemed to have tired of playing tour
guide, though she did an admirable job of
remaining polite.

"Well, that was fun, but I'm sure you need
to get back to your packing," she said in
duchess-speak, "so please don't let me keep
you any longer."

Which statement, Ruby thought, pretty
much translated to, *get your butts out of
here, now!* Any other time, she wouldn't
have blamed the woman, since technically it
wasn't her house to open up to strangers. If
Givens came back unexpectedly and saw
them hanging out together, he might be
justifiably ticked. But they couldn't leave
until they retrieved Luciana's paperwork.

And, fortunately, Luis had another arrow
in his quiver of excuses.

"We've got time," he said with a dismissive
shrug. "But here's something interesting.
Did you know that Ruby runs a Botanica
not far from my pawnshop? It so happens
she reads Tarot cards. I bet she'd be glad to
do a reading for you . . . right, Rubes?"

Ruby winced a little at the nickname but
did her own duchess nod. "Of course," she
agreed, reaching into her hoodie pocket for
the pre-stacked deck of Tarot cards. "We
could do a quick reading, just a little five-

card spread for fun."

Not waiting for Joan's reply, she took a seat on the closer of the two big black leather sofas since Joan's little gold purse was lying on the opposite one. The glass tabletop between the couches was the perfect place to lay out the spread.

Taking the cards out of their box, she began a swift but controlled overhand shuffle that, as she'd planned to do with Givens, left the "scary as heck" cards at the top of the deck. Then, divvying the cards into three piles, she swiftly restacked them but left the original cards as the top layer.

"All right, we're ready," she said with a bright smile. "Come sit down."

"Oh dear, I think not," the woman replied, giving her messy updo a seemingly nervous pat. "It's not . . . well, this voodoo stuff . . . it's not done around here."

"It's Tarot, not voodoo," Luis countered. "And Ruby was just here on the island the other night reading Tarot at a bridal shower for a whole gang of rich ladies. C'mon, be a good sport."

Even with that encouragement, Ruby was certain that the woman would refuse. And while that wouldn't be the end of the world, that would mean arrow number two was also a fire and miss. They were going to run out of subtle ploys to get the paperwork back. They'd probably have to do a grab and run, and hope it didn't end up a wrestling match on the estate's front lawn.

And then Joan shrugged.

"Oh, all right," she agreed, and plopped onto the sofa opposite Ruby.

Twenty-Four

Feeling suddenly nervous, Ruby shoved her glasses into place and dealt five cards from the deck facedown onto the table . . . three in a single row, and the other two arranged one above and one below. The spread looked a bit like a mathematical plus sign. Hence, its name.

"I call this the 'Adding Abundance' spread," she told the woman. "It's basically a snapshot of where you stand in your life."

She pointed to the line of three cards. "The first card will tell us where you were . . . the second where you currently are . . . and the third card, where you are going. The fourth card" — she indicated the one below — "tells us what's holding you back. And the card on top tells what's pushing you forward."

Joan frowned. "So I don't have to make a wish or anything?"

"Not at all. Now, let's see what our cards

are, and then we'll talk about them individually. Here's where you were," she said and flipped the first card over.

Now it was Ruby's turn to frown as she saw the cheery Ten of Cups card. It was one of the desk's most positive cards, with its depiction of a happy family rejoicing at a rainbow made of ten shiny gold chalices. Definitely *not* one of the scary cards that she'd stacked in her deck. She must have screwed up the shuffle.

Holding her breath, she flipped the next card over. "Here's where you are."

More like it, she thought as the Eight of Swords appeared. Again, it wasn't one of her scary cards, but its image of a bound and blindfolded woman in a red dress surrounded by swords indicated something serious afoot.

"And here's where you're going," she said and turned over the third card.

Justice. The same sword and scales-bearing female that was the lawyer statue JoJo had admired the other day. Ruby gave the card a quizzical look. Serious, but not scary. Definitely, she'd screwed up that shuffle big time.

"Uh, I'm going to grab a drink of water," Luis interrupted. "Anyone need anything?" Not waiting for a reply, he turned and headed off to the kitchen.

Joan huffed and got to her feet, cards forgotten. "Luis has no idea where anything is in there. Excuse me, I'd better check up on him."

"But what about your reading?" Ruby asked, hoping to stall her. It didn't work.

Joan gave her a cool look. "I'm sorry, I'm sure this is all a lot of fun, but I really need to make sure he doesn't make a mess in there. Terry likes things just so."

So saying, she smoothed her pink sheath dress and headed for the kitchen, too.

Ruby muttered a bad word and scrambled to her feet. At least Joan's clicking footsteps would sound a warning she was on the way. With luck, Luis would be swift enough to grab the bag and hide it before she caught him. First, however, she needed a look at the last two cards. *What's holding you back? What's pushing you forward?*

She flipped the cards over and scanned them, her heart suddenly racing.

The fourth card was one that had been in her stack that she'd prepared in advance . . . and, she feared, was far too telling. The fifth card had been a random draw, like the others, and hopefully spoke the truth.

She flipped those cards back over again and hurried off to the kitchen only to find

Luis and Joan in a virtual face-off. The former was holding the cereal box upside down.

Empty?

Joan wore an expression of cool confusion. Luis looked ticked, to put it mildly. Giving the box a shake by way of demonstration, he demanded, "All right, what did you do with the paperwork?"

"Paperwork?" She raised narrow, painted brows. "I'm sure I don't know what you mean."

"And I'm sure you do. When you walked out with the box of groceries, there was a bag of photocopies inside this empty cereal box. Now it's gone, and you're the only one who could have taken it. So hand it over."

She shrugged and gave a little laugh. "Darling, I know you're upset over your auntie, but this is ridiculous. I don't have any papers. Now, why don't you and Ruby go finish packing."

"Fine." He tossed aside the empty box and stalked past her. "C'mon, Ruby, let's see if she stashed those papers anywhere."

"Wait! You have no right . . ."

Joan clicked her way in the same direction, while Ruby stared after the pair in dismay. How had the woman known the papers were in that box, and that they had any importance? The other items in the packing container appeared untouched, so it wasn't as if she had dug through the boxed and bagged food and accidentally discovered the cache. Unless she had stumbled across the pages earlier that day, while she'd been alone in Luciana's place packing up things? That or maybe when she'd driven up to the guest house that night, she'd looked through the window and seen Luis with the pages and felt compelled to see what they were.

But none of that mattered at the moment. No matter how they'd somehow ended up there, the papers were now in Joan's possession. And despite Luis's threats, they could hardly tear apart the place searching for them. One call from Joan to the Palm Beach cops and Luis would be leaving the estate handcuffed in the back of a patrol car! And given her connection to Luis, there was a good chance that she, Ruby, might also be caught up in the same high society dragnet.

Muttering even more bad words, Ruby rushed out of the kitchen. She had to dial down things between Luis and Joan before someone dialed 911.

But when she reached the living room, the scene before her was not the one she'd expected. Rather than seeing sofa cushions flung about and potted plants overturned, she found Joan slumped on the sofa, face in her hands. Luis stood nearby, looking distinctly uncomfortable. The bag of papers, however, was nowhere in evidence.

"I didn't mean to spy," Joan was saying in a sobbing voice. "But I glanced through the guest house window earlier. I saw you and Ruby hiding those pages while you were packing up Luciana's kitchen, and things fell into place."

"What sort of things?" Ruby asked, sitting on the sofa opposite her.

The woman heaved a sigh. "I — I'd had my suspicions for a while. Mrs. Givens did, too. She finally confided in me. Of course, she didn't want to believe it . . . I didn't want to believe it either."

"Believe what?" Luis demanded.

"Mrs. Givens — Hilda — discovered that some of her money had been moved from one account to another, without her knowing about it. And some charitable contributions, well, they never reached the charities they were meant for. And then money — lots of money — began to go missing. She told me that your aunt was an accountant, and that Terry had been spending a lot of time with her recently. He'd made some bad investments, and . . ."

"What are you trying to say, Joan?" Luis asked as she trailed off.

Joan lifted her face from her hands and stared back at him. "I don't know quite how to tell you this, darling. I think Luciana was helping Terry embezzle from his mother."

The accusation hung there for a single shocking moment. Then Luis slammed a fist on the sofa back.

"That's crazy! No way was Aunt Lu conspiring with Givens and helping him embezzle. If anything, maybe she was working for Mrs. Givens gathering evidence against her son. Tell her, Ruby."

"Luis is right," Ruby promptly agreed. "That's why Luciana came to see me at the Botanica. She wanted me to read the cards and see if . . ."

She hesitated, and then finished, "She wanted to know if Mr. Givens caused his mother's accident."

Joan gasped and shook her head, the messy updo all but falling apart. "No, I could never believe that. The embezzling, maybe, but the other? I mean, they didn't always get along, but I know deep down that Terry loved his mother. Hilda's death was just a terrible, terrible accident. That's what the police told us."

Expression determined, she said, "I've

been thinking about this ever since I saw the paperwork. Now that Hilda's gone, surely there's no need to pursue anything. You know, legally. We can take the copies and all the notes and put them in Terry's shredder and pretend none of this ever happened."

Then, apparently seeing from their expressions that she and Luis were still not convinced, Joan went on in a pleading voice. "The money would have been Terry's, anyhow. He — He just took it a little early. There's no need to destroy his reputation now, when it won't help Hilda. Is there?"

Ruby exchanged glances with Luis. Joan had a point. Was it really necessary to pursue this? She'd have to ask JoJo, but she couldn't imagine who would even go after Givens. Likely not the police . . . not without Luciana's actual testimony. And as Joan had pointed out, he'd simply taken the money early.

Except that it wasn't going to be his money, a voice in her head reminded her. Luciana had very specifically said that Terrence had already received his inheritance and Mrs. Givens had changed her will to give everything to charity. But obviously Joan didn't know all this.

"We have to do this," the woman persisted,

rising from the sofa. "I've got the papers right here. We can do this now, and —"

As Ruby and Luis watched in surprise, she shoved aside the pillow behind her . . . and then picked up the next pillow, and the next. Her expression of dismay promptly morphed into outrage.

"It's gone. I had them here . . . and now they've vanished!" She rounded on Luis and raged on. "This isn't funny. Give me those papers back. We're going to burn them, shred them, just like we agreed."

"Me-OOOOOOOW!"

The ear-splitting yowl made them all freeze. Ruby was the first to react, turning in the direction of that strangely familiar cry. As she watched in disbelief, a sleek furry black form crawled out from under the toile chair.

Barely had Ruby gasped out "Ophelia?" when a second black feline — this one with a stubby tail — wriggled his way out, too. And behind him, he was dragging an equally familiar plastic bag filled with papers.

"Brandon? Ophelia? How did you get back here? And how did you get . . . oh, never mind," Ruby exclaimed as she rushed over to them.

The pair circled around her ankles, mewing, as she gave them each a quick pat and then grabbed the packet. She gave it a quick look. Definitely the same papers, the only difference being that the end of the bag now was pierced by a series of feline-sized fang marks.

"Ugh! I thought Terry got rid of those nasty creatures," Joan said with a shudder.

Ruby bristled. "Those nasty creatures happen to be my pets."

"Well, I suggest you remove your pets before I call Animal Control and report them as strays. Not that I would do such a thing," she smoothly added. "Not if you give me back the papers the little wretches stole from me."

Luis snorted. "You mean, the same papers you stole from *me*? And as for those cats, they used to live here. So as far as I'm concerned, they have as much right to be here as you do. Maybe more."

"Ahem," came a male voice from the vicinity of the front door. "Since I'm the only one who actually lives here now, maybe *I* should be the one making the decision about who is welcome in my house."

Terrence Givens shut the door behind him and strode through the foyer into the living room. His pale, disbelieving gaze took in all of them — felines, included — as he added, "Would someone care to explain what's going on here?"

Joan was the first to regain her composure. "Terry! Oh, darling, thank goodness you're home!" she cried and ran to him. "There's been a terrible misunderstanding, and I've been trying to protect you. But these people" — she waved wildly in Ruby and Luis's direction — "they're making things difficult. They're saying crazy things. And — And they brought cats with them!"

"Yes . . . *a-a-a-choo!* . . . so I see," he shot back, taking Joan by the arm.

Brandon and Ophelia, meanwhile, had ceased their circling and now flanked Ruby, green gazes fixed on Givens. The man sneezed again, and the cats let loose with twin hisses that, to Ruby's mind, spoke volumes. She clutched the papers more tightly to her, not sure what to do next.

Luis shrugged. "Looks like we've got a little impasse going here."

"And what does that mean?" Givens demanded. "I leave my home for less than an hour, and I come back to find it overrun by undesirables. Oh, I didn't mean you, darling," he hurriedly clarified, turning his attention to Joan. Patting her arm, he said in a solicitous tone, "What is this misunderstanding, and why do you need to protect me? Maybe you can make sense of this for me."

She nodded and put her free hand to her mouth, as if choking back sobs. "These two, they're accusing you of terrible things. I — I don't believe them, of course, but they make it sound so terrible. And I'm afraid they're going to try to smear your good name. If we can just destroy those papers, it'll be over with."

"You're not making sense, darling. Things? What sort of things?"

"Embezzlement things," Luis wryly answered for her. "Sometime before she died, your mother and my aunt discovered someone was dipping into Mrs. Givens's bank accounts. Aunt Lu put together the proof. Now we have to decide what to do with it."

Givens's pale eyes opened wide, and he began to sputter. "What the — ? Are you really saying — ? Are you trying to accuse me — ? Are you actually telling me you think I stole from Hilda?"

A series of emotions flashed over the man's blandly handsome features. *Shock. Outrage. Disbelief.* But not guilt, Ruby realized in surprise. She glanced over at the coffee table, where the Tarot card spread still lay. If those last two cards of Joan's reading that she'd peeked at were to be believed, maybe Givens was telling the truth.

Joan, meanwhile, was now clutching *his* arm. "Don't worry, darling," she said, tone fiercely possessive. "You don't have to confess to anything. Your poor mother is gone now, so it really doesn't make any difference anymore. She wouldn't want her own son to go to prison. We'll destroy the papers, and that will be an end to it."

Givens abruptly disengaged himself from her grip. "I don't have any idea what you're talking about. If someone was embezzling, I damn well want to know about it. Where are these papers?"

"I've got them," Ruby spoke up, holding up the sealed bag so he could see it. "And I'm pretty sure that Luciana and your mother were right. Somebody was embezzling from your mother . . . but it wasn't you. It was Joan."

TWENTY-FIVE

"I knew it!" Ophelia mewed in excitement at Ruby's announcement, hopping onto the arm of the black sofa so she could keep a better eye on things. "I knew the Joan person was the human rat that Philomena told us about! Even her name — Ratzen — has a 'rat' in it."

Brandon rolled his green eyes but jumped up to join her. "What do you mean, you knew it? I thought you thought it was Luis . . . though I knew all the time it wasn't."

Sure you did, Ophelia thought. Aloud, she merely said, "So what do you think they're going to do with her? Give her to the police people?"

"Maybe. But as long as she's here, keep an eye on her. She's sneaky like a rat, for sure."

And indeed, the Joan woman had casually strolled over to the black sofa and, with a sour look for the cats, picked up her small gold box. Opening it, she pulled out a small gold cylinder — *lipstick,* Ophelia knew it was called — and a little mirror.

Coloring her lips a bright red, she asked, "Terry, darling, are you going to stand there and let this awful woman accuse me of such a thing?"

"I don't know, *darling.* Did you steal the money?"

By way of answer, she snapped the lid back on the lipstick and stuffed it into the gold box, and then tossed the box onto the couch. She'd forgotten to close its top, however, and the lipstick rolled right out.

Something else rolled out, too . . . a small amber plastic cylinder, like the kind the old woman used to keep what she called her medicines in.

Ophelia squinted suspiciously at the little container as she recalled the last thing Philomena the koi had said. *It takes a pill to fix what's ill.* And if Joan was the rat, then maybe the medicine had something to do with it.

Joan, meanwhile, was giving the son a cold look. "I don't have to stay here and be insulted. Just remember all those times when I smoothed things over for you, the invitations I made sure you got, even when people knew you were on the outs with your dear mother."

She whipped about to face Luis. "And the same for you . . . darling." Giving her head a coquettish tilt, she went on in the same chill tone. "Have you forgotten I'm the one who hooked you up with those nice Palm Beach socialites? You know the ones I mean — the ones with no spare cash to pay the landscaper that week and afraid someone would find out? You have a nice little sideline business going with them, and it's because of me."

"Wait!"

This from the son, whose pale face was turning redder by the moment.

"Joan, would you care to explain how you seem to know the nephew of my late house-keeper so well?" Then, tone growing even more suspicious, he demanded, "And what's this about a side business? So help me, if anyone is using my house for anything nefarious . . ."

"Really, Terry, you know me better than that." The Joan woman's tone was cajoling, like a kitten trying to convince a grown cat to play. "Last year, I was attending this incredibly boring finance conference down in Ft. Lauderdale, and I ran into Luis at the bar. Of course, I had no idea at the time that he was related to Luciana."

She hesitated, then gave a careless shrug and went on. "We exchanged business cards, and I saw that he owned a pawn shop in West Palm. I didn't think much about it, until a friend of mine ran into a bit of difficulty trying to come up with some quick cash. I thought of him and gave my friend his number. Things worked out so well for her that I gave his number to a few other people I knew who got into trouble. I was only trying to help."

Ophelia frowned. She wasn't really sure why the Joan human would be giving numbers to other humans, but maybe that explained Brandon's adventure riding around that night in the picking up truck with Luis.

Luis, however, didn't seem much impressed with her story. He snorted. "Yeah, you're a real Oprah, helping all your rich friends like that. Don't forget to tell Terrence here that you got a cut of the action, too."

"So what? You made your money. You still owe me. Both of you do. Now give me the papers!"

If the Joan woman had been a feline, Ophelia thought, by now she would be hissing and baring fangs. Which would mean that the rest of the humans would be getting all hissy, too. But to Ophelia's surprise, Ruby calmly set the plastic bag containing the damning paperwork on the table.

"If Mr. Givens wants you to have the pages, they're yours. If he wants to keep things quiet about the stolen money, that's his call. But I think you've got something more on your conscience than embezzlement, Joan, don't you?"

So saying, she reached toward the Tarot cards still spread on the table and picked up the fourth Tarot card in her spread . . . a card that still lay face down. Flipping it over, she set it atop the financial papers and gave Joan a stern look from behind her black-framed glasses.

"Look familiar?"

Ophelia and Brandon exchanged glances. The picture on this one was a scary human skeleton wearing a metal suit. He rode a white horse and carried a flag with a white flower on it. *Death*.

"It's a trick," Joan snapped, though Ophelia could hear the uncertainty in her voice. "You're trying to rattle me, but it won't work."

"See here," the son swiftly broke in, looking a bit uncertain himself. "Are you trying to accuse Joan of something . . . well, something else?"

"I refuse to listen to this," the woman declared before Ruby could reply. "I'm going home now. Terry, when you're ready to be sensible again, you can call me."

She reached for the gold box, noticing then that it had spilled open. She said some bad human words and started to scoop everything back where it belonged.

Ophelia, however, was swifter. She bounded from couch arm to cushion, and with a single swat sent the brown cylinder flying off onto the tile floor.

"You distract them! Staircase plan!" she yowled back to her brother. "I'm going to get the pills and hide them until I can give them to Ruby. I'll be waiting for you in the picking up truck."

Leaping after the small plastic container, she gave another swat that sent it sliding toward the foyer, its contents rattling. She could hear the Joan woman shouting behind her, while Ruby valiantly tried to call Ophelia back. But the humans had all forgotten that she and Brandon used to play there, that they'd long ago mastered hitting every slide and turn and corner at full feline speed.

They weren't going to catch her.

Snatching the cylinder in her jaws, Ophelia

made as if to run into the kitchen. Joan and the son were behind her. At the last minute, she whipped about and instead made a beeline to the other, shadowy end of the foyer, where the staircase led to the rooms above.

Brandon was already in position, ready for a trick they'd done many times. She could see his one black ear sticking out from behind the baluster. "Get ready for the switch," he yowled at her.

Well ahead of the humans, she came skidding to a stop at the bottom of the stairway and momentarily ducked behind the baluster with her brother.

"Good luck," he purred, and then jumped out to take her place.

"There she goes, up the stairs!" came the shout as the son and Luis and Ruby all came rushing after her . . . or, rather, after Brandon pretending to be her.

Suppressing a snicker — it was hard to laugh with the cylinder in her mouth, anyhow — Ophelia slipped off into the shadows and quietly padded along the foyer. Fortunately, the humans had not thought to close the doors leading out to the courtyard. Making sure that the coast was clear — where had that Joan human gone, anyhow? — she bolted from the brightly lit room and outside into the darkness again.

Except that it wasn't totally dark. The lights inside the pool were glowing, as usual. Tonight, however, the full moon was high, its image spreading across the swimming pool's smooth surface, making it hard to see the scary fish that lay at its bottom. She would have liked to sit on the pool's edge and pat her paw against the water, so that she could watch the ripple running back and forth through the moon. But even though the days were pleasant, at night the water would be cold . . . unlike past days when the pool was kept artificially warm for the old woman to take her daily swim. And there was nothing worse for a feline than sticking a paw in cold water!

Besides, she had important work to do.

Keeping to the shadows, Ophelia made her cautious way to the far end of the pool. Her jaws were starting to ache from carrying the pill bottle, and so she stopped to set it down for a moment while she hurriedly surveyed the situation. As before, she'd exit the courtyard by means of the gate . . . except she couldn't carry the cylinder and still squeeze out. She'd have to leave the bottle beside the gate and shimmy beneath it first. Then she could reach back under the bars to snag the bottle and drag it out

440

after her.

Perfect. And once outside the courtyard, she'd run to the picking up truck where Zuki would keep anyone except Ruby from following after her.

Too late, Ophelia heard the sound of a bare footstep behind her. In a flash, she grabbed the bottle again. But she wasn't fast enough to get away.

"Gotcha!" the Joan female shrieked in triumph as she swooped down and captured Ophelia in a giant piece of cloth.

A towel, she realized as she struggled against it, recognizing the feel of the rough loops. The Joan was sneaky as a rat, indeed! While the others were looking inside, she'd been clever enough to look outside . . . and clever enough to use a towel against Ophelia's claws. And she'd been smart enough, too, to take off her clicking shoes, so Ophelia wouldn't hear her coming.

Ophelia gave her tail an angry flick . . . or tried to. She couldn't move because the human had her wrapped up tight, with only her head free. Her teeth were the only weapons left her. But if she tried to bite, she'd have to drop the amber cylinder. She might not be fast enough a second time to retrieve it before the Joan human did.

Trick her, like she tricked you!

Abruptly, Ophelia made a gurgling sound and went limp, eyes shut and head lolling over the human's arms. Joan gasped, and then softly laughed.

"All right, you nasty creature," she whispered. "Give me back my party girls."

Ophelia felt the human's fingers latching onto the cylinder. She remained limp, though her jaws were locked, holding the tiny bottle firm as the woman tugged at it. After a few unsuccessful pulls, she heard the woman mutter a curse as she released the bottle.

Ophelia felt herself being lowered as the human knelt on the paving stones. She sensed the towel loosening around her, but she kept herself deliberately limp, eyes still closed, teeth still clamped on the cylinder.

Wait. Wait. Wait.

Now she was on the ground, the towel falling away from her as the woman latched onto the cylinder and began tugging again. At that, Ophelia let her green eyes spring wide open, and she gave a throaty, unearthly growl.

The Joan woman screamed and let go of the pill bottle, leaping to her feet.

Ophelia scrambled to her paws, too, ready to flee . . . only to find that one back claw was tangled in the rough cloth. *Stupid towel!*

A second later, however, she had extricated herself.

And that was when the Joan human gave her a kick that sent her flying.

The impact to her side made her gasp, and the bottle fell from her mouth. She heard the skittering sound of the pills inside it as the cylinder hit the pavers and went rolling away. She should flip about so that she could land feet first, like a proper feline, she frantically told herself. But the kick had stunned her, knocked the breath from her so that she couldn't react.

And so she landed in the pool, upside down, splashing into the center of the shiny moon reflection, the impact sending silver water dancing skyward.

Cool water promptly enveloped her in a noiseless cocoon. She sank with frightening speed toward the bottom where the pointy-nose fish lurked. Eyes wide, she flailed her paws, desperate to flee it, to make her way to safety at the surface. At first, her efforts were in vain. But the more she kicked, the slower she fell through the shiny waters, until she began to rise again.

Just when she couldn't hold her breath any longer, she popped out onto the surface. Gasping, she sucked in fresh air, paws churning wildly as she strove to keep her head out of the pool. She should try to swim to the stairs, she told herself, but that end of the pool was a long way away. And her side hurt from being kicked. It was all she could do to keep herself afloat.

Brandon . . . Ruby . . . help! Come find me!

She kicked for a while longer, but her efforts didn't bring her any closer to the pool's edge. Worse, she was starting to shiver now as the chilly waters fully penetrated her fur. Her legs began moving more slowly, and she could feel herself sinking again, until only her mouth and nose were above water. She splashed a few moments longer, managing a final little mew — *help!*

She caught a last breath . . . and then she slipped beneath the surface.

She drifted down, down, down. Strangely, the water was clear and bright and shiny now, so that she seemed to be falling through liquid glass. And it felt warmer, too, like sitting on the old woman's lap back when she was just a kitten. She was dying, she realized, just like the ibis . . . just like Luciana . . . just like the old woman.

But it wasn't so bad. Not really.

Ophelia! Ophelia!

A soft familiar voice was calling her, and she looked around her, puzzled. And then, in the distance but moving closer through the bright water, she saw her.

Mom!

The old woman smiled as she drifted toward Ophelia. She was wearing the same long white nightgown she'd had on the morning they had found her in the water, but now her eyes were open, and her face was round and pink! Her white hair looked like a cloud, dancing in the water around her head. She extended a hand toward Ophelia, and her smile grew wider.

I've missed you, little one. Have you and your brother been behaving?

Mom, Mom, I've missed you, too, Ophelia mewed, raising her paws in return. *When you left, Brandon and I had to find a new home and a new mom. Her name is Ruby. She's nice, and so is our new friend Zuki. And even the roosters, and Philomena the koi.*

The old woman laughed, the sound like small bubbles of music surrounding her. *You've had an exciting time, my sweet Ophelia,* she exclaimed. *But now, you have to make a choice. You can come with me now, to a place where humans and animals live together. It's always warm and sunny, with bright colors and happy sounds. No one yells or fights or is ever hungry or hurt again.*

Ophelia opened her eyes wide. *Are — Are you talking about the Rainbow Bridge?* she asked in a small voice.

The old woman nodded. *People and animals call it by many different names, but yes. And it's a wonderful place.*

But what about Brandon and Ruby and Zuki? If I go with you now, I won't see them again . . . not for a long, long time.

She nodded. *That's true . . . and that's why you have to hurry and make a choice. You can come with me now, or go back to be with your brother and your new mom.*

But if I don't go, I'll miss you. And if I do go, I'll miss them. How do I choose?

The old woman's smile grew warmer, wiser. *I think you know that answer. It was my time to leave this world, but you're a young feline with many more adventures before you. And someday, when you're a very old cat, I'll see you again. And then we'll laugh and play together, just like we used to do.*

Ophelia nodded. *I — I have to go back. I can't leave Brandon by himself.*

I know. Give him a kiss from me. And don't be sad, either of you. This is how it was meant to be.

The water around the old woman started to shimmer, and she began drifting backward, away from Ophelia. But with the growing distance she started to change:

white hair turning long and dark, wrinkled skin turning smooth, lips rosy red instead of pale, limbs sturdy and firm. This, Ophelia realized, was how the old woman had looked many years ago, when she was in her prime.

Mom, Mom, you're young again! Ophelia cried in excitement as Hilda's beaming image grew smaller and smaller. *Mom, I love you! Goodbye, goodbye!*

I love you, too. I'll see you again, my sweet Ophelia. Ophelia . . . Ophelia . . .

"Ophelia! Ophelia!"

The frantic shouts were coming from somewhere beyond the pool. And then a large splash shattered the moon's reflection in its surface. She could see the lights along the pool's sides now, and something swimming toward her like a fast fish . . . a fish with dark hair with a blue stripe in it!

Mom!

An arm wrapped around her, and an instant later she was on the surface. Vaguely, she was aware that Ruby was holding onto her, swimming with her to the shallow end, and rushing up the pool steps cradling her. Then she was upside down for a moment as someone lightly shook her.

"Ophelia! Ophelia!" she could hear Brandon yowling. "Don't be dead!"

I'm not. At least, I don't think I am, she tried to yowl back, though she didn't know if he could hear her.

She was still cold, though Ruby had found the same towel that Joan had used to swaddle her and had wrapped her in it, holding her close. This time, she didn't mind the rough loops, though the towel really didn't help much, since they were both dripping with water. She heard another voice then, and she opened her eyes long enough to see the son coming toward them. He had a big blanket in his hands and was holding it up, ready to throw on top of them.

Ophelia squirmed and tried to call out a warning. But then the son draped the blanket over Ruby's shoulders, like he was trying to help. *So confusing . . . but then, she was so tired.* But with the blanket over her now like a tent, she wasn't quite so cold. She buried her face against Ruby's arm. Maybe she should try to sleep for a little bit . . . just until she was dry again.

But first, she raised a weak paw and, very softly, gave her new mom a gentle tap on her cheek.

"Is she alive?" Luis asked, tone anxious as he squatted down next to where Ruby

448

huddled under the blanket that Givens had brought her.

She nodded, trying not to shiver. "I'm pretty sure I pulled her out in time. I even turned her upside down and pressed her chest, but she didn't cough up any water. I think she might be in shock, though. I really should get her to the emergency vet."

"I can't leave . . . not until we get a few things settled here. But my aunt's car is parked behind the guest house. If you think you can make it alone, I've got her keys. You can take her car and go. Send me a text where you are, and I'll come meet you as soon as I can. The cops should be here any minute."

"All right. Do you think you can find my glasses for me? I pulled them and my shoes off before I jumped in, but I can't remember where I left them."

He quickly retrieved both items and then helped her to her feet, tucking the blanket more securely around her. "Come on, let's get your stuff and get you out the gate while the getting's still good."

"But what about Brandon and Zuki?" she asked as they exited through the gate, the cat in question trailing after them.

Luis bent and scooped up Brandon. "I'll put him and Zuki in the guest house until

I'm ready to leave . . . though Zuki is pretty busy at the moment."

He nodded in the direction of the portico, where Joan's red sports car was parked near the mansion's front door. Joan was awkwardly crouched atop the vehicle's hood, while Zuki sat patiently in front of it, pink tongue lolling. Seeing them, Joan gave a little shriek.

"Help! Call this filthy beast of yours off right now, or I swear I'll sue all of you."

"Don't worry, Joan," Luis called back to her. "Just sit tight for now, and try not to scream. The dog doesn't like that. Once the police arrive, she'll back right off."

Ruby gave a wry laugh. "Well, I can tell you what dog just earned herself a nice steak for dinner tomorrow night."

A few minutes later, she was sitting in Luciana's battered but serviceable sedan. Ophelia — almost dry now, and wrapped in an even larger towel — was carefully bundled in one of the empty packing boxes that had been placed in the car's front floorboard. To her relief, the cat seemed to be sleeping peacefully, but Ruby wasn't going to take any chances.

She was drier, too, now. At Luis's insistence, she'd hastily swapped her own soggy jeans and hoodie for a nearly new set of sweats belonging to his aunt, which were still in one of her dresser drawers. She'd given Brandon a quick kiss before leaving him in the guest house and rushing back out the door with Ophelia.

"There's an emergency vet on Old Dixie Highway," she told Luis now through the open window as she started up the car. "I'll text you with all the details. They'll probably want to keep her overnight."

To her dismay, she heard her voice trembling on the edge of tears. She hadn't realized until she'd seen Ophelia's seemingly lifeless body drifting in that pool how much she'd come to care about the little cat and her brother in just a few short weeks.

Luis gave her a reassuring pat on the arm. "I'm sure she'll be fine. That little *gata* is a tough cookie, just like her owner."

"Let's hope so." Then another thought occurred to her as she put the car into gear. "Since you did such a good job of finding my things, I don't suppose you stumbled across that pill bottle of Joan's that Ophelia ran off with, did you?"

"As a matter of fact, I did."

Triumphantly, he pulled a small amber pill bottle from his cargo shorts pocket. "Good old Joanie was crawling around on her hands and knees looking for it when I

451

ran out to the courtyard after I heard you yelling. She took off for the gate once she saw me. As soon as I was sure you and Ophelia were out of the pool, I sent Givens for a blanket and started looking for it, too. I always was the best one at finding Easter eggs when I was a kid. Turns out I haven't lost my touch."

He gave the container a shake, rattling its contents. "Something tells me that she doesn't have a prescription for these."

"What is it, Ecstasy or something?"

"More like something. Looking at the size and color, if I had to guess, I'd say they're roofies."

"Roofies? You mean, date rape drugs?" Ruby gave him a quizzical look, knowing she needed to get going but also certain she needed to understand just what was happening here. "Why in the world would she carry around something like that?"

"Some people use Rohypnol to take the edge off when they binge on cocaine. And then you get folks with really bad insomnia who use it to basically knock themselves out. I have a feeling coke's a little too old school for Joan, so it might be something as simple as the I-can't-sleep thing." He shrugged. "You can't get the stuff legally in the US, but that doesn't mean there's not plenty of dealers around. Of course, you can always head down to your neighborhood bar and use the pills as your good old 'knockout drug' if you're that kind of —"

He broke off abruptly and stared at the pill bottle in his hand, expressions of shock and then outrage flashing across his features. Ruby stared at the bottle, too, as a terrible thought occurred to her . . . the same thought that likely had just hit Luis.

Hadn't he told her previously that a witness supposedly had seen Luciana a few minutes before the hit-and-run accident wandering the streets looking drunk? Wasn't that what ingesting a drink spiked with roofies did . . . made the victim act like they'd had about ten too many mojitos?

And hadn't Mrs. Givens supposedly fallen and hit her head first, before she slipped into the pool and drowned? Had she swallowed a spiked drink, too?

She drew a steadying breath. "I was just trying to scare Joan with that Tarot Death card, but now I'm wondering . . ."

She trailed off, not quite wanting to voice the suspicion.

Expression grim, Luis finished the thought for her. "You mean, you're wondering if she had something to with Mrs. Givens's death and my aunt's accident? Yeah, I'm wondering that, too."

She saw his fingers wrapped tightly around the pill bottle, like they were wrapping around something else. Like Joan's throat.

"So that's why the cops are on the way, to arrest her on suspicion of murder?" she asked in a small voice.

He gave her a fleeing smile that held more anger than amusement. "Not unless they're psychic. The only thing I mentioned was embezzlement and illegal substances. We just upped the ante here, assuming we're right about Joan's involvement . . . and assuming anything can be proven."

Ruby bit her lip. Gut feelings might be stock-in-trade for Tarot card readers, but hard evidence was needed to charge someone with a crime. Unless Joan confessed, simply possessing the drugs likely wouldn't be enough to push for murder charges.

"At least we've got something to give the police that should make them reopen both cases," she declared. "Speaking of which, should they be here by now?"

"Actually, I should have said cop, singular. They do things a bit differently here in Palm Beach, especially when there's no cut-and-dried evidence. You remember good old George up at the guard house? He has a brother named Carson who's a Palm Beach police detective. He's coming out to have a little conversation with Joan. We'll see where it goes from there."

Ruby nodded. "If it helps, the last card in the reading — the one I didn't get a chance to show her — was Judgement."

She heard a faint mew then from the box on the floorboard beside her. "I'd better hurry. I'll let you know later about . . . well, everything."

EPILOGUE

JoJo grinned as she tossed a couple of shrimp from her spring roll onto the bricks near the koi pond. "I have to say, for a little cat that almost drowned a week ago, Ophelia sure is looking perky."

"She is, isn't she?" Ruby replied with a laugh.

Although perky wasn't exactly the word she would have chosen, she thought, watching the feline in question pounce on her unexpected treat and then kick it halfway across the courtyard. Positively feisty, was more like it.

Following a precautionary overnight stay at the emergency vet clinic, Dr. Olivia — the animal hospital's young, blond veterinarian on duty both days — had pronounced Ophelia to be healthy as the proverbial horse.

Your little kitty must have had a guardian angel looking after her, the vet had declared.

Near-drownings like these are serious. They usually mean major respiratory issues that require oxygen supplementation, sometimes even a ventilator for respiratory assistance. We gave her the oxygen, just to be sure. But Ophelia had no sign of water in her lungs. And all the lab tests came back normal.

To prove the vet's point, Ophelia's first action upon returning to the Botanica had been a celebratory leap and slide along the length of the cash register counter. The stunt had sent stacks of pamphlets and giveaway newspapers, along with a wide copper pot cram-filled with dracaena (aka corn plant, aka lucky bamboo) tumbling to the ground. Even after a meticulous cleanup, Ruby was still finding stalks here and there in the shop days later.

But while Ophelia had come through with flying colors, Ruby hadn't been sure, at first, that her bank account would survive the ordeal. She'd pulled out her credit card to settle up before bringing Ophelia home, feeling a bit lightheaded as she saw the four-figure total at the bottom of the itemized bill. But she'd truly almost fainted when the smiling clerk told her that the invoice had already been paid in full by someone who wished to remain anonymous.

Luis, she'd gratefully assumed, vowing to

pay him back.

What truly mattered was that the two cats and Zuki were safe and well after their adventure. She had puzzled for a couple of days over Brandon and Ophelia's startling appearance at the Givens estate. How'd they'd known something was up, let alone escaped the Botanica, she wasn't sure. Her best guess was that maybe they were jealous of Zuki getting all the road trips and so had hitched a ride in the back of Luis's truck along with the pit bull.

Figuring out the tangled machinations of Joan Ratzen had been far more difficult.

"Back to what we were talking about," she said through a bite of kung pao tofu. "Any chance that Joan is going to serve any time for Hilda and Luciana's deaths?"

"Without any evidence? Nope. Right now, all they could charge her with is simple possession because of the Rohypnol. That's three years tops, assuming the judge wants her to serve jail time. But I'm guessing it's her first offense, so she'd probably get by with a fine." JoJo frowned, pausing to draw a matching frowny face in her rice with a chopstick.

"Trying her for murder, or even manslaughter, will be a heck of a tough case to make," the attorney went on. "Even if she confesses to giving them spiked drinks, it was only random bad luck that both women suffered a fatal accident while under the influence. There's no real way to prove she deliberately put them in harm's way."

"No chance of jail, then?" Ruby asked with a grimace of her own.

JoJo shrugged. "If, heaven forbid, I were defending her, I'd get any charges knocked down to bodily harm and gross negligence. Worst case, we're probably talking a couple of months prison time, and then probation. The better way to make her feel the pain is a civil suit . . . assuming Givens is willing to go public about the embezzling. Unless we're talking millions, the DA probably won't pursue it."

Ruby set down her chopsticks, no longer hungry. "Wow. So not only does she steal from an old woman, she basically sets up two people to die, and all she'll get is a slap on the wrist."

"The law's the law. But look on the bright side. There's always karma."

Ruby sighed, then nodded. *Karma.* That and the Judgement Tarot card that had shown up in Joan's reading. Even if the law couldn't punish her, with the Judgement card hanging over her, the woman wasn't going to be totally off the hook.

"Sorry, Rubes, wish it was better news." With that, JoJo set down her chopsticks too and stood. "I've got a meeting in an hour, so I'd better get back to the mines. And I'll let Blake know you'll think about meeting the new guy in his building. What?" she defended herself when Ruby gave her a look. "You're obviously not interested in the hot guy that lives a few blocks away from you."

Meaning Luis, of course. It wasn't so much the "not interested" as the "not really compatible" thing. But JoJo didn't need to know that. And so Ruby shot her friend *the look* times two before answering.

"The *hot guy*" — she gave the words finger quotes — "has been busy handling details of his aunt's estate and helping his father plan a memorial service up in Cleveland. I've been busy here at the store. I haven't seen him since the night at the vet clinic, but that's okay. After all, I've got three pet children who require my undivided attention."

She finished that proclamation with a smile for the cats and Zuki, the latter whose patience was rewarded when Ruby tossed her the last bite of egg roll.

JoJo shook her head as she scooped the last of the empty wrappers and boxes into

460

the oversized takeout bag they'd originally come in. "I can't decide which to get you for your birthday next month, the *Crazy Cat Lady* T-shirt or the *Crazy Dog Lady* T-shirt. Maybe I should get you both."

Ruby grinned. "I think a T-shirt with just the word *Crazy* would cover it."

"You find that shirt, you buy me one, too," JoJo agreed as, laughing, they headed back inside, Zuki trailing after them.

"Thanks for lunch," Ruby told her friend as they reached the front door, and she switched the sign over from *Will Return* to *Open.* "And tell Blake I do appreciate the offer, but maybe later on."

"Sure," JoJo replied and gave her a quick hug before opening the door. "Don't mind us. We're just trying to look out for — oh!"

The startled cry, Ruby promptly saw, was because JoJo had almost stumbled into Luis. He was standing on the walkway beyond the door, and apparently had been reaching for the outside knob at the same time as JoJo.

"Sorry," he said and hastily stepped aside so that the pair avoided a collision.

JoJo gave him a sly smile. "No problem. I never mind bumping into a good-looking man." Then, looking over his shoulder to the parking area beyond, she asked, "Oooh, is that your ride?"

At his nod, Ruby looked, too. Her eyes opened wide. In the spot at the curb next to JoJo's little BMW was a silver Porsche convertible that looked like something Terrence Givens would drive.

"What happened to the pickup?" Ruby managed once she'd gotten past the first shock.

Luis shrugged. "Big Mike took it to fix the dinged-up front quarter panel and broken headlight. I usually keep the Porsche garaged, but I had to drive something."

Something, indeed. Apparently, Joan hadn't been kidding when she said he was making good money on the side with some of those pawn deals courtesy of the Palm Beach elite.

"Well, *I* like it," JoJo assured him when Ruby neglected to make the appropriate noises to indicate being impressed. "Anyhow, gotta go."

She started down the walk toward her own relatively pricey ride, though she paused when Luis wasn't looking and turned to catch Ruby's eye. *Hot,* she mouthed behind Luis's back, and then gave her favorite *oooh, burnt my fingers* shake of her hand.

Hoping she wasn't blushing, Ruby responded with a shooing gesture in JoJo's direction, then stepped aside so Luis could come in.

"I thought you already flew out to Cleveland for the funeral," she said as she closed the door after him, almost tripping over Zuki as she gestured him toward the counter.

He shook his head. "The service isn't until tomorrow. I had a few things to take care of so I'm not leaving until tonight. I thought I'd stop by here first and see if you have some sort of lucky charm for getting through TSA without the up-close and personal pat down."

Despite herself, Ruby smiled. "That's not a bad idea. I need to see if we have a supplier who can make up a candle or something just for that."

Then, sobering, she asked, "How's the rest of your family holding up?"

"Like you might expect. My dad's pretty broken up about it, but he's grateful he got to see his sister these past few years. And we had some news from the police. They found the truck that hit her."

"Thank goodness," Ruby breathed. "That's got to help your dad get some sort of closure." Then, as a thought occurred to her, she asked, "Wait! It wasn't —"

Luis shook his head. "No, it was just some

random guy on his way home after a night out with the boys. But Joan did admit that she drove over to the pawnshop that same night and used a tire iron to dent up my truck."

He picked up one of the previously abused lucky bamboo shoots and idly played with it a moment before continuing. "She claimed she was teaching me a lesson about some nonsense or another. We both know she was trying to throw a little suspicion my way, just in case her gamble worked and Aunt Lu met with a bad end. It was totally coincidental that the hit-and-run vehicle looked like mine."

"What about the truck owner?" Ruby wanted to know. "Did he confess to anything?"

"Only to being a coward. He claims Aunt Lu walked right out in front of him, and he panicked when he hit her and just kept driving. He said he didn't realize she died until he read about the accident in the paper the next day. And then he was too afraid of jail to come forward." Luis shook his head. "Since there's no toxicology, about all they can charge the guy with is failure to stop and render aid, and fleeing the scene of an accident with a fatality. It's not much, but it's something."

Another one walking virtually free, Ruby thought in dismay. They'd have to hope that karma did her number on the pickup driver, too.

Luis, meanwhile, had changed the subject. "So, how's Ophelia doing after her swim?"

"She's great, got through the whole ordeal unscathed. The vet was very impressed with her." She hesitated, and then went on. "I know you didn't want me to know, but thanks for taking care of the emergency vet bill. It really helped, not having to max out my credit card like that. But I do want to pay you back over time."

Luis raised a brow. "Much as I'd like to hog all the glory, it wasn't me. Our buddy, Terrence Givens, is your benefactor. After you texted me where you were, he asked for the clinic name. I heard him call and give them his credit card number."

"You're kidding? Mr. Terrence 'I-hate-cats' Givens?" Ruby gave a disbelieving snort as she shoved her glasses back into place. "Are you saying he actually paid an almost three-thousand-dollar vet bill out of the goodness of his heart?"

"Probably out of a sense of guilt, but yes. They were his mother's cats, after all, and he owed the old woman that much since he did a pretty poor job of keeping *her* safe. If he hadn't brought Joan around" — he paused, and his jaw tightened — "well, Mrs. Givens and Aunt Lu would both still be here."

Ruby gave a sober nod. "So he'll have to live with that . . . but maybe there's hope for him after all. I'll send him a nice thank you note and let him know I'll light a good luck candle for him."

"Maybe leave the candle part out," Luis suggested with a fleeting grin. Sticking the bamboo shoot back in the container, he went on. "Anyhow, I'm glad your kitty is fine. And maybe when I get back in town, you'll let me have a supervised visit with my cat."

"Sure, whenever you want."

"Great. So, uh, see you in a couple of weeks."

A few moments of awkward silence fell between them. He was wearing his work polo shirt with the pawnshop logo, and she could see the part of the tattoo on his biceps. Not enough to tell what it was, though she was pretty sure it was some small animal. Someday, she'd have to satisfy her curiosity and ask him what it was.

Fortunately, the bells on the front door chose that moment to jangle, dispelling the awkwardness and announcing a customer.

With that, Luis started toward the door, only to pause after a few steps and look back at her.

"By the way, it's there."

At her quizzical look, he gestured at the portrait of Rosa. Smiling, he clarified. "The resemblance to your sister . . . it's there. I saw the look on your face when you saw Ophelia floating in the pool and dove right in. Definite warrior queen."

"I talked to Philomena last night," Ophelia declared, sitting up straight with tail wrapped tightly around her as befitted making an important announcement. "I went outside in the middle of the night, after everyone was asleep, and called her."

She and Brandon were enjoying the sun while lounging near the koi pool following their unexpected Chinese food snack, courtesy of Ruby and JoJo. Zuki had gone inside with Ruby earlier but now had come back to the courtyard again, flopping onto the bricks for her own snooze. Brandon had almost fallen asleep, but at her words he opened his eyes wide again.

"You mean she actually stuck her head out of the water and talked? I thought she'd never come back again after you yelled and said all those bad things to her."

"Yeah," Zuki agreed, sounding hopeful. "I thought she'd be mad back. What did she say . . . what did you say?"

Ophelia gave her tail a little flick. "I told her she was a very smart fish, and that all her rhymes had come true. And then I told her I had a very important question. I wanted to know if that really was our old mom, Hilda, I saw when the bad Joan kicked me into the pool."

She'd already told both Brandon and Zuki about that mystical experience, explaining how she'd been given the choice to go with their old mom or stay with her brother and Ruby and all her new friends. They'd both been amazed at her account, wanting to know every detail.

Was Mom a ghost, like in the scary movies that Ruby liked to watch? Were you breathing underwater, or did you hold your breath? Could you hear us yelling for you while you were underwater?

She had answered every question as best she could, but she couldn't answer her own question . . . had she seen Hilda, or simply dreamed it?

"That's what I wanted to know," she explained now, "and I knew that Philomena was the only one who could say for sure."

Brandon's eyes grew wider. "So what did

Philomena say?"

"She told me that it really was our mom. She said that sometimes, when the moon is just right, when it shines a certain way on the water, all sorts of wondrous things can happen. But she also said I probably wouldn't ever see her again until someday when I die for real."

That sobering statement made everyone, including Ophelia, pause for an uncomfortable moment. She furrowed her brow, trying to remember if there was anything else. Yes, one more thing!

"Oh, and she also said that Rally the dog would come back."

Brandon and Zuki exchanged glances, and then burst into laughter.

"I don't know about you," the pit bull said, trying without success to muffle a snicker behind her paw, "but I'll sleep better tonight knowing that."

"Me too," Brandon chimed in, snickering, too.

Ophelia bristled. "Yeah, well," she huffed. Then, unable to hold back her own snicker, she agreed. "Yeah . . . me three."

When, after a few moments more silliness, they'd all composed themselves again, Zuki spoke up. "When I was inside a few minutes ago, Luis told Ruby that Joan confessed she was the one who smashed up his picking up truck. Just like she did all the other bad stuff to Luciana and to your old mom. So now we don't have to think any more awful things about him."

Then, as Ophelia and Brandon both heaved sighs of relief at this, she added, "You know, even though some bad things happened, I really did like riding around in the back of the picking up truck. Do you think we can try it again, sometime? Maybe have more adventures?"

"Maybe next time there's a full moon," Brandon suggested.

"You mean, a fool moon," Ophelia corrected. "Like on one of Ruby's Tarot cards. But next time, one of us should drive!"

ACKNOWLEDGMENTS

Few books are possible without the support of numerous wonderful folks. A flick of the whiskers to my fab agent, Josh, and his assistant, Jon, for all their hard work on my behalf. Big purrs to the lovely people at Midnight Ink, especially my editors, Terri and Sandy, whose input makes me a better storyteller. A special meow to my author buddy, Toni, who was generous in her referrals. Big head scritches to my real-life Brandon Bobtail and his sister, Ophelia — two feisty rescue kitties who were the inspirations for the fictional Tarot Cats. And finally, a big smooch for my husband, Gerry, who has always been my number one fan.

ABOUT THE AUTHOR

Diane A. S. Stuckart is the *New York Times* bestselling author of the Black Cat Bookshop Mystery series. She's also the author of the award-winning Leonardo da Vinci historical mysteries, as well as several historical romances and numerous short stories. Her Tarot connection is even more sprawling. She's been an on-and-off student of Tarot since she was a teenager, though she confesses to being more of a collector of decks than a reader. She will, however, pull out the cards for a friend on occasion.

Diane has served as Chapter President of the Mystery Writers of America Florida chapter, is a member of the Cat Writers' Association, and also belongs to the Palm Beach County Beekeepers Association. She lives west of West Palm Beach with her husband, dogs, cats — including the real-life Brandon Bobtail and Ophelia — and a few beehives. Visit her at www.tarotcats.com or at Facebook.com/BlackCatMysteries.

The employees of Thorndike Press hope you have enjoyed this Large Print book. All our Thorndike, Wheeler, and Kennebec Large Print titles are designed for easy reading, and all our books are made to last. Other Thorndike Press Large Print books are available at your library, through selected bookstores, or directly from us.

For information about titles, please call:
  (800) 223-1244

or visit our website at:
  gale.com/thorndike

To share your comments, please write:
  Publisher
  Thorndike Press
  10 Water St., Suite 310
  Waterville, ME 04901